'I hate you, Miles,' Diana said fiercely.

'Some people would say I was a model ex-husband,' he countered. Diana gasped. His smile grew.

'Generous,' he went on. 'Unobtrusive. Tolerant.'

'*Tolerant*? You?'

'Not a word of reproach about the way you've been running around the last two years,' Miles said, his voice hardening. 'You've made a good job of turning yourself into a rich man's house guest, haven't you, my pet?'

Dear Reader

Easter is upon us, and with it our thoughts turn to the meaning of Easter. For many, it's a time when Nature gives birth to all things, so what better way to begin a new season of love and romance than by reading some of the new authors whom we have recently introduced to our lists? Watch out for Helen Brooks, Jenny Cartwright, Liz Fielding, Sharon Kendrick and Catherine O'Connor—all of whom have books coming out this spring!

The Editor

Born in London, **Sophie Weston** is a traveller by nature who started writing when she was five. She wrote her first romance recovering from illness, thinking her travelling was over. She was wrong, but she enjoyed it so much that she has carried on. These days she lives in the heart of the city with two demanding cats and a cherry tree—and travels the world looking for settings for her stories.

Recent titles by the same author:

GOBLIN COURT
NO PROVOCATION
HABIT OF COMMAND
DANCE WITH ME

DECEPTIVE PASSION

BY

SOPHIE WESTON

MILLS & BOON LIMITED
ETON HOUSE   18-24 PARADISE ROAD
RICHMOND   SURREY   TW9 1SR

*First published in Great Britain 1993
by Mills & Boon Limited*

© Sophie Weston 1993

*Australian copyright 1993
Philippine copyright 1993
This edition 1993*

ISBN 0 263 77968 8

*Set in Times Roman 10 on 11½ pt.
01-9304-54354 C*

Made and printed in Great Britain

CHAPTER ONE

DIANA put her case down with a sigh. Athens airport at six o'clock in the morning contrived to be both bleak and busy. Everyone but herself seemed to have someone to meet them.

Two years ago, she thought wryly, she would have been full of trepidation, arriving on her own. She would have been worried about finding the hired car and more than worried about driving in a foreign country to a destination she had never visited before. But that was two years ago. These days she could handle it all.

She rapped sharply on the counter of the hire car kiosk to attract attention.

'Yes?' said a bored clerk, emerging reluctantly.

'Good morning,' said Diana pleasantly. You didn't, she had learned in these years on her own, go to war at once. It was something she had picked up from watching Max. 'I believe you have a car for me.'

'We're not open yet,' the clerk said, not listening.

She stood a little straighter and said firmly, 'A car to be ready on the arrival of the six o'clock plane from Hamburg. My name is Tabard. Mrs Tabard.'

The clerk just managed not to shrug.

'We open at eight.' He turned away.

'Booked,' Diana said softly, having also learned from Max that quietness was more intimidating than the most determined ranting, 'by Count Galatas.'

The clerk stopped dead. She saw with satisfaction that his shoulders twitched as if he'd taken an arrow between them. He turned back. She smiled at him.

'Ah, yes,' he said. 'I have a note from the Count's office.'

He disappeared briefly from view and reappeared with a set of car keys and a clipboard. He needed Mrs Tabard's signature, her passport, her driving licence and that was all. He shuffled the papers dextrously.

Diana got out her American Express card only to find it waved away.

'The car is to be charged to the Count's account with our head office,' the clerk said.

He gave her an assessing look which Diana noted with some amusement. He wouldn't be used to visitors of the wealthy Galatas family arriving on tourist flights, she guessed. He was too well trained for it to show, however.

'The car is a grey Citroën. It is in the car park. The Countess left a note——' he consulted his papers '——which is in the glove compartment.'

Diana stiffened. She had not expected a personal welcome. Still less had she expected a note from the Count's erratic sister. Susie Galatas was temperamental and unpredictable but she had shown a pretty consistent desire to avoid Diana in the past. Understandable in the circumstances, of course, Diana thought wryly, since Susie had never stopped wanting Miles Tabard.

The clerk didn't appear to notice. He handed her papers back along with a keyring and a slip of paper with the registration number on it. 'The oil, water and tyres have been checked and the petrol tank is full. We ask that you return it in the same condition.' He gave her a sudden flashing smile. 'Have a wonderful holiday, Mrs Tabard. Welcome to Greece.'

'Thank you,' murmured Diana, taken aback.

She blinked. The magic of the name of the great, she thought, was something that she would never have believed without the experience of these last two years. She didn't really approve but there were times when it was useful. Times like now when she had come straight from a decaying eighteenth-century palace where she had worked non-stop through four strenuous, dusty days. A holiday would indeed be welcome.

Not that she was likely to get one in Castle Galatas. The Count's secretary had been very clear: since they were old acquaintances, the Count would be grateful if Mrs Tabard would give him a preliminary estimate for some proposed renovations. Since they were old acquaintances, he hoped she would also be able to enjoy the hospitality of the castle for a few days' break as well. Which meant, as Diana well knew, that he expected the bill to reflect that old acquaintanceship. No matter that he and his sister had disapproved of her marriage to their childhood friend and had never taken much trouble to hide their coolness.

So she gave him a slightly rueful smile which made the clerk blink in his turn. He found himself summoning a porter to take Mrs Tabard's single suitcase and guide her to the rental car.

'That one,' he said to his colleague when they were out of sight, 'will give Susanna Galatas a run for her money if anyone can.'

The girl who had just joined him looked after Diana Tabard's trim figure critically.

'But the Countess is very beautiful,' she observed. 'And rich. And she has wonderful clothes.'

'But that one,' said her mentor wisely, 'has eyes a man could drown in.'

If Diana had heard him—or understood him—she would have been astonished. She thought of herself as very ordinary. Even these days when she knew she was more elegantly turned out than she used to be. It had been a matter of pride not to fall apart when Miles left.

So she had spent a lot of time and as much money as she safely could on her appearance. On the whole she was pleased with the result. But she would never have believed that anyone thought her a worthy rival to the glamorous Countess Galatas.

She tipped the porter and slid in behind the wheel of the car. It was new and spotless. Another tribute to the status of the brother and sister Galatas, thought Diana. She had driven enough hired cars these last two years to know that they normally showed the signs of a tough existence. This one, however, started smoothly at the first turn of the key and the engine was a whisper.

Diana grinned as she went up through the tight new gears. Normally the gears were soapy and the engine chugged. If she had needed any proof of the power of the Galatas family name here it was. She hoped, she thought suddenly, that she was never on the wrong side of it.

She hoped she was doing the right thing by coming here at all. She gave an odd, superstitious shiver. Only one way to find out!

She let out the clutch on a long breath and moved gently forward into the dangerous future.

The note in the glove compartment had proved to be a map. Susie had drawn it herself evidently. Diana turned it round several times and couldn't make head or tail of it. Perhaps the Countess had decided that the best way to avoid her brother's unwanted guest was to get her lost in southern Greece, Diana thought wryly. That would be very like her in Diana's experience. Miles, of course, would never hear a word against her.

Diana had cast the map aside and hoped devoutly that she knew where she was going as well as she thought she did.

Soon enough she got used to the car and found the large, clearly signposted road to Corinth. Ignoring Susie's instructions, Diana drove steadily south. Her eyes concentrated on the road. Her tired mind wandered.

She had never come to the castle with Miles. They had meant to; even planned to that last year. But with the coming of autumn, when the schedule in the kitchen said, 'Chris and Susie: Greece', she and Miles were in different continents. By that time they were no longer communicating except through solicitors. No longer, thought Diana painfully, even trying to pretend they had a marriage.

The sun was getting high. She extracted sunglasses one-handed from her bag and pushed them up her small nose. The glare of the metalled road was blinding. She nearly missed the turning off the main highway. She braked sharply and swung off on to the side road she remembered from poring over the Greek road maps Miles had left behind. Soon she was passing as many mule-drawn carts as lorries.

Miles, she remembered, always said the road to the Galatas castle was the last prehistoric route in Europe. So it must get tougher than this. Diana's mouth thinned. Miles had, nevertheless, negotiated whatever hazards the road presented without mishap from the day he got his driving licence. She wasn't going to do any less.

She quelled the treacherous flicker of trepidation. If Miles could do it, she could. It was the principle that had got her through the last two years.

Later, towards mid-morning, she looked at the petrol gauge. These last two years had taught her that on a road you didn't know you filled up whenever you could. She had never thought of that before. And Miles, of course, had never explained why he was putting petrol into a half-full tank. He had never explained why he was doing anything: he just did it. Silently, competently and, in the end, with a sizzling impatience that had kept Diana's nerves on the stretch for months, waiting for the final explosion.

The garage came into view. She drove into it and got out, stretching. The sun was like a physical presence at her shoulder after the greyness of Hamburg and London. She explained to the proprietor what she wanted in her few words of careful Greek and sat at a table in the shade with a coffee while her instructions were carried out by a teenage boy in overalls.

Diana closed her eyes, tilting her chair back until her head rested against the wall behind her. Miles, of course, had spoken fluent Greek. Well, he had been practically brought up by old Count Galatas after his parents split up. He and the old man's two grandchildren had more or less run wild at the castle in the school holidays from what she had gathered.

Diana took off her dark glasses. Maybe that was when Miles had got his taste for danger. She remembered one story of Miles and Chris diving off the castle battlements into the sea. The old Count had made them apologise to the fishermen who had pulled them out—and who, Diana thought, the boys must have frightened into heart attacks. And he made them chop wood as a penance. Nothing much there to deter a repeat performance, Diana had said drily.

Miles had been surprised.

'Repeat? Why should we? We'd proved we could do it. It's boring to repeat things. They become a habit. Where's the fun in a habit?'

Marriage, of course, had all too rapidly become a habit for Miles; one with no fun in it at all.

In a way, thought Diana, she'd almost expected it. The brilliance, the restlessness, the sharp sense of him always being on the edge of danger—they had all made him seem very strange and somehow intimidating. Even when they were first married and she was so in love with him that she could tell when he walked into a room with a hundred people between them, she had never felt quite at ease with him. Not as a wife should with her husband, Diana thought now.

There was a murmur at her elbow. She turned. It was the garage proprietor bearing a wooden tray with a glass of water, a smaller glass of some clear liquid and a dish of olives and little gobbets of fat bacon. He put it down and gestured, smiling.

Diana guessed what it was. She raised the glass to her lips and the smell of aniseed hit her like a blow. Ouzo.

Memory struck too, like a snake. Miles drank it every evening. A greeting to the night, he had said, laughing. Diana didn't like the taste much so she didn't usually join him. But later, when they kissed, it would still be there: the hint of aromatic heat and herbs that spoke of another country and all the foreign unguessable things in Miles's nature.

He could have been standing there with his lop-sided mocking smile. She could not have been less shocked if she had turned and found him beside her.

'This has got to stop,' Diana said to herself firmly.

She threw the spirit down her throat quickly. Her eyes filled with tears—due, she assured herself, entirely to the strength of the ouzo. She finished the water, thanked the proprietor and paid her bill.

She was not going to spend the rest of this, her first journey alone in Greece, with Miles as an invisible, mocking companion, she told herself. She had survived his departure. She was not going to fall apart now. She would put him out of her mind.

It should be a reasonably straight route from now on. Diana set off again, with determined confidence.

That confidence was hard won. She'd had none at all when she first met the Galatas family. It had been clear right from the start that any of Miles's friends who'd thought he might yet marry had had Susie Galatas picked out as the only candidate. He had been escorting her everywhere she wanted to go for fifteen years, and her brother was his best friend. And she was gorgeous. It would have been the ideal match—especially as Susie was wildly in love with him.

Or so they said. Susie herself denied it, of course. And Miles was very fond of her. Even after they were married he dropped everything whenever Susie rang, wanting to see him. It had been one of the first signs that all was not well with the marriage.

So why me in the first place? Diana bit her lip unhappily.

It always came back to that. It always had done, right from the first. She had never quite believed it. Miles was brilliant; to a modest history undergraduate he seemed utterly inaccessible.

At thirty-six, he was the youngest professor by ten years in the university. All his female students were in love with him. He wasn't classically good-looking but he had the proud, intense air of a visionary—and, it must be admitted, the body of an athlete, Diana thought wryly. They had had reason enough for their crushes, those devoted students of his.

Only she hadn't had a crush on him. She wasn't in his class and she had known him only by reputation. She had been overwhelmed with shyness when they were introduced. And after that first stammering exchange she had never expected to see him again.

Miles had decided otherwise. He chased her relent-lessly. Everyone noticed—most of them before Diana did. Even her elderly tutor had warned her uncom-fortably—and at the time inexplicably—about the dangers of relationships between sophisticated older men and innocent young girls. And she had been, thought Diana, horribly innocent.

She sighed, taking the car round a steeply sloped double bend with her new-won competence. Was it her innocence that had intrigued Miles? Had he always, in the private core of himself that he guarded from her, been secretly laughing at her naïve wonder?

Because, for Diana, Miles had been a revelation. She had not even attempted to disguise it. It had amused him, she remembered that. In fact he was usually amused; amused, sure of himself, passionate in a way that Diana had never even dreamed of. Even now she blushed if she strayed into too explicit memories of the passion between them. And in the end he had been passionate in his unrelenting hostility, too.

Diana's heart began to beat hard as she remembered those last terrible weeks. He had behaved as if she had betrayed him somehow. As if she had trapped him into marriage; as if she had set out to deceive him.

In the end she'd decided that he must suddenly have realised that the image he'd had of her when they married—whatever it was—was wrong and blamed her for it. It was the only reasonable explanation. But it still didn't answer the question which still haunted her after all these months, the beginning and the end of the whole thing: why, in the first place, why *me*?

The road forked. Without hesitation, Diana curved to the left. She had heard Miles talk about this road often enough. The steering-wheel was hot. Beyond the purring engine there was the heavy silence of the Mediterranean noon. Diana leaned forward.

Slowly, as the car breasted the hill, the sea came into sight—a glimmer of silver between two heat-hazed hills ahead. The road became stones and then sand. It climbed and dipped and the sea, glimpsed between outcrops of rock, came closer. It was the colour of ink at the horizon, paling to silver at the edge of the rocks where it furled along the shore below. In the distance she could hear the rise and fall of the tide against the rocks.

Diana sighed. Absolute peace, just as the Count's secretary had promised. No wonder Miles had loved it.

She stopped the thought abruptly. Miles again. She would *not* be invaded like this. She set her mouth angrily. She was never going to see him again and she had to get used to it.

The last she heard he was on the other side of the world, lecturing in Sydney. And for the next fortnight at least she was going to be here in Greece on a working holiday, to all intents and purposes alone. There would be the servants, of course. But Christos Galatas, or rather his shrewd secretary, had negotiated an undisturbed holiday as part of the package.

It was odd, thought Diana, how she could organise a solitary professional and social life without difficulty but was reduced to despair by the prospect of holidaying alone. Maybe she wasn't as strong as she thought yet.

But she would be, she promised herself. After all she had a life to live. She would have to shake off Miles's overwhelming shadow and find more than work to fill her days. He had.

Miles's friends seemed to expect him to marry Susie as soon as he and Diana divorced—as he probably should have done years ago. Her eyes felt gritty. The car jolted as it turned a particularly savage corner. Diana swore and then stopped, silenced by the vista before her.

It was the castle: a grim Venetian fortress, dark to the point of unreality against the splendid glow of sea and sky. Diana drew a long, appreciative breath.

Beautiful, yes, and with a near-vertical approach road. Diana laughed softly. Two years ago she wouldn't have contemplated driving up that suicidal road. At least Miles's defection had taught her to do things she was afraid of. Carefully she put the car into second gear and gunned the accelerator.

It went up the incline like a slightly unsteady bullet and came to rest—just—under an olive tree in the deeply shadowed courtyard. Miles's childhood home. There was no one about.

Diana crossed her arms on the steering-wheel and leaned her forehead against them. For no reason at all she felt like crying.

A woman came out of a small arched doorway. Diana sat up at once, confused. But it wasn't Susie, cool and polished, in one of her Paris outfits. It was a short square woman with greying dark hair and heavy brows.

'Mrs Tabard?' she asked in a heavy accent.

Diana got swiftly out of the car.

'Yes. I made good time.' She looked up at the forbidding walls.

The woman smiled and gestured to herself. 'Maria.'

She spoke at length. Diana's Greek gave out after the greetings. It was possible that Maria wanted her to have a meal.

'All I want,' Diana said slowly and with feeling, 'is a rest.'

Maria stared. A little desperately, Diana put her hands together and rested her cheek against them, making

snoring noises. Maria's face broke into a beam of delighted comprehension.

'*Hypno*,' she said, as far as Diana could make out.

There was no misunderstanding the imperative wave
with which she gestured to Diana to follow her, however.
She seized the overnight bag from the passenger seat and
set off across the courtyard into the cool darkness of
stone walls and winding stairs.

Diana was soon lost. Eventually they came to a wide
corridor with windows on one side and heavy unpol-
ished wooden doors on the other. Maria flung back one
of them.

'Bed,' she said proudly.

Over her shoulder Diana had a brief impression of a
tall room with a profusion of floor-to-ceiling Venetian
mirrors. She also detected a four-poster, a *petit point*
Louis-Quatorze chair and a monstrous Victorian
dressing-table. Diana blinked.

Maria, she saw, was unimpressed by this costly jumble.
She closed the door smartly and took her to the next
door in the corridor. She opened it with a flourish. This
was clearly the more impressive room in Maria's
estimation.

'Bath.'

It was indeed. It was a room of immense proportions,
fully as big as the bedroom next door, with a brass
Edwardian shower stall at one end and a bath as big as
a boat on huge brass claw feet in the middle of the floor.
In an attempt to reduce the air of vastness, presumably,
someone had surrounded it with a profusion of tables,
chairs and mirrors. There was even a quilted bathrobe
hanging on the door that led to the bedroom, presumably for passing guests.

Diana swallowed. Since she had entered her new profession she had become something of an expert in period bathrooms, and this was unique in her experience.

'Bath,' repeated Maria, a little impatiently.

'So I see,' Diana agreed faintly. 'I mean, thank you.'

Putting down Diana's overnight bag on a gilt chair, Maria swung energetically at a heavy brass lever sprouting from the edge of the bath. Water gushed from the central tap. It looked, thought Diana, like one of the water spouts from Notre Dame. Steam rose.

'Hot,' said Maria unnecessarily.

She adjusted the temperature with a number of expert tweaks. Then, under Diana's bemused eyes, she took a flagon the size of a stage prop from one of the glass-topped tables and swirled a liberal amount of oil into the water. A smell of white lilac infused the steam. Maria turned off the tap. Then, pointing to a pile of fluffy towels on a tapestry chair, she left.

Diana began to laugh. Maria was almost certainly right. She was hot and stiff and dusty. The scented water looked wonderful. Her long-delayed sleep could wait another ten minutes.

She stripped off her cotton jeans and shirt and let them fall to the floor. Her underwear was silk, beautifully cut and expensive, severely bare of the lace or bows she had favoured in the days when she had bought it as much for Miles's pleasure as her own. Not, she thought ruefully, that he had ever shown any signs of noticing. All he had ever wanted was to rid her of the delicate garments as swiftly as possible.

'*Stop* thinking about him,' she said aloud, sitting down in the middle of the 'boat' with a distinct splash.

She soaked for as long as she dared. It would be all too easy to fall asleep, she knew. She rotated her shoulders under the scented water, feeling the stiffness dissolve. A not unpleasant sense of unreality began to invade her. She got out at last, dreamily, wrapped herself in one of the large towels and padded through the connecting door into the bedroom she had been shown.

The shuttered darkness was cool. Diana drifted pleasurably to the curtained bed—and stopped dead. All her sense of well-being dropped from her abruptly.

For there was someone lying under the woven coverlet, one bare brown shoulder visible. He was face-down, a tanned arm flung up on the pillow round his sleeping head. The muscles were impressive and the tan the colour of fresh toast. He looked like a resting runner. He stirred, murmuring.

Diana's mouth went dry. Her hands closed convulsively on the knot she had made of the towel at her breasts. She took a step backwards.

He turned his face on the pillow. She could see the arrogant profile, the steep lids and the incongruous curl of hair that flicked round under his ear no matter what he did. Not that she needed to. She had already recognised those muscles. The shadows muted the Venetian red to chestnut but Diana knew the colour of his hair as well as she knew her own.

His lashes lifted gently and dropped at once. He was still unconscious, it seemed.

Diana pulled herself together. Carefully, putting one foot silently behind the other, she retreated, never taking her eyes off the bed.

It was the mirror that spoilt it. She had forgotten it was there and, catching sight of her own reflection's movement out of the corner of her eye, she gave an involuntary gasp.

It was enough. He had always, she thought bitterly, been a light sleeper.

He came awake, as he had always done, instantly. Diana froze. He turned his head.

There was a long, agonising silence. Her hands clenched so tight on her towel that the luxurious stuff marked her.

Very slowly he lifted himself on to his elbow. He surveyed her thoroughly. The key pattern coverlet fell away, revealing that his tan extended to his hips. Diana's thoughts scurried like rabbits let out of a cage. Only one clear message came through and that was one she didn't want: that he must have been working in the open for weeks to get so evenly brown.

Their eyes met. He gave a slow, sleepy smile. Diana felt something cold run up and down her spine and lodge solidly in the pit of her stomach.

'Unexpected,' Miles said huskily.

Her whole body was shaking with tension. He mustn't see it, she thought frantically. She knew she should move—turn her back on him and return to the sanctuary of the bathroom and her discarded clothes. Where was the strength of will she had spent the last two years nurturing? Hadn't she been congratulating herself on it only this morning?

But Diana could only stand and tremble. She felt that sensual regard envelop her like a warm breeze and despised herself.

With a suddenness that made her jump, he flung aside the coverlet and held out his hand. It was quite explicit. For a moment something inside her flared up in response to that wicked invitation.

Diana flinched. She was appalled. She shook her head vigorously. It must be because she was so tired—or the shock of finding him here—or the ouzo on the sunny road——

'God, *no*,' she said in a rag of a voice.

It seemed her hard-won poise had gone along with her strength of will. She bit her lip, struggling for composure, some semblance of dignity. He watched her, one eyebrow raised. He looked, she thought, amused. It was not surprising, or even out of character, but it made her feel ashamed.

'Why——?' he began softly.

But she interrupted him. 'I'm sorry,' she said. 'There's been a misunderstanding. I've only just arrived. No one was about except Maria, and I suppose she didn't understand.'

It came out high and breathless but at least she wasn't gibbering, Diana thought drily. Or asking what in the world he was doing here when he ought to be the other side of the world. Or screaming at him.

'It was probably my fault,' she went on, trying to sound composed. 'I've been travelling a long time and I'm tired. I must have got the wrong end of the stick. I'm sorry if I've disturbed you.'

His look of amusement deepened. He leaned back against the pillows, his hands clasped behind his head.

'You've done that all right.'

Diana blushed. She could feel the colour flooding into her face. Miles had always been able to make her blush, just by looking at her.

He watched with interest. She could—if she had been close enough and not shaking with reaction—have hit him.

'I'm sorry,' she said again coldly. 'There'll be a room for me somewhere. I'll go and——'

It was his turn to interrupt. 'Why bother? There's plenty of room here.'

It was, indeed, the biggest bed she'd ever seen in her life. Even with his six-foot frame stretched across it, there was space for several additional bodies. There was not, however, room enough for her.

'I wouldn't dream . . .'

'Why?' he said again very softly. He met her eyes, his own rueful. 'You're worn out. You said so. Maria goes to ground in the afternoon. God knows how you found her in the first place. She'll have evaporated by now. Why not give up and crash out till evening?'

Diana glared at him. 'Because you're here.'

'But not in exclusive possession.' His voice was bland. 'I've offered to share.'

Diana drew a long breath. 'I don't think that would be a good idea,' she said with a calm she was proud of.

There was a gleam in the brown eyes. 'Unrestful, you think? Well, there are remedies for that.' His voice was blatantly teasing.

Diana stopped even trying to play his game.

'You must think I'm an awful fool,' she said with heat. 'It would take nothing short of anaesthesia to get me into that bed with you.'

His lids dropped. He was laughing.

'I'll bear that in mind.'

There was no answer to that. Diana shrugged unwarily and caught at her towel just in time. Her blush redoubling, she turned away. She was conscious of his eyes on her shoulders above the bath-towel. How could eyes suggest so much? she thought in irritation.

He said idly, 'Where are you going to sleep? In the bath?'

'If I have to.' Her voice was grim. 'But I'll have a go at finding Maria first.'

'It might be easier to find Susie.'

His voice was mild enough, almost idle. But Diana knew him well indeed and she recognised a challenge when she heard one. She whipped round.

'Susie?' She was frankly appalled. It had never occurred to her that her undisturbed holiday would include a hostess who despised her. 'She's *here*?'

His mouth tilted wryly. 'It's her home.'

'But she hardly ever came...' Diana said, and stopped
dead on a shaft of memory.

It had been Christos, at a long-ago party, taking the
wind out Susie's sails. She'd been clinging to Miles's arm,
reminding him of the wonderfully simple life at the
castle—a life of course which Diana had never shared.
Diana had been rather grateful for Chris's intervention.

'You don't like the simple life, Susie,' he had said
dampeningly. 'No nightclubs, no shops, no friends to
party with. You never go to the castle any more.'

And Susie had looked adoringly up at Miles and said
softly, 'Neither does Miles.'

She hadn't said she'd live in a desert if Miles were
there. She hadn't had to. And here he was.

Diana stared at him. They must be here together. Her
mind worked frantically. The perfect secretary must be
less than perfect after all. She couldn't have known.
Unless...

She said carefully, 'Did you know I was coming?'

The lop-sided grin grew. 'Of course,' he said with
composure.

Her hands clenched tight into fists. He noted it, she
saw. His brows rose.

'I let Maria think that Susie had gone out and wouldn't
be back till after you got here. Whenever that was.' He
added thoughtfully, 'I didn't really think it'd be till this
evening. It was very silly of you not to have a rest in
Athens.'

Diana ignored that. 'You—told—Maria——'

'That when you arrived she was to bring you straight
up,' he said, watching her intently.

She opened her mouth to shout at him. Then shut it again. She couldn't think of anything devastating enough to say to express her feelings.

He watched her unblinkingly. He was still completely relaxed. It was only too obvious that he found the situation highly amusing and was interested to see how she would get out of it.

'*Why*?' she said at last in a strangled voice.

'Use your imagination,' he invited softly.

This can't be happening, she thought. It *can't*. It's worse than my worst nightmares. I'll wake up in a minute and find I've crashed the car... But she met his amused, level gaze and knew it was all too real.

'You're mad,' Diana said at last. She made a helpless gesture. 'I suppose you know why you're doing this.' She hitched her towel in front of her more securely. 'Are you going to tell me where I find my own room, or would you find it more amusing if I have to play hunt the thimble up and down this damned castle?'

One eyebrow flew up. 'In your bath-towel? Now that definitely has its attractions.'

'I'm glad to entertain you, of course,' Diana said with equal courtesy and untruth, 'but I would like...'

To her horror she found her eyes filling with unexpected, traitorous tears. She flung away from him quickly.

'The hell with you. I'll find Maria,' she said in a curt voice.

He spoke from behind her. For the first time he didn't sound amused.

'Diana...'

But she fled. She knew that voice and it was the one he used when he was determined to get his own way. She had learned to resist after a fashion—but not when she was tired, on the edge of tears, and wrapped in someone else's bath-towel. The odds, Diana thought, with slightly uncertain humour, had to be evened a little before she was ready to do battle with a master.

She locked the bathroom door and scrambled into her clothes. They looked even worse than they had when she arrived, wrinkling over her slightly damp skin. Diana didn't care. She had never had the clothes to compete with Susie anyway. And this was worse than the social embarrassment of being scruffy in the presence of the elegant Countess.

She found her with Maria's help. The Greek woman looked concerned, but she took one look at Diana's set pallor and uncurled herself from her comfortable chair. She escorted her to a heavy door and knocked.

Diana heard Susie's voice. A cold hand clenched round her heart. She had hoped not to hear it again.

'Come in.'

She did.

It was a huge room, full of flowers. They were crimson and purple and white, trailing from bowl to antique bowl so that it looked like a garden. In the middle of this riot, Susie lay on a chaise-longue reading a foolscap file.

There was a faint frown between the heavy brows. She looked up impatiently. As soon as she saw Diana her expression changed. It became cool and guarded. She did, however, stand up to greet her guest. Her unwanted guest, Diana reminded herself.

'Diana. I didn't know you'd arrived.' She brushed a scented cheek half an inch from Diana's. 'Good journey?'

But Diana wasn't playing social games. She found she was shaking. She drew a deep breath and said in a voice as cool as her adversary's, 'Susie, what is Miles Tabard doing in my bed?'

CHAPTER TWO

SUSIE seemed to go rigid. Her eyes not quite meeting Diana's, she said, 'I don't know what you mean.'

Diana said, 'I thought I was supposed to be here on a working holiday. *On my own*. Nobody said it was on my own except for my ex-husband.'

Susie was cool. 'And me.'

It was only a pin-prick but it still hurt. Susie had no doubt intended it to hurt, thought Diana. Susie was telling her that Miles travelled with her these days. Diana didn't entirely believe her but she still flinched from the message.

She said equally coolly, 'It wasn't you I walked in on, though. Was it?'

The heavy brows went up. 'Walked in on?'

Diana shuddered suddenly, remembering. Those mocking, knowing eyes. That careless invitation to which she had—oh, so nearly—responded.

Susie looked disgusted. 'For heaven's sake. You lived with the man for two years. There's no need to go on as if he's Sweeney Todd.'

Diana shook her fair head. 'It isn't that. You don't understand. I really did walk in on him, Susie. In bed. Maria just showed me into the room and . . .'

She couldn't go on. If Miles chose to tell Susie about her appearance from the bathroom wrapped in a towel, she couldn't prevent it, she thought. And if they were as close as rumour had it then he probably would. Eventually, anyway. But Diana couldn't.

Susie's eyes flickered. She shrugged.

25

'Since I take it he was in bed alone, I don't see what the fuss is about,' she said but her voice was strained. 'You did it daily up to two years ago.'

'It was different then,' Diana said bleakly.

She was remembering. Two years ago, they had been barely speaking. Four years ago they had been in love. Whenever she walked into a room where Miles was, he would turn his head and smile at her. She remembered the physical sensation like touching electricity, whenever she met the warm brown eyes.

When he'd invited her to bed then, it hadn't been a challenge, a way of watching her squirm. It had been tender, passionate, laughing and infinitely gentle. Tears threatened again. She turned her head, furious with herself.

Susie said curtly, 'Look, I don't know why there was a mix-up about your room. I'll sort it out. I've only just arrived myself. I haven't had time to talk to Maria yet.'

Diana ignored that. She said quietly, 'All you had to do was tell me you'd be here, Susie. I wouldn't have come.'

Something flashed in the black cherry eyes. 'You'd have preferred to be alone with Miles?'

This time Diana prevented herself from shuddering. 'I'd have preferred to be alone. Full stop.'

Susie looked at her carefully. 'I believe you would.' She sounded blank.

'I assure you I would,' Diana agreed wryly.

Susie shook her head. She sank down on the chaise-longue again. The rigidity seemed to go out of her.

'I didn't know you were coming,' she said at last. 'Nobody told me. I wasn't intending to be here myself but—well, something came up and I wanted to leave Athens.' A small, unhappy smile crossed her face. 'Not the ideal holiday for either of us.'

Diana took a decision. 'I'll go.'

At once Susie's head came up. She looked alarmed.

'You mustn't do that. They'll blame me. Chris is angry enough with me as it is.' She sounded genuinely worried.

'I'm sorry,' said Diana without much truth. On the whole she tried to help people out, but her charity towards Susie Galatas had diminished in direct proportion to the attention her husband had afforded the Countess in the year before they parted.

Susie said rapidly, 'Look, I don't know what's going on but I think Chris and Miles put their heads together. They'll never forgive me if I louse it up.'

Diana stared, bemused. 'Are you saying I was deliberately brought here under false pretences?' she demanded slowly.

Susie bit her lip. 'Miles may want to see you. He hasn't said anything to me, but... Is it so impossible?' she flashed with sudden bitterness.

Diana didn't believe it. In two years Miles hadn't written or made so much as a telephone call at New Year. He had asked for a meeting in the solicitor's offices a couple of times, of course, but Diana was fairly sure that was at her solicitor's instigation. Her solicitor had taken his moral obligation to attempt a reconciliation very seriously. In the end she had had to tell him frankly that she couldn't bear seeing Miles again that way.

'But if Miles——' she stumbled over the name '—wanted to get in touch he had only——'

'To write to your solicitor. I know. He said.' Susie sighed. 'I agree with you, that would have been the most sensible. What's the point in scratching over old wounds? But Miles——' She shrugged again. 'You know what he's like. He wants his own way. I heard Miles tell Chris he asked for a meeting three times and you wouldn't agree. That,' she added unnecessarily, 'annoyed him.'

So that was why he had conspired with Chris in setting this trap. Determination not to be bested by her evasive tactics. His determination was one of the things that Diana had most loved about him. Once. She bit back sudden, infuriating tears. Tiredness, she assured herself savagely.

When she had mastered her voice she said carefully, 'We had nothing to say to each other. It could only have been—painful.'

'You mean you couldn't face it,' Susie interpreted accurately.

Diana's eyes flickered. She didn't answer. Susie sighed angrily.

'Well, he's here now. And so are you. What are you going to do about it?'

'I—don't know,' Diana said in a voice that was hardly a voice at all. 'Look, Susie, I can't talk about this now. I'm so tired I can't think straight. Can you find me somewhere—anywhere—to lie down for a couple of hours? Maybe I'll start making sense after that.'

'But Miles . . .'

'*Please*,' said Diana with the quiet firmness that had worked so signally on the car rental clerk.

It worked on Susie too. She gave a small shrug.

'If that's what you want. I thought you'd like a room in the eighteenth-century bit, overlooking the terrace.' She hesitated and then said almost angrily, 'There'll be the whole castle between you and Miles. So you don't have to worry about him creeping up on you when you're asleep.'

Diana did not answer.

The room was exquisite. Diana looked round at the creamy hangings and delicate furniture and thought wryly how different it was from the room Miles inhabited. Or Susie for that matter. They were obviously on the family corridor. She wondered, briefly and painfully, whether they visited each other's rooms.

Though there was something in the other woman's manner that told her they didn't. She seemed angry, bitter even. Not like the successful rival confronting the old love.

'Oh, it's all so *difficult*,' she said aloud.

For the second time that afternoon she stepped out of her clothes. She was already more than half asleep as she slipped between the rosemary-scented sheets.

She didn't stir when Susie looked in an hour later. She didn't stir when Maria brought up her suitcase and placed it on the folding stool beside the bathroom door. Maria chuckled maternally and let herself out with only the minimum creaking of ancient hinges. Diana never moved.

She came wide awake, though, instantly, when the door closed behind Miles.

He stood with his hands behind him against the door, watching her sardonically.

'Recovered?'

Diana hauled herself up on the pillows, clutching the covers cautiously to her chest. She was wearing her underwear, which, she thought wryly, was better than a towel but not much. She schooled her expression. So much for Susie's belief that Miles would not invade her room, she thought. For all their shared childhood and Susie's own barely disguised predilection, she sometimes wondered how well Susie Galatas really knew Miles.

'Recovering,' she said coolly. 'I've got a lot of sleep to catch up on.'

'And you want me to push off while you do,' he interpreted softly.

She inclined her head. The fair hair was straining at the pins that kept it knotted at the nape. She winced. Miles saw it.

'Take them out,' he said.

Diana flinched. The sudden memory was vivid; too vivid. The times he had sat on the edge of the bed behind her, taking out the hairpins one by one; massaging her shoulders gently; kissing the back of her neck. Her eyes slid away from him as she fought the memory down.

'What do you want, Miles?' she asked.

His eyes were still on her hair. 'Why don't you take it down, for God's sake? You know it gives you a headache if you sleep with it up like that.'

Diana tensed. But she replied calmly enough, 'Thank you for your advice. What do you *want*?'

He came right into the room then and stood at the foot of the bed. He scanned her. It was odd, thought Diana confusedly, that a man with such a mobile, expressive face could be so completely unreadable when he chose.

'A talk,' he said at last coolly. 'A few words. Nothing more.'

Miles picked up a three-legged, fan-backed chair and swung it round so he could sit astride it, looking at her. He crossed his arms along the back and dropped his chin on them.

She watched him warily. He looked, thought Diana, irritated, like a scientist confronted with an interesting specimen.

'So speak,' she said curtly, looking away.

'Susie said you weren't staying.' He sounded indifferent. Diana mistrusted him thoroughly. 'Because of me.'

Diana was startled. She had not been together enough to make a decision like that, and Susie knew it. She had even urged her to stay. What game was the Countess playing? she wondered.

Though, of course, it was really the only sensible thing to do—to leave now before it all got recriminatory and hurtful.

Diana moved restlessly. 'So?'

His eyes were very steady. 'Is it true?'

She didn't know the answer to that even now. She burst out, 'What did you expect, for heaven's sake? That I would walk into the trap and say thank you?'

The brown eyes flickered. 'Trap?'

Diana made a weary gesture. 'What else would you call it? It was obvious what you planned. Getting me to a nice remote castle where I couldn't easily get away.'

His eyes narrowed. 'So I'm scheming against you? Planning a kidnap, maybe?' he said softly.

'What else is this?' she flung at him.

He put his head on one side, considering it. His fingers drummed on the fragile back of the chair.

'Why should I do that?' he parried.

Diana shook her head. 'That's what I said. It makes no sense. But Susie told me you and Chris conspired behind my back.'

His mouth slanted in an unamused smile. 'And you and Susie have been discussing me behind my back,' he pointed out, even more softly.

Diana curbed an instinct to apologise. He had always been able to do that: put her in the wrong so she backed away from what would have been a legitimate protest.

She glared at him. 'Don't I have a right to defend myself? Who else would tell me what's going on, for God's sake?'

That, she saw with satisfaction, got him on the raw. His eyebrows flew up as if she had astonished him. For a moment he looked as taut and dangerous as she had ever seen him. Diana's muscles locked in tension.

Then, with one of those bewildering changes of mood, he was laughing. The brown eyes, astonishingly, were warm, even caressing.

'You're growing up,' he said, propping his chin on his hands again. 'What else was I to do? I couldn't get past your damned obstructive solicitor.'

'Why should you want to?' Diana demanded harshly.

Miles looked surprised. 'You're my wife. We need to talk. Surely you can see that?'

She winced. 'Why? We never talked when we were married.'

For a moment he didn't answer. Then he said gently, 'We're still married.'

She was shaken with a gust of anger. He hadn't remembered they were married when he walked out two years ago. He hadn't wanted to remember since, either.

'And that gives you the right to manipulate me? Amuse yourself a little, maybe? At my expense, of course.' She couldn't keep the bitterness out of her voice.

Miles watched her, his face unreadable. But he said lightly enough, 'There's a certain humour in the situation certainly. Though you don't seem to see it yourself. So what are you going to do? Cut and run?'

Diana sighed, the anger draining out of her. Her head was beginning to thump. Absently she started to take out the hairpins.

'I don't know,' she admitted. 'I haven't thought much beyond this fortnight for weeks. Frankly, I'm too tired to climb back into the car and make a break for freedom today.'

Miles made an involuntary movement, quickly stilled.

'Do you want me to go?' he asked her unexpectedly.

Diana jumped. For the first time she remembered he was supposed to be in Australia. Had something gone wrong?

'What are you doing here?' she asked slowly.

Miles hesitated. 'We cut the lecture schedule. Steve's gone back to England for a holiday.'

Overwork, Diana diagnosed, hearing what he wasn't saying. Neither Miles nor Steve Gilman had any sense of self-preservation when they were working. They must have driven themselves to the end of endurance. Miles would need a holiday. And this was the home of much of his childhood.

She said, 'You shouldn't have to leave. This is your place.'

Miles shrugged again. 'I've never been a permanent resident. I can come back any time and resume my own holiday.'

Diana shook her head decisively. 'Not on my account. I bet you need this break.'

His mouth twisted in a small, private smile. She had learned to fear that smile. She never knew what it meant.

'Same old Diana,' he said softly. 'I wondered. I can see I needn't have done. Waifs and strays and needy persons this way.' He stood up suddenly, swinging the chair one-handed back to its place against the wall. 'Yes, I need a break. But I'm not on my last legs. I could go and play with the tourists on one of the islands if it would make you any happier.'

'No,' said Diana swiftly, making up her mind. 'No. I'll go. Oh, maybe not today. Or even tomorrow. But when I've got my breath back.'

Miles said without expression, 'Running away, Diana?'

She closed her eyes briefly. 'Is that so surprising?'

'Running doesn't help, you know,' he said gently. 'You have to turn and face the truth one day. Why not sooner rather than later?'

She made a helpless gesture. 'Don't.'

But he pursued his advantage ruthlessly.

'It would be such very public running, too. Susie's not the only one here with us, you know. Chris is down for a few days. And——' he hesitated '—an old boyfriend of Susie's. They'll talk if you pack your bags and bolt. Are you sure you feel equal to dealing with it? I thought you always wanted to settle our differences in private.'

It was true. Diana had fought to maintain the appearance of a united front for months after Miles had stopped speaking to her except in that clipped, cold way. She had taken his arm in public; smiled at him across dinner tables; pretended she knew where he was when people rang. He had accused her then of not facing up to things. And in the end he had made her face them. When he left her.

She felt the old sense of helpless incomprehension begin to take hold. She pushed it down firmly. She wasn't helpless any more. And she understood Miles only too well.

'Our differences are pretty public now, I think,' she said quietly.

He gave a little nod, like a chess player acknowledging an opponent's move.

'True enough. But Susie at least will demand a blow-by-blow account of what we've said to each other if you leave now,' he said at last carefully. 'You won't enjoy that, you know.'

It was true. Diana gave a little shiver. He knew her too well, this man.

'What do you want me to do, then?' she muttered.

He showed no indecent triumph. He didn't laugh at her capitulation. Indeed, he seemed to be choosing his words as carefully as if she had not given in at all.

'Give it a chance. Just a few days. We can be polite to each other that long, surely?'

Diana did not even try to meet his eyes. Miles could school his features like an actor, she had learned. And his expression was no clue to his feelings.

'I suppose so,' she said reluctantly.

'You won't see much of me,' he assured her, his tone dry. 'I'm in the fields most of the day. Or out on the boat.'

She said, 'I'll try to keep out of your way, then.'

He stood up at once. She felt a little spurt of resentment. Of course he would go, once she'd agreed to do what he wanted. And she wanted him to go, didn't she? After all she didn't want to talk to him. It was illogical to mind. It was just, she assured herself, that it was all too humiliatingly familiar.

'I'll see you at dinner, then.'

She thought he was going and felt the tension drain out of her. So it was all the greater shock when he took two long strides towards her. His arm snaked out and before she knew what he was doing he had flicked the last confining pins out of her hair.

It fell in a fair, feathery cloud. Diana felt it brush her shoulders and then, rigid with disbelief, felt his fingers looping it gently aside. As if they were still married, as if he had never hurt and deserted her, Miles Tabard bent and brushed his mouth against her exposed nape.

She gave a little gasp of outrage and jerked away from him. But he was laughing. And then he was gone.

When Susie came to fetch her before dinner, Diana was seriously reconsidering her decision.

Susie was wearing a simple cotton caftan with a bold geometric pattern in red and purple. Her hair was piled on top of her head in a coronet that made her look serene and royal. She was wearing, Diana saw, what were probably thousands of pounds' worth of platinum and rubies at her ears and wrists. Her bare feet were in chain-store espadrilles. She looked beautiful.

For the millionth time, Diana looked at Miles's childhood playfellow and thought, Why me?

But all she said was, 'You're looking very gorgeous. I take it exotic royalty is in this year?'

Susie laughed. She had very little vanity. And some-times, when they were not discussing Miles or romantic relationships, she could be very nice, Diana remembered.

'Be honest. You can't see me for the rubies,' she replied.

So she'd been right, Diana thought drily. She hadn't been certain because until she married Miles she had barely seen, much less owned, real jewels.

'They're lovely,' Diana agreed. 'New?'

Susie made a face. 'My grandmother's. We don't ask too closely how *she* got them. Are you ready?'

Diana glanced at her reflection. Normally she didn't wear much make-up but tonight, for some reason, she suddenly felt as if she wanted colour on her face. Armour, she thought wryly. Or maybe camouflage.

'Two minutes,' she said, reaching for the mascara.

Susie sat down on the love-seat. She watched Diana with a strange expression.

'You're beautiful, aren't you?' she said abruptly.

Diana was so startled that she nearly poked the mascara wand in her eye.

'You're joking.'

'No.' It was oddly sombre. 'You have the bones. And that look of vulnerability. As if you'd tremble into dust if a man laid a hand on you. I see why——' She stopped.

Diana turned, incredulous. 'Susie, that's nonsense,' she protested. 'I'm just a standard washed-out English blonde. No features, no colouring. Whereas you——' She gestured eloquently at Susie's ensemble.

Susie's smile was crooked. 'It's all detachable in my case. I *wish* I looked like a sea nymph.'

Diana was startled and more than a little embarrassed.

'You can't mean me. I can't even swim. It was one of the things——' She stopped, biting her lip.

Susie's brow creased. 'One of the things that made Miles feel protective?' she said in a light, hard tone. But there was an undertone to it that, if it hadn't been ridiculous, Diana would have said sounded like pain.

'One of the things that most annoyed him,' she corrected. 'Oh, I don't want to talk about him. Ever since I got off that damned plane, I seem to keep coming back to Miles. Let's drop the subject. And lead me to some food. I'm starving.'

Susie laughed again, her friendliness returning as suddenly as it had evaporated. She stood up. 'Stick close,' she said.

The castle was a jumble of buildings tacked on to the original Venetian fortress. Susie led her up steps, round turrets, down corridors until her head whirled. Diana could hardly believe it when at last they came out on to a ramparted terrace overlooking the sea. In the distance, the sun was setting behind the hills across the bay.

There were three men already on the terrace. Diana stopped dead. An old boyfriend of Susie's, Miles had said. But she had never heard that Dimitri Philippides was anything other than an old family friend. She looked quickly at Susie but the Countess's expression told her nothing.

Dimitri and Christos Galatas were sipping aperitifs. Miles was in the process of lighting a series of perfumed flambeaux. The scented smoke wafted across to them.

He turned, quick as a cat, when they set foot on the terrace. He caught Diana's eye and grinned.

'Against the mosquitoes,' he said as she raised her eyebrows. His voice was easy. For a moment they felt like friends again.

She laughed, tension temporarily forgotten. 'And I was going to congratulate you on a romantic idea.'

Miles grinned. 'Oh, I have those too.'

Diana caught her breath. But the others had not picked up that private, challenging message.

'Not before dinner,' said Chris. 'If you're going to start quoting Homer again, wait until I've had enough brandy to appreciate it. Hi, Diana, how are you?'

Dimitri was already bowing over Diana's hand. They had met before, both during and since her brief marriage. He had always been exquisitely tactful, however, and she liked him.

'Last night Miles gave us Odysseus's return,' he explained now, setting a basketwork chair for her. 'It was very—er—impressive.'

'It was very long,' corrected Count Galatas. He grinned at his friend. 'I keep hoping that his memory will go with advancing years. But it doesn't. Unlike mine,' he added with a sigh.

'That's because I keep it exercised,' Miles said smugly. 'You just sit about in those pets' parlour offices of yours, letting your secretaries do the remembering. You're going soft, Chris.'

Since Count Galatas ran a thriving international commodity business, this seemed unlikely. Chris, anyway, was not put out by these strictures.

'I like to be comfortable,' he said mildly. 'And that includes no narrative poetry until I'm sozzled enough to stand it.' He turned to Diana. 'I hope you had a good journey?'

The words were civil enough but there was none of that affection with which he had spoken to Miles. There never had been. From Chris Galatas's point of view his friend's new wife had always been an unknown quantity. She had never managed to prove herself. If he had conspired to get her and Miles here together, Diana thought suddenly, it must have gone against the grain with him.

She had wondered in the beginning whether it was some sort of influence from Chris that had persuaded Miles to leave her. Chris was currently on his third wife, an elegant woman with whom he spent the shortest possible time, and he did not have much use for women. Diana was pretty sure that Chris would have preferred Miles not to marry at all; to stay a free spirit. And if that was hopeless then he wanted him as a brother-in-law, not married to some English nobody.

She'd dismissed the thought soon enough, of course. Who knew better than she did that Miles had never been influenced by anybody? He did what he wanted—including discarding a wife who had become an encumbrance.

In the corner of the terrace a barbecue was glowing. Having tended his candles, Miles went to it.

'I'm chef this evening,' he announced to the company at large.

Chris groaned. 'Susie...'

But Susie was laughing. 'Oh, let him, Chris. You know he'll only criticise mercilessly if you or I do it.'

'Nobody cooks kebabs the way I do,' Miles agreed modestly.

Chris sniffed. 'Raw.'

'Rare,' corrected Miles, grinning. 'And properly marinated.'

Dimitri turned to Diana. 'We had them last night. I hope you like garlic?' he added with feeling.

Before she could answer, Miles sent her a flashing smile across the glowing coals.

'She learned to,' he said softly.

Dimitri looked startled. A well-shaped eyebrow flicked up.

Diana felt her cheeks burn in the darkness. She hastened to give them a cool explanation.

'Before I went to university I led a very sheltered life. I'd never even been to France. So—no garlic.' It struck just the right note of rueful amusement, she thought, pleased. And it made Miles frown quickly, which was even more pleasing.

Christos, who spent most of his working life in Paris, looked intrigued.

'How is that? I thought the English were in and out of France all the time.'

'Not,' said Diana drily, 'the rural working classes.'

Christos continued to look puzzled. 'But surely—those school trips that your educationalists are so proud of. Didn't you go to France with your school? To learn the language?'

Diana caught Miles looking at her speculatively. When they were married he had never discussed her background with his friends. He said she was too sensitive about it. But he had respected her wish and not referred to it. It was something she had corrected since.

She lifted her chin. Well, to all intents and purposes their marriage was over now. If her lowly ancestry upset them, it couldn't reflect on Miles any more.

'School trips take place during the holidays,' she said quietly. 'Or they did at my school. In the holidays I had to work.'

Chris said, 'Work? Oh, you English and your discipline! But surely it would have been work learning French in France?'

Diana smiled. 'Work to earn my bread,' she explained gently. 'My father was a gardener on a big estate. My mother did housework in the big house. My father had an accident and couldn't go on working. They let us keep the cottage but it was still difficult on just my mother's wages. I shouldn't really have stayed at school after sixteen but I was clever and they both wanted me to. So——' she shrugged '—we compromised. I stayed on and did my exams and took jobs in the holidays. So it was a long time before I encountered snails and garlic butter.'

There was a queer little silence. They were all looking at her as if she had sprouted two heads. All except Miles. He knew it all already, of course. And had his own views of her relationship with her parents.

'Tied to your mother's apron strings,' he had flung at her more than once.

She met his eyes now in the flickering candle-light. He was inscrutable.

Susie broke the silence. 'Well, there are no snails on the menu tonight. Only salad and the kebabs that Miles marinated in some poison of his own. Though, I grant you, that's probably eighty per cent garlic.'

They all laughed. Miles, Diana remembered with a pang, had always been a better cook than she was. Whatever he bothered to do, he did to masterpiece standards, of course. And tonight, true to form, he produced an excellent meal.

Dimitri filled Diana's plate and made sure her wine glass was topped up. In fact she would have preferred water but it seemed churlish to say so amid the general cordiality.

So Diana was feeling a little light-headed when Christos began to mutter over the brewing of Greek coffee. She had drunk it before and knew how to avoid the river silt at the bottom. But Christos was clearly adding vast amounts of sugar. So she refused it and continued to sip her resinated wine.

Under the cover of general conversation Miles said in her ear, 'Don't you think you've had enough?'

Diana jumped and half turned in her chair. He was kneeling just behind her chair, relighting a candle and using her as a wind-break to shield the flame from the light breeze that had sprung up with nightfall. She looked down at him haughtily.

'You've no head for it,' he reminded her pleasantly. 'As well you know. And if you carry on like this, Don Juan in the silk shirt over there is going to have lots of fun putting you to bed.'

She glared at him. Dimitri's exquisite grey shirt very probably was made of silk. It infuriated her that Miles should notice and mock him for it.

'Don't be disgusting.'

Miles looked pleased with himself. 'Don't want him to, Di?'

'That's not what I meant,' she began, recognising deep waters too late.

But he stopped her with that knowing, lop-sided smile of his.

'It's what you said. *I* don't think you fancy Don Juan half as much as you think you do.'

'I——' Diana bit her lip.

He had her boxed into a corner. If she told the truth, and said that she and Dimitri were not interested in each other, Miles would take it as a personal victory. But if she dissembled he was equally capable of calling Dimitri over from his conversation with Christos and telling him to take Diana to bed because she was tired.

She said fiercely, 'I hate you, Miles.'

He put his head on one side. The candle-flame threw the strong bones of his face into dramatic relief. For a moment he looked like a satyr—calculating and mischievous and quite heartless. His eyes were laughing but there was a distinct challenge in their depths.

'Now there you probably *do* know how you feel,' he allowed.

Her hands clenched round the stem of the Galatas family crystal. It was better than hitting the smile off his face and causing a scene.

'Not without cause,' she hissed under her breath.

The candle-flames were making little devils dance in his eyes. In the darkness they were as black as molasses, except for those little points of flame.

'That's a matter of opinion,' he countered. 'Some people would say I was a model ex-husband.'

Diana gasped. His smile grew.

'Generous,' he went on. 'Unobtrusive. Tolerant.'

'*Tolerant*? You?'

'Not a word of reproach about the way you've been running around the last two years,' Miles said, his voice hardening. 'You've made a good job of turning yourself into a rich man's house guest, haven't you, my pet? Since it was my money that paid for it, I might have been entitled to complain a bit, don't you think? Even put a stop to it, if I chose. But I've been mildness itself, you have to agree.'

Diana stared at him, uncomprehending. He might have been speaking a foreign language for all the sense he was making. She didn't understand him. But she knew that, in spite of the cool air, there was real heat licking through his indifferent tones.

She said in a low voice, 'You know why I took the allowance.'

'Your wheelchair-bound father,' Miles said without inflexion.

Diana said desperately, 'We'd *started* buying that house for them. I couldn't let it go when they'd got everything just where Daddy could use it...'

'Did it ever occur to you to get a job?' Miles asked, his voice deceptively mild. 'You were bright enough, as I recall. You might even have been able to contribute a bit yourself.'

Diana turned further round in the basket chair, staring at him. A *job*? She hadn't had a holiday in two years! 'What are you talking about, Miles?' she asked.

'Or did you think your pathetic struggle to get to university was enough?' His words bit. 'I admire that, of course. I always have admired it. But I don't think I care for the way you seem to have decided that you've had your share of adversity and now the world owes you a living.'

The light, amused voice had an edge like Toledo steel. Diana put her glass down on the terrace very carefully.

'I don't understand,' she said.

'No?'

She turned her head to meet his eyes fiercely. '*No.* I've done nothing... Why attack me like this? Suddenly?'

Their eyes locked with a force like a blow. Diana knew he felt it too; she could see it in the way his mouth twisted. But he was not admitting it.

'Now there's a lot of questions,' he mocked. He stood up. His shadow was long and menacing in the candle-light. 'It's not sudden,' he said with precision. 'It's not an attack. And I'm tired of you doing nothing. I've had enough. I give you fair warning. I'm not going to support you until you find some society playboy to take over your bills. I'm going to take you in hand. It's about time somebody did.'

Diana stood up too. Marriage to Miles had taught her a lot about disguising hurt. She said in a cool, dismissive voice, 'You will do nothing of the kind. I shall leave tomorrow.'

'You won't,' he corrected gently.

The others were moving away from the battlements, Christos pointing at the stars. A lecture on the heavens was clearly in progress. Miles gave her a slow smile. Diana began to wonder if she was going mad.

'You will stay,' he told her. 'And you will listen to me.'

CHAPTER THREE

DIMITRI walked her back down the stairs and passages to her room. He was obviously a frequent visitor. He had quickly grasped, though, that she wasn't, notwithstanding her embarrassing relationship to Miles, who regarded it as a second home.

'Susie thinks she runs the castle,' he told her.

They were strolling along a corridor. Their footsteps echoed queerly off the stone walls. Ridiculously, she knew, Diana was as tense as if they were being followed.

'Nominally it belongs to Miles but...'

This brought her attention smartly back to her companion.

'*Miles*?'

Dimitri gave her a surprised look. Although he had been angelically tactful, he was well aware that she and Miles had been married and were no longer.

'Didn't you know? He was practically brought up here.'

Diana shook her head. 'I knew that. His parents travelled all the time and Count Galatas was his godfather. I didn't know he had any claim...'

Dimitri made a rude noise. 'Godfather, my eye.'

Diana halted, staring at him. 'What do you mean?'

Dimitri looked faintly annoyed with himself. Then he shrugged.

'Well, if I don't tell you someone else will. I'm surprised they haven't already. Especially as you're here.' He paused and then said as if he were weighing his words, 'The old Count had two sons, you know. The good

46

brother who stayed at home and made money. Well, some of the time. Chris and Susie's father. And the bad brother who ran away to sea.'

Diana was bewildered.

'And was never heard of again?' she prompted, when he stopped.

'Oh, he was heard of all right. From all over the world. Sydney, Rio. New York. Valparaiso. You name it, Conrad went there. Or so my mother says,' he added conscientiously. 'He was—er—a free spirit.'

Diana began to see where this was leading. She drew a careful breath.

'And Miles was the result—according to your mother? Where?'

Dimitri cast her a look of mingled respect and deprecation. 'South America somewhere. He was a real nomad, Conrad. An explorer. Anne Tabard was a diplomat's wife or something. In some God-forsaken, mosquito-infested frontier town on the edge of the rainforest. Her husband was a lot older, I believe.'

Diana had met Lady Tabard. She examined her recollection of her ferociously sophisticated mother-in-law and found she didn't believe it.

'She must have been very bored,' Dimitri mused. Clearly he found it difficult to reconcile the two images as well. 'And Conrad was lethal with the ladies. A real heartbreaker, according to my mama.' He slanted a look down at her. 'She says he was exactly like your Miles.'

Diana did not rise to any one of the number of lures in that last, casual remark. Instead she said coolly, 'Is this all conjecture, or is there any proof? Does anyone know what happened?'

Dimitri shrugged. 'Conrad stayed with the Tabards on his way up the Amazon looking for some lost tribe.

There are letters, I believe. One imagines they had an affair before he went up-river.'

Diana shivered. 'Why didn't she go with him?' she said, half to herself. A sudden thought struck her. 'Or did she?'

Dimitri was astonished. 'From what I hear she wanted to get *out* of the place, not deeper into it. And Conrad wouldn't have been a good bet. He was always disappearing up glaciers and across oceans single-handed.'

Diana shook her head. For the first time she felt the stirring of some sympathy for her icy mother-in-law.

'Was there a scandal?'

Dimitri laughed. 'From the English? My dear, you have to be joking. Her husband was completely civilised. Conrad was nowhere to be found, of course. So old Galatas did the decent thing. Nothing acknowledged, needless to say, but there was always discreet support. The Tabards weren't well off. And eventually, all three got a share of the inheritance. Miles was particularly fond of the castle. So he got it. Chris got the fleet and the commodities business. Susie got shares and the jewellery.'

Diana felt strangely chilled. Half of her did not believe the story. She didn't want to believe it. Miles hadn't told her and surely he would have—at least in the days when they were close? Yet for some reason half of her found it all too convincing.

'What happened to him?' she asked at last. 'To——' she found she couldn't call him Miles's father '—to Conrad?'

Dimitri made a face. 'Who knows? He could be ruling some lost tribe somewhere. Or he could be dead. I don't think the family ever hear from him, anyway.'

Did Miles? Diana faced the thought painfully. He had never hinted at it. But then how much else of his private history had he withheld from her? She had told him everything and—— She caught her breath at the wave of desolation that swept over her.

Still, she thought. It made her angry. She ought to have got over it. She ought to be impervious to revelations about Miles Tabard by now. He was nothing to do with her any more. Was he?

Hastily, she said goodnight to Dimitri at her bedroom door. She was almost absent about it and his ironic look brought her up short. It had not occurred to her that he might want to kiss her goodnight. His expression told her that he had noticed. She closed her door in some confusion.

She went to the window. It was absolutely dark. She opened the french windows quietly. At once the honeyed scent of jasmine engulfed her. She stood very still. She could just make out the shapes of formal tubs which would no doubt hold geraniums. In the distance she could make out flashes of phosphorescence from the sea. She leaned her temple against the edge of the door, savouring the scents, the stillness, the distant lulling hush of the bay.

Why had Miles not told her? She could not believe he was ashamed. He wasn't ashamed of anything. He looked the world in the eye and dared it to criticise him.

Had Anne Tabard sworn him to secrecy? But other people seemed to know. Did he think it was none of Diana's business? Or had he thought it would give her a hold over him he didn't want her to have? The last possibility chilled her.

She rubbed her face tiredly against the frame. Or wasn't it true after all?

Dimitri and the Galatas family inhabited a social circle as small in its way as a village. Oh, they jetted all round the world but they met the same few people in each exotic stop-over. Like any other small community, they thrived on gossip, not all of it true. Maybe Dimitri's mother, seeing Miles's intimacy with the Galatas grandchildren, had put two and two together to make five.

And yet... And yet...

There was a sound below her. Diana froze.

The terrace was a long eighteenth-century affair that swept the length of one façade of the castle. Shallow steps led down not to a formal lawn, but an incongruous olive grove. Diana had seen it briefly earlier. Now she could just make out the trees in the dark. Trees and nothing else. The noise came again.

Silent-footed, she went outside to the edge of the terrace. Hands braced lightly on the marble balustrade, she scanned the shadows. It could have been some small animal. A lizard, say, although she had the vague idea that they were usually silent. Or——

She saw the pale gleam of a shirt-front among the trees and drew a sharp breath.

'Did I disturb you?' said Miles softly.

When didn't he disturb her? Especially coming at her without warning out of the scented night. He must have eyes like a cat's to make her out in this blackness, thought Diana. She found she was shaking.

'You gave me the fright of my life,' she spat back, finding her voice. 'I was just trying to convince myself that there were hedgehogs in Greece. Noisy hedgehogs.'

'I must be losing my touch.' The husky voice was amused.

He came out of the trees and ran lithely up the steps. His feet made no sound. He stopped in front of her. He didn't touch her.

'There was a time I could have got into any room off the terrace and not a soul would have heard me,' he told her softly in her ear.

Diana stepped back. 'Excellent talent for a cat burglar. Surely wasted on a physicist?' she responded tartly.

Her breathing was hurried. Deliberately she steadied herself. She saw his teeth gleam in the dark.

'Ah, but in those days physicist wasn't on my list. Too mundane. I was going to be a rock star. Jet pilot. Explorer.'

She was startled into a little laugh.

'What, *all* of them?'

'All of them,' he assured her solemnly. 'Maybe a brain surgeon in my spare time. Brain surgeons seemed to go down well.'

'Down well with whom?' Diana began, and found that he had moved imperceptibly so that now he was a good deal closer than she had realised.

'Use your imagination,' he told her huskily.

Her mouth was suddenly dry.

'Are you telling me you planned on being a vile seducer when you grew up?' she said, trying for a tone as cool and amused as his own. She didn't, she thought critically, do too badly either.

'Not vile,' he demurred.

He took another step forward. This time she saw it. She moved sideways and came up hard against a jasmine-entwined pillar. She put a hand against the cool marble to steady herself.

'I'm relieved to hear it,' she said politely.

'You ought to know without being told.' He was reproachful.

Diana flinched. She knew she was being teased. It was almost unbelievable. But she knew that provocative tone. She took firmer hold of her supporting pillar.

'I,' she told him lightly, 'never knew you in your midnight seducer days.'

'You missed something.' He was still laughing at her. In spite of the blackness of the night, she could feel his eyes on her, as vividly as a touch or the light breeze eddying up from the sea. She moved restively.

'I'm sure. I——'

'Mind you, getting out of the olive grove on to the terrace, without being caught, was only Phase One,' Miles said thoughtfully. 'And I seem to be out of practice there.' He reached for her. 'Let's see how we go on Phase Two.'

Phase Two had Diana breathless and shaking in seconds.

'Ah,' said Miles complacently, raising his head. 'It all comes back. Just like riding a bike.'

'Take your hands off me,' said Diana. She heard the tremor in her voice and despised herself for it.

'Keep your voice down. You don't want to wake the household.'

'I don't care if I wake the dead,' said Diana, really shaken. 'Take your hands off me *now*.'

Miles complied. His hands, she noticed, showed no disposition to linger. But he wasn't at all put out of countenance either.

'The trouble with you,' he said mildly, 'is you have no spirit of enquiry.'

Diana pushed past him. She took up a defensive stand behind a basket-weave chair, clutching its scratchy back like a lifebelt, and turned on him.

'I've plenty of spirit of enquiry,' she said grimly. 'Like what the *hell* you think you're doing, for a start.'

He gave a soft laugh. 'Me? I'd have thought I was easy enough to read. Reviving memories. Calling on my wife.'

'Ex-wife,' she interjected swiftly.

'Nope.' In the dark she could just make out the movement of the dark red hair. 'Not yet.'

She dismissed that with a gesture.

'Only because your damned solicitor was so inefficient he couldn't find you to sign the papers.'

Miles laughed again, quite kindly. It chilled her blood.

'Honey child, why do you think that was? I haven't been on the moon.'

Her heart gave a great thump like a pile-driver. Instinctively she put her hand to her side.

'I—don't understand.'

'He had instructions not to find me,' Miles said coolly, watching her.

For the second time that day, Diana felt the ground lurch under her.

'But—but why?' she managed at last. 'You were the one who left. You must want a divorce.'

'Is that why you asked for one?' he said swiftly.

Two years alone and the harsh months before them had taught Diana how to evade questions like that.

'Are you deliberately trying to be bloody-minded, Miles?' she demanded.

Yet again he disconcerted her. He propped himself against the balustrade and said thoughtfully, 'That's part of it, I suppose. The male need to look out for his own.'

She had a sudden vision of Dimitri's ironic look when she wished him goodnight and had an unwelcome revelation.

'Did you come here to make sure I was on my own tonight?' she said, furious. She saw his shoulders lift, and said between her teeth, 'I am not your own, Miles Tabard. I never will be.'

Again. She didn't say it. She didn't have to. It lay between them almost tangibly. She couldn't look at that casual, lounging body without remembering how completely she had been his own—once.

He remembered too, it was clear.

'No?' he said softly.

Diana felt as if she were in a whirlwind. 'I don't *understand* you,' she said in despair.

There was a pause. Then he said, 'I can see that. You don't know me very well, do you, Di?'

She winced. 'Did you ever let me know you?' she flashed.

Miles ignored that. 'You thought I'd let it go on forever? All this running around Europe after rich men. This great house. That palace. Do you ever go out with anyone who isn't a three-swimming-pool man, these days?'

If it hadn't been so hurtful, it would have been funny. Her job took her to the historic houses of Europe and the States; but, if their owners ever showed any personal interest in her, Diana Tabard was known for packing her bags and leaving.

There hadn't been anyone for her since Miles left. In her heart of hearts she knew there wouldn't be. It had hurt too much to risk again. But she wasn't going to tell Miles that.

She said in a strangled voice, 'You have no right to criticise the way I live.'

'You used to want to teach.' His voice was gentle, almost sad. 'Couldn't you have gone back to it?'

'When you left me, you mean?' Diana gave a hard laugh. 'I had to do something and I'd been out of university too long for a job to come up just like that. You didn't want me to stay on after we married.'

'So it's my fault?' He sounded resigned. 'I might have guessed.'

Diana flinched. 'It's nobody's fault,' she said in a voice like ice. 'It just happened. And I had to make the best of a bad job.'

He moved. 'You really think that is the best?'

Diana thought of the long hours, the travelling, matching colours till her eyes ached, the arduous processes of reconstructing paint and fabric.

'It's no picnic,' she allowed.

'Look,' Miles said in his most reasonable tone, 'give me a week of your time. Carry on with your holiday. Unwind. Take stock. If after that you want to carry on the way you are—well, it'll be your business. Only,' his voice grew grim, 'you won't do it on my money.'

Diana was instantly tense. 'The allowance...'

'Stops,' Miles said succinctly.

Diana thought of her parents' delight in their small house with its purpose-designed kitchen where her father could reach things and his conservatory where he could grow his plants. It was their independence which was at risk. She was building up a reputation as a consultant in her field but it was a slow business. She was almost sure she wouldn't be able to meet the payments on their mortgage out of her present income.

She said, 'What if I go tomorrow?'

'Then the allowance stops tomorrow,' Miles said, quite gently.

It was no choice at all. They both knew it.

He had always been like that, she thought with a flash of unwelcome memory. He didn't fight. He didn't even seem to *care* most of the time. But without raising his voice or taking any sort of stance he simply made it impossible for her to do anything except what he wanted.

He came over to her and took the light basket-weave chair out of her hands. She jumped. He bent and kissed her mouth lightly, almost insultingly. Diana went rigid.

Miles gave a soft laugh. He patted her cheek. He meant to denigrate her and he succeeded. Diana gave a small sound of protest.

'Quite right. Not a swimming-pool to my name; you'll have to change the entrance qualification,' he drawled.

And then his arms were round her like bands of steel. His hands in the small of her back hurt. He was kissing her with a bruising strength that was almost frightening. Her skin felt scorched. She struggled. Miles didn't seem to notice.

He had never kissed her like this before, not even when they were astonished by love and still exploring. Not when they were married. She had never been kissed like this in her life. It felt as if he was furiously angry, yet more with himself than her. It felt as if his mouth would sear deep into her and change her forever, as if that was what he was determined to do.

Earlier Diana had felt an electric echo of their old passion for each other. But this was nothing like that. Diana felt herself sinking in a sea of fire, appalled and helpless.

'*No*,' she said. She didn't know if she was addressing Miles or herself.

He let her go as abruptly as he had seized her. Diana fell back. Her mouth throbbed. Her whole body throbbed. Two years of careful independence and painfully cultivated poise cracked wide open in a moment, she thought. Her hands flew to hide her burning cheeks as she backed away from him.

'Don't ever do that again,' she said in a voice she barely recognised as her own.

He took a hasty step after her. Instinctively her hands went out to ward him off. He stopped dead. She could not look at him. She had the impression that he was

willing her to do so with every atom of his considerable personality. But she wouldn't give in.

She heard him draw a careful breath. 'Di,' he said in an undertone.

Her chin went up. 'You've made your point.'

He was preserving a careful distance. 'And what point is that?'

'That you still have—power—over me.' Her voice shook. The admission humiliated her and it was a worse humiliation that Miles would know it.

'Di,' he said again, softly.

'Get away from me.' There was real fear in her voice, fear of losing the last of her fragile self-possession.

He hesitated. She saw him debate and tensed. She saw him take that in, too, and fling up his hands, palms open.

'Hell,' he said explosively.

Before she realised, he turned on his heel and was running silently down the marble steps. He disappeared into the aromatic shadows while she was still fighting for composure.

It was not, Diana acknowledged wryly to her mirror the next morning, the most restful night of her life. In spite of her tiredness and the wine, her mind could not relax. Round and round it went: indignation at Miles's assumption about her life; bewilderment at how he arrived at his conclusions; fear that he would take action which would cost her parents their haven; indignation again that she should be caught in this trap.

Would he carry out his threat? It wasn't like him to be vindictive. But then two years of marriage had taught her that Miles didn't threaten anything he wasn't prepared to do. She must talk to him. Abandon her pride—and heaven knew there wasn't much of that left after last night—and make him understand the truth about

her visits to the grand houses, since he seemed to resent them so much. Explain about her job. Then maybe Miles would apologise and they could say goodbye.

Miles? her wiser self said tartly. *Miles, apologise?*

Two years of marriage had taught her that too. Miles had a simple philosophy: never explain, never apologise. He said it kept life uncomplicated. Perhaps it did, for him. For Diana, trying to guess his mood and assess his intentions in those last months, it had turned the marriage into a living nightmare.

She propped her hand on her chin, studying the too prominent cheekbones in the mirror. She didn't look so bad now. When Miles first walked out she had looked like a ghost.

She'd looked like a ghost the night of the Comem Ball. For weeks Miles had been coming home late, sleeping in his study, spending his weekends with Steve Gilman and his computer.

The only person he had seen outside his work was Susie, in London and signalling an emergency. He had run up to her West End hotel the evening of the day she telephoned. But then he always went when Susie summoned him.

The rest of the time he was so busy that he barely spoke. Diana was astonished when he'd announced that he wanted them to go to his college ball.

Her mouth twisted at the memory. She had tried so hard. She had even asked Susie to take her to her own exclusive dressmaker in London.

The dress was a drift of grey-green voile shot through with the faintest thread of gold. It left her shoulders bare and clung to the point where the skirt swirled at hip height. She had put her hair up for once, letting it curl on to her long neck in feathery curls. Miles loved

those curls. Or he had once said he did. She wore the jade drops he had given her as an engagement present.

Once she would have been delighted with the way she looked. But twenty months into marriage with Miles left her standing in front of him waiting for his verdict. The brown eyes had flicked over her once and come to rest on her naked shoulders.

'Did you decide against total nudity because of the temperature?' he asked neutrally. There was not the glimmer of a smile in the question.

Diana was stunned. The hard eyes told her nothing. That was when she sensed dislike for the first time. It was like a blow.

'I'll go and change,' she said quietly.

She put the dress and the jade away and never looked at them again. When she left the Oxford house they were still in their boxes in the bedroom that by that time she and Miles had openly ceased to share.

Yet yesterday—this morning—he had been almost as he was when they first met. He had laughed and teased her. He had made her feel—well, when she walked in on him in that bed and realised who it was, he had made her feel as if the years between were all in her imagination. As if he and she belonged together and had never been seriously apart.

'Careful,' Diana said to her mirrored image softly. 'Be very careful. You can't afford to be taken in again.'

There was a perfunctory scratch on the door. She looked up, startled. To her astonishment, Susie Galatas walked in bearing a tray.

'Maria said you were still asleep when she looked in. I thought you might like breakfast.' There was a constraint there. But it sounded as if she was genuinely trying to be friendly.

The tray was piled high with rolls. There was yoghurt too and a silver dish of honey as well as a steaming pot of coffee. Two cups. Susie—or someone—was intending to stay.

Diana swung round on her stool, her eyebrows lifting.

'Lavish,' she commented.

'Well, you ate little enough last night,' Susie said. She sent her guest a slant-eyed look. 'Did you think Miles had poisoned the food?'

Not that friendly, then. Diana side-stepped it with the ease of practice.

'Tiredness. I've been travelling too long.'

Susie poured coffee for both of them and took hers to the chaise-longue, tucking her feet under her.

'How was Hamburg?' she asked.

'Wet. But it should be rewarding.'

Susie nodded absently. 'It worries you that Miles is here, doesn't it?'

Diana made a great business of helping herself to yoghurt and swirling the dark golden honey into it.

'He's entitled,' she said carefully.

'But you're not happy about it.'

Diana avoided her eyes. Even if she knew what the truth was about her complicated feelings for Miles, she didn't feel like sharing them with Susie Galatas.

So she shrugged. 'He's human. We used to get on well enough, after all.'

Susie's eyes widened. 'You mean you'd go back to him?' she said blankly. 'After all you've said?'

Diana took a spoonful of yoghurt, not answering.

Susie looked troubled. 'Oh, God. It must be hell for you, being here with him. Look—if you want to go, I'll tell him. We won't be offended. Honestly.'

Yesterday, it would have been all that Diana needed to have her turned round and out of Castle Galatas in minutes. But Miles with his damnable blackmail had effectively cut off that escape route.

So she said casually, 'I can handle it.' She gave Susie a warm smile that was almost genuine. 'I'm going to snooze and rest, whenever I'm not working. If I know Miles he'll be flinging himself round the bay in a boat. Or running the marathon. We won't meet except at meals.'

Susie sucked in her bottom lip, shaking her head.

'For instance,' said Diana, taking more coffee, 'today, I'm going to lie on the terrace and not lift a finger all morning.'

Susie uncurled her legs and stood up. She still looked worried but there was an unusual gleam of amusement there too.

'Oh, no, you're not,' she said. 'Miles is taking us all fishing.'

Diana didn't resist, in the end. At least they would not be alone. Though the relief was short-lived when she saw the amount of luggage Susie and Chris considered essential for the trip.

'Good lord, are you going to *sleep* on board?' Diana demanded.

Dimitri, who was nearest, looked up and grinned. He took her hand and bent briefly over it. 'This is what the brother and sister Galatas consider essential fare for a civilised fishing trip,' he explained.

'The emphasis,' said Chris calmly, 'is on civilised. I am not Miles.'

Miles raised his brows. It fell to Susie to explain.

'Miles likes to kill his lunch,' she told Diana.

'I like my fish fresh,' Miles said.

Susie patted his arm. 'Squid still squirming. We know. We remember.'

They must do, thought Diana. A momentary bleakness touched her. A shared childhood gave an intimacy that nothing else quite matched. She shook off the shadow. 'Can I help?'

'Only by sitting and looking beautiful,' Susie said generously. 'Somebody needs to.'

'And you qualify,' Dimitri told her.

Susie turned away to supervise the picnic basket. Diana smiled. Her jeans were new, only because she had split her old ones climbing over antique fireplaces in Hamburg. Her striped blue shirt and bright scarf came from a chain-store and she wore neither make-up nor jewellery. But she did not protest, as she once would have done. She had learned that compliments were the social coinage with which men like Dimitri negotiated with the opposite sex. They were graceful and quite meaningless.

She saw Miles watching her frowningly. She lifted her chin and aimed a smile somewhere to his left.

'Can't I at least help carry this stuff to the boat?' she asked.

There was a general shout of laughter in which even Miles joined.

'I said civilised,' Chris reminded her. 'There's a hoist to get this stuff down to the bay. My grandfather had it installed.'

'And you and Miles rode up and down on it all week,' Susie recalled. '*How* angry he was!'

Once again Diana felt excluded. She covered up quickly.

'I'm going to be a complete passenger. You're not going to let me contribute at all.'

'Oh, we'll think of something,' Miles murmured.

Dimitri and Chris were hauling a rope tight while Maria and another girl were carefully stowing bottles in a wicker basket. Clearly nobody but Diana was intended to hear the barbed remark.

She looked at him then, schooling her expression. He looked friendly enough on the surface. But the brown eyes were masked. She knew that look. She had hoped—prayed—she would never have to see it again. Her heart sank.

And then, for some reason, she looked at Susie. She was watching them. Susie's beauty was always dark and dramatic but for a moment she looked almost ugly. Her mouth thinned, leaving her looking drained and shockingly old.

She must have overheard Miles's remark too. Diana realised it with a little shock. Heard it and been hurt by it. So Susie must still be in love with him.

She felt a brief spur of anger at Miles. Whether the rumours about him and Susie were justified or not, there was no need to hurt her gratuitously. Diana moved away from him unobtrusively, turning her back. She could feel his eyes between her shoulder-blades, though.

The others seemed unaware. They set off down the path to the boat, Miles first way out in front, then Susie with Dimitri and, last, Diana beside Christos. The other three talked of islands and charts and winds. She allowed her attention to wander.

It was very hot but the others had all brought jerseys, looped about them over long-sleeved shirts. All but Miles, who was wearing the lightest of T-shirts and looked as if he might tear it off at any moment. She watched him springing lithely down the uneven path. He looked superbly fit.

Not for the first time, Diana wondered what he was doing in Greece in May. He had said—hadn't he?—that he had been working in the open air. She had inferred that meant he had been there for some time. Whereas his lawyer thought he was in Australia on a lecture tour.

Had something gone wrong? She watched the solitary figure forging ahead as if impatient with the others' recreational pace. She had deliberately not kept up with his old friends in Oxford, but she had read that his book had been well received and that he and Steve Gilman were being given all sorts of honours in the scientific world. Nothing wrong there, surely?

Of course he drove himself and everyone else at a punishing pace. Diana wondered briefly if that had finally brought about a physical collapse. But she discarded the idea as soon as it was born. Quite apart from the muscular shoulders and the outdoor tan, it was no invalid who was leaping down the path like an Olympic runner.

Abruptly she caught herself. Well or ill, Miles Tabard was no longer any affair of hers. She reminded herself of that all the way down to the boat.

CHAPTER FOUR

THE boat trip was a revelation on a number of fronts, not all of them encouraging. For one thing Diana was surprised to see how relaxed and friendly Chris Galatas was. She thought wryly that it was probably because she and Miles were clearly no longer together.

For another, she was startled and dismayed to find how her heart quivered every time Miles leaped nimbly across the side of the boat. Had he always been this reckless? She watched him scramble over the top of the cockpit in the swaying launch as it curved round the bay, and had the sensation of being in a nightmare. He never seemed to lose his balance, even for a moment, but she found she couldn't bear to watch him.

He's nothing to do with me, Diana told herself again. She felt sick. She turned her back and concentrated on her conversation with Christos.

He was saying casually, 'I hear you're doing up Dieter's place, aren't you?'

The Hamburg client. Of course, she should have realised that Chris would know him. There were swift footsteps which she was almost sure were Miles running across the sloping roof. She swallowed, not looking round.

'I deal with the architect,' Diana said.

Christos took out some sunglasses and pushed them up his Roman nose. He grinned. 'I'm squashed. But I've known Dieter Schleger for a long time.'

Diana eyed him warily. 'What's that supposed to mean?'

'That if there was a gorgeous female tripping about renovating his crumbling tax-loss he'd be hot in pursuit.'

Against her will, she smiled. He was quite right about the reason for Schleger's purchase of his baroque mansion. The architect was open about it.

'I'm flattered,' she said with composure. 'But Herr Schleger doesn't know I exist.' She sat back, clasping her hands round her knees and looked at him thoughtfully. 'You and Miles seem to have an odd idea about what I do. I don't dine in diamonds and satin with the owners of the houses I work on, you know. I'm just as much a workman as the plumber or the person who puts tiles on their roofs. I wouldn't want it any other way. And I've never even *seen* your friend Dieter.'

Chris folded his hands over his stomach. A small smile played about his mouth. 'Wrong idea indeed.' He flicked her a look. 'I hope you won't mind having dinner with the owners here?' he added drily.

'Since you're so democratic in Greece, I'll make an exception,' she said demurely.

Chris gave a great shout of laughter.

Miles came sure-footedly down the deck towards them. As Diana had somehow known he would, he had discarded his T-shirt. His shoulders were as brown as polished walnut. The dusting of hair that formed a triangle on his chest had bleached to auburn. The bone and muscles beneath moved like oiled steel as he put one hand on the side and vaulted down to join them.

Diana caught her breath. One unprepared glimpse of the elegant machine that was her husband's body set her pulses hammering. She fumbled for her own dark glasses.

Miles smiled at her. 'Dazzled?'

For a moment she thought he had noticed her shameful reaction to his near-nakedness and was mocking her. She stiffened, angry and obscurely

wounded. Miles's eyebrows rose. Then, too late, she realised he was talking about the gleam of silver where the sun hit the water.

She pushed the sunglasses on with jerky movements, not answering.

Oblivious of the tension, Chris said, 'Not surprising. She's been locked in dark palaces for the last year. Needs the fresh air and sunshine.'

Miles laughed. 'Back to nature, that's what you need.'

Chris said, 'Not too far back. You be careful,' he urged Diana. 'He'll have you climbing masts and eating seaweed.'

Diana's confusion was under control now. 'So I gather,' she said coolly. From behind the protection of her dark glasses she said to Miles, 'When did you develop this Boy Scout streak?'

Miles eased himself down beside her. He spread his arms along the side of the boat, stretching behind her. It was the merest brushing of flesh against the material of her shirt. Diana went still. The warm skin felt like fire against the masking cotton. She felt his eyes on her.

'Oh, it's always been there,' he said easily. 'You didn't see it in England because I don't like wet tents and sausages.'

Chris shuddered. 'I don't understand English education.'

Miles kicked him with a bare, bronzed foot. 'You don't understand education at all, you philistine. When did you last read a book? All you do is make money. Look to the whole man, my friend. Look to the whole man.'

'I conserve my energies,' Chris said with dignity.

Miles laughed. 'Too right. If your car broke down, how far do you think you could walk?'

Chris grinned suddenly. 'As far as I had to. Shut up, you monster. And stop waving your biceps about. You're not going to make me feel inferior. Or Diana either.'

Miles's laughing eyes surveyed her deliberately.

'Diana's a different kettle of porridge altogether,' he drawled. 'You're just lazy. And if you aren't ashamed you aren't proud of it either. Now, Diana thinks it's a good thing to be frail and let people take care of her. Don't you, sweetheart?'

The attack was unexpected but the weapons weren't. It was what Miles had said on that devastating last night.

'I'm not your insurance policy,' he had said to her with that killing quietness. 'You picked the wrong man for a father substitute.'

Even now, it could still hurt. But she had been on her own since then. She had rebuilt her confidence. Miles was not going to put her down again.

'I thought real men like to take care of women,' she told him sweetly.

Miles gave that crooked, mocking smile she had once feared so much.

'*Real* men like their ladies to be equals,' he said softly.

Diana leaned forward casually, so that she broke that delicate friction between their bodies.

'Desirable behaviour is spearing squid and tightrope-walking on fast launches?' she enquired neutrally.

Even though they were no longer touching, she could feel Miles's body tense as if she had surprised him. Chris was chuckling.

'She's right, you know. You wouldn't like a girl to play your games as well as you do yourself, Miles.'

Diana flung him a grateful smile. Miles reached out a lazy foot and kicked him gently again.

'You're supposed to be on my side,' he complained.

Chris flung up a hand, the stub of his cigar between his fingers.

'Not me. I'm a fully paid-up neutral.'

'You're a fully paid-up coward,' Miles retorted. But there was a smile in his voice.

Why, thought Diana, *why* does he sound so tolerant, so friendly when he's teasing Chris and so cold when it's me?

Chris was smiling too. 'I initiate. I create. I inspire,' he said. 'That's work. I just don't like getting my hands dirty.'

Miles flung back his head and laughed. Chris turned to Diana.

'Do you like getting your hands dirty?' he appealed. 'When you're consorting with your plumbers and tilers and whatever, do you take the tools out of their hands and cover yourself with dirt?'

Miles sat upright suddenly. She felt his arm tense along the wood behind her, even though they were no longer touching.

'It's a fascinating thought,' he drawled. 'Dirt, darling?'

Diana didn't look at him. The endearment was like a touch; her blood leaped at it. Even when she knew it was a mockery of everything they had once felt. Correction, thought Diana wryly; everything she had felt.

'Dust rather than dirt,' she said with an effort. Even without looking at him she could feel Miles's eyes on her.

He said slowly, 'I thought you were an interior decorator. An adviser.'

Diana sent him a brief, carefully unfocused smile over her shoulder. She didn't want to meet his eyes. He was too close.

'When you're talking about restoration, it gets a bit basic, I'm afraid. More than pretty ideas and swatches of materials, anyway.'

'You mean those palaces of yours put you on a daily rate and make you bring your own sandwiches?' His voice was full of unholy amusement.

She made herself laugh a little. 'No sandwiches when I'm examining historic fabrics. But you've basically got the idea.'

Miles chuckled. 'Do you enjoy it?'

Diana considered. It was better than thinking about his uncomfortable nearness.

'Most of the time,' she said honestly. 'I'm getting quite good, which is nice. I'm not very keen on having to sell myself but more work comes in these days from recommedations. And of course,' she added with a flicker of malice she couldn't repress, thinking of his strictures last night, 'you meet a very nice class of person.'

Miles's eyes went blank. She looked full in his face and saw they had gone as brown as madeira, bright as the sunlit sea and quite without expression.

'A very nice class of plumber,' murmured Chris, 'is exactly what this castle needs. If we entertain you royally, do you suppose you could give us an introduction, Diana?'

Before she could answer Susie had come and claimed Miles. It didn't seem to Diana that he went reluctantly. She relaxed her tense shoulders against the side of the boat with an almost audible sigh of relief as he went. But it didn't stop her looking after them with something like regret.

Miles and Susie fished noisily from the side of the boat for the rest of the morning. Dimitri came and sat beside her, pointing out landmarks as they rapidly went past. Chris dozed. From the corner of her eye Diana watched the anglers.

Dimitri followed the direction of her gaze. He stopped talking about the coastal landscape.

'I think this time she's going to get what she wants,' he said softly.

It was obvious what he meant. Diana didn't try to pretend she didn't understand. She looked at Susie's animation and thought she detected a hint of frenzy there. Diana, who knew how Miles could remove himself at a stroke when he felt like it, felt suddenly sorry for her. If Susie wasn't as confident as she looked, Miles could hurt her badly.

'If it is what she wants,' she said.

Dimitri looked at her pityingly. 'Diana, how old are you?' he asked.

'Twenty-six,' she said, startled.

'And you have heaven knows how many degrees and run your own business?'

'Well, sort of,' Diana said cautiously. 'It's not quite as grand as you make it sound but...'

He waved the *caveat* aside. 'No matter. My point is that you have a lot to learn.'

She stared at him. His mouth twisted a little and he said gently, 'You think you're bright. And sophisticated. And up to a point you are. But you're no match for Susie. She can't spell in any language and she wouldn't know how to run a cocktail party without help, much less her own business. But she's got you taped and hog-tied.'

'I don't understand,' said Diana, pardonably.

'No. You wouldn't. Because Susie is a Clever Woman,' Dimitri said, stabbing the air with his finger to make his point. 'And you're not.'

'Thank you,' said Diana, ruffled.

He grinned. 'It's a compliment, you know. Clever Women are manipulators. Men don't like that. When,' he added with sudden gloom, 'we notice it's happening.'

He cast a thoughtful look at the cheerful pair and their fishing lines.

'Now I'd say Susie was being a bit obvious this time. But there's no sign Miles has noticed.'

'Miles,' said Diana with bitterness, 'notices everything.'

Dimitri lit a cigarette. He gave her a faint smile.

'Then we should be in for an interesting time.'

But Susie and Miles seemed in perfect harmony. In fact, as Diana watched, they seem to become more and more of a couple. It was easy to attribute it to their shared childhood, of course, but that was too easy. Miles had shared his childhood with Chris as well and they sparred relentlessly. Most of the time it was good-humoured, but just sometimes Diana thought she heard an edge to the teasing. There was no edge at all when he teased Susie.

And there was no teasing in his voice when he fell into step beside her on the way back from the boat.

'Why did you let me think your job wasn't serious?' he asked.

Diana's shoulders stiffened. 'I don't recall discussing my job with you at all.'

'Precisely.'

'So you leapt to conclusions and I'm to blame?' Diana stopped dead and turned towards him. The dusty stones sputtered under the abrupt movement. 'Would you have believed me if I'd said I was interested in the houses, not the titled owners? When did you ever believe my unsupported word, Miles?' she said with a bitterness she couldn't hide. 'Nobody else thought I was chasing the jet set. Why did you? And I don't notice you apologising,' she added acidly.

He stared at her with a very strange expression.

'You want an apology?' he asked softly, at last.

Diana turned away, feeling somehow defeated. 'I don't want anything,' she said wearily.

'Now that I doubt,' said the quiet voice at her shoulder.

She began to walk again, her shoulders slumping. 'What do you want from me, Miles? I've told you I won't stand in the way of a divorce. You need never see me again. And once my business is really solid I can take over the payments on the house.'

He made a sharp movement. 'That's not important.'

'Isn't it?' She was wry. 'I thought it was the thought of my swanning around Europe on your hard-earned cash that was the cause of this—farce.'

'If you thought that, you've even more to learn than Dimitri thinks,' he told her softly.

She was confused. 'More than...?' Then she understood. 'You were listening. Eavesdropping. On a private conversation.' She was almost incoherent with the rage that consumed her.

Miles was unrepentant. 'You said yourself I notice everything.'

'How dare you? You had no right...'

'You're my wife,' he said flatly.

'That doesn't give you the right to spy on me——' she began hotly.

He interrupted, 'Maybe not the right. What about necessity?'

'I don't know what you're talking about,' she cried.

'I know you don't.' He was odiously calm. 'Dimitri was right. A *lot* to learn.'

'I hate you,' she said, knowing it was childish but unable to suppress it.

'Possibly.' He didn't sound concerned.

She flung round on him, stopping again. 'Look, now you know I'm a solid citizen who does a decent job of work for her bread—will you let me go?'

'No.'

She swept on, hardly heeding. 'You wouldn't really let my parents be thrown out of their house. They never did you any harm.'

'I said no.'

Her voice rose. 'You used to like them. And it won't be forever. Just another couple of years.'

'If you leave the castle, the allowance stops,' he said implacably.

Diana gave a little sob. 'How can you be so cruel?'

'To insist you have what is obviously a much needed holiday?' His crooked smile didn't reach his eyes. 'Where's the cruelty in that?'

'I can't bear it,' Diana said involuntarily.

'Yes, you can. You bore it very gracefully today. And you'll continue to do so, if you want that allowance.' His voice softened suddenly. 'Look, all I want is a week. Is that so much to ask? I won't hound you, I promise.'

She looked away.

'I don't seem to have much choice, do I?'

His voice hardened. But all he said was, 'You're learning.'

He was as good as his word. He did not seek her out. And when she said she didn't want to go fishing the next day he was the only one of the group who didn't protest.

Diana should have relaxed. Instead, she got more tense. She found herself jumping at odd noises; looking for him, even when she knew he was out in the bay; waiting. The third night she even locked her bedroom door. There was no need. She was undisturbed.

She spent the mornings going round the apartments that needed restoration. Neither Chris nor Susie showed much interest, to her surprise. She began to wonder uneasily if Dimitri was right when he said the castle belonged to Miles.

It seemed inconceivable that she shouldn't have known. It seemed inconceivable that Miles would have arranged to employ his estranged wife to restore the rooms. But nothing about this visit was going the way she expected. It could be that both the holiday and the commission were Miles's idea. Not that he ever said anything that hinted at it. But Diana remembered all too clearly how good he had always been at keeping his own counsel.

The afternoons, theoretically at least, she spent dozing on the terrace outside her room, under the shade of the vines. In fact she sat and stared unseeingly at the bay, her mind turning over and over old estrangements. It was not restful. She began to look strained.

Oddly enough, it was Chris who remarked on it first. It was at the evening meal on the fourth day of Diana's stay. They were on the battlemented terrace looking over the northern stretch of water. On this occasion they were eating spit-roasted lamb from the kitchen and Maria was waiting on them.

'You're looking tired. Are we working you too hard?' Chris said.

Diana shook her head. 'I enjoy it.'

Miles looked up sharply from his discussion with Susie over the wine.

'Come to any conclusions yet?' Chris asked.

Diana hesitated. 'It's going to cost a lot of money,' she said bluntly.

Miles gave a soft laugh. 'In character.'

Diana tried not to wince. She turned to him slowly. 'I'm sorry?'

He smiled at her innocently. 'She was a very expensive lady, by all accounts. The Princess, I mean.'

She met his eyes and saw a lot more than innocence in them. She wondered if the others did too, and shivered.

Chris said tolerantly, 'Well, she had a lot to compensate for—living here in the middle of nowhere with a chap she didn't really know. And a foreigner.'

'An old foreigner,' Miles reminded him. There was an edge to his voice.

Susie said indignantly, 'He wasn't old. He was forty. You're nearly forty, after all.'

'That made him old enough to be her father,' Miles said evenly.

Something troubled Diana. She said slowly, 'And how old was she? The Princess?'

Susie shrugged. 'Who knows? They didn't exactly have birth certificates. She was the last daughter of the Bey, and his favourite. That was why they were so angry when she helped our ancestor escape. And then ran away with him.'

Miles said, 'Family legend says she was twenty. She could have been three or four years either side of it.'

And I was only just twenty-two when you married me, Diana thought, disturbed.

Chris said easily, 'Well, she must have been a strong character. She created quite a salon, you know. It was some achievement, getting civilised people to come out into the wilds of Greece in the middle of the eighteenth century. But she did it. And collected all that expensive furniture that it's going to cost a fortune to put right.'

He sent Miles a quick look. Diana looked at him searchingly for signs that it was going to be his bill. But Miles, as ever, was inscrutable.

She said, watching him, 'It could. If you want to do it properly.'

Chris made a face. 'What do you mean by properly?'

She hesitated. Did they really want a lecture on restoration techniques?

'Well, take the upholstery. I could get the furniture re-stuffed, mended. But if you want it to last another two hundred years looking as it should, you'd need to re-embroider. It's all skilled hand-work. So it's expensive.'

Susie had been looking at Miles too, she discovered. Now she said suddenly, 'We don't want to turn the Princess's rooms into a museum, you know, Diana. I'm sure you're very skilful but this isn't for show. Just for the family's private satisfaction. There's not limitless money to spend.'

Diana was taken aback. It was friendly enough on the surface but underneath there was more than a hint of annoyance. And had there been the faintest emphasis on the word 'family', pointing out that Diana was an outsider?

She said gently, '*I'm* not spending any money at all, Susie. Or saying that anyone else should.' Across the terrace her eyes met Miles's. 'You asked for my views. There they are.'

Miles lifted one eyebrow and his mouth quirked. He looked carelessly amused. There was something in his eyes, though, that was neither amused nor careless.

Diana rapidly averted her eyes. She looked round at the others steadily. She did not say what she was thinking because it was clear from their expressions that they, like Miles, recognised it: I'm not in your employment and

if you speak to me like that again I won't help any
further.

Susie frowned. But at once she was laughing again.

'Of course. It's frightfully kind of you to spend your
holiday going over our mouldy old rooms.'

Diana chose to accept it as a tacit apology.

'It's as well to realise from the first what a big under-
taking restoration often is. It can get completely out of
hand,' she said.

'Because it's done by enthusiasts, I suppose,' Susie
murmured. 'People with lots of knowledge and degrees
and no common sense.'

So it hadn't been an apology.

Before she could answer, Miles intervened. 'Don't you
like enthusiasts, Susie?' he said lazily.

She gave a husky laugh and put a hand on his arm.
'I like *practical* people, darling. You should know that,'
she said into his eyes.

Her hand with its scattering of jewelled rings looked
very small against the white sleeve of his shirt. It also
looked as if she was very used to touching him. It gave
Diana a queer little stab. She looked away, not wanting
to think about why it hurt.

Chris turned to her. 'Well, you sound eminently practical to me.'

'Oh, she does,' Miles agreed. 'You'd better get her to
take you round the apartments tomorrow and explain
the options.'

Was his tone unduly meaningful? Had Chris just received his orders? Or was she being paranoid? Diana
said at random, 'It's not all in my field. I might mislead
you.'

'Ball-park figures,' Chris said and grinned at her expression. 'Don't look so worried. I'm a rich man.'

'Oh, she knows that,' said Miles, his voice hard. 'Don't you, darling? Or you wouldn't be here.'

There was a nasty little silence. This time Diana knew exactly why she was hurt. It made her angry. What right had he to call her a gold-digger? And what reason?

She said coldly, 'I'm here because I was invited. For a holiday. I don't have to tout for business, Miles. I'm an expert. If the *family*——' and she emphasised it just as Susie had '—want to make the room look pretty, without restoration, then they don't need me. I'm too expensive.'

'Surprise me,' mocked Miles.

But Chris intervened, defusing the anger that sparked between them, barely below the surface.

'We'll talk it through tomorrow. I'm not giving myself indigestion fighting over our heritage at this hour,' he said firmly.

Miles spent the whole meal being impeccably polite. Diana, wincing from barbs that she felt she alone understood, could only be thankful when it ended. She excused herself while Susie and Dimitri were brewing coffee. Miles was watching them critically.

'You said it yourself, Chris. I'm tired. I've got a lot of sleep to catch up on,' she murmured. 'I'll slip away now, if you don't mind. I—er—don't want to break up the party.'

The look he gave her held a good deal of comprehension, she thought. But all he said was, 'Sleep well.'

She lost herself returning to her room. She wasn't particularly worried. Since she'd arrived in the castle, she thought wryly, she never seemed to get where she was going at the first attempt. But she always found her way in the end. She was tranquil about it.

Her tranquility disappeared abruptly when she saw Miles standing in the corridor outside her room.

'What are you doing?' she began.

He turned to look at her. He seemed very tall in the shadowed corridor. His shirt was blindingly white against the deep tan of his throat. His hair was longer than she was used to. It brushed the deep collar, like one of those eighteenth-century dandies whose portraits had surrounded her all morning. Except that he was warm and breathing and there wasn't inches of brocade and velvet between those powerful shoulders and the world, she thought involuntarily. She drew a shaky breath.

He scanned her face. 'You're going to do it, aren't you?' he said slowly.

'I don't know what you mean,' she said.

'Chris. You're going to do his silly little ancestress's boudoir.'

'Your silly little ancestress too,' Diana flashed before she thought.

He put his hands on her shoulders. She went still. He turned her slowly so that her face was turned to the light. The deep-set eyes were unreadable.

'You've caught up with that one, have you?' he murmured. 'I wondered when you would. Yes, it's true. Bastard that I am, I share the genes of the Princess whom George Galatas brought home from Turkey. The enemy in the house.'

There was deep bitterness there. Diana was startled. So startled that she forbore to challenge him on the ownership of the castle and whether he was the one who would be paying for her expert services, for all his clever byplay with Chris.

'What do you mean?' she said instead.

'It isn't quite the romantic story Susie wants to believe, you know. She was a brat and spoilt rotten. Hence the French furniture and the Italian paintings.'

Diana said with an odd breathlessness, 'It's a beautiful set of rooms. I'll be glad to do what I can.'

Miles surveyed her. 'Do you feel empathy with her? The Princess? Do you go in that room and sense her poor little exiled spirit calling you?'

His scorn was like a burn. She flinched inwardly. She would not let him see how it affected her, though.

'No,' she said with composure. 'I go into that room and sense a strong odour of rotting horsehair, just like anyone else.'

He gave a brief, unamused laugh. 'She came to a bad end, you know, the Princess. She drove him too far once too often.'

'I know nothing about her,' Diana said defensively.

'Oh, you should look her up. There's plenty of stuff in the library here. Some of it's even in English. She has had her biographers. Attracted by the romance, of course. When they find out the truth, they tend to lose heart.'

'The truth?' said Diana, suddenly wary.

'That she was a calculating, poisonous bitch. She may have been only twenty but she took poor old George Galatas like a professional.' His voice was bitter.

Diana thought, He doesn't sound as if he's talking about people who have been dead for two hundred years and more.

'He was a quiet soul. Something of a scholar. He wrote rather a good book on the Great Bear. Heaven knows what he was doing on that expedition to Turkey. He was no soldier. He was ransomed, you know. It wasn't a dashing escape. She smuggled herself on board, into his stateroom. It damned nearly caused another war.'

Diana said quietly, 'She must have been very much in love with him.'

His laugh was soft and chillingly cold.

'Oh, I don't think so. She didn't have much of a future at home and she didn't fancy life on her own in Europe. She was used to the best, too. George was the ideal solution. So she seduced him and made him marry her. And then made his life hell.'

Diana thought, He's talking about himself. About us.

She said harshly, 'You've never been seduced in your life.'

'No,' he agreed softly.

Their eyes met. It was almost brutal. Diana gasped. He slanted her a mocking look.

'She came to a bad end, you know. She was killed by brigands. Or that's the story. Her body was found by the roadside anyway. It could have been the lover she thought would take her away with him. Or it could have been George himself.'

Oddly shaken, Diana said, 'That's—horrible.'

He said, 'No more than she deserved, some say.'

She looked at the cold, handsome face. 'Do you believe that?' It was a strangled whisper.

Miles gave a slow smile. 'I believe that very young women can sometimes be careless—shall we say?—about how their activities affect others.'

Diana winced.

'And, whether he did it or not, I think poor old George had suffered enough by the time she died. He was something of a mathematician; he did good work after she went.'

Diana felt as if her heart would stop. She flung up her head defiantly and met the predator's gaze as bravely as she could.

'As you have?' she suggested.

Just for a moment the ice in his eyes moved. It didn't melt but it cracked and shifted to show a volcano of feeling that had her retreating involuntarily before she realised it.

Miles gave a soft laugh. It wasn't a pleasant sound. 'Oh, we're fellows, all right, George and I.'

Diana stared at him, mesmerised. The eyes were like a hawk's, clever and pitiless. He moved. She closed her eyes, then felt his fingers, like fire, against her cold cheek.

'I see you agree with me,' Miles murmured.

He drew her against his body, so that she could feel the height and strength and fierce energy there. And then, quite slowly, he let her go. Bewildered, and more than a little afraid, she opened her eyes. His smile was crooked.

'Interesting,' he said.

His hands dropped. Then, abruptly, he made her a quaint little mock-bow and strode past her without another word.

CHAPTER FIVE

DIANA was shaking when she closed the door of her room. In her wildest imaginings she had never expected that passionate outburst from Miles. She knew it was passion. It was there not just in his words but in every line of his body. She knew his body language very well. She had learned to read it during the long silences that were the graveyard of their marriage.

But passion could be deceptive. She had learned that too.

There was no use trying to sleep. Diana pulled on her pretty cotton night things and opened her windows wider. The night was windless. There wasn't even the faint breeze from the sea she had grown used to. The scent of jasmine lay heavy in the humid air.

The scent triggered her memory. Was it only two nights ago that Miles had come to her out of that olive grove? He had reminded her—briefly and shockingly—of how it felt to be in his arms.

She had thought herself safe after two years of hard-won independence. But one potent reminder of what was lost to her had destroyed all that. Diana clutched her elbows, standing statue-still in the warm air. She no longer felt safe.

She was not still in love with him. She couldn't still be in love with him. It was out of the question.

She had been in love, all right—desperately in love. She had been frightened of how much she loved him. When Miles, against all the odds, seemed to love her, she had hardly dared to believe it.

She sighed. Well, he had said he loved her. They probably meant different things by the words. Certainly he had soon grown bored with what little she had to offer a man of his intellect. He had spent more and more time with his research colleagues.

The only time he'd allowed himself to be diverted, Diana remembered painfully, was when Susie rang him with one of her long, passionate phone calls. He would drop everything then. It was his unsophisticated wife who bored him, not the glamorous childhood friend.

So first he grew bored, then impatient, as Diana grew more and more hesitant, more and more afraid of losing him—and, in the end, downright hostile.

She shivered, remembering. There had been a terrible upsurge of anger. She hadn't seen it coming. She was so bewildered, so miserable that she hardly knew what she wanted any more. And she hadn't been reading him right for days. She had lurched from mistake to mistake, hardly daring to open her mouth, and when she had tried to talk to him about it he had rounded on her with such rage that it had appalled her.

'I'm not your insurance policy,' he had said, looking at her as if he despised her.

She had fled to what had once been their room. By then she'd had sole possession, and it had become her sanctuary from the rage in him she didn't understand. So when he'd come to her there later, she had been utterly unprepared. Unprepared and so vulnerable to his fierce caress.

Diana closed her eyes, not wanting to remember. Not able to block it out.

From somewhere she had mustered the self-respect to ask him to leave. Miles had stopped still as if he had walked into a wall. And then he had turned and was gone. Permanently, as it turned out. Without another

word. Diana remembered feeling as if she had fallen off
the world.

'*Never* again,' she said out loud.

She had not realised how hurt she still was. Seeing
Miles every day was making it all too plain. She was hurt
and angry. It was anger that made her retaliate against
Miles's every barb, anger and a queer, perverse determination to prove to him she did not care any more.

Diana sighed wryly. All she had succeeded in doing
was convincing herself, woundingly, that she did still
care.

'I wish to hell I didn't,' she murmured.

She looked at the night sky. It was more overcast than
the last one she had looked at. She swallowed. Why had
he kissed her like that? Was it planned? The Miles she
knew never used to do anything without planning it. Yet
she had sensed in that astonishing, passionate moment
the other night that he had lost some sort of hold over
himself.

He wouldn't like that, she thought. Could that account for his suppressed anger tonight? She shook her
head. How could you tell with a cool, guarded man like
Miles? How could you tell, even if you loved him?

That stopped her.

'I *don't* love him,' she said aloud.

She went back to bed. But her dreams were troubled
and she woke early.

There was no one about. There was not even the smell
of coffee in the kitchen, it was so early, though the sun
was already warm. Diana decided to risk a cautious ex-
posure to its rays. Perhaps she might be soothed into a
doze, making up a little for the sleep she had lost, she
thought wryly.

She was not alone. Christos was already there, stretched out on his lounger. He looked up at her approach and, seeing her, stood up.

'Going to risk our sun after all?' he asked.

Diana smiled, indicating her sun-cream. 'Blocked from all its rays, yes.'

Chris set a lounger for her. 'You are so admirably cautious. And well organised,' he remarked.

He returned to his reclining luxury. Diana sank down on to the lounger and closed her eyes. It was possible to doze, after all. Though the images of Miles kept coming back.

Eventually she said softly, 'Chris? Can I ask you something?'

'You can try,' he said drowsily.

'You know Miles better than anyone.'

He turned his head towards her. 'I wouldn't say that,' he murmured, his tone dry.

She shook her head, answering the implicit comment. 'I don't know him at all any more. If I ever did,' she added in a painful undertone. 'I wondered—he seems—oh, I don't know. *Angry* somehow. Is there anything wrong?'

'And you say you don't know him?' Chris shook his head. 'I know what you mean. I've seen it too.' He hesitated. Then, seeming to choose his words with care, he said, 'He tells me he's been overworking.'

Diana listened to the carefully neutral tone.

'Don't you believe him?' she asked.

Chris shrugged. 'Oh, I believe him. He's always overworked, as long as he's lived. It's in his temperament. And it was clear that book of his was going to be the beginning of the work cycle, not the end. He's been flogging round the world lecturing. They both have. I believe the other guy's in hospital. Nervous exhaustion, Miles said.'

'Oh, *no*.' Steve Gilman was an easygoing Devonian whose slow speech hid a lightning mind. Diana would have said he was the most stable man in the world. 'Do you think Miles blames himself?'

Chris shook his head, his mouth tightening. 'I don't know. He hasn't talked about it. Won't tell me anything unless I drag it out of him.'

Diana looked down at her hands. 'Maybe he's told Susie.'

'No,' said Chris unequivocally. 'No, he's not talking. He simply turned up in Greece saying he wanted to work in the fields. And that's all he's said. Except the facts about Gilman. And that only when I pushed him. And,' he added with a glimmer of a smile, 'I'd fed him the best part of a bottle of Armagnac.'

Diana was blank. 'But—what's happening to the lecture tour? Is it over? And what about his research? His work is his life.'

'Not any more,' Chris said grimly.

He swung his legs round and sat up suddenly. He faced her, his arms resting on his knees. He took his sunglasses off and Diana saw that his face was set in worried lines.

'He's done what he said he was going to do, I gather. Ever since he's been here, he's played in the fields. Susie came down to be with him as soon as she heard. My office in Athens is full of telexes from people wanting to get in touch with him. He won't even read them. He hasn't opened a book or sat at a desk since he's been here.'

Diana was horrified. 'But—I've never known him like that.'

'Nor have I,' Chris said heavily. 'I'm told that he has some date to speak in Moscow. Major stuff—unity of the east and west scientific establishments—UN-sponsored. He won't talk about that either. They're frantic to get in touch with him. It's in seven weeks' time. Miles won't even say for certain whether he's going or not. I'd bet the whole of the Galatas line that he hasn't started his paper for it, though.'

'Something's happened,' Diana said with conviction. 'He'd never let people down like that.'

Chris rubbed a hand over his eyes. He looked worried.

'I know. I agree with you. But I can't help thinking...' He trailed off.

'What?'

'There's a streak in our family,' he said slowly. 'We have a taste for danger. Living on the edge. Usually we channel it—making scientific discoveries, punting on commercial risks, like me. But if things go wrong—if we're angry, or indignant about some injustice—it can turn into real recklessness.' He gave her a quick look. 'Miles told you about my uncle Conrad?'

Diana bit her lip. 'That he was Miles's father? I know. Miles didn't tell me, though.'

Chris looked astonished. But all he said was, 'By all accounts he was the worst of the lot. Got a lot of people killed when he lost his temper. My grandfather always said Miles was very like him.'

Diana said, 'Miles isn't reckless.'

'What else do you call his attitude to the Russian lecture? He could be throwing away his whole pro-fessional reputation. And he doesn't seem to care a fig.'

'There'll be a reason,' Diana said with conviction. 'Miles doesn't do things without a reason. And his career is the most important thing in his life.'

Chris was watching her narrowly. 'I think—just at the moment—something else must be more important.'

She stared. 'Like what?'

He shrugged. 'How should I know? I've told you, he's not talking to me. I wondered whether he'd discussed it with you.'

Diana flushed in comprehension. She looked away. 'He wouldn't. We're only just polite. You've seen it.'

She looked at him in appeal. He looked back steadily, nibbling one arm of his sunglasses. He said nothing.

'We—we aren't *friends* any more,' she offered desperately.

'It's new to me that you ever were.' Chris's tone was dry.

That hurt. 'You're right, of course,' Diana said in a small voice.

He snorted, his exasperation evident.

'Diana, friends don't tear each other to bits. The man was in love with you. Crazy-deep in love. That also,' he said with precision to her disbelieving expression, 'is a Galatas family characteristic.'

There was a step on the spiral stair that led to the ramparts.

'What is?' said Miles behind them.

Diana was appalled. She felt her face flame. Even though she didn't for a moment believe that Miles had loved her like that—if at all—she could still hear the words echoing in the air. If Miles had heard them he would think she *did* believe and... His inevitable mockery was too terrible to contemplate.

Chris gave her a look of comprehension and turned to Miles.

'Persuading lovely ladies to take their clothes off,' he said with absolute calm and a complete disregard for the truth. 'I've been telling Diana she should borrow one of Susie's bikinis and try to lay the foundations of a tan.'

'She burns,' Miles said coolly. 'Anyway, Susie's clothes wouldn't fit.' There was an indefinable distaste in his voice.

He doesn't want me sharing anything of hers, Diana thought suddenly. She lay back on her lounger, her blush subsiding. She had seen many things in Miles's face when he looked at her, but she had never detected distaste before. It made her feel strange.

Miles looked down at them. 'What about a drink?' he said pleasantly. 'I've just been helping Maria with a new barrel of retsina. It wants tasting.'

No sign there of the wilful recluse Chris had described, Diana thought.

Chris shuddered. 'Retsina is for picnics,' he said firmly. 'We can do better than that, Miles. I'll investigate the cellar. What do you feel like, Diana?'

'I don't want any wine.' Even to herself, her voice sounded unnaturally high and breathless. She saw Miles give her a searching look. 'Mineral water would be nice.'

'Back in a trice,' Chris said. And was gone.

Miles took his lounger. He stretched out at once. Diana watched him.

He was browner than she would have imagined possible with that red hair of his. Close to, she could see tiny freckles across his nose and cheekbones. There was a dusting of them along the backs of the muscular arms as well. She remembered his body so well. Even now she was tempted to lean across and carry one warm palm to her cheek.

Hurriedly she put her arms behind her head.

Miles said idly, 'Were you getting the authorised version on our very own princess?'

Diana said, 'No.' It came out rather short because she was still shaken by that humiliating impulse.

Miles raised his eyebrows. 'Matters nearer home, perhaps?'

'Perhaps.'

He sighed. 'I do wish every conversation didn't turn into a fencing match,' he said drily. 'What were you talking about?'

'Ourselves,' Diana said evasively.

He looked at her sharply. He would recognise the evasion, she knew. He was too intelligent.

'Di—I wish——' He stopped, then said abruptly, 'Come swimming with me this afternoon.'

It was an order, not an invitation. She was oddly shaken by it. They had never swum together before. They had never really holidayed together, she realised. Miles had always been too taken up with his work. And she had never had the confidence to insist.

'I'm not a strong swimmer,' she said.

Miles knew that already. He brushed it aside. 'Then we'll sit in the boat and look at fish.'

Diana said suspiciously, 'No killing things?'

He laughed. 'We kill to eat, you know. You're no vegetarian.'

'I don't go on holiday to kill things,' she said stubbornly.

He grinned. 'All right. No fishing. No big game shooting. That suit you?'

It was so absolutely Miles that in spite of her uneasiness Diana could not prevent herself laughing.

Miles turned his head on the pillow of his lounger. It was very near her own. Too near. She saw his eyes: warm brown and teasing. It was so like the brief, vanished happy time that Diana could have cried.

Her face must have changed because Miles said urgently, 'Don't look like that, love. I'm not a monster. I only want——'

But Diana hardly cared what he wanted when he was looking into her eyes and smiling like that. It was too much of a threat. One healed heart and two years' independence were on the line.

She tore her eyes away and said hurriedly, 'All right. I'll swim.'

He reached for her hand. 'You'll enjoy it.'

She tried to withdraw from his grasp. But he had always been stronger than he looked, and weeks of open-air work had given him a grip like iron. He looked down at their clasped fingers, a small smile playing about his mouth.

She found herself saying on impulse, 'Miles, do you own this place?'

His eyebrows rose. 'Why?' he asked softly. He didn't loose her fingers. 'Does it matter?'

'Yes,' she said, trying fruitlessly to remove her hand.

'Why?' he asked again, his eyes intent.

'Because I feel as if there's some sort of conspiracy with me as the only one who doesn't know what's going on,' Diana said frankly. 'And I don't like it.'

Abruptly he released her.

'I see.'

He was silent for a moment. The steep lids dropped, veiling his expression. Then he shrugged, a brief, devastating movement of tanned shoulders. Diana averted her eyes, swallowing.

'Do you?' she persisted.

'Own the castle? Oh, yes,' Miles said indifferently.

Indignation swamped her other feelings. 'Why?' she demanded.

His smile was crooked. 'Because my grandfather left it to me.'

Diana could have hit him. 'I don't mean that and you know it. Why this elaborate charade? Why make Chris offer me the job here as if it were his house?'

He looked at her curiously. 'Would you have come if you'd known it was mine?'

'Of course not.'

Miles shrugged again. 'There's your answer.'

Diana said through gritted teeth, 'You're impossible. How dare you manipulate me like that?'

Miles said slowly, 'I needed to know——'

'Know what?' she demanded.

The crooked smile was rueful. 'How important the glamour had become, I suppose.'

Diana stared at him, disconcerted. 'What?'

'The glamour of your crumbling palaces. The three-swimming-pool men,' he elaborated. He gave a short laugh. 'My mama married a man she thought was glamorous. When she found he was only an ordinary man after all, she imported some foreign glamour. Specifically, the man who became my father.'

He sounded completely indifferent, Diana thought, shocked. And yet... And yet...

He was not looking at her. His eyes were shadowed, in spite of the immaculately cool voice.

'It must have been the best time of her life. Flying down to Rio to watch him play blackjack, then dancing through the night to Carioca crooners. Then back in his own plane to the marital breakfast table. Real high life.'

Diana said swiftly, 'They don't play a lot of blackjack in my crumbling palaces.'

Miles laughed, but differently, as if he really was amused. 'I should have thought of that.' He reached for her hand again, and Diana let him take it without resistance. 'But people told me you were flitting from rich man to rich man. And I'd seen it before. So I had to be sure.'

'People? Who?'

But he didn't hear her. 'You can't blame me for being—concerned. Rich men and castles. I know more about that sort of life than you can begin to imagine. And, believe me, it's not for you.'

Diana stared at him, half puzzled, half affronted. Was he warning her off her friendship with the Galatas family?

'Not for working girls?' she asked sweetly.

'Not for a girl who likes order and stability,' he said quietly.

'As I had when I was married to you?' she gibed.

He winced, letting go of her hand. Diana snatched it back and stood up. How dared he patronise her? From somewhere a volcano of rage seemed to be pushing at the top of her head. She stopped fighting it.

'From what I hear you haven't been exactly a model of order and stability these last weeks—have you, Miles? Dishonoured commitments and unwritten papers,' she said savagely. 'Don't you dare preach to me, you—you playboy. Don't you *dare*.'

He stood up too. Unforgivably, he was laughing. 'Playboy? Darling . . .'

But she could hear Chris coming up the steps again. It sounded as if Susie and Dimitri were with him. With her flushed face and over-bright eyes, Diana knew she couldn't face them. Especially not with Miles standing there looking like a laughing devil.

She turned on her heel and fled.

She managed to compose herself for lunch. But she was quiet and kept out of Miles's way. Susie was in a mood.

She had been for a walk with Dimitri and it was clear that they had had a fight. Everything he said she contradicted loudly and flatly. And when she asked him to drive her to the village, as Chris had put an embargo on her driving the car herself, Dimitri said swiftly that he was going water-skiing.

So that took care of the boat, Diana thought with an inward sigh of relief. If Dimitri was using it to water-ski, there was no possibility of Miles taking her out in it for the sort of tête-à-tête he obviously had in mind.

Across the wooden table, Miles met her eyes and gave her a slow smile. It was not reassuring.

Chris said, 'I'm sorry, Dimitri. Miles is using the boat this afternoon.'

Miles said lazily, 'Don't worry. It can wait.'

Diana expelled a little breath she didn't even know she had been holding. So her reprieve was confirmed.

But it wasn't.

'Diana wants to practise her swimming,' he continued blandly and untruthfully, 'but I can just as well take her to the little beach to the east. No one will disturb us there.'

There was an odd silence. Looking round, Diana saw that it was not just to her ears that it had sounded like a command. She looked down at her plate, blushing furiously.

Chris said, a shade too heartily, 'Susie, you'd better tell Michalis to drive you.'

Miles nodded, as if satisfied. I'll kill him, thought Diana, acutely embarrassed.

Susie's eyes were blank. Her heavy brows almost met. She said to Miles, 'So I certainly shan't disturb you.' There was an edge to it.

Once again, Diana recognised, she had been outmanoeuvred. She balked at making a scene—especially since she was sure that all the other participants would join in with enthusiasm. So she borrowed a bikini from the general cache, put her own shorts and shirt over it, and allowed Miles to lead her sedately down the rugged path to the east of the castle.

He met her with a large cartwheel hat, which he set on her head.

'Thank you,' she said between her teeth.

He was laughing. 'Better than frying your brains. I've brought your sun stuff too. Chris gave it to me. Was he oiling your back for you this morning?'

Diana disdained to answer that one. He laughed.

He took her hand again. She did not withdraw it. The ground was stony and her ankle would have turned too often without that support.

It was hot and the insects buzzed. The sparse bushes at the margin of the beach smelt like herbs in a kitchen—warm and aromatic. There were poppies among the long, waving grasses.

'It's beautiful,' Diana said involuntarily.

Miles looked round, then up at the castle, lowering over them like a Transylvanian fortress.

'But exposed. I've got a better idea,' he said. 'We'll go round the headland.'

Diana looked at it doubtfully. It looked pure granite.

'There's a path?' she asked.

'We swim,' he said succinctly.

She was alarmed. 'I couldn't. You know I don't really swim. I get in a panic if I can't put my feet on the bottom.'

'You won't with me,' Miles told her softly. 'Come on.'

And before she could say anything more he was running her into the little waves. The water struck cold and she spluttered. She was still spluttering when she felt him flip her on to her back and his hands came under her armpits.

'I'll tow you round,' he said in her ear. 'You can practise your swimming later.'

Diana was helpless. She turned her head in the water, glaring at him.

'I'll never forgive you for this.'

'Add it to the list.' Miles was not obviously repentant. 'Relax, for heaven's sake, I won't let you go. Trust me.'

'Great,' she said with irony. 'I've got real reasons to trust you, of course.'

'Don't start bitching mid-ocean,' Miles said comfortably. 'You can tell me what you think of me when we land. Much more satisfactory.'

He swam with lazy, powerful strokes that took them out of sight of the castle in minutes and had them landed in a small, almost enclosed bay almost as fast.

Diana gave a sigh of thankfulness as her feet touched the bottom. She stood up and waded out, looking around her. Her anger dissipated in sheer shock. It was beautiful, too, but it looked the loneliest place in the world. The beach was a great swath of white sand, bordered by tall rushes and overlooked by the sheer cliff.

She turned on Miles.

'Why have you brought me here? What are you doing?'

He gave her his old, lop-sided grin. He looked tough and capable and terrifyingly strong.

'Use your imagination,' he said softly.

She stared at him, mesmerised. The cotton of her soaked shirt plastered against her body in the faint breeze that came from the sea. Diana was oblivious. He came towards her. She closed her eyes. The hard brown hands were cool from the sea. The air hummed. He was quite slow and very gentle about it. But there was no way she was going to escape.

Diana screwed her eyes tight, tight shut so that red caverns danced before her inner vision. It was no use. His salty mouth closed hungrily on her own and her every sense opened to him.

CHAPTER SIX

IT WAS getting dark when they got back to the castle. The sun was only just visible above the distant hills and the moon was already high. The sea shifted and glimmered behind them, giving off little salty breaths of breeze.

The half-dark somehow made them seem much closer together. Closer and alone.

Diana climbed the cliff path without touching Miles. It was an effort she would not admit. She was shivering. This time there was no sun to dry off her clothes as soon as she emerged from the sea.

Miles said something under his breath. She ignored it. And when he offered her his hand over a difficult stretch she pretended she didn't see it. She was in turmoil.

There were lights in the kitchen and the corridors. But nobody was about. Presumably everyone had gathered on the battlements already. Diana was grateful. She knew she couldn't face anyone yet.

'I'm going to my room,' she told Miles, not looking at him.

He looked at her bent head.

'I take it that isn't an invitation,' he said drily.

Her head came up at that.

'As always, you are right,' she agreed, pushing a strand of damp, loosened hair back off her neck.

His mouth twisted. 'You look like a schoolgirl.'

Diana turned carefully, her eyes just missing his. 'Hardly a schoolgirl. As you've just demonstrated.' She

100

kept her voice level with an effort. But the bitterness showed—bitterness and acute humiliation.

If I don't get away from him this minute, I'm going to start howling, thought Diana. She set her jaw grimly.

'I need a shower. I want to wash my hair before I present myself at dinner.'

Miles was not deceived. 'Going to ground, Di?' he challenged softly.

That did get her looking at him. Her grey-green eyes were glacial with hurt and indignation.

'Why should I do that?' she asked.

He touched her cheek. 'I can think of any number of reasons. None of which I like,' he said ruefully. 'Trying to pretend it didn't happen?'

Diana's eyes flashed. 'Happen? *Happen*? Like an act of God or something? Nothing happened that you didn't intend right from the start.'

'Are you so sure of that?' Miles asked quietly.

Her eyes hated him. 'You took me to a deserted beach. And jumped on me,' she said with precision. 'As you planned to do. Do you deny that?'

Miles winced. But he said mildly, 'I thought the jumping was mutual.'

Diana drew a sharp breath.

'Wasn't it?' he insisted.

He had more than a grain of right on his side. But Diana was too angry to be honest and too hurt to be fair.

'I don't recall being offered a choice,' she flung at him.

She turned away abruptly, afraid that the threatening tears were going to spill over. Tears of temper, she assured herself feverishly. Tears of temper.

'Di——'

But at the old name she whipped round. He was the only person who shortened her name, ever. It used to be a sign of affection. Suddenly she couldn't bear it.

'Don't call me that,' she said furiously. 'Don't ever call me that again.'

The handsome face registered no reaction whatsoever. But the piercing eyes narrowed, interested. Oh, lord, she had given herself away. She had shown too much.

She scrabbled for some sort of composure.

'I don't know what you think you're trying to do, Miles. Surely, we're both agreed, there's no future for us.'

The steep lids drooped, then lifted with startling suddenness, catching her nearly off-guard. Diana drew back.

'I don't remember discussing the future. Sometimes the present can be fun,' he drawled.

'Not for me,' she retorted. 'I'm not like that. You ought to remember that, at least.' For the first time since the beach she looked him in the eye. 'No one-night stands, Miles. Not for me.'

'Not with your husband?'

He was amused, Diana realised in outrage. He had torn her carefully constructed world to shreds with those long, clever fingers and he thought it was funny. Her rage suddenly went several notches deeper, and cooled to a cutting edge.

'That's a fiction,' she drawled in her turn. 'We both know it.' She saw his jaw tighten and felt a harsh, angry triumph. She went on, 'And before you remind me that your allowance pays my parents' mortgage you can forget it. From now on we won't take another penny.'

The brown eyes flickered and went absolutely impenetrable. 'I thought you couldn't afford it on your own.'

He sounded faintly interested. 'How are you going to explain it when they lose the roof over their heads?'

Diana swallowed. 'They'll understand,' she said desolately. 'They love me.'

That earned a fierce silence. She could feel his anger beating at her. She held herself very straight, braced in every nerve for his next move.

Miles didn't move. He didn't say anything either. His eyes flicked up an down her without noticeable expression.

She thought, He's trying to make me feel guilty. I won't. I won't. I won't let him play on my feelings the way he used to. She set her teeth.

At last he said softly, 'A gesture, Di? At any cost?'

She lifted her chin.

'You don't seem to understand, Miles. After today——' Her voice trembled. She steadied it with an immense effort and went on bravely, 'After today I want you out of my life completely. It's obvious we can't be friends...'

'And why do you think that is?'

She ignored him. '... as today's events have proved. So I don't want to have to see you, or hear about you, or think of you ever again.' She made a violent gesture which contrasted sharply with the level voice. It revealed all too clearly the strength of her feelings but she was beyond caring. 'Finish!'

Miles surveyed her. He pursed his mouth. 'Dramatic,' he commented.

For a moment Diana, who had never raised a hand in anger in her life, seriously considered hitting him. Miles took in her white face and the glittering intensity of the green eyes and seemed to sense that she was on a knife-edge of control. His voice gentled.

'We'll talk about it tomorrow.'

It was somehow the final insult, that gentleness. Diana took a spontaneous decision.

'No, we won't. I'm leaving tomorrow,' she flung at him. 'You've no hold over me and you can't keep me here.'

Miles considered that.

'Isn't running away rather pointless?' he asked.

She was so angry she could have screamed. Instead she gave him a fierce, mocking smile and said, 'I wouldn't know. You're the one who runs, Miles.'

She turned her back on him and started to go inside.

'*What*?'

He was in front of her suddenly, as quick as a panther—and as dangerous. All the careful negligence was gone. His eyes drilled into hers. Diana glared back, refusing to quail.

'*You* went,' she reminded him, her voice low and bitter. 'I didn't.'

He stared, his face fierce. 'You told me to.'

She pushed her drying hair back with hands that shook.

'Miles, you'd just said I'd got the wrong man if I wanted a father substitute,' she said, her voice raw. 'I was devastated. And then you thought I'd fall into your arms...' She shuddered, remembering. 'Yes, that night I was angry too, and I wanted to be left alone. That *night*, Miles. I didn't expect you to walk out on me forever. It was you who chose to do that. And, having chosen,' her voice was suddenly ragged, 'keep to it. Now get out of my way.'

He stood back without a word.

When she got to her room, she tore off her clothes as if they were infected. She would, she promised herself, burn the shorts and shirt. The borrowed bikini was a different matter. Even in her present rage, Diana recognised that she couldn't burn someone else's clothes.

She looked at herself in the mirror with dislike. The bikini was tiny and sophisticated in cut, brilliant in colour. Suddenly she saw what Miles had seen—her breasts half revealed by the jade stuff, artfully piped with black to emphasise the contours it covered. The tiny briefs laced round her pale hips, the lacings an evident invitation. She turned away, her mouth twisting with distaste. The whole garment was designed to be taken off by someone else—all the fastenings stood out, black and blatant.

Maybe Miles wasn't as much to blame as she thought. She should never have worn it.

She went into the bathroom and began the slow process of running a bath. As the steam began to rise, she untied the black strips from around her neck and scrambled out of the briefs. The bikini fell. Diana assiduously avoided her image in the mirrors with which the room was plentifully provided.

Her body felt different. She did not want to see the evidence. She wondered whether she would ever be comfortable looking at her own naked body again. Even alone in the privacy of her steamy bathroom she felt her colour rise at the thought.

This, she told herself grimly, was ridiculous. This was running away indeed. Deliberately, she turned to face a mirror. There were very faint marks on her thighs. The shadow of a bruise on her throat. Her breasts were tender. It could be the sun, she reminded herself. It had been burning hot and she had had no protection from it. Except Miles's body when—— She gave a little moan, seeing herself flush.

But it was the mouth that really gave her away, she thought, wincing. It looked swollen and vulnerable. You might miss the shadows on her skin, but that mouth told its own tale.

She closed her eyes, ashamed to remember. What marks had she left on Miles? What had *happened*? They never treated each other like that in the old days.

And then it all came back in an unwelcome rush. Diana sat limply on the edge of the bath, wishing she didn't have to remember.

How long had Miles held her mouth in that first desperate kiss? A minute? Longer? Until he knew she was his, anyway. It had left Diana weak, startled as much by her own response as his action. When he lifted his head, she couldn't look at him. Her breathing was swift and shallow. He ran his palms down her arms, barely touching the skin. Her breath caught, and she shivered.

Miles took her hands and carried first one and then the other to his lips. He just brushed a whisper across her knuckles; but the kiss he pressed into the palm was passionate.

Something clenched hard inside Diana. She felt as if she was taking painful, dangerous steps up a critical staircase. It left her dizzy and afraid—and with no choice but to go on.

He tucked a straying wisp of the damp fair hair behind her ear. He was very gentle then. He trailed his fingertip over her cheekbone, her nose, her chin. Diana's lips parted. He touched the finger to her lower lip. Diana gasped.

Behind them the ocean was almost silent. The breeze had dropped, leaving the air like warm honey. On the hill behind them birds twittered. There was a buzz of insects and, far out in the bay, the distant chug of a motor on the still air. They were utterly alone.

Miles traced her mouth with his thumb. He looked intent, absorbed. Oh, there had been times when she thought she would drown in those warm, laughing eyes. Diana swayed towards him. It was another step up that perilous ladder.

Miles held her very lightly. His mouth drifted butterfly kisses over her face. Diana trembled and his hold tightened. But he didn't stop. She felt his tongue briefly against her temple and then, with infinite care, between her lips. She gave a long, long shudder and put her arms round him. Another step.

He picked her up then. Diana had forgotten how easily he could do it. It had always alarmed her. She would cry out, feeling insecure and half annoyed. This time was different. She felt languorous in his arms, utterly safe. But she knew he remembered her old trepidation because he laughed down at her—with something that was not laughter at all in the brown eyes.

Slowly, almost dreamily, she lifted one hand from his shoulder and ran it along the smooth brown jaw. Miles turned his head, so that her drifting fingers touched his mouth and kissed them.

That was when things changed. That was the moment when she leaped the rest of the staircase and didn't know where she'd reached—the moment she stepped on to the thunderbolt and was flung into the heavens.

They were kissing before Miles lowered her to the ground. They were both shaking with impatience. The scraps of clothing were torn away, flung behind them as they locked together in a need too great for tenderness. Diana's throat arched and she drew Miles to her like a vice, crying out. In the end she heard him cry out too.

'Oh, lord,' said Diana wearily now, drooping on the side of her bath.

They had ridden the thunderbolt, all right. Together. When the explosion came she had been clinging to him, sobbing, holding him with fierce love. Oh, Miles had had every right to say it was mutual.

It was total defeat. There was nothing she wouldn't have done, nothing she wouldn't have agreed to, with his head dropped against her breast. She had felt utterly peaceful.

Utterly—she said it to herself now deliberately—in love.

She put her fingers to her tender mouth. It was her own fault, of course. All those brave statements of independence, all that insistence that he couldn't hurt her any more—it was all a disguise to cover the fact that she had never, not for a moment, stopped loving him. Not when he was angry, not when he was cold, not on the evenings he went to Susie without a word of excuse or explanation, not even when he looked at her with that indifference that hurt worse than anything else.

She looked at him and she was hungry for his love. It was hopeless.

Wearily she got into the bath and closed off the taps. She lay back, trying to unknot her tense muscles. There must be something she could do. She had got over him before, she told herself desperately. Her brain went round and round. If she didn't see him again; if there was nothing left connecting them, not even the allowance; if she never saw his friends or went to places where he had been... But there was no avoiding the truth. She was in love with the man and would be till the day she died.

'I've just got to take damned good care he doesn't find out,' she told herself out loud. 'If he doesn't know already, that is. Which, knowing Miles, he probably does.'

It was not a comforting thought. It drove her to dress carefully in one of her prettiest silvery green dresses and make up her face with care. It wasn't much of a suit of armour but it was something. And it had its effect.

A little silence fell when she joined the others on the lamp-lit battlements. Chris and Dimitri rose, staring at her. Miles was already on his feet in the shadows, his expression indecipherable.

Susie was an empress in scarlet and gold at the far end of the table. She greeted Diana warily, but her words were cheerful enough.

'Well, you don't look like a girl Miles dragged over sand and ocean half the day.'

Miles made a small movement, quickly stilled. He began to pour Diana a drink.

'You look very lovely,' he said slowly.

Susie said with an odd harshness, 'Did he make you swim till you dropped?'

Diana said carefully, 'I'm not a strong swimmer. But he got me there and back.'

Miles was giving her a glass of ouzo. The smell brought back older, sensuous memories. She gave a quick shiver, hurriedly repressed.

'Didn't I just?' he murmured, for her ear alone.

Diana pretended she didn't hear.

Christos said, 'Miles swims like a dolphin. He always has. But he's not very good at remembering that other people can be scared. I hope he didn't take you out of your depth, Diana?'

Miles stepped back, a small smile playing round his mouth. 'Did I?' he asked.

Diana glared at him. 'No.'

He gave a small nod. 'I thought not.' He sounded smug.

Susie said stiffly, 'Tomorrow you can take me climbing through rock pools and leave poor Diana to bask.'

Miles laughed softly. 'Tomorrow she's leaving.'

There was an outcry. Diana sat down and let it fly over her head. The others resumed their seats, arguing.

'Darling, *must* you?' wailed Susie.

'If you stay another three days, Dimitri can fly you back to London himself,' Chris said. 'If you're pressed for time that would save you a day's travelling at least. You've got room for a passenger, Dimitri?'

'With the greatest of pleasure.'

Miles frowned heavily. It was that really which decided her. She wanted to get away from him, true. But she also wanted to demonstrate how little she cared for him or his disapproval. She wanted quite desperately to do that. And if he didn't want her to fly with Dimitri—as he plainly didn't—here was the ideal opportunity.

'If you're sure...' she said hesitatingly.

Dimitri took her hand and kissed it.

'Positive,' he said caressingly.

Miles made a noise suspiciously like a snort. Diana felt a small glow of satisfaction.

'Then that's settled,' Chris said affably. 'Tomorrow Susie goes rockpooling with Miles and Diana basks.' He met Miles's look with amusement. 'And now we eat.'

In fact the next morning Diana was still so exhausted after one of the worst nights of her life that she did exactly what Chris foretold. She took her basket-weave chair under an olive tree out of sight of the windows and tried to concentrate on a popular novel. In the end she dozed off.

She woke to find Dimitri sitting at her feet, wearing a quizzical expression.

'Miles clearly wore you out yesterday,' he said drily.

Diana, well aware that he was fishing, managed not to blush.

'Swimming isn't my forte,' she told him calmly.

He laughed. 'So you said. So there wouldn't be much point in my asking you if you wanted to come out in the boat with me?'

'Not if I have to swim back,' she agreed. She stirred. The air was getting uncomfortably hot. There would be a breeze out on the bay. 'On the other hand, if all I had to do was to sit under a sunhat and watch *you* swim...'

Dimitri grinned. 'Deal. Come on, then, before Susie decides she and the rest of the world want to come too.'

There was an edge to his voice, Diana noticed. She went with him thoughtfully.

When he had had his swim and was back on board the gently rocking boat, she said carefully, 'Have you had a fight with Susie, Dimitri?'

He was stretched on the cover of the cockpit, exposing an already impressive tan. He kept his eyes closed but he made a face.

'You noticed?' he asked.

Diana said, 'Not really. I just wondered.'

He sighed, sitting up. 'She's being an absolute fool,' he said explosively. 'I have told her—but when did Susie ever listen to anyone else?'

'Except Miles,' Diana said quietly.

Dimitri gave a harsh laugh. 'Oh, she doesn't listen to Miles either normally. At the moment she's all sweet agreement because she thinks if she hangs on his every word he'll——' He stopped abruptly.

'He'll what?' Diana prompted, keeping her voice light. 'Fall in love with her? Marry her?'

Dimitri looked embarrassed. 'Lord knows.'

Well, it was more or less what she had worked out for herself. 'And will he?' she asked.

Dimitri was startled. 'You're better placed to answer that than I am, surely?'

She said evenly, 'I haven't seen Miles for two years until this week. I don't think I know him very well any more. If I ever did.' He gave her a look of considerable sympathy. More to herself than him she said, 'But I've never realised until . . . I suppose I always hoped, in the back of my mind somewhere, that we could try again. Have another chance. Stupid, of course, but fantasies usually are, aren't they?'

Dimitri looked at her soberly. 'Hope can be cruel,' he agreed.

She shook her head. 'Do you know—until yesterday I didn't even know I was still hoping?'

Dimitri came down from the cockpit roof and eased himself on to the deck beside her.

'Are you sure there really is no hope? I don't know Miles very well but, well, he clearly—er—cares for you.'

'He fancies me,' Diana corrected him brutally. It was like pressing on a bruise. She said it again with fury.

Dimitri was not shocked. He even looked a little amused. 'Who would not?' he said politely. 'But for Miles it is more than that, I think. And he is not happy.'

'If he isn't happy it's more likely to be his work—or even Susie—than anything to do with me. It always was.'

Dimitri nodded slowly. 'I see. But people change.'

'Not Miles,' Diana said with absolute conviction. She gave a little shiver, remembering his driven hunger on the beach. 'He wants me to do what he wants. He gets fighting mad when I don't. But he doesn't care whether or not I'm happy or bother about the things that interest me. He doesn't love me.'

'I see,' Dimitri said again. 'And this is why you were leaving so soon?'

'Yes. It must seem childish,' she admitted, 'but I was desperate to keep out of his way.'

Dimitri sighed. 'If it is childish then we both need to grow up. I too share this feeling.' He looked at her with a sudden flare of mischief lighting his sombre expression. 'Shall we run away together?'

Diana smiled. 'Where? Kathmandu? The ends of the universe?'

He shrugged. 'It would take that far to forget, I agree. But for today we could go just a little way.'

She stared. 'Are you serious?'

His smile faded. 'I'm serious about not wanting to sit down to lunch with Susie while she curls herself round Miles,' he said with suppressed violence.

Diana swallowed. 'Me too.' She touched his hand sympathetically.

'Right.' He stood up. 'That settles it. The Caves of Hippolytus. We'll go there for the afternoon. And we won't go home till dark.'

He started the outboard motor and turned the launch in a curving arc out of the bay.

Diana came to her feet unsteadily and went to stand beside him at the wheel. The salt spray in her face was not unpleasant.

'What are the Caves of Hippolytus?' she shouted above the noise of the engine.

Dimitri grinned. 'The stuff of adventure. Wait and see.'

It was quite a long journey. Out on the open sea, in the relatively sheltered gulf, the wind whipped the waves to a surprising height. The sun was still fierce but in the distance ominous purple clouds were massing on the horizon. She saw Dimitri glance at them a couple of times.

At last he cut the engine and guided the little boat carefully in between some rocks that stuck out of the water like icebergs. He moored them in the shelter of a sea cavern three times the height of a man.

'The Caves of Hippolytus,' he said, his voice echoing queerly.

Diana looked round. The waves slapping against the side of the boat also echoed in the rock dome.

'What are they?' she said in a whisper.

'Local legend says that Hippolytus was washed up here after his father had called up a wave to overturn his chariot and drown him,' Dimitri said. He was playing with the radio in the control panel. There was a quick sputter of Greek and he cut the connection. 'There. Now the coastguard know where we are. I've asked them to let the castle know. Just in case.'

Just in case Susie had missed him and was worried, Diana saw with compassion. Poor Dimitri. As long as Susie was with Miles, she wouldn't have any thoughts for anyone else.

He helped her out of the boat and around the shingly floor of the cavern. 'There's a whole network of caves,' he explained.

Diana looked round curiously. 'Inhabited?'

He shook his head. 'No. The tide comes up too high. Good for fishing, though. The caves are a sort of honeycomb of rock and water. There are quite big pools in there where you can't get a boat but you can get quite substantial fish.' He smiled. 'A couple of developers thought they could exploit the caves as a tourist trap. But they're too dangerous.'

'Dangerous?' Diana was surprised. She looked round at the calm cavern and the gently lulling sea beyond.

'Only at high tide, in bad weather, when you don't know what you're doing,' Dimitri told her fluently. 'You're safe with me.'

'Of course,' Diana said politely.

They scrambled through a tunnel into a bigger cave. It was weird, looking up through the spiral of rock to the sky. The clouds were moving quite fast now. When they got back to the main cavern, the water was slapping more agitatedly against the boat.

Dimitri looked at his watch. She knew he was going to say they ought to go. She suppressed the little lurch of the heart that told her she wasn't ready to go back and confront Miles.

Some piece of machinery on the boat began to beep. Diana jumped. Dimitri said, 'It's only the radio. I'll go and answer it. We should move soon anyway.'

'Let me have one last look round,' Diana pleaded.

He hesitated. But he clearly saw something in her face that swayed him. 'All right. Ten minutes,' he agreed.

And he waded out to the boat.

Diana turned and went down a tunnel they had not traversed before. She was glad of the moments alone. She liked Dimitri, but all afternoon she had been looking at him as if he were a ghost and Miles, the unseen, absent presence, was the real companion with her. It was not a pleasant feeling.

She wandered along the edge of another rock-locked pool and through a darker, damper tunnel. The floor sloped sharply and so did the ceiling. At times she was bent almost double. She had no torch so she couldn't see anything. But in the distance she heard water against rock and knew she would come out into another enclosed pool.

When she emerged it was as if it were a different day. The sky was gun-metal-grey and even in its shelter the water was violently agitated. The waves on the open sea were going to be quite something, Diana thought.

She squinted up. The rocks looked like granite: wet, sheer and deadly. High above her head there was a pinnacle like an angry finger stabbing at the sky. Well, if she got trapped there was no way out up the cliff-side, she thought wryly. Time to go back.

It was only as she tried to make her way back through the longest tunnel that she realised she wasn't going to be able to do it. The water was too high.

She felt a flutter of panic, but suppressed it. Dimitri knew where she was. She didn't think the caves were so extensive that he wouldn't be able to find her.

Eventually, said an inner voice. When the water goes down. And how high is it going to come first?

She went back to the pool. The water was definitely higher now. And it had begun to rain in great drops. Diana found the highest dry place she could locate and sat on the ledge, looking at the rising water. She was shaking, although it was hardly cold.

There was a brilliant flash and then she heard thunder in the distance. Rain fell harder. She brought her knees up to her chin and watched the pool below. She thought quite suddenly, I'm not going to get out of this.

She thought of Miles. Running away from him looked as if it was going to get her killed. He had been right, she thought with desperate irony. Running away never paid. If she ever had the chance, she would tell him.

Stop it, she said to herself. This is melodrama. You're not going to suffocate in the open air. You're not going to drown either. Bodies float and there's lots of stuff to hang on to, like the handrail in a swimming-pool. You're going to get wet and cold and miserable and it serves you right. But you're *not going to die*.

You can't afford to die. You've got to tell Miles you love him.

Diana jumped so hard that she nearly fell off her ledge. *Tell* Miles . . . ? What was she thinking of? But suddenly it seemed the most important thing in the world.

She dropped her head in her hands. If only she could see him once more; touch him...

She did not know how much time passed. The storm got nearer, bringing with it the strange illusion of human voices. Then, in a sudden lull, she realised there *were* voices. They were above her head. She looked up, astonished.

There were figures on the cliff. She couldn't make out who, through the driving rain. Except she had the crazy feeling they were fighting. She stood up, craning to wave. No one seemed to take any notice of her.

One of the figures detached itself and began to swarm up the pinnacle. Then he was standing on it, straight as an arrow, arms extended to a point above his head. He was going to dive into the enclosed pool.

A hand went to her throat. It must be incredibly foolhardy. Even without the wind that was now whipping up the water, a dive from such a height into that heaving water would have been the height of recklessness.

In her head she heard Chris say, Our family have a taste for danger.

The man on the pinnacle seemed to fall in one graceful, uninterrupted arc. He cut into the black water as cleanly as a knife. As he plummeted, she saw the flash of copper hair. She backed against the wall of granite behind her and screamed aloud.

CHAPTER SEVEN

DIANA strained forward, agonised. Diving from that height, Miles must have gone right to the bottom. Was it deep enough? There must be a real risk that he would injure his head badly.

All thought of her own danger disappeared as she scanned the heavy sea below her. There was no sign of him. Diana began to rock backwards and forwards, her lips forming a silent prayer.

Please let him be all right. Please, I'll do anything. *Please.*

Then there was a splash. Diana stopped rocking, her eyes wide and tearless, fixed on the water. Another splash. Then a regular series of them. A smooth head appeared among the rhythmic spray. Miles powered towards her with fast strokes that sent the foam flying.

Diana went to the edge of her ledge. He trod water beneath her, shaking the water out of his eyes. His head and shoulders streamed. The copper hair was nearly black with water. He rubbed a powerful hand across his face to clear his vision, and Diana saw that his eyes were dark and sharp as daggers.

'What the hell,' he said, not attempting to disguise his temper, 'do you think you're doing?' He was breathing hard.

Diana didn't answer. She was too busy reaching a hand down to him. He barely touched it, hauling himself up the side of the chimney easily enough. Safe on the ledge, he turned to her.

118

'You have no *sense* sometimes,' he said furiously. He pulled her against him roughly. She was shaking with cold and the aftermath of fear. He cursed when he felt the tremors that shook her.

'Didn't you know it was dangerous? Wandering off like a four-year-old at a picnic.'

'I know,' said Diana, huddled against him, her lips against the cold, soaked skin of his shoulder. 'I know. I didn't think.'

'So you damned well should have.' Miles was looking rapidly round her eyrie, assessing the place. 'Not much shelter here.' He hesitated. 'Have you tried climbing?'

Diana raised her head and looked at the rock wall behind them. In his arms her trembling had quieted. Now her expression was rueful.

'There's a limit to how far I can climb,' she said. 'This is it.'

'They'll be back with a rope in half an hour or so,' he said, half to himself. He looked down at her assessingly. 'Very cold?'

She nodded. She was still held against the comforting strength of his body and she was not at all anxious to let him go.

'Not up to swimming?' he asked.

She looked down at the surging water, thought of the black tunnel, and shuddered. Miles detached her clinging hands and set her gently back against the rock-face. He surveyed their position narrow-eyed.

She started shivering again. Her finger-ends, she noticed with faint interest, were turning blue. In contrast—and in spite of his soaking—Miles looked warm and alive. He hunkered down in front of her.

'Look, Di, I know it goes against the grain, but you'll have to trust me.'

She looked at him blankly. He sighed as if he was trying to curb impatience.

'I can get you out of here,' he told her clearly. 'If you trust me. I can tow you through the cave in a life-saving hold.' His eyes gleamed briefly. 'The way I got you out to the beach. There's still air in the corridor. It will take ten minutes at the outside. Maybe less. But we'll both be at risk if you panic or try to fight me.' He took her icy hands. 'Will you trust me?'

Diana looked at the turbulent sea below them. There was no one on the headland above them now. They would have gone for help as Miles said. The storm clouds were racing and the wind was very cold.

She tried to force her icy lips to smile. 'There's n-not a lot going for us here,' she agreed. 'I'll have to.'

His eyes flickered. But his only response was to aim a playful fist at her cheek in a mock punch. 'That's my girl.' He took her hand, pulling her upright. 'Come on.'

'N-now?'

'Nothing to be gained by waiting,' Miles said in a practical tone. 'I'd take your skirt off. It won't be nice waterlogged and it could get in my way.'

It was a dress. Diana hesitated only momentarily. His gaze was almost clinical as he held out his hand for the scrap of cloth. He dropped it casually behind him.

'It'll be safe. We can collect it at low tide if you're specially fond of it.' He slipped off the ledge into the surging water. Bracing himself one-handed against the rock-face, he held the other up to her. 'Come on.'

The water was worse than before, boisterous as well as cold. Her feet touched the bottom and she staggered, sinking. She bit her lip till the blood ran, grabbing for him instinctively. His hands were as steady as hawsers.

'Don't think,' he instructed unemotionally. 'Let yourself float. Relax.'

It wasn't the easiest instruction in the world to comply with, Diana thought, amused in spite of her alarm. The water bumped her against him uncontrollably. Her own lack of ease in the water didn't make it any easier. But in the end he had her floating on her back, held against his chest.

Looking over his shoulder, he took them with steady strokes towards the rock passage. They seemed, to Diana's fluttering senses, to cover the distance in half a dozen sweeps of one powerful arm. As they plunged into darkness she gave an instinctive gasp that she wasn't quick enough to suppress. At once the arm that held her tightened.

'Don't think,' Miles said calmly. 'Relax.'

He kept on saying it as they swam and bumped their way through the little passage. The water was very high and it seemed to Diana that they were in imminent danger of scraping their faces on the roof.

Once she felt Miles hit the rock wall and flinch, swearing. But he was right. It didn't take much over ten minutes.

Dimitri was waiting in the boat. He wasn't alone. Chris was there, looking surprisingly grim. So were a couple of strangers who turned out to be fishermen.

They hauled her on to the launch and plied her with rough towels, rougher brandy and fishy-smelling sweaters. Dimitri was conspicuously silent while Chris gave crisp instructions into the radio. No one, Diana saw from her huddle in the cabin, seemed to be paying much attention to Miles.

She tried to say as much. After all, he was cold too and probably twice as exhausted, even though he wouldn't have been as scared. She looked across at him, pulling his own shirt over his damp shoulders. He looked brisk and, she thought, taking in the tense jawline and hard profile, angry. The words died on her lips. Thunder started in the distance.

The boat came to land on a small beach. Chris's limousine was waiting, though for once his driver wasn't in immaculate uniform. She gave him a faint smile as the man came forward anxiously to help her. She got up the beach under her own steam, though.

She hesitated before getting into the car. It seemed sacrilege somehow—the pristine ivory leather seats and her tarred and fishy garments. Miles came up the beach at a run.

'Get in,' he said sharply.

It was beginning to rain again, great drops like coins that spattered on the Mercedes's bonnet and were converted into steam. Diana did as she was told. She held open the door for him too but he had already turned away. She sank back.

Dimitri crunched up the shale towards her. He leaned on the door, bending to make out her expression.

'You are all right? Truly?' he asked.

Diana nodded. A great weariness was beginning to settle over her. Dimitri looked down to the beach to the others.

'Miles is astonishing,' he said in an odd voice. 'I had no idea he could be so——' he hesitated '—dramatic.'

Diana gave a little laugh that broke in the middle.

'Neither did I.'

'No,' Dimitri agreed. He swung into the back of the car beside her. 'He has surprised all of us, I think.'

Miles finished his consultation with Chris and ran lightly back up the beach to the car.

'The castle,' he said to the chauffeur. 'The Count will take the boat back.'

He got in and the car rocked gently up the unmade track. Miles looked round at her.

'You're cold and a bit shocked but I think that's all. We'll have a doctor look at you but I don't think we need to run you into the clinic as an emergency. Do you?'

Diana shook her head violently. 'Of course not. I was just stupid. It was you...' She remembered that brush with the rock wall and winced.

'I'm OK,' he said curtly.

Dimitri said, 'I've never seen a dive like that. Have you always dived?'

They began to discuss the local swimming. Diana's head spun. The car was warm and superbly sprung. She began to droop sideways.

She awoke to find herself being carried. She thought she was being pulled out of the car. 'Dimitri?' she said, still three-quarters asleep.

'No,' said Miles grimly. 'Think again.'

She was long out of the car. He was taking her down the corridor in the castle. He shouldered open the door to her room. Diana's eyes focused with difficulty.

Miles dropped her on the lace-covered bed and began to strip off the odorous sweaters. Her cold fingers closed over his own, trying to stop him.

The sherry-brown eyes glinted down at her. 'Quite apart from the fact that we've been married for years, if you believe you came out of the sea anything other than effectively naked, you're living in fairyland,' he told her brutally.

She flushed, turning her face away, hating him again.

Miles took no notice. He peeled off the jerseys with his customary efficiency, ridding her of the scraps of despised underwear. He flung a robe at her.

'Put that on. I'll run you a bath.'

She huddled into it, glaring at his back. Protest was clearly going to be useless. He slammed the bathroom door.

Diana rubbed the shivering flesh on her arms. She couldn't remember Miles like this, she thought. Oh, he'd been angry before, but never with this glittering danger as if at any moment he might lash out. He was always so cool, so remote. The sense that he might be at the edge of his control was almost frightening. Diana examined her feelings. No, not frightening—exciting.

Miles came out of the bathroom. The front of his shirt was damp again, revealing the muscles that had held Diana so securely. The dark red hair was curling uncontrollably after its soaking. Diana's mouth went dry. Miles bent and picked her up again, though she protested.

The bath was steaming. He slipped the robe off her shoulders and held her hand while she got in, then trickled water down her back out of a big sponge. Almost at once she felt the shattering cold along her spine begin to melt. His touch was quite impersonal, but Diana didn't feel impersonal at all. That was exciting too. She tipped her head back, closing her eyes, and gave herself up to the luxurious sensation of his hands on her again.

He said nothing, playing the warm water over her steadily.

After a while Diana opened her eyes and tried to behave sensibly. She said with a little difficulty, 'I can do that. I'm all right now. Shouldn't you have a bath yourself? You got as cold as I did.'

She met his eyes. They gleamed. He didn't look impersonal after all.

'Are you inviting me to join you?' he asked.

Heat flooded her cheeks and she sat up straighter. 'No,' she choked, though her flesh trembled at the thought. Could he see that? She turned her head away, furious with herself. And ashamed.

'Only in salt water?' Miles laughed down at her. 'Cold salt water? You may have a point.' But he handed her the sponge, searching her flushed face. 'You're sure you're all right?'

She nodded, still conscious of that burning blush. His hands left her without apparent reluctance.

'Then get into bed when you're finished,' he said practically. 'I'll have a hot drink sent up. You probably need food too.'

She shook her head. Miles took no notice.

'Don't fall asleep in the bath either,' he instructed. 'I'll be back to make sure.'

His last threat had Diana out of the water and huddled in a nightshirt under the bedcovers in five minutes flat. Which was just as well because, true to his word, he was back in less than ten. He brought a tray of food.

Diana looked at it with loathing, hugging her arms round her knees.

'I don't want anything to eat,' she said militantly. 'I told you so.'

Miles slanted a look down at her. 'Maybe not. But it stops anyone else thinking you do and bringing it up.'

Diana stared.

'I can do without any further interruptions,' he explained, putting the tray down on a distant table.

Diana's mouth went dry again. 'Why?' she said to his back. It came out as a croak. She cleared her throat and tried again. 'Why?'

He turned back to her. His smile was wry.

'There are too many people around. Haven't you noticed? When I arranged to get you here I hadn't bargained on a damned houseparty.'

His eyes were very bright. They searched her face as if they saw secrets there that not even she was aware of.

Diana felt that treacherous excitement begin to burn again. She could not tear her eyes away from his.

'Wh-what do you mean?'

'Whenever I look for you, you're with somebody else. Whenever I get you alone, someone interrupts.'

Except on the beach. Neither of them said it, though Diana's cheeks were suddenly on fire. His expression was rueful.

'Or I get you alone and we don't talk,' he agreed. 'Don't you think we need to talk, Di?'

She moved restlessly. 'You were never very good at talking as far as I remember,' she muttered.

He grimaced. 'Guilty as charged,' he said, to her surprise. 'Those last weeks I was hell to live with, I know. I'd let work get out of hand and...'

'Not just weeks,' Diana said without thinking. 'And not just work.'

'...I didn't know what to do about us. *What* did you say?'

He looked so startled that she felt the easy colour rise again.

She would have given anything to recall her betraying words. But it was too late. She would have to admit to his face what he must already know, Diana thought resentfully: that she had never understood the hold Susie had over his affections and had been bitterly intimidated by the other woman's glamour and sophistication.

She lifted her chin and met his eyes defiantly.

'It had been going wrong for months and you know it.'

Miles's eyes were shrewd. 'And?'

Diana swallowed but her chin went higher.

'And when you didn't come home at night you weren't always in the Physics building,' she flung at him.

His face went absolutely still. She had the feeling that behind the mask the clever brain was racing. But his expression gave no sign of it. As usual, she thought bitterly.

'Did you think I was unfaithful, then?' he asked at last softly. 'Out on the town? Cheating on you?'

To Diana's wincing ears it sounded almost like a taunt. She flung her hair back and met his eyes proudly.

'I thought it was probable, yes,' she told him in a level voice.

The brown eyes flickered.

'Who with, for heaven's sake? I was spending all my waking hours with a computer and Steve Gilman.'

'Not,' said Diana with precision, 'all.'

Miles gave a sharp exclamation, abruptly cut off. His eyes burned into hers. She met the look unflinchingly. She was not, after all these months dealing with life on her own, going to let him intimidate her, she thought with determination.

At last he expelled a long breath. 'I see. Whatever happened to trust?' His voice was bitter.

Diana said quietly, 'Trust has to be earned.'

He winced. 'You thought I'd let you down? Lied to you?' He sounded incredulous.

She hesitated. Had she ever thought Miles was lying? He kept his own counsel and he never explained what he was doing or why. But lying?

'Not exactly,' she said.

'Then what are you talking about?'

She found she was twisting her hands together. It was an old sign of agitation, and Miles would recognise it as such. She stilled them.

'Well, you didn't exactly tell me the whole truth about your life, did you?' she said. 'I didn't know about your father, for example. Or that you owned this house. Or that Chris and Susie were your cousins, not just friends.'

He was watching her with a curious expression. 'All that stuff was important?'

She shook her head vigorously. 'No. Don't you see, Miles? If you'd told me it wouldn't have mattered a row of beans. What mattered was that there were big bits of your life that you didn't want me to know about. Secrets, Miles. They're not good for mutual trust.'

He said softly, 'But these are all things you've found out in the last week. They weren't the reason we broke up.'

Diana shut her eyes. 'We broke up,' she said with an effort, 'because we didn't have a marriage any more.'

There was a long, sizzling silence.

Then Miles said, 'Didn't we? How did you come to that conclusion?'

Diana opened her eyes and found he was strolling towards the bed. Like a stalking jaguar, she thought, with a little rush of alarm.

She said hurriedly, 'Look, Miles. You worked. We hardly spoke. Not for weeks. For over a year. And then when Susie rang you—you dropped everything and went to London to see her.'

He stopped as if she had felled him.

'Susie?' he echoed softly.

There was an expression in his eyes that made her heart flutter frantically. She went on, almost gabbling, 'Of course you were fond of her. I knew that. And you knew her better than you knew me. She's more your sort of person. She's got the same background. I could see that even before I knew you were cousins. But you didn't say why she needed to see you or when you'd be back—or if you were coming back——'

'Susie,' he said again on a long breath.

He gave no sign of having heard a word she'd said, Diana thought. She pleated the edge of the coverlet with fingers that trembled imperceptibly.

'You thought I was having an affair with *Susie*.' It was an accusation.

She glared at him, in spite of her tremors.

'It seemed a reasonable deduction.'

'Did it?' Miles was grim. 'Why didn't you ask me, for heaven's sake?'

'I thought I did.' She winced, remembering the stilted conversations, Miles's harsh, impatient answers. 'You didn't seem to be making a secret of it.'

He passed a hand over his face. 'Dear heaven,' he said wearily. 'I didn't realise. It never occurred to me. What made you think of Susie?'

Diana looked down. She could, of course, have told the literal truth and said, She did. But it wasn't the whole truth, and somehow she didn't feel that less than the whole truth would do.

So she said carefully, 'You were obviously close. And she's gorgeous. And everyone else seemed to expect you'd marry her if you married anyone.'

He shook his head, wordlessly.

'And even when you weren't talking to me you went to her whenever she called,' Diana finished simply.

'I—oh, lord, yes, I suppose I did,' Miles said as if it was wrenched out of him. 'And I suppose from your point of view I'm still doing it, aren't I?'

Diana flinched.

He said urgently, 'Look, I'll get rid of her. I'll get rid of them all. We'll be alone with some time to ourselves. We'll just take it as it comes.'

She shut her eyes. Being alone with Miles with time to themselves would, she thought, just about take out all her defences. Could she afford it?

As if he sensed her inner turmoil, he said carefully, 'No promises. No pressure. Just a holiday we both need. After all, we always got on well enough, didn't we?'

She could have screamed that once he had withdrawn into himself they had not got on at all. And her every day had been a nightmare—to say nothing of the empty nights. But she was shaking with reaction already. She didn't think she could take a full-scale confrontation about his personal isolation.

So instead she said carefully in her turn, 'It's difficult to get on badly with someone who may just have saved your life.'

He made an abrupt, dismissive gesture. 'Will you stay with me, Di?' His voice was low.

Her defences were pretty flimsy things after all.

'Yes,' she said.

CHAPTER EIGHT

SLIGHTLY to Diana's surprise, Miles wasn't triumphant at his easy victory. Nor did he attempt to take immediate advantage of it.

Instead he touched her cheek very lightly with the back of his hand.

'Sleep,' he said. 'You need it. You look like a ghost. We'll talk later.'

He went noiselessly from the room without waiting for an answer. Which was just as well, Diana thought wryly, because she hadn't the faintest idea what she would have said to him. He seemed to have her in the palm of his hand again.

She sank back among the pillows, disturbed. Oh, she knew it all, the faint tremors that radiated out from the spine through her whole body, the hunger for his touch, the fear... She screwed her eyes tight shut. That was the awful thing: the fear that he would turn away again, with his remote, polite smile, and remove himself into the far distance.

'I couldn't take that again,' Diana said aloud.

She turned her head into the pillow, shaken. Take it *again*? What was she thinking of? Dropping her independence like an old pair of jeans she had no further use for, and going back to Miles? Even if he wanted her—and he hadn't said he wanted her—that would be foolhardy in the extreme. Surely she wasn't going to let her heart run away with her again?

She fell asleep telling herself she would not be such a fool.

She didn't know what it was that brought her awake. She had been dreaming, some sad, familiar stuff where she huddled, shivering in a darkened doorway, waiting and afraid. When she awoke, she was still entangled in the webs of the dream, bewildered and desolate.

At first she didn't know where she was. She lifted her head and looked round, rubbing the back of her hand across her eyes like a child. Her face, she found, was damp with tears from the dream. The strange shapes of unknown furniture startled her. She sat up.

'Did I disturb you?' said a soft voice from the window.

Diana gave a small silent scream, her heart jumping. She swung over to look in the direction of the voice.

Out of the grey and lilac shadows, Miles strolled. He was like a shadow himself. She could not see his face, only the lithe, beautiful shape of his body and the characteristic tilt of his head. Her blood seemed to stop, then suddenly to start thundering at a new and audible rate.

She said his name. It was a voiceless whisper.

'Yes.'

She could tell from his voice that he was smiling. She shut her eyes, reaching for her common sense, her resolve, her sense of self-preservation.

'You shouldn't be here,' she said.

'An interesting proposition.' The husky voice was amused. Amused and determined. 'Why not?'

There was a soft rustle of cloth. Diana's eyes flew open. But she already knew what she would see. He was shrugging himself out of the pale shirt. It dropped unheeded. Oh, the times she had watched him do that! The times she had picked up the misused shirt the next day, holding it against her face, remembering their laughter and the crazy passion they incited in each other.

Diana scrambled up among the bedclothes with a small moan of panic.

'*No,*' she said, pushing the pillows away in an attempt to get off the bed and on to her feet.

But Miles turned neatly and took her by the shoulders, hauling her across the bed to where he stood at its head. In the cool shadows, his hands were like fire. She shuddered with a feeling she would infinitely have preferred not to recognise. There was no doubt that Miles recognised it. He laughed softly as she put her hands against his chest, trying to lever herself away from him.

He kissed her. Her protest shuddered into silence.

The terrifying thing, Diana thought muzzily, was that it was all so *familiar*. It was nothing like those crazy, calculated minutes on the beach. This was what she knew, what she had grown used to—the absolute physical rapport, a refinement of sensation so exquisite that it was almost a pain.

In all the bleak days of her independence she had never once looked for another lover. And here he was, proving again, unequivocally and unforgettably, exactly why. It would have been pointless. Only Miles had ever made her feel like this, Diana thought. Only Miles ever could.

If he leaves me again, I'll die, she thought. She had just enough presence of mind not to say it aloud.

Their clothes fell in their accustomed tangle. Their bodies moulded into the accustomed attitudes. There was, perhaps, a new intensity. He did, perhaps, hold her more fiercely as she ran her lips over his skin. Diana heard him catch his breath. His throat arched. She was trembling wildly, out of control. She gave herself up to the feelings that swept them both into the whirlwind.

The next time she awoke, she was smiling. She turned lazily, filled with a sense of sunshine and well-being that she had not had for months.

The shutters were open. The Attic sun streamed in like wine, blasting colour out of the elaborate hangings. Diana stretched like a cat, looking at the room through half-closed eyes. It was a ridiculous room for a climate like this, she thought. She must make Miles get rid of these tapestries and weighty furniture.

She turned towards him, reaching out a hand for the support of his shoulder. But she was alone.

It disconcerted her. She sat up, her eyes flying open. Perhaps he was in the bathroom?

But no. The bathroom door was open and no sounds came from it. A chill touched her. She pulled the coverlet up to cover her breasts, scanning the room for clues that he had been there, that it had not all been a dream.

There was nothing. The tangle of masculine clothes had gone from the rug beside the bed. Her own cotton nightdress had been draped modestly over the end of the bed. Apart from that, you wouldn't think Miles had been there at all.

All Diana's doubts surged back like an unwelcome revelation. Had he said he loved her last night? Had he said anything at all last night? He had said her name on that shaken little note of laughter and passion which had delivered up her soul to him. But of his thoughts, his own feelings, he had said nothing. He had kept his own counsel. Just, Diana reminded herself, growing colder by the minute, as he used to.

She scrambled off the bed, pulling the coverlet self-consciously round her. But there was no one else in the suite. She put her head out of the door: no one else in the corridor. There was no one on the terrace either. And nothing that could be construed as a message.

Diana dressed swiftly and went looking.

She found Christos Galatas on the battlements. There was no sign of anyone else, though the sun was so high that it had to be mid-morning. Christos was looking pre-occupied and not very pleased.

'Miles has gone,' he said tersely.

Diana stopped as if he had hit her.

'Gone?'

He looked at her narrowly. 'I was going to ask you if you knew. But obviously you didn't.'

She put out a hand and lowered herself into a seat blindly. She felt numb.

Again. He had left her again. Without a word, or a kiss or so much as a note to say where he was going. I don't believe it, she thought. But then, at a deeper, harder level, Yes, I do.

And yet, after last night, how could he? She would have sworn that he was as moved as she was. Even though he hadn't put it into words, she knew how he had trembled under her hands. Surely that meant something? *Surely*?

Nothing, Diana thought, was ever going to hurt her again as much as this second desertion.

Chris was speaking. ' . . . taken my damn fool sister with him.'

She drew a sharp little breath. Wrong again; something could hurt worse. She gave a sudden, harsh laugh. She'd thought if Miles left her again she would die. Well, this was where she found out how you went on living with a second mortal wound.

Chris looked at her for a narrow-eyed moment. 'Has he gone to write his Russian paper?' he asked.

Diana winced. But she said coolly enough, 'I have no idea why he's gone. Or where.'

'He didn't tell you?'

She shook her head. 'Miles never told me much when I was married to him. Now . . .' She shrugged.

'He seems to think you're still married to him.'

The pain round her heart was so bad that she felt as if the life blood was being squeezed out of it.

'Not,' she said grimly, 'for long.'

To his evident consternation, she insisted on leaving that day. He wanted Dimitri to fly her back to London but the other guest was nowhere to be found, so Chris abandoned that. He would not, however, hear of her driving the hired car back to Athens.

'You're upset,' he said flatly. 'You'll have an accident.'

'I am not upset,' Diana said.

She had packed with murderous speed. She was now holding on to her temper with the greatest of difficulty. She had to keep reminding herself that Chris was not responsible for his cousin's careless seductions.

'I've had a wonderful holiday,' she said with vicious politeness, 'and now I need to go back and get on with my life.'

'Miles will kill me,' he said gloomily.

But he ordered the chauffeured limousine to take her to the airport. He even accompanied her.

'What are you going to do when you get back?' he asked as they came into the Athenian suburbs.

'Work,' she said. 'Put my affairs in order. Get a divorce.'

He bit his lip and said nothing for a moment. Then, 'Why did you marry Miles, Diana?'

She drew a careful breath. She had asked herself that too in the last few hours. She knew the answer and there was no point in dissembling, furious though it undoubtedly made her.

'Because I was in love,' she said crisply. 'And Miles was so sure it was the right thing.' She shrugged. 'We seemed to fit. Then.'

Christos nodded. 'And Miles was in love,' he supplied.

Diana swallowed and set her jaw, looking out into the dusty streets.

'No,' she said. 'I very much doubt it.'

Chris sighed. 'Then you're wrong,' he said at last. 'Miles was so in love that it showed. Frankly, I envied him.'

He paused. She said nothing. He sighed again. He did not mention the subject again.

Diana hardly noticed the flight home. It was late and crowded and not all the Count's influence had succeeded in locating a first-class seat on a tourist-class flight. She was wedged into the window seat that his influence did manage to procure, flanked by a worried mother and a restless nine-year-old whose interest in herself didn't diminish until she was climbing into a taxi outside Heathrow.

Her little house was cold and dusty. Diana went round putting on lights and radiators. After the brightness of Greece it seemed cramped and dark.

Stop it, she told herself. This is the home you made for yourself when Miles left you. It's what you want. You're comfortable here. You're safe.

Ah, but am I happy? Will I ever be happy again?

Self-pity, she told herself grimly, will get you nowhere.

She went through her post like a whirlwind. When she had answered everything, she ran through the messages on the answering machine. Nothing from Miles, of course. Everything else was easily dealt with. Too easily. It was early afternoon and she had nothing to do to take her mind off the confused and painful thoughts that were churning away at the back of her mind.

She walked round the house with an undrunk mug of coffee in her hand, formulating plans and discarding them as soon as she thought of them. She went to put music on the stereo and her hand fell on the Bach English

Suites. Miles's favourites. She stuffed them back into the rack and played Charlie Parker loudly and defiantly.

When her thinking took her nowhere, she went looking for something stronger than coffee. There were the eight-week-old remains of a bottle of Sancerre in the fridge. She threw it away with a grimace and investigated the drinks cupboard. She drank so rarely that she couldn't remember what was there. She looked at the array of bottles with distaste: gin too sweet, brandy too dry, whisky was only for cold weather, ouzo...

She stopped dead. She had no idea how it had come there. She wouldn't have bought it and she couldn't have brought Miles's bottle from the marital home when she moved her things. Surely she couldn't.

'It's a conspiracy,' Diana said, shaking with fury.

With shaking fingers she took the bottle out of the cupboard and marched it into the kitchen like a prisoner under guard. There she twisted the top off viciously and flung the stuff down the sink. The warm smell of aniseed rebounded on her. She set her teeth, flinging the empty bottle into the swing-bin so hard that she heard it shatter.

'I will get him out of my life,' she vowed. 'I will be free. I *will*.'

Without thinking further she picked up the phone and dialled her lawyer. Joan was an old friend who had helped her set up her consultancy.

'Joan,' she said as soon as she'd identified herself, 'I'm divorcing Miles.' For some stupid reason the tears began to seep out of her eyes. She stuffed the back of her hand in her mouth to stop herself whimpering. She mastered her voice. 'Will you act for me?'

'Are you sure that's what you want?' Joan Dryden asked cautiously after a startled pause. 'Do you want to talk about this?'

'No,' Diana said curtly. 'I just want it over with as soon as possible.'

There was another pause. 'Er—well, that will depend on Miles as well, of course,' Joan ventured.

Diana gave a laugh that didn't—quite—break.

'I've seen Miles. He's got no grounds to contest a divorce.' She swallowed something huge and jagged in her throat. 'He's left me twice now.'

'Well, he's off lecturing, that's his job. You have to be reasonable,' Joan said with infuriating calm.

'He's off with Susanna Galatas,' Diana said coldly.

'Oh, lord,' said Joan, suddenly less the lawyer than the concerned friend. 'Oh, Diana, I'm so sorry. What a bastard.'

I will not cry, Diana told herself. She swallowed again.

'He was always close to her,' she said, her voice a model of indifference. 'He may even marry her. I don't care. I just want shot of him, Joan.'

'I don't blame you. I'll start drafting,' her friend said. 'Are you all right? I mean do you want me to come over or anything?'

'No. I'm going to see my parents,' Diana said on another of her instantaneous decisions. Her voice suddenly thickened. 'But thanks, Joan.'

She prepared more carefully for her visit to her parents the next day. If Miles was serious about his threat to stop her allowance, she would have to see if there was any way that between them they could carry on paying the mortgage. And she didn't want them to detect her own devastation. Not least because she didn't want to admit it herself.

They were delighted to see her. Her father was cooking in his skilfully adapted kitchen. He sent her out to talk to her mother, who was gardening.

Constance Silk hugged her, then held her a little away from her.

'Did you have a good holiday?' she said, searching her face. 'You don't look very brown.'

'Mum, I saw Miles,' Diana blurted, breaching all her prepared resolutions.

Mrs Silk sat down on a wooden bench that circled a pear tree and placed her trug under it. She was heart-breakingly unalarmed.

'Did you, now? I'm glad.'

Diana subsided beside her and took hold of herself rapidly. 'Don't be.'

Her mother looked faintly amused. 'Did you have another fight?'

One of the most difficult things to deal with since Miles had walked out had been, in Diana's experience, her mother's bland determination that it was a temporary interlude, resulting from Diana's losing her temper with a busy man she didn't appreciate.

Diana closed her eyes briefly. 'Mother, Miles and I fought all the time.'

Mrs Silk shook her head at her. 'You're the most contrary girl. You and Miles head over heels as you are, I'd have thought you could find something better to do than quarrelling.' And, having delivered her considered view, which Diana knew would not be repeated, she sat back and said comfortably, 'Now tell me how Miles is.'

Diana straightened her shoulders. She shielded her father a good deal but experience had taught her there was not much point in trying to hide things from her mother.

'Miles is getting tired of paying my allowance,' she said. 'We're going to have to look at the mortgage again. I'm not sure I can keep it up. Or not for long. I'm sorry.'

She waited for an outbreak of emotion. None came.

'You must have made him very angry this time,' Constance Silk said thoughtfully.

Diana decided to tell her everything. Or at least all the facts. The emotions she couldn't handle herself yet. She certainly wasn't going to try and explain them to someone else.

'I told him I didn't want to have anything more to do with him,' she said with a hint of defiance.

'Ah. I see now,' her mother said at length.

Diana stared. This was superhuman self-control.

'See what, Mum?'

'The solicitors in Oxford sent someone over last week. Wednesday, was it? Thursday? He said Miles thought the present arrangement was unsatisfactory. So he was going to pay off the mortgage entirely. Dad and I had to sign some papers. I thought,' said Constance Silk with the confidence of a woman who never bothered her head with such things, 'it was probably something to do with tax.'

'Pay off...?' A terrible fear took hold of Diana. 'You mean the house is in his name now?'

Mrs Silk looked shocked. 'Oh, I don't think so, dear. You'll have to ask your father. The solicitor brought the deeds back. Dad and I went into town and put them in the bank. It made a nice trip for him.'

Diana felt as if she had taken a step into quicksand. 'I don't understand.'

Mrs Silk sent her a shrewd look. 'I suppose Miles didn't want Dad and me to be mixed up in whatever fight you're having now,' she said comfortably. 'Very sensible of him.'

There was a shriek of triumph from the kitchen. Constance Silk stood up, looking pleased.

'Devil's Food Cake,' she said. 'It's a recipe he got out of a magazine. If you tell him you're on a diet I'll never speak to you again. Anyway, you look as if you could do with some more flesh on your bones. No one would think you've had a holiday.'

In the kitchen Frank Silk was swinging the wheelchair deftly from one counter-top to the other. His face was red, as much with pleasure as with the heat from the oven. On the baking tray stood a rich-looking chocolate cake. Diana looked at it with real admiration, repressing sternly the tears that pricked at her eyes.

'When can we start it?' she asked.

'I'll make tea now,' said her mother. 'It'll be cool enough by the time the kettle's boiled. Go and sit in the fresh air and I'll bring it out into the garden.'

Frank buzzed the wheelchair briskly down the specially constructed path and swung round to a stop under the pear tree. Diana dropped to the ground beside him. He looked down at her fondly.

'So you had a lovely holiday with Miles,' he said. He and Constance managed to communicate telepathically, Diana thought sourly. 'How is he?'

Her father had been shocked and angry when Miles left her. He seemed to have got over it now.

Diana said carefully, 'Fit. Very tanned.'

Frank nodded. 'Good. The last time we saw him he was looking like a ghost, I thought. Working too hard.'

'Yes,' said Diana automatically. She was trying to assimilate this piece of surprising news. 'Er—when was that, Dad?'

Her father thought about it. 'Oh, quite a while now. Couple of months. Before he went to Australia. He dropped in to say he'd be out of the country for a bit.'

Diana choked. 'How often have you been seeing him?'

It was Frank's turn to be surprised. 'Every month or so, I suppose. Didn't he mention it?'

Diana could have screamed. Instead she drew several long breaths and said in a careful voice, 'We've parted, Dad. We don't see each other.'

'But you've just been on holiday together,' he pointed out.

'Not,' she said between her teeth, 'voluntarily. If I'd known he was going to be there, wild horses wouldn't have got me to that damned castle.'

He looked worried. 'Oh, dear. I had no idea.' He bent down, peering into her face. 'But I thought... I mean your mother said... Aren't you getting back together again, then?'

Very slowly her hands closed into fists. She could feel the nails digging into her palms. But she said calmly, 'No, Dad. Not the last time I looked.'

He shook his head. 'I'm sorry,' he said simply. 'You're never going to be happy without him, you know.'

She winced. It was too horribly close to what she felt herself.

'Nor happy with him,' she said quietly.

He smiled at her affectionately. 'You're just going through a bad time,' he said. 'Marriage is a difficult relationship. But when Miles put that ring on your finger he meant it to stay there.'

She took it off that night when she got back. She thrust the ring deep into her handkerchief drawer, not looking where it fell. She should, she knew, have taken it off years ago. If she had really wanted to be free, she would have done.

'Heaven help me,' she muttered.

She began to work. It was late and she was tired but she knew if she went to bed she wouldn't sleep any more than she had slept last night. And the night before that, her hurt heart reminded her, she had slept dreamlessly deep in Miles's arms. Until he had left her.

She was at her desk, poring over a sketch plan by the light of an angled lamp, when the doorbell rang. She jumped, looking at the clock. After nine. Joan Dryden making house calls?

She picked up the entryphone. 'Hello?'

'And where the hell have you been?'

Even through the distorting device she could hear the menace in his voice. She clenched her hand round the instrument until her knuckles showed white.

'Who is that?' she demanded in as cool a voice as she could manage.

'Don't play games with me,' he advised softly. 'Let me in, or I'll raise the neighbourhood.'

He would too. It was a small residential square, with the house fronts facing inwards over a pedestrian path and the central shrubbery. It would be all too easy for him to bring the residents of all twelve houses out into the communal garden. He would probably, thought Diana in helpless anger, enjoy it.

She punched the entry button with quite unnecessary viciousness. At least she wasn't going to go down to the ground floor and let him in.

He came up the stairs two at a time. She listened for his steps as she had listened for them so many times before in the house they had shared.

I am not going to be sentimental, she vowed. And I'm not going to let him persuade me or browbeat me or seduce me. Particularly not seduce me.

She switched on the wall-lights as he got to the top of the stairs. He stood there looking round the open-plan sitting-room, pushing his hands through his hair.

'Sitting in the dark?' he mocked with a nod to the light-switch where her hand still lingered. 'Moping?'

Diana glared at him. 'Working,' she said coldly, indicating the desk and its workmanlike lighting arrangements. 'I didn't realise how late it had got.'

He gave a brisk nod. 'Then you won't have eaten. Get your coat.'

She stared at him. 'I'm sorry?' she said in a voice of ice.

'So you should be. Get your coat.'

She wasn't going to allow him to browbeat her, Diana reminded herself.

'I won't,' she said.

Miles gave her his most charming smile. He was looking at his most implacable.

'Then come as you are and freeze.'

'I'm not going anywhere with you.'

'Yes, you are,' he said positively. 'You're coming to have dinner. And then you're coming home with me.'

Diana retreated behind a sofa. 'This is my home.'

'You would be there now if I hadn't missed you at the airport,' he said, ignoring her.

Diana suddenly felt a surge of kindness for the small jumping bean who had sat next to her on the horrible flight. At least his company seemed to have camouflaged her arrival. If she had known Miles was in the crowd waiting for her she would have been frantic.

'You delude yourself, Miles,' she said. 'I would never have gone back to your house in any circumstances.'

His eyes narrowed. 'That isn't what your body was telling me two nights ago,' he said softly.

Diana flinched. So she'd found something else that hurt more than anything had ever done before or could do again, she thought with a touch of hysteria. How many more such records was she going to have to break before Miles got out of her life forever?

She said, 'I'd rather we didn't talk about that.'

'I'm sure you would.' He was grimly amused. 'We're going to talk about it, nevertheless.'

She might be determined not to be browbeaten but she knew her limitations, Diana thought. She made a despairing gesture.

'All right. Have your say. And then go away.'

'Only if you come with me.'

She closed her eyes. 'For the last time, Miles. *No.*'

'The night before last...'

She opened her eyes and glared at him. 'The night before last I behaved like a fool and a tramp.'

He might just as well not have been listening to her. He stretched out a hand and cupped her cheek as if they were lovers about to fall into each other's arms. His eyes were warm.

Damn him, thought Diana, suddenly sharply afraid of herself. She stepped back, wrenching her head aside.

'I've started divorce proceedings,' she said harshly.

That at least managed to get his attention, she saw with satisfaction.

'You've *what*?'

Prudently she didn't repeat it. It was all she could do to stand her ground. His eyes weren't warm any more. They were flaming. She thought suddenly, I've never seen him lose control of himself like this before. He will hate losing control.

He didn't touch her. But she felt the blast of his anger like a water-cannon. If she hadn't been holding on to the back of the sofa she could almost have staggered under the force of it.

'Don't bully me, Miles,' she flared.

He looked her up and down measuringly. 'Two nights ago, you were going mad in my arms,' he said levelly.

It was an accusation. Diana's face flamed.

'I——'

'You told me you loved me,' he said relentlessly.

Heaven help her, she probably had. She'd felt the love all right, Diana thought with a stab of misery. With her guard down like that, she'd probably been stupid enough to tell him as well. She shook her head at the thought.

'I assure you, you did.'

She gathered up the tatters of her pride and met his eyes.

'Very possibly,' she said in an even tone. 'In the heat of the moment one says these things. I'm afraid I don't remember.' Her shrug was a masterpiece.

Their eyes locked. His darkened.

Then he said softly, 'I don't believe you.'

She shrugged again, looking away.

'You were never much of a liar, my dear Diana. Especially not in bed,' he drawled.

If he had meant to be cruel, he could not have hit her with more precision.

Her voice like ice, she said, 'It's called sex, Miles. Chemical attraction. Of which you and I have rather too much for our own comfort. It's pretty ephemeral. It doesn't replace liking and trust. And you can't build a marriage on it.'

He stared at her. The handsome face looked gaunt suddenly.

'I won't let you get away with that,' he said.

Quite suddenly Diana realised that she was at the end of her tether. If he didn't leave, and soon, she was going to break down and start begging him to stay. And then he'd leave, without a backward look, until the next time...

'I can't bear it,' she said. 'I've had all I'm going to take from you, Miles...'

It was the wrong tone to take, the wrong thing to say. He was too near, the mood was too taut, they were too alone in the quiet house. He stepped round the sofa, his expression black.

'Now there you're wrong,' he said quite gently. And took hold of her.

Diana would have said she knew all there was to know about the way she and Miles made love. She would have been wrong.

There was none of the gentleness they were used to. None of the slow savouring of the delights of the senses. They were both hurt and angry and, both in their particular way, driven to the limit.

Diana didn't know who astonished her most—Miles, no longer silent and immaculately controlled, or herself, as fierce in her demands of their bodies as he was. When they fell back, gasping, she felt as if she had run through fire—and not wholly escaped the burning.

Miles was breathing hard. He reached out a long arm for her, drawing her back against his body.

'Di.' His voice was slurred but the amusement was back. If it hadn't been she might not have reacted as she did. But she was not in any case to be laughed at, with her heart still pounding and the bruises beginning to appear.

She wrenched herself away from all that dangerous warmth and laughter. He was never going to hurt her again. Never.

'My point proved, I think,' she said coldly. 'Sex, Miles. And nothing else.'

CHAPTER NINE

THIS time it was Diana who left. She stumbled into some clothes and drove her car to Joan Dryden's. She was, she freely admitted, lucky that the windy streets were empty at that time of night.

Joan took one look at her and sent her to bed with a hot drink. The next day she even came back to the little house with her distressed client. But Miles had gone by then.

The sitting-room still looked like a battlefield. A chair was on its side and papers were everywhere. Joan's eyebrows went up to her hairline.

'I'll get a "no molestation" order,' she said practically.

But Diana said swiftly, 'No. Don't do that. He won't be back again.'

Joan looked at her narrowly. 'You're sure of that?'

Diana thought of the bleakness in his eyes when she had looked down at him with that parting shot.

'I'm sure.'

Joan shrugged. 'Well, you know your own business best,' she said doubtfully. 'I'll get on to his solicitor anyway. He's still using Hendon, I presume?'

'I suppose so.'

Diana must have sounded as depressed as she felt. Joan touched her arm.

'What you need is a bit of forward planning. Go and look at the order book and see whether you can pay the bills,' she said bracingly. 'That'll put a bit of ginger into life, especially if you can't. Take care of yourself.'

Diana saw her off, then went slowly back indoors. Take care of yourself, she thought wryly. Well, she'd been doing that, hadn't she? Since long before Miles left, too. Miles had never wanted to take care of her. He'd been too impatient, too—other than in those moments of devastating passion—remote. She'd broken her heart on that remoteness. All the passion had done was hide it.

She was, Diana assured herself, better off taking care of herself and not looking, hopelessly, for love that wasn't there. Passion was no substitute. All it did was disguise Miles's deep indifference, and her own need to protect herself from him.

She took Joan's advice and listed all the work she had accepted and all that had been offered while she was away. She gave the computer some parameters and told it to prioritise. It came out with a schedule that, even assuming minimum travel, was full for six months.

'At least I won't starve,' Diana said wryly.

She looked uneasily at the papers on the Princess's apartment. She didn't need Miles's work. On the other hand, it would look like running away if she didn't at least attempt a report of sorts. And Miles wasn't going to have the satisfaction of having got her on the run, she told herself.

She would send him a nominal bill which she would be quite glad if he never paid. And then the whole relationship would be behind her.

The report on the Princess's apartment was typed and printed off by midnight.

She stood up, stretching her arms above her head. The queer silence of the small hours made her feel very alone. She bit her lip. Not alone. Lonely. For Miles. Her very skin called out for his touch. She lowered her arms abruptly.

'This has got to stop,' she said aloud between her teeth. 'It's over. I am never going to see him again. I don't *want* to see him again. I've got to get on with my life on my own.'

For the next four weeks she made a valiant attempt to do just that. She worked fourteen hours a day, leaving the answering machine as a barrier between her and the outside world. Miles neither wrote nor tried to call her. She was, Diana said to herself, thankful.

She went to see her parents on brief, irregular visits. She had checked with the solicitor and they were right. The house was in their own name now. At least Miles wasn't going to hold that over her head.

She had a faint suspicion her parents were still seeing Miles, though. It crystallised one Saturday evening when, watching a science programme on television about a new discovery, her father said cheerfully, 'That's over my head. Miles will have to explain it to me.'

Diana sat bolt upright. 'Dad——'

But her mother interposed smoothly, 'There'll be stuff in the Sunday papers, I shouldn't wonder. We'll look.'

At once she got up and began to fuss about evening drinks and Diana felt the opportunity to challenge her slip away. It was frustrating. She would, she thought grimly, have it out with both of them in the morning.

But Constance Silk had a heavy programme for her in the morning. She had to plant out seedlings, gather flowers for the house, go to the farm for cream. Diana did it all with a grim efficiency that must have told her mother that she wasn't going to avoid interrogation. Constance stayed serene.

'Your father's papers?' she suggested, receiving the carton of cream with a word of thanks.

'All right, Mother,' Diana agreed. 'I'll go to the village shop for you. *Then* we'll talk.'

'Of course, darling,' Constance agreed with the calm of a woman who had the next diversionary tactic well planned.

Diana laughed in spite of herself. But her mother wasn't going to get out of it, she promised herself. But in the end it was not Constance who diverted attention from the subject.

Diana strolled back along the metalled road with the papers under her arm, enjoying the scents of the June countryside. They were, she thought, utterly unlike the hot herbal smell of the Greek cliffs. They were heady and sweet—too sweet. And the road began to give off an odd sheen as if the tar was melting. The papers were very heavy. All of a sudden Diana realised she didn't feel very well.

She got home somehow. One look at her face and Constance Silk had her sitting on the doorstep with her head between her knees. Her father's wheelchair whirred agitatedly.

'No need to get in a flap, Frank,' Constance said calmly. 'She's got a touch of the sun, that's all.'

And, sure enough, she felt better after lunch. She drove home, forgetting the incident.

The following morning, however, was different. Diana awoke late and heavy-eyed with the feeling that something horrible was imminent. It was. She was sick.

It didn't last long. She recovered and went through the rest of her day as if it had not happened, though it was an effort. She had a strange feeling of exhaustion, which was infuriating with all the work she had to do. And when the same thing happened the next morning she lost patience with herself.

She hardly ever went to the doctor, so he was a stranger. He turned out to be young and horridly cheerful. He listened to her tale of the accident in Greece and the chance of slight concussion with an air of tolerant superiority which made Diana want to hit him.

'Well, we'll see what the tests say,' he conceded at last. 'But I'd say it was a slight touch of pregnancy, Mrs Tabard. Congratulations.'

Diana could never afterwards remember how she got herself out of his surgery and home. She must have driven but she had no memory of the journey. She felt cold. Panic, she knew. Panic and a strange, frightening sensation of being caught up in events over which she had no control.

For the moment the doctor had suggested it she had recognised it as the truth. She would wait for the test results, of course, but in her heart she already knew. She was carrying Miles's child.

'And what do I do *now*?' she asked her blank computer screen, feeling no less blank herself.

She thought about telling her parents, and shuddered. They would be overjoyed. They would also expect her to go back to Miles. She shuddered again, more deeply. She couldn't bear it. She *couldn't*.

There were occasions—short, ecstatic and unforeseeable moments—when he wanted her with a physical passion that, if you were very gullible, looked like love, Diana allowed. Felt like love, even. But then he would go away and not want her. He might want Susie Galatas, or some other worldly sophisticate who could match him, in those moods. But he wouldn't want Diana. And that would break her, she knew.

Diana tipped forward and leaned her hot forehead against the top of the computer screen. If you were very gullible or very much in love...she mused. If you were very much in love you saw what you wanted to see and only counted the cost afterwards. As she had counted the cost in the last two years.

'I can't do it again,' she said aloud. 'I wouldn't survive another blast.'

And yet. And yet...

Didn't Miles have a right to know that she was expecting his child? She knew if she were advising someone else she would disapprove violently of a woman not at least telling her child's father. Yet if she told him, what could she expect? Worse, what would she want?

Diana closed her eyes.

Face it, she told herself with fierce contempt, what you want is your fantasy back. Miles loving you. Miles wanting the baby. Miles holding your hand through all the things you're scared of: doctors and clinics and the whole bureaucracy. And getting ready for the baby. You don't want to do it alone. But it's more than that. You want Miles. Haven't you got any backbone at all? Haven't you learned *anything*?

The arguments went round and round, not just that day but all the days that followed. The results of the test came but Diana was not surprised at the result. She still didn't know what she was going to do. She put off going to see her parents that weekend. Constance's eyes were too sharp.

Every morning she woke up with the conviction that it would be all right if she told Miles. He was a civilised man and he would be considerate and helpful in a practical way. And then during the day she would lose her nerve. She would start to imagine herself taken over by him again, as he took charge of the situation. Or, worse, living with him, trying not to beg him to love her.

She could have found out where he was easily enough. If he was writing his paper for Moscow he was probably in Oxford anyway. Or Joan Dryden could have talked neutrally to his solicitor. Diana stayed silent.

She lost weight. Knowing it was bad for the baby, she began to watch her diet in a distracted way. She worked like a demon, and spent the small, sleepless hours knitting secret garments for a February baby. She knew that the time during which she could hope to keep her secret was running out.

And then Susie Galatas turned up, out of the blue, unannounced, standing on Diana's doorstep in glamorous scarlet with diamonds in her ears and round her slender wrist.

'Oh,' said Diana, conscious of bare feet and jeans and enormous hostility.

Susie's eyes gleamed for a moment, then were swiftly veiled.

'Busy?' she asked, following Diana into the sitting-room.

Diana took the excuse gratefully.

'I'm afraid so. So I don't want to be rude, Susie, but it's a quick coffee and goodbye, I'm afraid,' she told her uninvited guest.

Susie sat down in Diana's Victorian chair and inspected her bracelet.

'I think you were so sensible not to go back to Miles,' she said. 'Chris thought you would.' It was not quite a question.

Diana felt her face freeze into a mask. 'Milk in your coffee?'

Susie crossed exquisite legs. 'Of course, living here in Oxford you'll have heard the gossip. About him and the wife of the man he was working with. Yes, milk and a little sugar, please.'

Diana stirred milk and several teaspoonsful of sugar into the brew with unnecessary viciousness.

'That's why they cancelled the lecture tour, you know. The boffin found out that his wife was having an affair with Miles and had a breakdown.' She took the coffee and sipped. 'Personally, I always thought that was why Miles wanted you to go back to him—to knock the rumours on the head. Though why he bothered...' She shrugged. 'I suppose he must have wanted to go on working with the husband.' She put her head on one side. 'What do you think?'

'I think you've got a poisonous tongue and a worse mind,' Diana said.

It was a great release to say it. Susie looked astonished.

'Steve and Hilary Gilman are Miles's friends. That's not the way he treats friends,' Diana continued quietly.

Under the perfect make-up, Susie flushed.

'You know him so well, I suppose?'

'Well enough to know he doesn't cheat friends.'

Susie gave a trill of laughter that sounded forced. 'Oh, they'll have hushed it up. The husband's gone into some academic nut-house,' she said cruelly, 'and the devoted wife's gone home to hold his hand. So Miles went to the castle to play peasant and look for some longer-term cover before he went back on the academic circuit: you.'

Diana looked at her with dislike.

'If it were true—which it isn't because Miles doesn't do things like that—he wouldn't need cover,' she said in a light, hard voice. 'Academics run off with other academics' wives all the time. It's a licensed university sport.'

Susie was pitying, and her tone was triumphant.

'Miles doesn't do things like run off with people,' she said. 'I agree. He travels light. He doesn't want a lady cluttering up his life. He's not into permanence.'

Unwarily, Diana shut her eyes. 'He was into permanence once.' She wasn't talking to Susie.

Susie made an angry noise. '*Darling*. How blind can you be? Miles didn't marry in thirty-six years. He'd had hundreds of women after him. Some of them were devastating. He didn't marry because he didn't need to. When he saw you—well, frankly, darling, none of us could understand it. Until Chris said it had to be the only way he could get you. Then it made sense.' She pulled out a packet of cigarettes and lit one with unsteady fingers. 'That was how it was, wasn't it?'

Diana whitened.

There had been a night—nights—when Miles had taken her back to her graduate house and sat drinking coffee with her until the small hours. He had wanted more, urged her, demonstrated beyond any doubt that she wanted more as well. It had all been so new, so strong. She had hesitated.

Ironically, she had said to Miles that all that there was between them was sex. And here was Susie telling her the same thing.

'That's all,' said Susie, her eyes like diamonds. She drew rapidly on the cigarette. 'If you'd gone to bed with him, you'd have got rid of him inside three months like the rest of us.' She sounded furious.

Diana drew a careful breath. Susie was jealous, she told herself. Jealous and angry, though heaven knew why. Miles seemed to be more committed to her than he had ever been to his wife. But she knew the expression on Susie's face. The Countess was hurt and she wanted to lash out at someone. Diana could even sympathise with it, reluctantly.

She said gently, 'That's all in the past, Susie. There's no point in raking it over again. Now, was this only a social call or did you want me to do something for you?'

'The Princess's room,' said Susie, 'the man you told us to go to. The Italian? He says we need to have the paint made up specially if it's to be authentic. In England. *He* recommended *you*.'

Diana closed her eyes. That was undoubtedly Francesco trying to do her a good turn professionally after she recommended him to Castle Galatas. She cursed all friends.

'I'm really terribly busy. I couldn't fit you in for ages . . .'

Susie said swiftly, 'A weekend. That's all it would take. The Italian said so. You take photographs and scrapings of the existing paint and then come back and commission some firm you know here. They can ship the paint out to us without your ever going near them again. It needn't take long. Dimitri could fly you out.'

It was true. Diana glared at her.

Susie said stiffly, 'Miles told me to get it finished. He doesn't think I've got the sticking power. I—need help.'

It was that unvarnished statement that persuaded Diana. It couldn't be easy for the Countess to ask for help from someone she'd always despised. And Diana had some fellow feeling for her. Miles was an impossible taskmaster.

'All right,' she found herself saying. 'One weekend.' She put a hand over her stomach in an instinctive protective movement that Susie didn't notice. 'But soon.'

As Susie promised, Dimitri flew Diana out to Greece. He piloted the plane himself with another man whom he introduced as his navigator. He was friendly enough but businesslike. A laughing, holidaying Dimitri was, Diana realised, a different proposition from the serious man of affairs.

They landed at a small, private airstrip. The Galatas Mercedes was there to meet them. Dimitri handed her into it, bade goodbye to the navigator and got in beside her. He looked tired and preoccupied.

Diana said, 'Do you often spend weekends here?'

He shrugged, looking out of the window at the passing landscape. It was a uniform golden brown now; the green of spring had disappeared. It was very hot, too.

'I used to,' he said evenly. 'Lord knows why I've come this time. I don't know what game Susie's playing.'

He turned and Diana could see the pain in his eyes. It was a pain she was not a stranger to. She had an impulse to touch his hand, and curbed it. He wouldn't want pity any more than she did herself.

'I want her to marry me, you know.'

She nodded. 'Yes. I thought you did. I'm sorry.'

'I nearly asked her in the spring. She seemed as if she was changing, calming down a bit. Not chasing round all over the world the way she has been. This last winter I thought, At last. But——' He shrugged. 'Miles came back and she ran to him, just as she always does. As if they're still *children*.'

Diana's heart lurched. 'I'm sorry,' she said with difficulty. 'But I don't think he thinks of her as a child.'

He gave a brief laugh. 'He does,' he contradicted her. 'Because that's what she is. She refuses to grow up.'

Diana thought of the intensity she had sometimes detected in Susie Galatas. With sudden insight, she said positively, 'It won't be enough for her. She wants a husband. Children. I'm certain.'

This time his laugh was gentler. But he shook his head. 'She lives in a fantasy world,' he said.

There was only Maria to meet them when the car swept into the courtyard. Maria looked worried and was uncommunicative in the extreme. Diana was surprised, then decided that Maria must be embarrassed by what she could not help knowing about the circumstances of her parting with Miles. Whatever the reason, Maria's eyes didn't quite meet hers. And even before the chauffeur had taken their cases out of the car the housekeeper disappeared back into the kitchen muttering about supper.

The chauffeur led the way into the eighteenth-century part of the house. Dimitri was puzzled.

'I always have the tower room under Chris,' he objected. 'So I can listen to the sea.'

The chauffeur was wooden. 'The Countess said you were to have the lilac room, overlooking the terrace.'

Dimitri made a face. 'Susie pointing out she'll do as she pleases in her own house,' he deduced. 'She can be so childish sometimes,' he muttered, though Diana wasn't sure whether she was intended to hear.

He shrugged, anyway, and went in. The chauffeur led Diana round the corner of the corridor. She found that she, at least, was in the same room as before. So Susie was only playing power games with her rejected suitor.

Diana unpacked her overnight case briskly. Her kit for taking paint samples was the largest thing in it, she thought wryly, shaking out her creaseless lace and muslin. She sat down in front of the flower-framed mirror and unpinned her hair. She was brushing it with smooth, rhythmic strokes when, to her consternation, the door from her bathroom opened. She dropped her brush with a clatter and jumped to her feet.

'Who...?' she gasped, thinking, Not Miles. Please don't let Susie have betrayed me to Miles after all.

But to her amazement it was Dimitri. His face was like thunder.

'Do you know what that woman has done?' he almost shouted.

Diana was astonished. 'Maria?'

'Maria!' he spat. 'Of course not. The witch of the castle. Susanna Eleni Penelope Galatas.'

Diana prepared to be soothing and sympathetic. 'No. What?'

He seized her by the hand. 'Come with me.'

He marched her through the bathroom to the bedroom on the other side. It was full of flowers too.

'The lilac room,' Dimitri said grimly. 'Susie clearly thinks you and I should console each other.'

Diana quailed before his ferocity. If he was right, Susie, she thought, had been very unwise.

She said feebly, 'There must be some mistake.'

'No mistake. Susie,' said Dimitri with barely repressed violence, 'has played her last game with me. I bet she isn't even here.'

Diana stared. 'What? But she asked me for the weekend.'

'And me. She has set us up, my dear Diana, for a romantic weekend *à deux*.'

Diana sat down suddenly on the side of the bed. Her head was whirling unpleasantly. 'I don't believe it.'

He flung away and punched the bellpush in the wall as if it were a personal enemy.

'All right. We'll take statements,' he said grimly.

And when Maria arrived, knocking cautiously, he flung open the door and almost dragged her into the room.

'Where's the Countess, Maria?' he asked her without preamble.

Maria looked unhappy. She sent Diana a faintly apologetic look and launched into a flood of Greek. Dimitri's face darkened even more, if that were possible. He turned back to Diana.

'Unavoidably detained. She rang Maria this morning. I,' he said, 'am going to talk to her. Now.'

He stalked out, banging the door behind him. Maria looked after him with consternation. Diana put an alarmed hand to her suddenly tremulous stomach.

'I'm going to be sick,' she said on a rising note.

And Maria, taking one look at her white face, had no trouble at all in leaping the language barrier.

She wasn't in fact sick. But Maria put her to bed as tenderly as if she had been. Dimitri, Diana thought muzzily, would have had to wait an unconscionable time for his dinner.

The next morning she was awakened early. There were alien noises, loud and angry, which brought her up on one elbow. Straining her ears, she thought she caught Miles's deep tones. It was, she thought wryly, a product of pathetic wish-fulfilment. Oh, lord, would she never get him out of her blood? The slightest confusion in the distance and she thought it was Miles calling her.

The noises got louder. Yet it was hardly day. Beyond the open french windows, the dawn was streaking the horizon. Diana pushed her hair back, bewildered. And then she heard her name being called indeed, but not by Miles.

The door to her room was flung back and Susie rushed in. She was dishevelled and breathless, her sunburst scarves flying.

Diana sat up, startled. Her modest broderie anglaise nightdress slipped off one shoulder.

'What is it?' she demanded.

'When you didn't get to the flat, we thought Dimitri must have had an accident. We checked but no one knew anything. It never occurred to us that he would have brought you straight here. We were frantic.'

Diana plucked the only word out all of this which made any sense.

'We?' she said with foreboding.

Susie ignored that. Her eyes slid sideways.

'Susie, what have you done?' Diana asked in dawning alarm.

But there was no need for an answer. The door to the bathroom was pushed open and Miles strolled in.

For a timeless moment there was absolute silence in the opulent bedroom. Across the flowers and the heavy furniture Miles met her eyes, his expression unmistakable. Diana took in the naked hunger in one appalled second. She hauled the strap of her nightdress back into place with fingers that shook.

A quick glance told her that Susie, wringing her hands, was oblivious of that instantaneous, blazing signal. Diana's mouth was dry. She swallowed.

Susie turned to Miles, palms outspread.

'They were here together all night,' she said. 'I was going to tell him I'd marry him. I thought he loved me...'

Miles didn't speak. Something flickered in Susie's eyes. She whirled, draperies flying. 'Where is he?' Her voice rose to screaming-pitch. 'Bitch! Traitor! Where is he?'

Diana got out of bed. If she ever told Miles the truth about her night here with Dimitri, she knew she couldn't do it in front of a hysterical Susie. She was shaking. But she took hold of her courage and her common sense and faced the fierce Countess.

Susie screamed. And went on screaming. The look she turned on Diana was pure hatred.

Miles stepped between them. He looked cool and about as approachable as the moon. Had she imagined that blazing look? Would he believe his cousin's melodrama? And would he care?

There was a sharp crack as his hand connected with Susie's cheek, but his voice was gentle. 'That's enough, Susanna,' he said firmly. 'You're leaping to conclusions again.'

Susie's hand went to her reddening cheek. She didn't look glamorous and sophisticated any more. She looked like the child Dimitri called her. She was crying in great gulping sobs, like a schoolgirl.

'He—he . . .'

'You don't know what's happened yet,' Miles said, still in that steady voice.

But Susie was looking at Diana now and her expression was murderous.

'Oh, yes, I do,' she said fiercely, and made a dart at Diana.

Not expecting it, Diana flinched away and stumbled, cracking herself against the side of the bed. She gave an exclamation of pain at exactly the same time as Miles said in quite a different voice, '*Enough*!'

CHAPTER TEN

DIANA flinched at the iciness of it. If Miles had spoken to her like that, she thought, she would have turned and fled. Susie, though she stopped screaming, showed no such inclination.

She stared at him for a moment, her dark eyes huge.

'Oh, *Miles*,' she said heart-rendingly. And flung herself into his arms.

Diana flinched again, as his arms closed round the vibrant figure. She caught sight of the little tableau in the mirror behind them. They looked like three other people, actors on a screen, she thought. If she had been white before, she was now as pale as milk.

Susie was weeping over his shirt-front, heedless of her eye make-up. She seemed genuinely distraught.

'They were *here*, Miles. All night. Together.'

Miles was impassive. He detached Susie's clinging hands without visible emotion, propelling her into a chair. Susie's weeping redoubled. She clutched at him but, though he didn't slap her again, he ignored her. He turned decisively to Diana.

'Well?'

There was no blaze of desire in his face now. He was utterly controlled. Diana made a helpless gesture. She looked at the cold, handsome face and could not believe that they had ever been close, that he had ever lost control in her arms.

Her throat clogged. She couldn't speak. She shook her head.

Behind Miles, Susie said, 'You see, she can't deny it.'
She sounded both wretched and triumphant.

Diana said, 'Miles please——' It was not much more
than a whisper.

He did not take those cool eyes off her.

'Diana tells the truth.' It was very quiet, his dangerous
quietness. He spoke over his shoulder to Susie, but it
was Diana he was looking at. 'Even when it isn't what
you want to hear. Only the truth.'

It was not, she thought, looking at the handsome, indifferent face, a compliment. Yes, she must have been
mistaken earlier. He looked like a man who would never
desire her again.

'They're *lovers*,' said Susie. 'She and Dimitri.' It was
an accusation.

Miles looked at Diana levelly. 'Is that true?'

Her throat hurt. She shook her head. 'No,' she
managed in a rasping voice she didn't recognise as her
own.

The brown eyes stayed cool. He didn't say anything.
All he did was give a little nod, as if that was what he
expected. It didn't seem as if he cared at all. Susie gave
a shriek.

'You don't believe her. You can't,' she cried.

She sounded like a child. Miles turned to look down
at her. He looked like a judge, calm and determined.

'Susie, I've known you a long time but I know Diana
better.' He sounded tired. 'I know the sort of woman
she is.' His voice gentled. 'There's no doubt, my dear.
If Diana says she and Dimitri didn't sleep together, then
they didn't.'

Diana froze in astonishment. She held her breath as
he turned Susie's mascara-streaked face up to him.

'My dear,' he said again, very gently, 'this has got to
stop. You're not fourteen any more. And I can't rescue
you from every situation you can't handle.'

Susie stared at him.

'I have my own life to lead, you know. And I'm afraid you're beginning to make that difficult.' His voice was kind but quite implacable. 'My own wife thinks I'm having an affair with you, Susie. I'm very sorry, my pet, but this nonsense has got to stop.'

Susie looked shattered. 'But she hates you, Miles,' she said, in a panting voice. She seemed on the verge of hysteria. 'She wouldn't have come to the castle if I hadn't sworn that you wouldn't be here and I didn't know where to get in touch with you.'

Miles looked like stone. His lips barely moved as he said, 'I know.'

'Oh, lord,' said Diana, unheeded.

His eyes flicked up and down her briefly. She could not discern any expression on his face at all. Then he turned back to Susie.

'That's still our business, Susie. Not yours. Just as your problems with Dimitri aren't my responsibility.'

Susie looked stricken. He had clearly shocked her. What he said must have registered for once, Diana thought, suddenly sorry for her.

'I never...' Susie began.

'Oh, but you did,' he corrected. His voice was gentle. But weary. 'Every love-affair, every failed job, every slight, every missed plane and unbooked hotel room—they've all been my responsibility to sort out, haven't they? And if I didn't come at once, then you went crazy.'

Susie stared at him, silenced, her mouth working furiously. She no longer looked remotely attractive. Diana couldn't bear it.

'Why?' she said, stepping forward impetuously. She was shivering. 'If you loved Dimitri, why on earth didn't you tell him? He wanted to marry you, for heaven's sake. Why keep dragging Miles into it?'

For the first time since he had slapped her, Susie's eyes left Miles. She turned to Diana, her mouth twitching. She looked distraught. But she looked fierce as well.

'Because he's *mine*,' Susie ground out. 'There were years when he didn't belong to anyone but me.'

'You're wrong,' Miles told her evenly. 'I don't belong to anyone. I never have and I never will.'

Diana's head went back as if she'd been hit. Susie saw it and laughed. There was something hectic in her laughter. She seemed to have lost all sense of normal restraint.

'Did you think he was yours, then? He wasn't. Never for a minute. You're so pleased with yourself because he says you tell the truth, aren't you? You think you're going to get him back. But you're not.'

Diana thought, This can't be happening. People don't *say* things like that, even if they think them. And with a sudden huge compassion, She's going to feel appalled when she realises what she's done.

But for the moment Susie was on a high. The spite and envy were wincingly obvious.

'He never trusted you. Never. He knew you thought he was old and boring. He knew you went out with his students, dancing with them, spending the night with them while he was working.'

She came close up to Diana and hissed into her face, 'He knew because I told him.'

Diana felt the world begin to sway again. She closed her eyes.

'That wasn't true,' she said quietly, opening them again.

The horrible streaked mask of a face grinned at her.

'I told him I'd seen you,' Susie said in triumph.

The look of venom was horrifying. Diana's heart lurched. She put a hand to her throat.

'Seen me?'

'The green dress at Lalande's. Solange showed it to me and said you'd bought it. It was one of a kind, of course. I knew that. I knew Miles would too. I told him I'd seen a girl who looked like you and wearing a green cobweb Lalande coming out of Simon Herriot's flat at five in the morning. One of the nights he didn't come home, of course. You even told me when they were. I pretended that I didn't think it could be you. I said I didn't think you'd ever been to Lalande. I said I was *sure* you couldn't afford one.'

And I, thought Diana, was so delighted with myself for wearing it on the night of the college ball. A surprise for Miles, who liked me to dress up. Out of character for me but a peace-offering to him, for a night that was intended to be a reconciliation. Reconciliation? Oh, lord! How he must have mistrusted me. She remembered the look on his face.

'You were very clever, Susie,' she acknowledged. Her heart hurt. She put a hand to her side. Her pulses were fluttering wildly. 'I played right into your hands, didn't I?'

Miles moved suddenly. He said, 'Understandably.' His voice was harsh. 'Tell me, Susie, did it ever occur to you that there might be occasions on which you weren't entitled to have your own way? Ever?'

Susie turned to look at him. 'You don't understand...'

He took a step forward. He looked, Diana thought with a sudden thrill of alarm, almost murderous.

'Oh, but I do,' he said, too gently. 'You have no scruples at all, do you? I knew you were clever and spoiled and didn't have enough to do with your time, but, God help me, I never dreamed of anything like this.'

'You shouldn't have married her,' Susie said obstinately. 'She didn't fit in.'

His eyes narrowed. 'And you told her so, I suppose?'

Susie gave him a smile that was pure malice.

'I didn't have to.'

Miles went white. Susie's eyes flickered. Watching, Diana saw her begin to realise what she had done. She backed away from him.

'She's not stupid. She could see it for herself,' she gabbled. 'It was obvious. She could never give you what you wanted. What you were used to.'

'What I wanted?' he repeated in that mild voice that sent ice down Diana's spine. 'And you told her that was you, I suppose?'

Susie quailed. 'Not—not exactly.'

'What, then?'

Susie's head came up. 'I didn't tell her anything,' she said softly. 'She could *see*.'

He took a stride forward. 'There was nothing to see—unless you told her some fairy-story to dress it up.'

Susie gave a harsh laugh. The sudden sound was almost shocking. Diana's sense of unreality increased.

'Don't be a fool, Miles,' Susie said contemptuously. 'She saw what any woman would have seen. You didn't go near her for days, but when I said I needed you, you rushed to my side. You don't have to be a genius to work out where your priorities lay.'

He said quite gently, 'Not my priorities. My desire to minimise your nuisance value.'

Susie winced. There was a perfectly horrible silence. Diana's head began to swim.

'You know,' Miles said musingly, 'until I met Diana I thought most women were like that. Attention-seeking,' he explained with a cruelty that was all the worse for the considered, judicial tone in which it was uttered. 'Self-willed. Trivial. Making trouble and requiring other people to sort it out. Basically a nuisance if a man let them get too close. Where I went wrong,' he concluded thoughtfully, 'was in not realising you were a dangerous nuisance. You really don't have any glimmering of a conscience about all this, do you, Susie?'

Susie stared at him for an uncomprehending moment. Her eyes blinked convulsively. Then, all of a sudden, she whirled on Diana.

'You!' she was shouting. 'It's all your fault. You've turned him against me...'

Diana had a snatched vision of a harridan's face with flying hair and vengefully reaching hands. She cried out just as there was a wild shriek and Miles caught Susie. He lifted her off her feet and away from Diana.

But it was too much for Diana's uncertain hold on consciousness. Her blood began to thump until it was a pain in her head. She put out an uncertain hand. She thought she heard Miles cursing, fluently and at length. She wasn't sure why or whether it was her fault again. But she felt too faint to care.

She put out a hand to the chair-back. Missed. And toppled sideways on to the rug.

When she returned to her senses the sun was shining brilliantly through her open window. She lay for a moment, bemused. The wafting curtains and the elaborate furniture did not belong to the simple bedroom she had inhabited since she and Miles parted. Then she caught the scent of jasmine and everything came back with a rush.

'Oh, good grief,' she said aloud, sitting up abruptly.

'You're awake,' a voice said with satisfaction.

She knew the smooth tones. Her heart clenched. She turned her head. Miles was sitting on the chaise-longue with his long legs stretched out in front of him. The cushions at his shoulder were flattened. He looked as if he'd been there some time.

The white anger that he had shown Susie had gone. He looked tired but his face was no longer pinched and burning. She gave a shuddering sigh of relief.

He stood up and strolled over to the bed.

'Better?' he asked.

Diana met his eyes and found a message in them that brought the blood surging into her cheeks.

'Er—yes,' she said distractedly. 'Thank you.'

He touched the back of his hand briefly to her cheek. 'Good.'

Did he sound amused? Diana was confused. Surely he had been angry—cold and angry, just as he had been on the night he left, as if he couldn't bear to see her... Her thoughts stopped abruptly as she remembered everything that Susie had let fall. For no reason that she could think of she flushed again.

'Well enough to talk?' he asked lightly.

'About what?' she asked, wary.

'Us. Don't you think it's time?'

Her eyes fell. Was this where he agreed to a divorce? It was what she wanted of course, she told herself. Her heart plunged at the thought.

She said past the constriction in her throat, 'Not here. Not now, this minute. Let me get up and collect myself.'

There was a little silence. 'Time to get the armour back on, Diana?' he asked, an edge to his voice.

She didn't look at him. 'A few clothes, anyway.'

He gave a short bark of laughter. 'Well, that makes sense, I suppose.'

Diana didn't pretend to misunderstand him. She lifted her eyes. 'If we're going to talk sensibly, you have to promise to...to...'

'To keep my hands off you,' Miles supplied coolly.

Diana stiffened. She refused to blush a third time.

'Well, you haven't been very good at that in the immediate past, have you?' she reminded him.

And I have the consequences to prove it, she added silently.

Miles's eyes narrowed. But all he said was, 'Granted. OK—a nice neutral discussion in full armour with a ton of garden furniture between us. That make you feel safe? Or do you want a chaperon?'

Nothing would make her feel safe with Miles. Her own heart betrayed her over and over again, she thought wryly.

But she said with composure, 'That won't be necessary. Thank you.'

'I'll get Maria to make up a breakfast tray. I'll be out on the terrace when you're ready.' He nodded to the open window.

'Very well.'

Their eyes locked. Diana clenched her fingers over the coverlet. She lifted her chin defiantly. He looked at her taut fingers. His mouth twisted. Then he shrugged imperceptibly, turned and walked out on to the terrace.

As soon as the curtains billowed behind him, Diana darted out of bed, seizing a handful of clothes at random from her suitcase, and bolted into the bathroom.

She took a long time over her bath. The early morning nausea to which she had become accustomed passed as she dallied in the lilac-scented water. She sank her shoulders under the warm water, relaxing her muscles deliberately. If she was going to negotiate with Miles, she would have to be as calm as she could manage. Calm, controlled and unemotional.

Diana laughed bitterly. Was she ever going to feel unemotional in the same room as Miles?

Anyway, she had to try. She put on a cool cotton blouse and workmanlike jeans. She brushed her hair till it shone and pinned it on the top of her head. Peering at her image in the mirror, she wasn't pleased with her pallor. She didn't look as well as she had when she left Greece, and there was no way to disguise it.

Was it possible that Miles would be able to detect her pregnancy? Might he even suspect it already? And, whether he suspected or not, what ought she to tell him, now that they were to talk about their future?

Diana bit her lip. She didn't know. And there was no disguising that either. She shook her head, sighing. She hadn't been particularly clear-headed on the issue in the first place. Seeing Miles had only thrown her into greater turmoil.

Straightening her shoulders, she went out to him. The lemon grove in the distance looked golden yellow under the early morning sun, with the grey-green olives and nearly black cypresses behind them. It looked like a magic grove, Diana thought. The contrast between the beauty and the tense interview before her was all too sharp. She set her teeth.

Miles stood up as soon as he saw her. He had been sitting at the white ironwork table, frowning into the middle distance. A tray containing bowls of yoghurt and honey, sweet rolls and a steaming coffee-pot stood in front of him. His expression, Diana registered, was carefully neutral.

'Breakfast,' he said, indicating the tray. 'Maria's most anxious that you keep your strength up.'

In spite of her determined cool, Diana jumped. She didn't want to examine the possible implications of Maria's concern. She saw his eyes narrow again and said quickly, 'That's kind of her. I got the impression that she didn't approve of me yesterday. She wasn't terribly welcoming.'

'She thought you were here on a dirty weekend with Dimitri,' he said coolly. 'She didn't approve.'

Diana gaped. 'Why...?'

His eyebrows rose. 'Because you're my wife,' he said. 'She's old-fashioned like that.'

Diana said hurriedly, 'I didn't mean that. I meant why did she think it.'

He shrugged. 'It looked a bit like that, you have to admit. People don't believe in those sort of coincidences. Susie thought the same.'

Diana swallowed. 'You didn't,' she remembered.

His eyes were very steady. 'No,' he agreed quietly. 'I didn't.'

Diana decided she didn't want to examine the implications of that either. She sat down. She chose the chair furthest from his own. She watched him register it and the thin mouth slant at her choice. She reached for coffee.

'Susie—er—rather sees things from her own perspective, I think,' she said with constraint.

Miles sat down too. 'Black,' he said absently. 'Doesn't she just, though? And then spreads it around. It's amazing that people still believe her.'

Diana said gently, 'She believes herself. That's what makes it convincing.'

'I suppose so.' He sent her a long look. 'She did quite a number on us,' he said carefully.

Diana didn't answer immediately. She poured two cups of coffee and gave him his. She swirled milk into her own and stirred it, concentrating. She said slowly, 'If things had been right between us, Susie couldn't have done a thing.'

His face was mask-like. He didn't touch his coffee. She could feel his eyes on her, even though she wasn't looking at him.

'So what was wrong?' he said softly at last.

Diana tensed. She stirred the spoon round the boat-shaped coffee-cup as if her life depended on it. The sun was beginning to warm the back of her neck. It was going to be a blistering day, she thought irrelevantly.

'Don't you know?' she muttered.

He lifted his shoulders. 'I have my theories,' he said in his most cynical voice. 'I'd be interested in yours.'

Diana winced. 'I'd say we were incompatible from the start,' she told him. Her heart felt scorched by the lie. But she couldn't afford to give him any weapons. Least of all her unsuppressed love. 'It was just wrong.'

He didn't answer at once. Instead, he stretched his long legs out in front of him and turned his face up to the sun.

'I wouldn't say that,' he drawled at last. 'In fact in the early stages I'd say it was just about as right as it could be.' He flashed her an amused, under-browed look. 'Or don't you remember?'

Diana put her spoon down very deliberately. 'I remember.' She still wouldn't look at him.

'A marriage of true minds,' he said softly. 'To say nothing of hearts. Or bodies.'

He reached out and took her wrist in a light clasp. Diana jumped, her eyes flying at last to his face. But she didn't pull away. Under his fingertips, her blood was racing.

'I wasn't talking about sex,' Diana said in a stifled voice.

His thumb moved gently, soothingly over the frail wrist.

'Neither was I,' he insisted.

He sounded amused again. Diana tore her wrist away.

'Don't *do* that,' she said raggedly.

'Why not?'

She rounded on him suddenly, her eyes meeting his in desperation.

'It's just a game to you, isn't it?' she cried.

Miles looked blank. 'What?'

'Susie's a nuisance. So were your other ex-girlfriends. I, on the other hand, know my place better and keep out of the way when I'm not wanted.' She was bitter. 'Do you think I find that flattering?'

He sat up very straight. 'I wasn't intending to flatter you, no.' He still sounded unforgivably amused.

Diana pounded her hands on the arms of the chair. 'You don't *care* about any of us, do you?' His eyebrows flew up. 'You manipulate me. All of us. You're no better than Susie,' she flung at him. 'You just decide what you want and then move people around like chess-pieces until you get it.'

There was a pause. He did not, she noticed, try to deny the accusation.

Then he said levelly, 'If that were true, I haven't been very successful with you, have I?'

No word of affection, she noted. This was awful. Diana shut her eyes. She remembered Susie's allegations about his partner's wife. All of a sudden they didn't sound so unlikely.

'When she told me you wanted me back for camouflage, I didn't believe her,' she said almost to herself. She shook her head. The pain was almost physical.

Miles said impatiently, 'What on earth are you talking about?'

'Did you think I wouldn't hear about it?' She opened her eyes. She was trembling with what she assured herself was temper. 'Steve's ill, isn't he? That's why you had to cut the tour short. And Hilary's the problem, isn't she?'

He stared at her for a long moment as if she were speaking in a foreign language.

'Hilary?'

'Oh, don't try to pretend,' Diana said in a fury. 'I know what you want, Miles. Steve got suspicious, didn't he? And you need Steve's work. So you had to convince him.'

Something flickered in Miles's eyes. 'Hilary Gilman's the problem,' he said on a slow note of discovery. He almost sounded as if he was laughing again.

Diana felt as if he'd hit her. She swung round with her back to him.

'At least you admit it,' she said in a suffocated voice.

'I admit nothing,' Miles drawled. 'It was you who said Hilary was the problem; not me. The only problem I've had with Hilary is when she flung it in my face that I was halfway human when I was married to you and the sooner I got you back, the better for all my colleagues.'

'*What*?'

He put his hands on her shoulders and turned her gently round to face him.

'Listen, my—— Listen, Diana. Hilary Gilman's a friend.' He paused. 'Or she was. At the moment she blames me for Steve's illness.'

Diana said fearfully, 'Irreversible breakdown?'

'Good lord, no.' Miles stared down at her. His hands fell away from her shoulders. 'Where did you get that idea? He picked up a virus. It was bad enough, heaven knows. He was pretty well exhausted already. When he couldn't shake off the virus he got badly depressed. That's why we cancelled the tour. Depressed about his *work*,' he said gently. 'Nothing to do with an imaginary fancy I had for his wife.' He added reflectively, 'Hilary said it was my fault because I'd been driving us both so hard. I do that when I'm trying to forget.'

'But Susie said——'

'Susie!' His eyes narrowed. 'All right, tell me. How did Susie dress it up for you? I'd driven Steve to paranoia and was consoling Hilary?'

Diana shook her head. 'She said you'd been having an affair. That when Steve found out he had a nervous breakdown. That that was why——' She broke off.

'Why?' he prompted.

Her eyes fell. 'Why you wanted me back.'

'Ah. That accounts for the crack about camouflage,' Miles said affably. 'I wondered. He shook her gently. 'I'm surprised at you, Diana. You ought to know me better than that.'

She scanned his face. There was something there she didn't understand. It wasn't unkind but it was un-yielding—a sort of amused determination. She felt her heart flutter and pressed her hand instinctively to the place where their child lay.

He feathered his thumb across her lips. Diana gave a long sigh.

'Yes,' she agreed. 'Yes, I suppose I did. If you'd wanted Hilary, you wouldn't have tried to keep it a secret. No matter how much you needed Steve's professional co-operation.'

His eyes glinted. 'Well, thank you, ma'am,' he drawled. 'An endorsement of my integrity, if not my sexual morals.' He was teasing.

For some reason that made her blush. She said hur-riedly, 'I didn't really think...I mean I told Susie you wouldn't do anything hole-and-corner, no matter what she said.'

'You know me better than she does,' he agreed. 'And if you weren't blinded by jealousy you'd know that I don't care a row of beans for Hilary Gilman either.'

Diana tore herself away from him. 'I—am—not—jealous.'

Miles did not attempt to hold on to her. He looked at her for a moment, taking in her ruffled breathing and over-bright eyes. Then he shrugged, very slightly, and sat down again, patting the chair beside him.

Diana ignored that. He smiled crookedly. He looked up at her, the brown eyes narrowed against the sun. He looked singularly unagitated, to add to her fury.

'Yes, you are.' He sounded pleased.

Diana glared at him. 'And you are the most arrogant, complacent, *unprincipled* man I've ever met.'

'Would you say I was unprincipled?' Miles asked mildly.

'I just did,' Diana pointed out. She took a couple of calming breaths and said more quietly, 'I know you think it's funny, Miles. But I'm fresh out of a sense of humour where you're concerned.'

He smiled up at her. 'Interesting.'

'It isn't interesting,' Diana contradicted him. She had a horrible suspicion she was all too close to tears. Where was the strong, self-determining character she had been so proud of becoming? 'It's a damned nuisance. And very discouraging,' she admitted on a sigh.

He shook his head. 'On the contrary. It's the most encouraging thing I've heard in a long time.'

Diana stared at him suspiciously. His smile slanted.

'It's a sign that you care,' he explained quietly.

She scanned his face. He wasn't laughing any more. He stood up again suddenly. Diana tensed. But he made no attempt to touch her.

'You do care, don't you?' He might have formed it like a question but it was a statement of fact and they both knew it.

Diana made a small, despairing gesture, turning away.

'Diana——'

She closed her eyes, screwing them up tight against the threatened tears.

'Don't make me admit it,' she begged. 'You've taken everything else. Leave me my pride.'

Miles said softly, 'Will your pride feel better if I tell you I love you? That I haven't had a day's happiness since we parted? That I'll do any damned thing you say to get you back?'

Diana whirled, suspecting him of some dark mockery. But the brown eyes were unguarded. His smile twisted.

'Don't look so incredulous. Everyone knows but you.'

She felt as if the cool terrace tiles were shifting beneath her feet.

'Everyone?' she echoed.

He stood very still. 'Chris. Your parents. My mother.'

Diana thought of her parents' bland refusal to acknowledge that their parting was permanent. Was it more than a determined attempt to ignore the hurtfulness of the parting? Did they really believe that Miles wanted his wife back? Did they have reasons to believe it? She remembered that she had suspected they had been seeing him. What had he said to them?

'And they know you well enough to know when you're telling the truth?' she asked, almost of herself.

He said harshly, 'What have I ever done to make you mistrust me so much?'

At least that was something she had an answer to.

'You left me,' she said with spirit. 'You froze me out for weeks before you went. How do I know what you were doing those evenings when you said you were in college? You could have been seeing Hilary Gilman or Susie or any one of a hundred other women even then. How do I know you weren't?'

'Because you know me,' Miles said. As if it was obvious.

That stopped her. 'Do I?'

'You know you do. Better than anyone.' His voice was gentle.

'But——' All her hesitations were in her eyes. 'The women you knew—they were all so much more polished than I was. Sophisticated.'

'And you thought I was attracted to sophisticated women?' He shook his head, his eyes alight with laughter—and something more. 'After all the trouble I took to get you in my net?'

'It seemed reasonable.' Diana was defensive.

'More reasonable than the self-evident fact that I'm crazy about you?' Miles demanded evenly.

Diana gasped. Somewhere inside she began to tremble uncontrollably. He mustn't see it.

'Not self-evident to me,' she managed.

'All right. Maybe I made the wrong moves when we were together. But here, in the castle—what did you think I was doing when I kept carrying you off and making love to you?' Miles said in exasperation.

Diana swallowed. 'I thought it was a calculated attempt to make me come back and pretend. So you had the freedom to do whatever you wanted. Including walk away from me when you had more important things to think about.'

He raised his eyebrows. 'Calculated?' he echoed. 'You must think highly of my powers of acting.'

Diana flushed. 'We respond to each other. We always have,' she muttered. 'That doesn't mean . . .'

'That I'm honest or that I care for you?' he suggested softly as she hesitated.

'Miles,' she said at last, hanging on to the rags of her composure with resolution, 'you've got to understand—when you left me, I was devastated. I knew something was going wrong but I didn't know what I'd done. I fell apart. When I managed to piece my life back together again, I promised myself that no one would ever be able to do that to me again. Just because you happened to be here . . .'

She stopped as Miles made a rude noise. 'I didn't happen to be here, my darling. It was very carefully planned,' he said deliberately.

She stared.

'The commission to do the Princess's room was my idea. Chris didn't want to get involved to begin with but I pushed him. I knew I needed to see you, and your solicitor wouldn't let me near you. Even your parents wouldn't give me your address and they wanted us to get together again. But they said it was up to you to decide when you wanted to see me. And you didn't. So—I took steps. All right, manipulation if you like, but I was desperate.'

He didn't look desperate, Diana thought. He looked cool and confident and utterly in control.

'I thought if I could get you here alone... But I reckoned without Susie.' His tone was rueful. 'With her usual impeccable timing, she announced she was coming here herself. She'd had another of her misunderstandings with Dimitri. The castle has always been her bolt-hole. In a way she has as much right here as I have, so I couldn't bar the door against her. I tried to talk her out of it but...' He shrugged. 'So I got Chris to bring Dimitri down as well and see if he could do a bit of discreet patching up.'

Diana said, 'But she virtually ignored him.'

'That's love for you, my darling,' Miles said lightly. '*You* virtually ignored *me*.' He eyed her hopefully.

She winced, refusing to rise to the bait.

'Why didn't you cancel my visit, then? If all your stage management was going wrong.'

His mouth quirked in self-mockery. 'I couldn't bear to wait another day. And anyway——' he looked down at her with that wicked challenge she recognised '—not all my stage management went wrong. I told Maria to make sure when you arrived that you were brought to me and only me.'

Diana knitted her brows, remembering. She stiffened.

'You mean it wasn't an accident, that first time when Maria showed me into your room?' she asked.

The brown eyes danced. 'Well, I wasn't supposed to be in bed. Or at least not asleep,' he temporised. 'You arrived earlier than I'd allowed for. I did tell you at the time,' he reminded her.

'*Oh*!' she exclaimed in outrage.

He seized her hands, cupping them in his own and stroking them.

'Nothing else was planned,' he said rapidly. 'When I saw you—I lost my head. You were so beautiful. And you looked more fragile than the last time I'd seen you. Fragile and hurt. I thought, I can't play games with this woman. It's too important.'

'I hated you,' Diana said under her breath.

'It showed.'

'Making me want you like that.'

His hands stilled. 'Did I?'

She swallowed hard, raised her chin and told him the truth. 'At once. Just by turning over and holding out your hand. I was so *ashamed*.'

Miles looked down at her, not saying anything. She could feel the beat of his blood in the hands holding her. Her mouth was wry. 'I'd got rid of all that, hadn't I? I was strong and independent and I didn't need anyone. And then all of a sudden there you were, proving it was all a sham. I was furious. And scared.'

He frowned quickly. 'Scared?'

'I thought, I need him. I probably can't live without him. And I can't have him.'

'Oh, my darling,' he said, pulling her into his arms.

He kissed her fiercely. After a longer time without oxygen than she would have believed possible, Miles raised his head.

'Calculated?' he asked, though there was a faint tremor below the amusement.

Diana put up a wondering hand and touched his face. 'No. I accept that was spontaneous——'

'Passion,' Miles supplied, 'is the word you're looking for.'

Diana gave a slow, sweet shiver. 'Passion can be deceptive.'

'Not between us,' he said positively. 'If we'd listened to our feelings instead of other people's neat, logical lies, we'd never have parted. Or fought as we have these last weeks.'

Diana smiled into his eyes. 'It didn't feel like fighting all the time,' she murmured.

His eyes were intent. 'No?'

'Just most of the time,' she amended mischievously.

His arms tightened painfully. 'Oh, lord, I remember. You seemed as if you wouldn't talk to me, or even look at me most of the time. And then—that day on the launch, when you said something about walking tight-ropes on boats, I thought, She is looking at me, after all. There's hope.'

Diana blushed. 'Well, you scared me.'

'And you scared me in those damned caves,' Miles said with feeling. 'I thought, What will I do if she's hurt?' His voice rasped.

She shivered again. 'I know. I felt the same when you dived. I thought you were going to kill yourself. And I knew if you did that was the end. Until then I hadn't realised I was still—hoping. That scared me too, in a different way. I was pretty horrid to you after that, wasn't I?'

'I forgive you.'

'And I listened to Susie's malice.'

'I forgive you that too,' Miles said, kissing her eyebrow thoughtfully. 'She's very convincing, as I know to my cost. She kept telling me I was too old for you. That I'd spoilt your life.'

Diana made a small sound of distress. 'Did it seem to you that you had?'

Miles's smile was crooked. 'Not at first, no. But you were such a gentle girl. You wouldn't have told me. And I was working like a demon. When I came home in the small hours sometimes you used to look at me as if I were a stranger.'

'Whenever I saw her, Susie kept hinting that I wasn't really sophisticated enough for you,' Diana said in a small voice. 'When you stayed away so much—it seemed as if she was right.'

He compressed his mouth. 'I kept expecting you to find someone else,' he said quietly.

Diana stared. At last she said slowly, 'But you said this morning you trusted me.'

'I do. In a way I always did. But I was never sure I'd been fair to you, gathering you up into marriage the way I did. You'd hardly had time to look round at other men. And I was nearly old enough to be your father.'

There was real pain beneath the light tone. This, she saw suddenly, was important. This was the heart of their misunderstandings. And it needed careful handling. Any hint of sentimentality—still worse, compassion—and she would lose his trust forever.

Diana held herself away from him, her eyes glinting. 'Not unless you were extraordinarily precocious,' she said.

He laughed then. 'You always said that. But Susie...'

'Susie,' Diana said thoughtfully, 'said you'd only married me because you couldn't get me any other way.'

A gleam came into Miles's eyes. She found his fingers were busy with the pins in her hair.

'Susie has a commonplace mind,' he said mischievously. 'There were lots of other ways I could get you.' He chuckled as her eyes flashed, and listed them. 'Kidnap. Blackmail. Torture. Tickets for the Venice Biennale. Or plain seduction.'

Her hair fell free over his hands. He fanned it out pleasurably.

She said with a little difficulty, 'But you never did. Not before we were married.'

He looked down at her. 'Because I wanted you to be sure,' he said simply. 'I knew the moment I saw you. But you—you had no experience, no knowledge of the world. It was a much bigger gamble for you than me. Then—when Susie dropped clues that you were seeing other men, men more your own age—well, it was no more than I was braced for already. Do you see?'

She felt humbled. She should have made him more sure of her love than that. She took his face between her hands.

'Yes. I see. And I felt young and naïve and out of my depth so I retreated behind my pride.'

'Pride's a killer,' he agreed, kissing her.

So this was where she had to ditch her pride, Diana realised. Miles had made all the declarations so far. If they were to go forward, this was where she had to take some risks of her own.

She said painfully, not looking at him, 'Why did you leave me? After we'd spent the night together here, I mean. I—it felt as if you'd abandoned me again.'

He looked horrified.

'Oh, lord, my darling, I never thought of that. All I could think of was getting Susie and her troubles out of my hair. I took her to Athens. I told her she and Dimitri had to sort out their problems on neutral territory. Then when I came back and you were gone—I couldn't believe it. Not after that night.'

She hadn't believed it either, that apparent betrayal—not after that night. She drew a deep breath. This needed all her courage.

She cleared her throat. 'Er—Miles?'

'Mmm?' He was looking at her with a warmth that she would never have believed possible. Her whole body went into a slow burn, under that look. She could feel the blush rising.

She shut her eyes. 'I love you very much and please will you make love to me?' she gabbled.

He stood very still, then his arms went round her, tightening painfully. He gave a low laugh, and hoisted her into his arms in a sudden movement that made her squeak with alarm.

'At once,' he said solemnly.

Rather later, when the cicadas had joined the sun and there were faint, distant sounds of activity in the courtyard, Diana raised her head from his smooth brown chest and said, 'Miles, where are we going to live?'

He smiled, curling her hair round his fingers.

'The Moon? The Garden of Dreams?'

She kissed his nose. 'I'm serious. Do you want to go back to the old house in Oxford?'

'Not necessarily. Not if it has bad memories for you,' he said quietly.

'It doesn't,' she assured him. 'Only...'

'Or I suppose an interior decorator wants something more stylish. A Finnish ranch with a sauna on the roof?' he suggested.

'You know perfectly well I'm not that sort of decorator. Though I'll need my own study this time,' she warned.

'Certainly,' said Miles, closing his eyes. 'Whichever room you want. I believe in female liberation. As long as you move your own things.'

Diana tickled his ribs. 'Not in my condition,' she said gleefully.

He sat bolt upright, tumbling her off his chest. She looked up at him innocently.

'Are you...?' He stopped and started again. 'Are you telling me...?'

'We'll need a nursery. The small room next to the top-floor bathroom, maybe. There's another manipulative Galatas on the way.'

He bent over her, kissing her as if he would never stop. Eventually she called a halt, breathless and laughing.

'You don't mind?' she asked, her last fear gone.

He was honestly amazed. 'Di, it's wonderful.' He paused suddenly. 'As long as you don't?'

She shook her head. 'I was scared when I first found out. I kept thinking that everything would be all right if only I had you to hold my hand. Now I've got you——' she kissed his shoulder '——everything will be all right. Just as long as you're with me.'

Miles tightened his embrace. 'Forever,' he told her seriously. 'Forever.'

Next Month's Romances

Each month you can choose from a wide variety of romance with Mills & Boon. Below are the new titles to look out for next month, why not ask either Mills & Boon Reader Service or your Newsagent to reserve you a copy of the titles you want to buy — just tick the titles you would like and either post to Reader Service or take it to any Newsagent and ask them to order your books.

Please save me the following titles:	Please tick	√
HIGH RISK	Emma Darcy	
PAGAN SURRENDER	Robyn Donald	
YESTERDAY'S ECHOES	Penny Jordan	
PASSIONATE CAPTIVITY	Patricia Wilson	
LOVE OF MY HEART	Emma Richmond	
RELATIVE VALUES	Jessica Steele	
TRAIL OF LOVE	Amanda Browning	
THE SPANISH CONNECTION	Kay Thorpe	
SOMETHING MISSING	Kate Walker	
SOUTHERN PASSIONS	Sara Wood	
FORGIVE AND FORGET	Elizabeth Barnes	
YESTERDAY'S DREAMS	Margaret Mayo	
STORM OF PASSION	Jenny Cartwright	
MIDNIGHT STRANGER	Jessica Marchant	
WILDER'S WILDERNESS	Miriam Macgregor	
ONLY TWO CAN SHARE	Annabel Murray	

If you would like to order these books in addition to your regular subscription from Mills & Boon Reader Service please send £1.80 per title to: Mills & Boon Reader Service, Freepost, P.O. Box 236, Croydon, Surrey, CR9 9EL, quote your Subscriber No:................................ (If applicable) and complete the name and address details below. Alternatively, these books are available from many local Newsagents including W.H.Smith, J.Menzies, Martins and other paperback stockists from 14th May 1993.

Name:..

Address:..

....Post Code:................................

To Retailer: If you would like to stock M&B books please contact your regular book/magazine wholesaler for details.

You may be mailed with offers from other reputable companies as a result of this application.
If you would rather not take advantage of these opportunities please tick box ☐

Helpless against the avalanche of emotions, she waited, everything in her wanting Marc Ballantyne to kiss her, yet not wanting it to happen at all.

'It's too soon, Marc.' It was abrupt, urgent.

'Perhaps…' he drawled darkly.

She shivered as he took her hand, the exquisite rasp of his tongue against the soft skin of her inner wrist freezing any further protest in her throat.

Then in one movement his hands shifted, deftly removing the clip from her hair, his fingers tangling in its silky mass, gathering it up and letting it fall away.

Ally closed her eyes, breathless with expectation, and the last thing she heard before his mouth took hers was his muted, 'Perhaps not…'

Leah Martyn loves to create warm, believable characters for the medical series. She is grounded firmly in rural Australia and the special qualities of the bush are reflected in her stories. For plots and possibilities, she bounces ideas off her husband on their early-morning walks. Browsing in bookshops and buying an armful of new releases are high on her list of enjoyable things to do.

Recent titles by the same author:

DR CHRISTIE'S BRIDE
CHRISTMAS IN THE OUTBACK
THE FAMILY PRACTITIONER

THE BUSH
DOCTOR'S RESCUE

BY
LEAH MARTYN

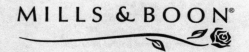

MILLS & BOON®

*All the characters in this book have no existence outside the imagination
of the author, and have no relation whatsoever to anyone bearing the
same name or names. They are not even distantly inspired by any
individual known or unknown to the author, and all the incidents are
pure invention.*

*First published in Great Britain 2005
Harlequin Mills & Boon Limited,
Eton House, 18-24 Paradise Road, Richmond, Surrey TW9 1SR*

© Leah Martyn 2005

ISBN 0 263 84320 3

*Set in Times Roman 10½ on 12 pt.
03-0705-48213*

*Printed and bound in Spain
by Litografia Rosés, S.A., Barcelona*

CHAPTER ONE

'GET out of this department! Now!' Marc Ballantyne's voice rose to such a pitch that his charge nurse half expected the paint on the walls to blister.

'And the jury's still out on *your* performance as well, sunshine!' The senior registrar rounded on the department's other resident, Ben Anderson, thrusting a warning finger at his chest.

'Who shook his tree?' Ben muttered with an expressive roll of his eyes as Marc Ballantyne slammed his way out of the resus unit.

Oh, lord. Nerida, the charge nurse, tightened her lips. They were short-staffed and under stress and Marc's attitude wasn't helping.

She slipped out quietly. Her nurses were more than capable of clearing up and preparing their patient to go to ICU.

Blessed are the peacemakers, she thought wryly a few minutes later as she went along to Marc's office. Tapping on the door, she went in. 'I thought you could do with a coffee,' she said, placing the mug on his desk.

'You haven't put arsenic in it, by any chance, have you?' He looked rueful as he turned from the window, ploughing his hands through his hair and locking them at the back of his neck. 'Thanks for this, by the way.' He threw himself into his chair and made an effort to smile. 'Are you not having one?'

'Perhaps later.' Nerida folded her arms and looked at

him. 'What are you going to do about this situation with Sonia?'

His jaw clamped. 'I won't have her in my department. I've given her so much leeway, it's ridiculous.'

Nerida gave a little shake of her head. 'You know what a vicious circle it is for the interns, Marc. They're all sleep-deprived. But if they don't work all the hours demanded of them, they may as well whistle for a place on any of the training programmes.'

'You're breaking my heart, Ned,' he countered grimly. 'But all right.' He held up a hand in compliance. 'I'll apol-ogise to the team and take Sonia through the basics *again*.' He blew out a long breath born of frustration. 'Did you see what a dog's breakfast she made of that intubation yester-day? Despite all the guidance I've given her, she *still* doesn't know the difference between the oesophagus and the trachea.'

Nerida winced. Privately she agreed that Sonia's practi-cal skills left a lot to be desired. But surely it wasn't too much to ask for a semblance of harmony in the department? The doctors and nurses were supposed to be a team after all.

'Is it just possible your own attitude is causing some of this flak?' she said with the forthrightness of long friend-ship.

A dark eyebrow shot up. 'You mean my people skills are lacking?'

'Just lately,' Nerida said honestly. 'You're bone weary yourself, Marc. Why don't you take a holiday?'

He snorted. 'I'm beginning to think a permanent one from this place might be in order.'

'Leave McAuley?' Nerida's eyes widened. 'Where would you go? Another teaching hospital?'

He shrugged. 'Probably not. Actually, I have a strong urge to go bush.'

'I'd no idea you were thinking like this.' Nerida eased herself onto the corner of his desk. She gave a half-smile. 'Only that I've a husband and kids I'm nuts about, I'd be tempted to come with you.'

'We've worked together for a while now, haven't we?' he drawled with his slow smile.

She nodded. It would be strange not to have his presence about the place. 'Are you really serious about this?'

'More with every passing minute, Ned.'

'Um—when do you think you might leave?'

He jerked a shoulder indifferently. He felt raked with fatigue, both mental and physical, as well as being stuffed to the gills with hurt and disillusionment. 'Soonish.' His jaw worked for a second. 'I've nothing to keep me here now…'

'You're in early!' Ally's head came up, several fronds of honey-blonde hair drifting across her cheekbones.

'Couldn't sleep.' Her friend and colleague Rosie Tennant blocked a yawn. 'And that is absolutely the last time I go out with a farmer!'

'Uh-oh.' Ally rolled her eyes, recalling similar conversations from their nurse-training days. She pushed her chair away from the computer terminal and got to her feet, turning to slot several files back into their homes. 'No sparks, then?'

Rosie's breath came out on a scornful huff as she plonked down on one of the high stools behind the nurses' station. 'All he could talk about were his damned cows. For instance, did you know,' she mimicked in lecturing fashion, 'that grass-fed beef is tastier and more healthy than grain-fed? But on the other hand, grain-fed is more tender. And organic beef can be a third more expensive by the time it reaches your plate but—'

'Enough!' Ally laughed good-naturedly and held up both hands for mercy. 'I get the picture. But I think you're generalising. All farmers are not like that, for heaven's sake!'

Rosie made a face. 'Well, I don't aim to find out.'

'Not regretting making the move here from the big smoke, are you?' Ally's light tone masked a faint anxiety. Their rural hospital couldn't afford to lose any staff, let alone an experienced nurse like Rosie. And after all it had been on Ally's suggestion that her friend had come to Hillcrest in the first place.

'After battling the bumper-to-bumper traffic in Sydney every day? Not likely!' Rosie stretched languidly and the top button on her uniform shirt popped open. 'Oops.' She gave a rueful chuckle. 'Must have shrunk in the wash. When's our new MO arriving?' The question was distorted by another huge yawn. 'Have you heard?'

'Not until next week, apparently.'

'And today's only Friday. Oh, well, we've coped for ages with dodgy locums in and out of the place so I guess a few more days won't kill us.'

'As long as it doesn't kill any of our patients,' Ally replied thinly. She was heartily sick of the raw deal the hospital staff had been handed. And the way the funding had gone to the pack since the Jamesons had left. It wouldn't have been what they'd wanted for Hillcrest at all.

Noah and Erika Jameson were the popular family practitioners who had been looking after the health of the residents of the little border town for the past five years. But now, with Erika set to pursue further training towards a specialty, the couple and their two small children had relocated to Melbourne.

'Wouldn't you just love to see that ''for sale'' sign disappear off the Jamesons' surgery?' Rosie gathered up her fall of dark straight hair and expertly tidied it into a respectable knot. 'To the right person, of course.'

'Mmm.' Ally sent her contemporary a quick, dry look. 'And one who'll stay in the place for more than five minutes.' She stifled a yawn herself and thought, Heavens, it must be catching. 'That's me squared away. Like to take the report now?'

'Yep.' Rosie slid from the stool and turned towards the staffroom. 'Just give me a tick to swipe on some lipstick.'

If what he remembered from his brief time in rural hospitals was right, the cook would already have breakfast on the go. Purposefully, Marc Ballantyne strode up the ramp that led to the hospital's rear entrance.

Erika had told him to make himself at home, so he guessed breakfast would surely come under that invitation. And he'd been travelling for most of the night, wanting to put as many miles as possible between himself and the hollowness of his life in the city.

In a faintly weary gesture, he lifted his hands, running his fingers around his eye sockets and down over the slight roughness of new beard along his jaw.

On the wide back verandah, he hesitated and looked around him. Everything was clearly signposted and even if it hadn't been, he thought wryly, the aroma of grilled bacon would have led him unerringly to the kitchen. And he was starving.

Palming open the swing doors, he jerked to a stop, the unexpectedness of what he saw paralysing him for a second, until his responses kicked in.

The chef was on the floor, slumped against a kitchen cupboard. Marc's breath hissed through his clenched teeth and in a few short strides he was at the man's side.

Instinctively, he hunkered down, bending towards his patient. And then he reeled back, icy daggers of alarm shooting up his spine.

In a split second he knew he was dealing with an emergency of no small order.

The chef's colour was glassily pale, he was blue around the lips and—horror of horrors—he was still gripping the electric knife that had obviously short-circuited, the force from the bolt of electricity having thrown him to the floor.

How long had the man been down? Marc's expression became tight. He needed absolute calm and clear thinking here. Anything less could undoubtedly lead to him becoming a casualty himself.

His gaze flew over the kitchen, seeking some kind of implement that would act as an insulator against the charge of electricity. His eyes lit on a broom against the wall. Hopefully, its long wooden handle would do the job. In a couple of strides he'd grabbed the broom and in one well-aimed upward thrust disconnected the electric plug from its socket.

Throwing the broom aside, he slammed his hand against the emergency button, hoping like mad there would be someone at the end of it to answer his call.

'OK, mate—it's just you and me,' he grated, dropping beside his patient to begin CPR.

Help was not long in coming.

The doors flew open and the two senior nurses arrived with a small crash cart.

'Oh, my God— Jason!' Ally's horrified gaze meshed with Marc Ballantyne's. 'What's happened?'

'He's been electrocuted.' Marc's response was terse. 'I'm a doctor. I'll need to get an airway in. Could I have some help here, please?'

In a heartbeat they were working like a well-oiled team.

'I'll take over the CPR.' Relieving Marc, Rosie began counting the rhythmic beats of resuscitation in her head.

'Defib's charging.' Ally slapped the tube into Marc's waiting hand, holding their patient's head steady while he deftly positioned the airway.

'Right. Run the oxygen now, please,' Marc rapped. 'Let's start at ten litres per minute.'

Ally's stomach tightened into a clenched fist as Marc took up the paddles. Their only option now was to try to shock Jason's heart back into rhythm. Please, God, it would work.

'OK, everyone clear, please.' Marc's jaw tightened as he discharged the paddles.

Ally felt for a pulse and shook her head.

'Shocking again.' Marc's controlled direction seemed to echo round the big old-fashioned kitchen.

'No output.' Ally felt her nerves pull as tight as a bow string.

'Dammit!' Marc swore under his breath. 'He should be coming out of it. Shocking again!'

'He's back,' Ally confirmed, husky relief in her voice. 'We have a pulse.'

Marc's face cleared. 'Good work, people. Now, let's get some fluids into this big guy. And could we organise a trolley and get him into Resus so I can examine him properly?'

'I'll go.' Rosie left the scene at great speed.

Ally began to prepare the IV line. Suddenly the bizarre nature of the situation struck her, activating a tiny frown. Her eyes skimmed over her companion, registering an imposingly broad-shouldered physique, olive complexion and dark close-cropped hair.

She couldn't miss the blueness of his eyes. They were startling in their setting of dark lashes. Her gaze continued to take its fill, noting high cheekbones and a wide mouth that looked as though it was made for smiling but at the moment had forgotten how.

'What a welcome for you,' she said jerkily. 'But we understood you weren't arriving until next week.'

'Sorry?' He stared moodily at her.

Disconcerted, Ally pulled back from his sudden scrutiny. 'Aren't you the new locum?'

'No.' His mouth flattened in a thin smile. 'Marc Ballantyne. And you are?'

'Um…Ally Inglis.' Ally took his outstretched hand. It was just the whisper of skin against skin, almost gone before it had happened, yet Ally felt as if all her senses had sprung to attention.

She blinked uncertainly. Just how did Marc Ballantyne happen to be here? That he was a highly skilled doctor went without saying. She doubted Jason would be alive if it hadn't been for this man's early intervention.

'Oh, my stars! What's happened here?' Two kitchen workers arrived and stood transfixed.

Ally snapped her wits together and briefly explained things. 'But we're pretty sure Jason will recover fully.'

'Just don't touch any of the electrical equipment until the power people give the OK,' Marc added tersely.

'Thank heavens for the Aga, then.' Jan Yardley, the more practical of the two women, began unfurling her clean pink overall. 'Jason's probably already done the breakfasts and left them in the warming oven.' She turned to her companion. 'Come on, Tina, look snappy. There are patients waiting to be fed.'

'What if there's not enough cooked food?' the much younger Tina said hesitantly.

Jan bustled across to the big old-fashioned stove. 'Then we'll just have to improvise.'

Suddenly the place was alive with purpose and within seconds the orderlies had arrived with the trolley, their presence making the kitchen seem suddenly overcrowded. Jason was lifted gently onto a board.

Marc looked at Ally, taut preoccupation in his expression. 'I imagine, like all rural hospitals, you're short-staffed, but would you mind assisting?'

'Yes, Doctor, of course,' Ally acknowledged in her polite professional voice. Officially she was off duty but that meant nothing. It was an emergency after all.

'Does our patient have family to be notified?' Marc asked, as they entered the resus room.

'Rosie, my colleague, will have done that.'

He received the information with a brief nod.

'Jason's wife is on her way.' Right on cue, Rosie popped her head in and handed the chart to Ally. 'Are you OK to stay on? It's just that a couple of walking wounded have arrived—'

'I need a senior nurse here.' Marc swung round from the bedside, his tone brooking no discussion.

'It's fine,' Ally said quietly. 'I'll stay.'

Rosie's raised eyebrows conveyed volumes before she said crisply, 'OK— I'll get the shift up and running.'

Marc began to scribble on Jason's chart. 'He has entry and exit burns on his left hand and right foot. It's obviously been a bad shock. We'll need him on a heart monitor for the next two days at least.'

Poor Jason. He'd been in the job only a few weeks. Ally eased her neck and shoulders. It had been a busy night and she was dying for a shower and bed. 'He's regaining consciousness, Doctor.'

Jason was indeed regaining consciousness, panic and distress in his eyes.

'You're in hospital, Jason,' Ally said calmly, lifting his

wrist and looking down at her watch to check his pulse. 'You've had an electric shock. This is Dr Ballantyne. He found you just in time.'

'Looks like you've some dodgy electrical equipment about the place, mate.' Marc's hand tightened on the young man's shoulder. 'This gadget here is helping you breathe, OK?'

Jason's eyes squeezed shut and then opened.

'Pulse is fine,' Ally reported.

'In that case, I think we could extubate.' Marc explained to their patient what he was about to do. 'I think there's a good chance you'll be able to breathe on your own, Jason.' He turned to Ally. 'Stand by with the oxygen, please, but let's hope he won't need it.'

Ally noticed the man's fingers were gentle. Mentally, she gave him a tick of approval. In her time she'd seen extubations carried out with all the finesse of pulling nails with a claw hammer.

'Jason, I want you to cough when I've got rid of this contraption,' Marc said. 'Go for it. You won't damage anything.' In a few deft movements Jason's tube was removed. He looked uncomfortable for a few seconds until he coughed as Marc had requested.

'OK, let's have a listen to your chest now.' Marc dipped his head, his face impassive in concentration. 'Good man.' He gave a guarded smile and placed the stethoscope to one side. 'You're breathing well.'

'Thanks, Doc.' Jason's voice was a bit rusty. 'I guess I've been lucky, haven't I?'

'You have.' Marc's lips compressed for a minute. 'Obviously I'm going to have to put in a report to the Workplace Health and Safety people and all the electrical equipment will have to be thoroughly checked.'

Jason looked anxious. 'Probably just a one-off.' His gaze went to Ally. 'I'll still have a job, won't I, Sister?'

'Of course you will.' Ally hastened to reassure him. 'None of this is your fault. And I'm sure Jan and Tina won't mind helping out until you're fit again.'

'So, Doc…' Jason rolled his bottom lip between his teeth. 'How long will I have to stay here?'

'Probably for a couple of days.'

'Two days…' The young chef shut his eyes with a snap and dropped his head back.

'I know that probably sounds like a damn nuisance…' Marc's tone softened. 'But, remember, you've had a hell of a whack to every part of your body. To cover all the bases, we'll put you on a heart monitor. That's nothing to be concerned about. It's like a little clock radio that will warn us in plenty of time if there's any problem.'

'Jason's wife is here.' Rosie poked her head in.

'Two minutes.' Marc flicked a hand backwards. 'I'd like the fluids kept up until the end of shift.' His dark head was bent close to Ally's as he scribbled on the chart once more.

'I'll pass it on.'

'Thanks for your help,' he drawled, straightening and pocketing his pen. 'Now, is there somewhere in this town I can buy breakfast?' His slow smile went all the way, pleating interesting grooves in the lean planes of his face and activating the tiniest indentation in his cheek.

Heavens, the man actually had a dimple! Ally blinked at the absurdity of her thoughts, feeling an odd little glitch in her heart rate. She made a small face. 'Nothing will be open yet. But I'm off duty now and I live only a few minutes away. I'm sure I could rustle up something.'

His jaw tightened for a moment. 'Thanks, but I imagine I'll find somewhere open if I look hard enough.' He'd already noticed her slim gold wedding band. And there was no way he wanted to be tripping over a welcoming husband when Ally Inglis got home after her stint of night duty. No way.

'Honestly, it's no trouble,' Ally said, hearing the insistent quality in her voice as though it belonged to someone else.

Marc paused and then thought, Oh, what the hell. Some home-cooked food sounded wonderful. 'If you're sure I wouldn't be intruding?'

'Not remotely.' Ally took a thin breath. The timbre of his voice had been almost intimate, distracting her, raising possibilities she hadn't thought about in ages. She hoped the surge of heat she felt wasn't obvious. 'I'll just make sure the shift knows what's going on with Jason before I leave.'

'And I'll have a word with his wife.' At the door, Marc swung back to his patient. 'I'll be in later to check on you, Jason. Don't go anywhere.'

Back at the nurses' station, Ally filled Rosie in.

'So, his name's Marc Ballantyne.' Head tilted, Rosie considered the information. 'And he's not the new MO?'

'Apparently not. And he asked to make a couple of phone calls so I've pointed him in the direction of Sister's office.'

Rosie made a click of disapproval. 'He could be ringing Alaska! We don't have the funds to subsidise phone calls for every man and his dog.'

'For heaven's sake, Rosie, get over it.' In a weary gesture Ally pushed an escaping curl behind her ear. 'He's offered to pay for them. And I've invited him home for breakfast as well.'

'You've what?' Rosie's eyes flew wide. 'You're letting him into your home after five minutes' acquaintance? Are you nuts, Ally? You know nothing about his background. He could have been struck off for some reason!'

'That hardly matters, does it?' Ally countered the other's dismayed outburst blandly. 'He asked if there was some-where he could buy breakfast so I offered. It's as simple as that. Anyway,' she justified herself, 'it's the least we can do. He saved Jason's life in there.'

'I'm not disputing that. But, Ally…' Rosie made an open-handed plea. 'This is so unlike you. Are you sure you know what you're doing?'

Probably not, Ally thought, and shrugged inwardly. For the past couple of years she'd more or less jogged along with no great highs or lows, intent on just keeping afloat. But the fact was, she *had* moved to Hillcrest in an attempt to start over. Perhaps it was time she got on with it.

'What if he comes on heavy?' Rosie asked in a tone meant for her friend's ears only.

Ally sent her gaze upwards. 'He won't. But even if he did, I've done a course in self-defence.'

'I don't believe we're having this conversation,' Rosie muttered, flinging some paperwork down beside the com-puter. 'I know!' Her head came up, her hand fisting against her chest in excited relief. 'We'll have a code system. I'll call you a bit later and if it looks like he's being trouble, you can say you've got a rat problem and need the pest control to come round as soon as possible.'

Ally sent her friend a speaking look. 'And then you'll come and save me, will you?'

Rosie tsked. 'Don't be dumb. I'll call the police.'

'Oh, good grief.' Ally shook her head. 'Look, Rosie, just cool it, OK? Now…' She turned her attention to Jason's chart. 'Dr Ballantyne would like Jason to remain on the heart monitor and his fluids kept up until the end of shift, please.'

Rosie made a prim little moue. 'So we can expect the good doctor in later to check on the patient?'

'That's what I gathered,' Ally agreed. 'Now, if you don't need me for anything else, I'm out of here.'

Ally felt all fatigue vanish as she left the hospital precincts and headed towards the car park. Having checked Sister's office and finding Marc still engrossed in his phone call, she'd taken the chance to freshen up and change out of her uniform.

Now she swung her gaze over the parked cars, stopping at the only unfamiliar vehicle. That was probably *his*, she decided, noticing the Jaguar's dusty paintwork and interstate registration.

Her full lower lip made a reflective moue. Rosie had serious concerns about him. But based on what? He'd acted quite professionally. But on the other hand…

Out of nowhere Ally felt a flicker of unease. Perhaps after all it hadn't been the brightest idea to have invited Marc Ballantyne into her home on such a short acquaintance.

'Sorry to keep you waiting.'

His soft apology sent shivers down her backbone. She swallowed. 'No problem. I just got here myself.' Ally reined in her edginess with a taut smile.

'Good.' His gaze slid over her, dropping from her cloud of fairish hair to the soft curve of her cheek, to her mouth unadorned with any lipstick and finally to the slenderness of her body in its simple navy T-shirt and faded jeans. His eyes glinted momentarily. 'I left my personal cheque at Reception for the phone calls. I hope that's OK?'

'Fine.' Ally waggled her keys restively. 'Shall we go, then?'

'Sure you're OK about this?' Marc frowned. He'd picked up on her unease. Hell. Why had he gone along with any of this? His jaw clamped for a second. 'I'm a friend of the Jamesons'.' He felt the need to explain. 'Well, at least of

Erika's. We trained together at the Prince Alfred in Melbourne. We still stay in touch.'

'I see,' Ally murmured, although she didn't, quite. 'We're really missing Erika and Noah. You knew they'd returned to Melbourne?'

'Mmm.' He shifted his position slightly as if to relieve tense muscles. 'When I told Erika I'd be passing through Hillcrest on my travels, she urged me to call at the hospital.' The side of his mouth turned up in a dry smile. 'I think her exact words were to make myself at home. And that's why I was in the kitchen. I was about to invite myself to breakfast.'

'Oh—terrific…' Ally felt the weight of indecision slip from her. 'Then it was our lucky day, wasn't it?'

CHAPTER TWO

ALLY looked across the rim of her tea mug at Marc. They were sitting in her back garden under the pergola.

Inviting him home hadn't raised any problems, she thought with relief. Marc had proved an undemanding guest, prowling around the garden while she'd made a huge bacon and mushroom omelette, and then he'd helped carry the place settings and food outside.

She asked lightly, 'So, are you on holiday, then?'

Marc felt a sliver of uncertainty. How much or how little to tell? He was by nature a private person yet it didn't seem right to sit here enjoying Ally's hospitality under the guise of being a casual holidaymaker. He looked down, one blunt finger tracing a pattern on the outdoor table. 'I guess I'm playing hooky to some extent.'

So, was that a euphemism for burnout? Ally took a careful mouthful of her tea. The health profession was rife with it and she was in a better position than most to recognise the signs.

From the cover of her lashes, she noted the charcoal smudges around his eyes had deepened. 'Why not stay on here for a bit?' The words had tumbled out before she could fully consider what they meant. 'The scenery's great and the folk are friendly.'

'I'd gathered that.' Marc raised his mug in a solemn little toast. 'That was the best food I've eaten in days. Thank you for your hospitality, Ally.'

'It was just an omelette.' She shrugged off his thanks

20

with a stilted laugh, unwilling to delve into the reasons she'd let this man into her personal space so readily.

'So.' Marc's eyes narrowed slightly over her. 'Ally is a shortened version of what? Alicia, Alison?'

Ally winced. 'Allegra. But no one calls me that,' she added, her grimace relaxing into a smile.

'As a name it's rather grand.' Marc found himself smiling back at her. 'I like it.'

'Hmm.' Ally made a noncommittal moue. 'But rather more fitting to someone tall and statuesque, I think.' She gave a cracked little laugh. 'Somewhere along the line I suspect my mother thought I might turn out to be an exotic dancer or something.'

'Or a presenter on one of those high-powered lifestyle shows,' Marc suggested with a dry chuckle.

'Oh, please!' They both laughed and then locked startled, wary glances. Ally felt herself warm uncomfortably. Why on earth was she directing all this attention on herself? When the phone rang, she thanked heaven for the reprieve and sprang to her feet 'Excuse me for a minute.'

What the hell are you doing, Ballantyne? Marc smothered a groan of self-derision. He'd been practically flirting with her! She was *married*. The word hammered in his brain like drumming rain on a tin roof and he shook his head. What kind of fool would start down that path? Not him. Not again.

'I don't believe you've done this!' Ally hissed when Rosie identified herself as the caller.

'Hey! Take a chill pill, all right?' Rosie defended herself. 'I gather your guest is still there?'

'Yes. And you can relax about his credentials,' Ally said with some satisfaction. 'He's a friend of the Jamesons. He and Erika trained together at Melbourne's RPA.'

'Well, that's a turn-up!' Rosie sounded almost excited.

'Makes easier what I wanted to tell you. We've just received a fax from the so-called locum. Sorry and all that, but he won't be joining us.'

Ally wailed her frustration. 'What are we supposed to do now?'

'Um...' Rosie hesitated. 'Don't suppose you could talk your Dr Ballantyne into staying around, could you, Ally?'

'You've changed your tune. You were all for getting him out of the place earlier.'

'That's before we knew he was respectable,' Rosie countered glibly. 'Couldn't you just test the water with him?'

'No, I couldn't!' Ally felt a wild flurry of mixed emotions engulf her. 'He's on leave. He certainly wouldn't want to start wearing our problems.'

'Well, just ask him, honey,' Rosie wheedled. 'What've you got to lose?'

Just her entire composure, Ally thought despairingly as she put down the phone. As if she could ask Marc Ballantyne something like that!

Unless... She remembered he'd told Jason he'd be back later to check on him, so perhaps he'd consider staying around for a few days longer. But that was just a drop in the bucket. They needed a permanent medical officer in the town. And why was it all down to her? Surely it was about time that damned board got off its butt—

'Is everything OK?'

Ally jerked her head up and turned, every nerve ending leaping with awareness. Her brows sprang together in sudden accusation. 'You startled me!'

'Sorry.' Planted against the doorframe, Marc stood his ground. And there was a definite degree of reproach in his body language. 'You were gone a long time. I just wondered if you'd had bad news or...'

'No.' She shook her head, feeling suddenly foolish. It

was all Rosie's fault, she snapped silently. Putting all those crazy ideas in her head about Marc Ballantyne. 'Well, not personal bad news,' she qualified, biting the edge of her bottom lip. 'But kind of upsetting.'

'Can I help?'

A dozen responses were juxtaposed in her head. This was the opening she needed. But would it be fair to take it? Did she dare take it?

'Look, why don't we go outside and sit down again?' When she hesitated, Marc curled a dry smile at her. 'I promise I won't bite.'

'Sorry, I overreacted.'

He shrugged. 'You were deep in thought and I scared the daylights out of you. It was a pretty normal reaction. Coming, then?' He reached out and touched her arm, as if emphasising the invitation. 'We can probably squeeze another cup of tea from the pot.'

'All right.' She took a shaky breath. Even that light-as-air brush of contact with him had been enough to throw her right off balance all over again.

Marc lifted the teapot and managed to refill their mugs to just halfway. 'It might be a bit strong but at least it's still hot.'

'Thanks.' Ally took a mouthful, feeling the warmth ironing out her nerves. 'The locum we'd expected has decided not to take the job after all.'

Marc's dark brows snapped together. 'That was the phone call?'

'Well, not from him exactly.' Gaze lowered, Ally laced her fingers around her tea mug. 'It was Rosie from the hospital. They'd had a fax.'

'So what will you do now?'

Ally laughed a little hollowly. 'Keep shunting the serious cases over to the regional hospital at Warwick, I suppose.'

Sitting sideways in his chair, Marc stretched out his legs and crossed them at the ankles. 'How long have you had to do this?'

'On and off since the Jamesons left. Although we did have the odd locum who stayed for more than a couple of days.'

Good grief. Was that the best the department could do? Marc stared pensively into the residue of tea in his mug, remembering. 'Have a really good look around the place while you're there,' Erika had said when he'd called her earlier and filled her in about his role in the emergency with Jason. 'You might decide Hillcrest is the environment you're looking for.'

Dumb idea, Erika, his mind protested now. Very dumb. 'You just want to flog your practice to me,' he'd come back jokingly at her.

'Well, that, too, eventually, if it would work for you. You've already done the hard part and made the break from big-city medicine.'

'That's a bit simplistic,' he'd pointed out. 'How do I know Hillcrest is what I want?'

'You don't until you try it. But you've already made a connection with the place. You've saved someone's life.'

He'd made a sound between a snort and a laugh. 'And that ties me to the place for ever, does it?'

'Of course not!' Erika had tutted. 'But surely you must have felt needed.'

He digested that for a minute. And then realised Erika was right. He couldn't say he'd felt exactly *needed*. But he'd certainly felt on a high, in charge of his own world, able to see the process through to a successful outcome for Jason.

'The area to be covered would seem a big responsibility for a sole practitioner.' He'd voiced his doubts.

'Not so much now.' Erika's response was reassuringly bright. 'There's another GP practising out of Wattle Flats, Shaun O'Connor. Him being there took quite a load off Noah and me, especially when I needed time off with the bubs. Think about it, Marc, that's all I'm saying…'

Well, there was no law against that, he supposed now. He lifted a hand, rubbing at the new growth of stubble on his jaw. As if he'd suddenly made a decision, he swung back so he was facing Ally across the table, feeling the merest flicker of excitement licking along his veins. 'Is there a decent motel hereabouts? I'd like to break my travels for a couple of days—at least over the weekend.'

'The Lavender Farm motel,' Ally said without hesitation. 'They have cabins rather than motel rooms. But they're up-market and very comfortable.'

'So, is it an actual lavender farm?' Marc looked intrigued.

'Oh, yes.' She leaned forward, eagerly. 'Both a lavender farm and a vineyard. And they run a restaurant on the place. The food is divine and the view to die for.'

Marc grinned. 'Not their PR person on your days off, by any chance, are you?'

'It's a small community. We like to do what we can for one another.' She swept a hand through her hair, leaving the short curls on top sticking up and ruffled, and he felt an insane desire to finger-comb them back. Slowly and gently…

'Looks like the Lavender Farm it is, then.' Marc shook his head as if to clear it. Pushing back his chair he got to his feet.

'You'll love it.' Ally stood quickly. 'Just continue straight on out of town for about three k's. You'll see the sign.'

They began walking along the path at the side of the house to the front gate.

'You shouldn't be bearing all the problems of the hospital yourself.' Marc backtracked on the conversation, the unfamiliar surge of male protectiveness in his gut taking him unawares. Opening the gate, he went through it and then stood, leaning his arms across the top. 'Isn't acquiring suitable staff a matter for your board?'

Ally shrugged. 'They try.' But not very hard, she added to herself. 'All they can do is advertise and if no one suitable replies…'

'Where did you train?' Marc regarded her steadily, recalling how very professional she'd been earlier. And how she'd instinctively known what he'd needed and when, as though from long practice.

'St Vincent's in Sydney,' she replied shortly. 'I stayed on, working mostly in A and E. I came here about eighteen months ago.'

Marc's expression narrowed. She'd said *I*, not *we*. He had to find out. 'And your husband, does he—?'

'He died,' Ally intercepted, feeling as though ice water had been flung over her.

'Sorry.' Marc cringed inwardly. 'I noticed your ring and just assumed…'

'No need to apologise.' Her smile was forced. 'I'm fine,' she insisted. 'Moving on, as they say.'

But the throaty edge to her voice, and the fact she unconsciously began twisting her wedding ring back and forth round her finger, confirmed Marc's observation that Ally Inglis wasn't fine at all.

'I'll, uh, get back to the hospital later today and check on Jason.' Adroitly, he switched the conversation back into safer channels.

'That's very kind of you.' Ally lifted a hand, shading her

eyes against the vividness of the morning sun. 'We probably haven't even thanked you for what you did. It was very remiss of us.'

He made a dismissive movement with his hand. 'I happened to be in the right place at the right time.'

'But what if you hadn't been?'

Marc's jaw tightened. 'Ally, don't go there, all right? Jason will recover and that's all that matters. Wouldn't you agree?'

She nodded mutely. She supposed he was right. 'I'm on days off now. So, if you have any concerns, it'll be best if you address them to Rosie.'

At her words Marc felt as though all the colour had gone out of the morning. Somewhere in the back of his mind he'd banked on seeing Ally again. Now he felt like a child whose favourite toy had been snatched away. 'When will you be back on duty?' He hated the desperate sound in his voice but it matched the way he felt. He clenched his jaw. God, he was pathetic.

Ally drew back from the intensity of his gaze. In an instant the air between them had tightened somehow and she was flustered, unsure. 'I'm back on an early on Monday.'

'A long weekend, then.'

Her green eyes flashed. 'I've just come off two weeks of night duty. I've earned it.'

'Hey, I wasn't criticising. I've been there. And now I feel doubly guilty.'

'Why?' Ally bit the inside of her cheek. She shouldn't have flared up like that.

Marc glanced at his watch and sent her an almost rueful smile. 'Because it seems I've extended your shift by another couple of hours. I should have realized...'

'It's OK.' Distractedly, she half turned, catching a pink

hibiscus from the tall shrub flowering beside the front gate and cradling the blossom in her hand. And wishing like mad she had the confidence and sophistication to chat normally with this man. She'd possessed it once. But now she was so out of practice...

'Right. Well, thanks again for breakfast.' Marc took his leave abruptly, walking the few paces to where he'd parked at the kerb. Opening the door of his Jaguar, he swung in, looking back at Ally as she climbed the front steps into the house. He tried to look away but couldn't. The gentle lifting of her small neat bottom beneath the snug-fitting jeans was altogether too compelling.

He swore under his breath. For his own peace of mind, the sooner he was out of Hillcrest, the better. Only a fool would tumble out of one unsuitable involvement into another. Setting his jaw grimly, he started the engine and gunned the car into escape mode.

Why was he getting so uptight anyway? Deliberately, he relaxed his hands on the wheel. The ball was entirely in his court. If he chose, he could end his tenuous connection with the hospital and with Ally Inglis and be gone on his way long before she came back on duty. Unless...

CHAPTER THREE

MARC lingered over his coffee, looking out through the glass wall of the restaurant.

Ally had been right, he thought. The scenery was picture-postcard material. His gaze travelled outwards, to the mass of lavender bushes with their dark purple spiky blooms, lifting higher to take in the rows of grapevines on their trellises and beyond them again to the blue of the mountains.

There was something about the place, a gentleness that had already begun seeping into his soul. Wincing at his overblown thoughts, he lifted his cup and swallowed the last of his coffee.

He'd had no trouble getting a booking and the long, warm shower had felt heaven-sent. After that, he pretty much remembered nothing other than crashing out on the big comfortable bed and sleeping like the dead for what had seemed like hours. He checked his watch. It was almost three o'clock.

Time he went back to the hospital.

Would he show or not? Rosie shot another look at the round-faced clock above Reception. If he didn't get here soon, she'd be off duty and that would ruin her plan. Despite Ally's misgivings, Rosie intended asking Marc Ballantyne to consider doing a locum for them.

Hearing a car door slam, she spun round hopefully but it was Diane Castaldi, her replacement for the late shift, making her way slowly across the car park towards Reception.

'Hi.' Diane pushed through the glass doors, greeting Rosie with a distracted smile. 'Do I have time for a quick shower before handover?'

'Go for it.' Rosie flapped a hand. 'I can hang about for a bit.'

'Thanks. I've been to the gym.'

Rosie raised a dark brow. 'I'd gathered that.' Diane was still in her exercise gear, her uniform trousers and shirt dangling on hangers over her arm. 'How's the weight loss coming?' Diane was trying to lose the extra kilograms after two babies in less than two years.

'Not off, that's for sure,' she said glumly. 'They told me once I stopped breastfeeding, the weight would fall off.'

'It's only been a month, Di,' Rosie said bracingly. 'You're being too hard on yourself.'

Diane made a face. 'I leave *that* to the gym instructor. I'll be as quick as I can,' she promised, turning towards the showers.

'See you back at the station,' Rosie called after her. 'Like a cuppa?'

'And a piece of cake if there's any going.' Diane swung a rueful look over her shoulder. 'I need the energy boost.'

There was no one at the nurses' station when Marc arrived. He looked around him, eyes narrowing briefly, as a nurse approached at breakneck speed from the end of the corridor.

'Sorry…' She came to a breathy stop. 'Is someone looking after you?'

'Not yet.' Marc gave a contained little smile. 'I'm Marc Ballantyne. I'm the MO who attended at the chef's mishap this morning.'

'Oh…' Diane looked baffled, hurriedly scraping a still-damp fringe to one side. 'I've just come on duty so I'm not up to date—'

'Dr Ballantyne!' Rosie swept out from the kitchenette adjoining the station. 'You're here to check on Jason.'

'Ah…yes.' Marc took the file she handed him, absently stroking his chin as he pored over the information.

'Tea's made,' Rosie said in a muted aside to Diane. 'I'll be with you in a tick for handover.'

'Oh, OK.' Still looking puzzled, Diane made her way behind the counter. 'No hurry.'

'Jason's looking good.' Marc handed Rosie the file with a brief nod. 'Bring it with you, will you, please?'

'Certainly.' Rosie gave him one of her special smiles. 'Like the good old days, having a doctor about the place again,' she said as they walked towards Resus. 'I'm Rosie Tennant, by the way. We didn't actually get time to introduce ourselves this morning.'

'It was rather full on, wasn't it?' Marc's mouth softened almost imperceptibly.

You couldn't by any stretch of the imagination call it a smile, Rosie decided, but Marc Ballantyne appeared far more approachable than he had this morning.

She studied him covertly as he talked quietly to Jason. He'd shaved, of course, and obviously slept. Her gaze flicked over his chinos and black polo shirt. Nice pecs. Athletic. In fact, he scrubbed up rather well.

'I think we can let you go to the ward now, Jason.' Marc scribbled something on the patient's notes and handed them back to Rosie with a slight lifting of his brows.

'I'm off duty now so I'll pass it along.' Rosie's gaze flicked up and met his. *Please, stay and do a locum for us,* she wanted to blurt, but of course she couldn't. Somehow, she had to be subtle about it. Except that was never her strongest attribute, she reflected ruefully.

'Even though he's doing very well, I'd still like to keep Jason another couple of days,' Marc said as they walked back up the corridor together. 'I'm staying at the Lavender Farm motel over the weekend so feel free to call on me if there are any problems. I've left my mobile number as well.'

'Thanks.' Rosie stopped and held the chart to her chest. 'I'll make sure it's noted. Could I get you a coffee?'

'Ah, no, thanks.' He lifted a hand and rubbed the back of his neck. 'I had a snack earlier.'

Rosie tried to think on her feet—anything to keep him there a bit longer. 'You've travelled a long way?'

'From Newcastle. I've had a hectic couple of weeks, clearing out my desk at McAuley and handing over to the new Senior Registrar.'

'So you're at a loose end.' Rosie chose her words carefully.

'And loving it.' His mouth softened again. 'Is there anywhere I could get a game of squash at short notice?'

'There's a gym-cum-sports centre at the top of the main street.' Rosie's eyes flickered over the hard-muscled length of him. 'I dare say someone will take you on.'

He nodded and spun away. 'Have a good night, then.'

'Damn!' Rosie's muttered expletive bounced off the opposite wall as she watched Marc stride purposefully towards the exit. She gritted her teeth in frustration. 'Good one, Rosie!' she berated herself. 'You're such a wimp! That's the last Hillcrest will see of that particular doctor!'

Restlessness was eating Marc alive. He went out to the front deck of his cabin and looked out. It was another perfect autumn day. Bluer than blue mountains, smoky wisps of clouds on the horizon, the air crisp and glassily still.

Taking in a huge breath, he let it go and thought how very strange life was sometimes.

On Friday, when he'd reached Hillcrest, he'd been ready to drop with fatigue, physical and mental, wondering what on earth he was going to do with the rest of his life. Now, only two days on, he had a very clear picture of what he wanted to do.

And he had to tell someone.

'Oh...' Ally opened her front door and inhaled a ragged little breath. 'Marc, hello.'

'Hello, Ally. I hope you don't mind me crashing in on your days off, but I'm here on a mission.'

At her puzzled look he flashed her a dry smile, the movement demonstrating both a perfect set of white teeth and the fine creases beneath his eyes which until then she hadn't noticed. Creases, she decided, that added another dimension to the powerful appeal of his masculinity.

And suddenly her body was stiff with tension. Almost jerkily, she lifted her hands, bunching her cloud of wayward hair off her shoulders and letting it spiral away. 'You'd better come in, then.'

'Thanks.' He looked her over fleetingly. 'Not interrupting anything, am I?'

'No.' She swallowed, suddenly conscious of the short white towelling robe she was wearing, with nothing much underneath. 'I slept late and I was just reading the Sunday papers...'

His mouth pleated at the corners. 'I would've rung but your number wasn't in the book.'

'It's unlisted. I depend on my mobile mostly.'

He nodded. 'I've come to invite you to lunch.'

'Lunch?' Ally stared at him bemused.

'Mmm.' Marc indicated his watch with a jab of his index

finger. 'In another half-hour it'll be noon. And I believe
the Lavender Farm has a superb menu for Sunday lunch.'

His glance slid over her, a question in his eyes, and a
taut smile touched his mouth. 'Quite honestly, I need you
to take pity on me. I hate to eat alone.'

In an instant Ally had talked herself into accepting, deciding it would be ungracious to refuse his invitation—and
what harm could it do anyway? 'All right, then.' She was
conscious of holding herself tightly, turning towards the
bedroom. 'Give me five minutes to get respectable.'

'Only five?'

He grinned, a cool, lazy, challenging grin, and Ally
blinked, finding herself wrinkling her nose at him and grinning back. And then feeling terribly flustered with the relief
of just being normal with a man again. It felt overwhelming. Crazy. But good.

So good, it was almost scary.

Head lowered, she dived for cover into her bedroom.

Oh, lord, what on earth was she doing? In a second all
her doubts and misgivings came rushing back. A jolt of
panic shot through her and in a little gesture of self-
preservation she crossed her hands over her chest, only to
feel her heart revving like mad.

'Oh, come on!' she murmured bracingly. 'Lighten up,
Ally. Just get yourself dressed, for heaven's sake!'

But her mouth felt parched and her heartbeat was still
drum-heavy as she pulled on a pair of seersucker trousers
and a sporty crop top. Her make-up was minimal—mois-
turiser, a hint of mascara and lipstick. A few tendrils escaped as she scooped up her fall of hair and secured it with
a butterfly clip.

She drew in a quivery breath, automatically shoving her
feet into rope espadrilles and plucking a dusky pink over-
shirt from its hanger in the wardrobe.

Taking a steadying breath that came up from her toes, she opened the door of her bedroom and took the few steps out into the lounge.

At her entrance, Marc turned from the window and raised the briefest smile. 'All set?'

Her throat closed for a second and she licked her lips. 'I'll just get my mobile,' she responded weakly.

A few minutes later they were in his car and on their way to the motel.

'How's your weekend been so far?' Ally stole a glance at Marc as they drove. From the moment he'd arrived at her house, he'd seemed remarkably upbeat. In fact, she could scarcely believe the change in him since Friday.

'Great.' He turned his head, sending her a contained little smile. 'How about yours?'

Ally lifted a shoulder. 'Sleep and more sleep. But it was what I needed.' She laughed, a complex, brittle sound. 'That probably sounds utterly boring.'

'On the contrary. I'm well aware of the recuperative powers of sleep. I was in need of it myself.' He flicked her a glance, a warm glint in his blue eyes. 'We sound like a couple of geriatrics, don't we?'

Ally responded with a wry look. 'Not unless we've both gained another forty years. Although sometimes it feels like I have.' Her mouth turned down. 'Comes with the territory, I guess.'

'Have you thought about switching careers?'

Ally hesitated, hearing his question like a giant resonance in the air. 'No—not really.'

But she had. For weeks after Simon had died, everything about hospitals had spooked her. Eventually, she'd asked to be moved from the A and E department but even that hadn't helped.

Then her sister Anne had phoned from Hillcrest. 'Instead

of moaning, get out of that place,' she'd advised practically. 'Look, Ally, Dirk's been transferred. We're moving to Toowoomba so I'm going to have to give up my job here at the hospital. Why don't I put a word in for you?'

On a terrible downer that day, Ally had responded doubtfully, 'It'll take more than a change of scene, Anne.'

'But it's a start,' Anne had persisted. 'It's a caring community and the Jamesons are absolute gems. You'll begin healing.'

And in some ways, ones she hadn't realised, she supposed she had, Ally admitted silently as they turned into the road that led to Lavender Farm.

'Quite a crowd.' Ally brought herself back to the present with a snap, her gaze running over the collection of vehicles, including a couple of tourist coaches, surrounding the sprawling stone building. 'Will we get a table, do you think?'

Marc smiled crookedly. 'I booked on the off-chance you could join me.'

Leaving the car, they made their way up a slight incline, almost brushing against the lavender bushes that edged the gravel walkway.

Feeling a lightness she couldn't explain, Ally pointed out the little gift shop and the section of the building that was set aside as a wine-tasting facility.

'I haven't had a chance of sampling any of the local wine yet,' Marc said. 'Any suggestions?'

'I've not tasted all their varieties. But one of the blended whites might be nice with lunch.'

Everything was perfect. Marc acknowledged his thanks, as the waiter showed them to their table and then shortly afterwards brought their wine. About the only thing missing were candles, but if he invited Ally here to dinner one evening, he was sure candles would be part of the idyllic setting.

Would the lady accept, though? That was the point. With the chilled wine tasted and poured, Marc lifted his glass in a gesture that invited Ally to do the same.

Her glass clinked gently with his, while their gazes caught and lingered. Just long enough for her to notice his fingers. They were tanned, strong, capable-looking.

'To big decisions,' he said, then pulled back, his hand jerking a little as he lifted his glass to his mouth.

Ally's eyes widened and she wondered what was coming next.

Marc smiled a bit sheepishly. 'I've decided to stay on in Hillcrest for a while.'

Ally took a careful mouthful of her wine and set her glass back on the table. 'Take an extended holiday, you mean?'

'No, not a holiday.' His jaw tightened for a moment. 'I've been liaising with the Jamesons. I'm staying on to do a locum. Perhaps with a view to something more permanent.'

Then it *had* been a big decision. Suddenly, Ally was drenched with uncertainty. And guilt. 'I hope you weren't feeling pressured. I probably made our frustration with the situation at the hospital rather evident.'

'That you did, Sister.' He curved her a dry smile. 'And Rosie kept dropping hints like lead weights when I was at the hospital to check on Jason.'

Ally gave a smothered groan. 'I might have known she'd stick her nose in.'

'Hey, none of that influenced my decision.' Without warning his hand reached out and touched hers. 'I went about things very carefully.'

Ally reclaimed her hand, as if to define her own space. Her thoughts were spinning. 'So you've seen the board?'

'One member.' Marc lifted a shoulder. 'I had a long session with Cameron Strudwick yesterday. By all accounts, I'd take over the Jamesons' practice and have visiting rights at the hospital. Cameron got back to me this morning. Apparently, my credentials checked out all right.' He cocked an eyebrow and sent her a wry grin. 'Now I just have to find the money to get things up and running. But that shouldn't be too much of a problem.'

Ally's fingers tightened on the stem of her glass. 'I guess congratulations are in order, then.'

'Thanks.' Hell, she didn't look like she was congratulating him at all. Marc looked down broodingly into his wine.

Surely he should have waited to see if he liked the set-up before he made such a life-changing decision? Ally teased her lower lip, a tiny frown marking her forehead. For starters, he'd have to get most of the Jamesons' patients to come back to the surgery to make the whole exercise worthwhile, otherwise he could find himself in deep financial trouble...

'What is it, Ally?'

Ally's gaze snapped up, her eyes widening in query. 'Sorry?'

He stared at her for a long moment. 'You look less than enthusiastic about my news. I thought you'd be pleased at the prospect of offloading some of the responsibility at the hospital.'

Ally suddenly felt boxed in, vulnerable. 'You said that as though your decision had something to do with me. Surely you should be looking at the bigger picture. What if the whole thing fails—or you hate the place—?'

'Ally, if I fall on my butt, I'll pick myself up and move on.' The glint in his blue eyes warned her off any further questioning of his decision.

'Fine.' She folded in her bottom lip, pointedly reaching

over to pluck the menu from its stand. 'Perhaps we should choose what we'll have for lunch, then, so you can be on your way. I'm sure you have things you need to be doing in connection with taking over the practice, even temporarily.'

He'd offended her somehow.

Marc concentrated on his lunch. She'd hardly said two words to him after they'd ordered the lime and chilli chicken with an avocado side salad that Ally had recommended.

Raising his head, he let his eyes rest on her for a few seconds. The stream of sunlight through the glass wall of the restaurant made her hair shine, and her lowered gaze sent her eyelashes into silhouette against her flushed cheeks. She forked a portion of chicken to her lips and followed it with a tiny curl of lettuce, every movement mesmerising him and leaving him to dwell on the other possibilities that hands and lips could have…

Hell! Where on earth did he think he was going with those kinds of thoughts? Marc placed his knife and fork neatly together on his plate. He wasn't ready for anything like a casual affair. Abruptly, he swiped his mouth with his serviette. And on the scant bit of interaction he'd had with her so far, he'd guess Ally wasn't up for that either.

While they waited for their coffee, he set out to resurrect the conversation and they ended up having a rambling discussion about everything and nothing.

She shouldn't have come out with him. Disappointment settled like a hard lump in Ally's chest as she left Marc to pay the bill and walked outside into the sunshine.

Pausing beside the wooden fence, she looked out across the fields of purple and green then drew her gaze in to watch a dragonfly flex its wings, to fold and unfold them in perfect symmetry. The tiny creature looked so gauzy and light, its legs slightly bent as if it could take flight at any moment.

Ally's mouth turned down. Perhaps that's what she should do. Move on before things got any more complicated. Suddenly, her breath felt fluttery. She'd have to be unconscious not to recognise the growing chemistry between her and Marc.

Not that she wanted to do anything about it…

She shook her head as if to clear it, turning as Marc made his way along the path towards her. 'Um, thanks again for lunch,' she said awkwardly, as they walked back to his car.

'Thanks for your company,' Marc returned, and then winced. His remark had sounded facetious, as though he was blaming her for the less than easy atmosphere over lunch. 'Did you have any plans for this afternoon?' he plunged on, determined to clear the air one way or another.

'Plans?' Her echo had a husky edge to it.

'I have the key to the surgery.' He unlocked the passenger door, his gaze narrowing down on her. 'I thought of taking a look over it so I can get an idea of the layout. Care to come along?'

Ally took a deep breath. She felt slightly ashamed. She hadn't put herself out over lunch. She'd let Marc do all the running, make all the conversation. It was a wonder he hadn't dumped her back at her house in double-quick time. Instead, he was trying to plough on, trying to salvage something from their outing… She threw him a small smile. 'Consider me your guide, Dr Ballantyne.'

On the drive back to town, Ally began telling him a little of the surgery's history. 'Noah bought the old Queenslander and had it refurbished as a medical facility several years before Erika came on the scene.'

Marc threw her a dry look. 'She came here as his locum, I believe. And they later married.'

'A match made in heaven, according to their receptionist.' Ally gave a snip of laughter.

'Do you believe in such a thing?'

Ally averted her gaze to stare through the side window. 'No, Marc— I don't.'

His mouth twisted with faint mockery. 'That makes two of us, then.'

As they crossed the strip of lawn to the surgery Marc stopped for a moment, taking in the unique character and charm of the old home. 'It's larger than I thought,' he said.

'The original plan was that there'd be two doctors, but that didn't eventuate until Erika came on board.'

'Is there a practice nurse?' Marc unlocked the front door and they went inside.

Ally shook her head. 'They seemed to manage without one. But Jenny McGill, the receptionist, is pretty hands-on as far as running the place.'

'Would she continue to work with me? That's *if* I took it on permanently,' Marc qualified, taking in the high-ceilinged consulting room with its pastel lightness and big windows.

'You'd have to ask her.' Ally flicked him a puzzled glance. Was he already doubting the decision he'd made? 'Are you having second thoughts?'

'You sound like it matters to you, Ally.' His look was guarded and cool. 'Does it?' Somehow they were standing far closer than they needed to be, looking into each other's faces.

'The town needs a doctor,' she justified, suddenly flustered. 'But if you feel you'd be taking on too much...'

'I didn't say that,' he stated baldly. 'I asked whether it mattered to you if I stayed.'

It shouldn't but she knew deep in her heart it did. She took a shallow breath, almost desperately looking around as if to find a way out. The slatted blinds were slightly open, the afternoon sunlight casting shadows across his face and making his expression hard to read. Only his eyes seemed clear, the question he'd asked reflected deep within them.

Time seemed to stand still, the probability of a kiss making the air around them as thick and smouldering as the atmosphere before an electrical storm.

Ally's hand went to her heart, feeling its crashing throb through the thin stuff of her top. She felt her safe world tilt and emotions she'd painstakingly hidden away begin stirring, clamouring for light and fulfilment.

Helpless against the avalanche of emotions, she waited, everything in her wanting Marc to kiss her yet not wanting it to happen at all.

Watching her, Marc felt as though an invisible punch had landed in his solar plexus, robbing him not just of oxygen but of reason as well. Trancelike, he imagined tracing the outline of her lips with his fingers. Was her mouth really as close as it seemed, slightly parted as if waiting, wanting…?

'It's too soon, Marc.' It was abrupt, urgent.

'Perhaps,' he drawled darkly.

She shivered as he took her hand, the exquisite rasp of his tongue against the soft skin of her inner wrist freezing any further protest in her throat.

Then in one movement his hands shifted, deftly removing the clip from her hair, his fingers tangling in its silky mass, gathering it up and letting it fall away.

Ally closed her eyes, breathless with expectation, and the

last thing she heard before his mouth took hers was his muted, 'Perhaps not...'

Ally opened her mouth, giving him entry, lost in the urgency of the moment, loving the vital male taste of him, the warmth of his arms around her and the heavy weight of his body that pressed lingeringly against hers.

Marc felt intoxicated, as though he was swimming leisurely through warm treacle toffee. There was no urgency now, only a gentle slow exploration and the subtle female scent of her. Their mouths sipped, tasted and went back for more as though they were possessed of an unquenchable thirst.

A soft little moan left Ally's throat. She felt cocooned, as liquid and insubstantial as air. And she wanted this never to stop.

Only it did.

Without warning, a male voice called from Reception, 'Marc! You in there, mate?'

As one they reeled back.

Ally's eyes blinked open dazedly. 'Who is it?' She put her hand to her throat, oblivious of the way her shirt was drooping off her shoulder.

Marc swore, one hand raking his hair. 'Probably Cameron. I'll get rid of him.' His voice came from near the door. 'Wait for me.'

CHAPTER FOUR

WELL, what else did he think she was going to do?

Ally felt as though she was coming out of a dream. Agitatedly, she finger-combed her hair into some semblance of order and replaced the clip.

She took a deep breath and let it go, pressing her hands against her burning cheeks. Now what? Feeling as though her legs belonged to someone else, she went to the window and peered through the slats. Cameron's dark blue Land Rover was parked outside.

How long would it take Marc to get rid of him? she fretted, yanking her shirt back into place and straightening the collar. What if he couldn't? Oh, lord. She slumped back against the examination couch and frowned down at her watch, listening to the drone of male voices go on and on...

'Finally!' Marc muttered in relief, throwing Cameron a casual salute as the board member took off in a cloud of gravel. Closing the front door, he stood against it, taking a steadying breath before he went back to Ally.

When the door of the consulting room opened, Ally levered herself sharply away from the edge of the couch. Suddenly and without warning she felt dismally self-conscious. She looked up, seeing wariness in Marc's expression. She moistened her lips. 'Everything OK?'

He gave a shrug. 'You tell me, Ally.'

She met his gaze unflinchingly, although inside she was quivering. 'Let's not have a post-mortem.'

His eyes flinted briefly. 'No, let's not. Something positive may have come out of this afternoon anyway.' His mouth quirked. 'The latest research says kissing is supposed to be good for you.'

Was he trying to be funny? Ally shook her head. She had no ready response to his words. In fact, she was beginning to feel completely drained. Lacing her fingers across her chest, she said jerkily, 'If you've quite finished here, I've a dozen things to do before work tomorrow.'

'I get the message.'

She could barely keep up with him as they walked outside to his car.

Ally's heart was all but leaping against her chest wall as she slipped into the hospital for the start of her early shift on Monday.

She'd tried for most of last night to get Marc out of her head but he wouldn't go. She bit her lip, shoving her bag into her locker in the staffroom. They'd hardly exchanged a word on the way home and then he'd been almost abrupt when he'd left.

'See you tomorrow,' he'd said. 'I'll be in early to sign Jason's release.'

Well, she had to expect to run into him professionally, if nowhere else, Ally decided grimly after she'd taken the report and got the shift sorted out. Perhaps, if she concentrated hard enough, she could forget the kisses they'd shared.

And perhaps nothing.

It was just after eight when Marc pushed his way through the outer glass doors of the hospital entrance, past the big earthenware pot of greenery and made his way across the tiled foyer to the nurses' station.

His mouth clamped. She was already there, her fair head

bent over her paperwork. He squared his shoulders. He'd play it by ear, for the simple reason he didn't know what else to do.

'Morning, Ally.' He leaned on the benchtop separating them.

Ignoring the kick in her heart, Ally looked up, meeting his gaze as coolly as she could. 'Good morning. I have Jason's release ready for you to sign.'

A dark brow etched tauntingly. 'Trying to get rid of me?'

She flushed. 'I didn't want to hold you up, that's all.'

'I'm not one of those doctors who rush in and out of the place, Ally. Get used to it, OK?'

'Sorry.' The hollow feeling in her stomach intensified. 'It won't happen again.'

'You didn't sleep well?'

No thanks to him. Ally brought her chin up. 'I slept fine, thanks.'

Marc's mouth curled slightly and he snapped up the file from the counter top. 'Let's spring Jason out of here, then, shall we?'

Arranging for someone to cover the station, Ally accompanied him along to the ward.

Marc's examination was swift but clinically thorough. 'So, what do you reckon, Doc?' Jason looked up hopefully.

'I'd say you're as fit as a Mallee bull, buddy. Be thankful you're young and in good shape.' Marc ran his eyes over the chart and added a final notation. 'A couple of days' R and R at home, though, I think. And then you can come back to work.'

'Cool!'

Ally managed a professional smile. 'I'm sure you're longing to get home to your wife, Jason.'

'Yeah.' He gave a grin, one shoulder flexing under his white T-shirt in a slightly embarrassed shrug. 'Can't wait.'

'Well, that's one couple who are going to have a happy reunion this morning,' Marc said mildly, as they made their way back to the station.

Ally turned her head, tilting her chin towards him almost defensively. 'Lucky them.'

'Indeed. How is Jason getting home?' Marc handed her the file. 'Is his wife coming for him?'

'Apparently their car's in for a service.' Ally slipped behind the counter, marginally more relaxed to be back in her own space. 'We've arranged a cab for him.' She placed Jason's file beside the computer. She'd log in his details later. Holding herself very stiffly, she asked, 'So, do we take it you're on staff now?'

'In a locum capacity for the present,' he offered briefly. 'The Jamesons have agreed to lease me the practice on a month-by-month basis until I decide whether this is where I want to be.'

So in reality he was on loan to the community of Hillcrest, leaving himself free to bale out when it suited him, like the others. She'd bet he had his running shoes unpacked already. She felt suddenly vindicated. 'I knew you hadn't taken enough time to think things through.' Her tone was made harsh by the sudden tightness in her throat.

'So you can say, "I told you so", can't you?'

Ally flushed. She'd sounded so petty and self-righteous. She swallowed uncomfortably. 'Um, I need a coffee. What about you?'

'Sounds good.' He managed a taut smile and followed her through into the adjoining kitchenette.

Ally made the coffee quickly and handed him the steaming brew, strong and with a dollop of milk because she'd noticed that had been how he'd taken it at the restaurant yesterday. 'So, when do you hope to be operational at the surgery?'

'Not for a couple of weeks yet. I'm off to the Sunshine Coast this morning to spend a few days with my parents and catch up with my sisters in Brisbane. They're both married with kids and I haven't met the latest baby yet.'

She nodded, unwillingly warming to him, a vivid picture springing into her mind of him sprawled on the floor with kids all over him, patiently explaining the intricate workings of a toy or assembling a doll's house for a little girl. 'So you're Uncle Marc to how many?' she asked, hearing the question tumble out, startled to realise she really wanted to know.

'Four. Antonia, Lily and Daniel, and the baby is Jack.'

'Nice names.' Ally felt an odd little ache deep with her. 'Family is what it's all about in the long run, isn't it?'

'Mmm. Warts and all, I guess.' Marc took another mouthful of his coffee and wondered about the drift of their conversation. He'd sensed a softening in her and that was odd when she'd fallen just short of being hostile with him earlier.

He frowned down into his mug. Should he try to get her to talk about what was obviously bugging her—or leave well enough alone? Again that feeling of protectiveness surged into his gut.

He swallowed the last of his coffee, holding the empty mug against his chest. He hated the thought of her being upset or unhappy, and if he'd been the cause of it, albeit unknowingly, then he needed to rectify things before he took off.

'Ally—why don't you just spit it out?'

She brought her head up, finding his moody gaze unflinchingly on her. She didn't pretend to misunderstand him. But how could she begin to explain that her response to his kisses had overwhelmed her, disturbed her, left her thoughts in turmoil, her body aching for the touch of his all over again?

And shamefully, most of all, that she'd never experienced anything like these feelings before. Not even with Simon, whom she'd married...

Neither was she ready to admit to Marc that everything about his rough-hewn masculinity, so different from Simon's almost model looks, called to something deep within her. Something so basic, so earthy, it scared the life out of her.

'I...think I was taken unawares yesterday,' she explained lamely.

'When we kissed.' Marc looked at her for a long moment, than said steadily, 'It was inevitable, though, don't you agree?'

She nibbled her bottom lip. 'I suppose...yes.'

'So it was probably a good idea we got it out of the way.'

'But where does that leave us?' She put her mug back on the counter top with an anguished little thump.

'I don't have any instant answers, Ally.' He leaned over and placed his empty mug next to hers. 'It was nice, though.' There was a gleam of amusement in his eyes.

'And fraught with repercussions,' she put in crossly.

'We've done nothing to be ashamed of.' Marc's tone was steely. 'Why are you beating up on yourself like this?'

She shook her head mutely, feeling as though she was floundering around in deep, unknown waters with nowhere safe to place her feet. Abruptly, she collected the mugs and began washing them at the sink.

'Are you in a hurry to get away?' she found herself asking.

'Basically, my time is my own,' Marc said, and then

grinned. 'And I can't tell you how good that feels. Did you want me for something?'

'Well, there is a patient, Owen Phillips, age seventy-two.'

'History?' Marc parked himself against the bench and proceeded to listen.

'He had a stroke about three months ago, resulting in paralysis down the dominant side of his body.' Ally took a strip of paper towel and dried her hands. 'He's been away in Brisbane, first in hospital and then for rehab.'

'And now he's back home?'

'Yes. Well, not exactly home. He's been here in our nursing-home facility for the past couple of weeks.' They walked back through to the station and Ally pulled the file.

'But there's no reason for him to be here?' Marc homed in on her problem correctly.

'None at all. For starters, it's a drain on our funding and it's doing Owen no favours either. He should be reclaiming his independence.'

Marc cut to the chase. 'So why won't he go home?'

'He'd be on his own. He's a retired teacher, widower, one son working overseas, but we could arrange modifications to his house, even some home help and Meals on Wheels. And transport is already in place for him to continue his rehab here twice a week.'

'Sounds like he's scared to try himself out.' Marc stroked his chin thoughtfully, as he speed-read the patient notes. 'Has he talked to anyone about the stroke itself? How it actually happened and so on?'

Ally shrugged. 'You know how busy things get in a big teaching hospital. Probably no one had the time—but he did receive very good physical care,' she emphasised.

'Possibly there's a residue of post-trauma,' Marc said, as if he was testing his thoughts out loud. 'He won't open up to you?'

'Rosie and I have tried but he refers to us as *the girls*, as though we'd have no concept of his problems. But I think perhaps he'd talk to you.'

'Because I'm a doctor?'

'No!' Ally gave a small impatient tut. 'Because you're a man!'

'Ah!' Marc's lips twisted thoughtfully. 'Let's see if we can get your Owen Phillips sorted, then. Care to come with me?'

Ally looked doubtful. 'Perhaps if I just introduce you and then fade.'

'And leave me at the mercy of your old chauvinist?' he countered, fixing his blue gaze on her.

'Like you haven't dealt with difficult patients before, Doctor. I'm sure you can more than hold your own.'

Ally saw his mouth quirk with humour and acknowledged the almost painful lurching of her heart as it thundered out the rhythm of physical attraction. Accompanying him along the corridor to the nursing-home annexe, she consciously steadied her breathing, resolving to use the time while he was gone to pull things into perspective and put her sensible head back on.

They found their patient in the sunroom. He was carefully and neatly dressed and reading the morning paper.

Marc raised an eyebrow. Owen Phillips had the youthful glow of someone who controlled his weight and exercised regularly. He'd guess the stroke had come as a rude shock to the elderly man.

'Mr Phillips, this is Dr Ballantyne,' Ally said brightly. 'He'd like to have a chat with you.'

'Good morning, Mr Phillips.' Marc leant forward and held out his hand. 'Or may I call you Owen?'

'No law against it, I suppose.' Owen's faded blue eyes

ran over the imposing male figure. 'You're new around here, aren't you?'

'Yes.' Marc took a chair beside his patient. 'Sister Inglis tells me you've had a stroke.'

'Couldn't even sign my own name.' Owen shook his head mournfully. He folded his newspaper, placed it to one side and tilted an enquiring look at Ally. 'Morning tea's a touch on the late side, isn't it, Sister?'

Marc covered his mouth to hide a burgeoning grin and Ally's raised brows spoke volumes before she said patiently, 'We're a bit short-staffed in the kitchen at the moment, Mr Phillips. I'll get someone to chase it up for you.'

With Ally's departure, Owen seemed to sense the importance of Marc's visit. 'So, Doctor, are you going to examine me?'

'I don't think that'll be necessary, Owen.' Marc relaxed his frame into the easy chair. 'You've had your clearance from the Royal Brisbane. I'd say, just by looking at you, you're well on the way to an excellent recovery.'

'I got a terrible shock when it happened,' he confessed. 'Woke up in the middle of the night for a pee and my arm and leg felt as weak as a kitten's. I knew then something was wrong.'

Marc nodded sympathetically. 'Has it been explained to you just what a stroke is?'

The elderly man shook his head. 'Can't remember. Maybe someone did, maybe they didn't. It's something to do with a blood clot, isn't it?'

'Exactly. A stroke happens when a clot blocks a blood vessel or artery in the brain. It interrupts the blood flow and the body is suddenly out of whack.'

'They airlifted me to the city,' Owen hurried on. 'I didn't want to go. The girls could've looked after me here.'

'You needed specialist treatment, Owen.' Marc spread

his hands in explanation. 'What we call a multi-disciplinary approach. And while our nurses here are highly trained, there are no facilities in most rural hospitals to back them up—not even a doctor in some cases. You must see they had no alternative than to send you on.'

'I suppose...' Owen went quiet for a minute. 'I was pretty down, I can tell you.'

'Depression is all part of the stroke syndrome.' Marc leant forward, his hands linked between his knees. 'When your body won't do what you want it to, you feel robbed of self-respect. People want to help you all the time and you feel like yelling at them to get off and leave you alone.'

'My word! That's it, Doctor!' Owen's eyes held new respect. 'I felt helpless—couldn't even wash myself properly or get my pants on.' He swallowed and pressed his lips tightly together.

'But life is much better for you now, right?' Marc suggested. 'You're able to cope and I believe you're going great guns with your physio.'

A tiny flicker of humour showed in Owen's eyes. 'Young Damon keeps me hard at it.'

'You realise once you go home you'll still be able to come back in for your rehab sessions?'

Owen fiddled with his leather watchband. 'The girls mentioned something about that.'

'Then you also know your home will be fitted with safety rails so you won't go falling. In the bathroom and toilet as a matter of course and anywhere else you'd like them. You could oversee their installation with the builder.'

'I do miss being at home,' Owen said quietly. 'I suppose I could give it a shot, couldn't I?' He seemed to be considering his options out loud.

'You certainly could.' Marc leaned back in his chair and steepled his fingers under his chin. 'I'd say you're more than ready to give it a shot. In any case, have a chat with Sister. She'll have a wealth of information you'll be able to tap into.'

'Will *you* be staying around, Doctor?' Owen's brows were furrowed in concern.

'I'll be practising in Hillcrest for quite a while,' Marc surprised himself by saying. 'I'm on leave for the next couple of weeks but I'll check up on you when I get back.'

Owen seemed content with that, looking up eagerly when one of the ward workers arrived with his morning tea tray.

Ally was just putting the phone down when Marc made his way back to the station. He looked pleased, she thought, a little spiral of awareness snatching at her composure. 'How did it go?'

'Piece of cake. He actually admitted it might be a good idea to go home.'

'I knew it! He listened to everything you told him like you were God, didn't he?'

'Moses, at least.' Marc gave a soft chuckle. 'But he's a proud old guy, Ally, and it's a generational thing with men of his age.'

Ally snorted. 'Like thinking the nurses are still the doctors' handmaidens?'

Marc looked blank. 'Aren't they?'

Ally felt like whacking him with one of her computer printouts but couldn't help the smile that nipped her mouth. 'Cameron will have told you about the flat that goes with the job, I imagine?' she sidetracked quickly, almost painfully aware her mouth was too dry, her heart skipping a mad dance of its own.

'Yep.' He sent her a lazy smile, parked himself closer and asked softly, 'Going to kiss me goodbye, then?'

She managed a strangled laugh. 'You're quite the joker this morning, aren't you?'

His eyes lit with devilment. 'Scared we'd frighten the patients?'

They'd probably frighten themselves more. Ally felt heat rush to her face, all her resolutions to be thoroughly professional around him running away like sand through a sieve. She managed a saccharine smile. 'I've things to do, Dr Ballantyne. See you in a couple of weeks.'

Marc stepped back, his amused gaze roaming over her flushed cheeks. 'You bet you'll see me.' He flung her a casual salute. 'I'll bring you back a present.'

Marc felt a new spring in his step as he strode along the lattice enclosed veranda. It was amazing how surprising life could be when you opened yourself up to it.

Even exhilarating wouldn't be too strong a statement.

Crossing the car park, he tossed his keys in the air and caught them. He felt as though he'd negotiated his way through the prickly bushes and found the beautiful garden beyond. Opening the door of his car, he gave a jagged laugh at his flowery analogy.

He belted up, ignited the engine and reversed quickly out of his parking space. Beyond the thorns, he'd found the real Ally Inglis and she was warm and funny. And delectable.

And suddenly he felt the kind of sensation you wanted to cling to, yet at the same time run like mad from its potency and danger.

'Would you believe that old coot wants to go home this afternoon?' In the staff kitchen, Rosie slapped a tea bag into a mug and poured in boiling water.

'Well, he can't,' Ally responded calmly. 'He'll have to wait until the safety rails are in place, at least the ones in his shower. Maintenance said they can get someone over there tomorrow.'

'Well, will *you* tell him that? He obviously thinks you're marginally more intelligent than the rest of us.' Rosie discarded the tea bag and rummaged in the jar for a chocolate biscuit.

'Mmm…'

Rosie's dark head tipped sideways, her almost black eyes full of speculation. 'You haven't taken in a word I've said, Ally Inglis, and you've been wearing that goofy grin all day. What gives?'

'Nothing. I have to get back to work.' Her colour high, Ally rose to her feet, throwing aside the magazine she'd been pretending to read.

'My God!' Rosie's dark eyes gleamed. 'Marc Ballantyne hit on you, didn't he?'

'No one hit on anyone. And that's a disgusting expression.'

'Yeah, yeah.' Rosie flapped a dismissive hand. 'But I did warn you, didn't I? So, how did you spend the weekend?'

Ally shrugged indifferently. 'Sleeping mostly.'

'With him! Oh, my stars! This gets better and better.'

Ally stifled a mock yawn. 'When you've quite finished writing this ridiculous script of my life, perhaps you'd run through our list of home helps and see who's available for Mr Phillips?'

Rosie gave a throaty chuckle. 'Let's send him Mavis O'Donoghue. She won't take any of his nonsense. He did kiss you, though, didn't he?' She reverted to their earlier topic determinedly.

'Who, Mr Phillips?'

Rosie clicked her tongue. 'Babe Ballantyne! Who else would I be—'

'Oops, there's the buzzer,' Ally cut in hastily. 'Check if Mavis is available, would you, please, Rosie, and get back to me? If she is, we'll put our heads together and see what we can organise.'

'Will do. And don't think you're off the hook about that other matter,' Rosie called back darkly.

CHAPTER FIVE

'I'LL leave this in your safekeeping, Ally.' Mavis O'Donoghue waggled the house key on its length of cord and then placed it on the counter top at the nurses' station. 'I've given the locum's flat a good going over and got in a few groceries, like Cameron asked me to.'

'I'm sure you've done a brilliant job, Mavis.' Ally smiled at the plump little woman, thinking the hospital board was really pulling out all the stops to keep its locum happy. 'And thank you so much for fitting us in.'

'To tell you the truth, I'll be glad of the extra money.' Mavis leaned over confidentially. 'I'm off to England in a few months to see my daughter Karen, and air fares don't come cheap. But, then, I haven't seen her in two years.'

'You must miss her terribly.' Ally's look was soft.

'She's my baby—and my only girl.' Mavis blinked a bit. 'Some days I just feel in terrible need of a hug.'

'Oh, Mavis…' Ally leaned over and patted the older woman's hand. 'I'm sure you'll have a wonderful trip and I'll put any overtime your way where I can.'

'Would you, love?'

'Of course. You're one of our most valued workers.' Unobtrusively, Ally slipped the key into the side pocket of her trousers. She'd pop across to the flat after work with the casseroles she'd made last night. At least then Marc would have something on hand for hot meals over the coming week.

Today was Thursday and she expected he'd be back from

58

his leave some time on Saturday—or even Sunday, if he really intended stretching his vacation to its limits.

And when he returned, things would be back in perspective. Ally had promised herself to recognise what had happened for what it was. A few hot kisses between a man and a woman, nothing more.

And certainly not the sensual coming together that had rocked the foundations of her world.

'Oh, Mavis, before you go?' Ally caught the inside of her bottom lip. 'Um, how are you getting along with Mr Phillips?'

'No problems.' Mavis flapped a hand. 'Once we'd got ourselves sorted out.' She hitched up her large patchwork shopping bag. 'He's really a nice old gentleman when you get to know him.'

'Oh, good.' Ally's tone was softly amused. Owen was obviously on his best behaviour. But with a gem like Mavis to do his donkey work, who could blame him for wanting to keep on the right side of her?

When she got home, Ally took her time to shower and change and then organised the goodies she was taking to Marc's flat. It was almost five when she pulled up outside.

Juggling her basket on her hip, she pushed the key into the lock and opened the front door on the freshness of pine-scented furniture polish. She smiled. Mavis had done her usual special job.

Closing the door softly behind her, Ally walked through to the kitchen and placed her basket on the counter top. Something outside caught her attention and she moved closer to peer through the window. Her heart did a tumble turn.

Marc's car was parked in front of the garage. And he was already out, retrieving something from the boot.

Not giving herself time to think, Ally snatched open the back door, her trainers noiseless as she crossed the deck and took the five steps to the concrete path. 'Hi,' she called, her voice coming out throatily.

Marc swung a look upwards over his shoulder and unfolded slowly upright. His heart thumped against his ribs and he felt the slow burn of desire warm his body. She looked even lovelier than he remembered. So fresh and alive. 'Hello, Ally.'

'When did you get back?' she asked, crossing her arms around her body as if to shield herself.

'A few minutes ago.'

She gave a little frown. 'We didn't expect you until the weekend.'

Blue eyes regarded her levelly. 'Is there a problem?'

'No.' She sucked in her bottom lip quickly. 'Of course not. We've had the place cleaned and aired and I was just delivering some food for your freezer.'

'Sweet of you.' He bent back to his task and pulled out a crate of books. Looking up, he saw the back door wide open. 'Good.' His mouth kicked up in a crooked smile. 'I won't have to juggle with keys.'

'Can I help bring in something?'

He shrugged. 'Couple of carry bags there, if you wouldn't mind. They're not heavy. Thanks.'

They returned up the path together and with every step of the way Ally was conscious of his presence, aware of him in a way she hadn't been aware of a man since—well, since Simon. But there any similarity ended.

There was a vitality about Marc, a different kind of maleness she couldn't explain. But one that called to every feminine part of her.

'Just dump it all in the lounge for the moment,' he said shortly. 'I'll sort it out tomorrow.'

'Oh, OK.' Ally smile was a little uncertain as she placed the carry bags on the floor next to the sofa. 'I'll…um…get on with unpacking the stuff I brought for the fridge, then.'

'And I'll just get my suitcase from the car. Won't be long.'

He was right. He wasn't long. Ally was conscious of him passing the kitchen door on his way to the bedroom, heard the thump of his case on the floor and then he was back. Right behind her. She straightened as he approached. 'All squared away?'

'For now.' He put a brown paper carrier bag on the bench beside her. 'What did you bring?' His look was youthfully curious and she tipped back her head and sent him a prim little look in return.

'A couple of different casseroles and a spaghetti sauce. I did some Basmati rice as well. I hope you like it. And I've put everything in meal-size containers so they'll stack easily in the freezer.'

'Thank you, but you didn't have to go to all that trouble.'

'It was no trouble. I like cooking.'

'You must let me pay you for the ingredients.'

'Don't be silly,' she said with an embarrassed little laugh. 'It's just meant as a neighbourly gesture.'

'Then you'll have to come and share it with me,' he insisted. 'Every evening, until we've eaten it all.'

Of course she couldn't and she wasn't even going to allow herself the possibility. 'Well, we can think about that later.' Full of confusion, Ally dipped her head and continued stowing the containers of food in the freezer.

'At least I can offer you a glass of wine.' His lips kicked up in a twisted smile. 'I nipped into the bottle shop on the way here.'

'Snap!' Ally laughed, suddenly short of air. 'I brought wine, too.' She pointed to the long slim bottle in her basket.

He peered closer. 'What kind did you get?'

'White. What did you?'

'White, too—and red.'

She wrinkled her nose at him. 'Show-off.'

He chuckled. 'Which white are we drinking, then?' Grabbing both bottles, he waggled them in front of her, almost holding his breath while she vacillated, her unconscious little gesture of nibbling at her bottom lip sending blood rushing through his veins with indecent haste.

'Yours, I think,' she said finally. 'It's one of the nice local ones.'

They took their wine and some cheese and crackers Mavis had thoughtfully provided, and went out onto his back deck. There was already a round wooden table in place and Marc unfolded a couple of canvas chairs that had been stacked against the railings.

When they were seated, he raised his glass. 'Cheers,' he said briefly.

'Cheers,' Ally responded, glad he hadn't gone into flowery thanks or speeches about starting out in his new job. 'Do you have everything you need?' she asked. 'I only ask because the shops are open late tonight.'

'Everything I need is right here,' he said in a curiously gruff voice. 'And I include you in that, Ally. You've been tremendous.'

She felt a gentle tide of warmth wash over her skin at his words. She couldn't think of anything to say in return, nothing sensible anyway. So she took a careful mouthful of her wine and remained silent.

Finally, Marc cleared his throat. 'Ally, I need to ask you something. Nothing too terrible,' he emphasised quickly, seeing her startled look. 'How would you feel about coming to work at the surgery with me?'

She looked at him in blank astonishment. 'Leave my present job?'

He shrugged. 'Could be the change you were thinking about.'

'What about Jenny McGill's job? She's been the mainstay at the surgery for ages.'

Marc helped himself to a wedge of cheese. 'This doesn't affect Jenny's job. I'm creating a new one.'

'You've spoken to Jenny?'

'At length. She's happy to continue in her present role.'

Ally looked at him, her gaze slightly wary. 'I don't know what to say. You want me to be your practice nurse?'

More than anything. But he couldn't tell her that. Instead, he flipped a hand dismissively. 'Should be a pushover for you, Ally. There'll be enough hands-on medical procedures to keep you busy. Any emergencies I'm called to, I'd expect you to accompany me where necessary, so there could be a fair bit of overtime involved. And the budget will stretch to it. I've made sure of that.'

Ally rubbed at the pattern on her wineglass with the pad of her thumb. 'When do you need to know?'

'Yesterday.' Marc's eyes seemed to track over her features one by one before he went on. 'I realise I'm rushing you, but I need things settled. I want to make a go of this but while I was away I realised I'm going to need all the professional expertise I can muster to make it happen.' His mouth turned down. 'Would it leave a gaping hole in the staffing arrangements at the hospital if you transferred over to me?'

'No one's indispensable,' she said with a dry smile. 'But, as a matter of fact, we've had a recent enquiry for employment from a senior nurse, Brooke Jeffreys. She's new in town. Her husband's transferred here with the police department. She's very keen to get on at the hospital.'

Marc stroked a hand across his chin thoughtfully. 'Would she fit in? I imagine you run a pretty tight ship.'

Ally shrugged. 'We can't afford to be ultra-choosy. But she seemed friendly and her credentials were excellent.'

Marc pursed his lips slightly and nodded. 'Ultimately, it has to be your decision, Ally.'

'But you can't give me any permanent tenure, can you?'

'No, I can't.' He fell silent, but after a moment he started to speak again. 'If things go well, I'd have no reason to quit. But I'm used to working with good nursing back-up. And I'm not too proud to admit I'll need it if I'm going to make the most of this opportunity. I don't want to let anyone down, especially the people of Hillcrest.'

It was a huge decision and Ally agonised over whether she was ready to make it. Yet everything was urging her to take this chance he was offering her.

It would be a challenge and she'd probably end up not having a moment to call her own, but in the long run might not that be a good thing? There was no use pretending she hadn't fallen into a rather comfortable rut working at the hospital. Even with all its frustration.

But what of her relationship with Marc? They'd be working very closely together, both in and out of the surgery. Her pulse speeded up at the thought. Circumstances beyond their control had already linked them, tangling them in a heat of shared awareness. And once she'd seen him again this afternoon, all her protestations that she could remain detached had been shattered like eggshells under the tread of a heavy boot.

Lifting her glass, she took another mouthful of her wine, looking out from the deck to the strip of lawn, the orderly row of citrus trees along the back fence and the clothesline, a bit lopsided from years of use.

It all looked so familiar, so Australian. Yet she felt suddenly in wild country, an untravelled road ahead of her. Did she have the courage to take it?

Suddenly she straightened in her chair. Of course she did! Like a spark on tinder, her resolve took hold. For heaven's sake! She was barely thirty and life was for the living and the doing. She took a deep breath. 'OK, Dr Ballantyne,' she said decisively. 'I've thought. I'll accept your job offer.'

'Thank you...' Marc let the air out of his lungs in a relieved gush of breath and for a second he felt guilty for almost hijacking her. His gaze raked her face. Her smile was a little unsteady and he could see the soft wash of colour on her cheeks, as though the decision had somehow unnerved her. 'You won't regret it, Ally,' he promised. 'We'll make this work. Just see if we don't.'

'I'll put my resignation in tomorrow,' she said with hardly a tremor. 'If the supervisor can replace me quickly, I could probably start in a week's time.'

'Excellent.' Marc drained his wine and set his glass back on the table. 'Then I'll enlist Jenny's help to get things ticking over until you're ready to come on board.'

When his mobile rang, they looked blankly at each other for a second until Marc sprang to life, patting his back pocket urgently. 'Hell.' He cast a look around. 'Where did I leave it?'

'I seem to remember you putting it on the kitchen bench when you brought the wine in.'

'Ah.' He moved quickly inside, while Ally waited. When he returned, she raised her brows in query.

'That was the hospital.' Marc's clipped tone indicated he was already in professional mode. 'There's been an MVA on the Mount Alford road. Only one car involved. Pregnant woman trying to get herself to hospital. Too much speed. Car swerved and she hit a tree. Fortunately, she appears only shocked. She managed to dial the emergency number and the ambulance base contacted the hospital.'

'Is an ambulance going out?' Ally got quickly to her feet.

'Apparently they're both on other calls at the moment. The base will get one there as soon as they can. Meanwhile, I'm it.'

'*We're* it,' Ally corrected.

'You're coming with me?'

'I joined your staff not ten minutes ago, Doctor. Of course I'm coming.' In a flash she'd swept up the remains of their food and wine and returned them to their various homes. 'I'm parked out the front.' Ally hooked an arm through the handle of her basket, car keys already jangling in her hand. 'I'll take my car and meet you at the hospital. They'll have a trauma kit ready for us.'

'See you in a few minutes, then.' In a flash, Marc felt his years of training in emergency medicine kick in. Slamming the back door, he took the steps two at a time. His car was unlocked and he threw himself in behind the steering wheel, the familiar rush of adrenalin hitting him as he reversed out of the drive at speed.

You wanted rural medicine, he reminded himself with a faintly grim smile. And now you're in it right up to your neck.

He had no idea where this Mount Alford road was, and less idea where to find his patient. And it was almost dark. Despite all his misgivings, he suddenly felt on a tremendous high. What the hell was he worrying about when he had the remarkable Ally Inglis in his corner?

Di Castaldi was waiting for them in Reception. She handed over the emergency kit. 'I've taken the precaution of including a midwifery pack as well,' she told them. 'The base said the message was a bit garbled but they did get a name—Tiffany Fields. And she said she could see the mountain quite clearly before the accident so I'd guess she's come to grief where the road runs parallel with the base of Mount Alford.'

Marc raised a startled brow. 'That's brilliant, Di. You're obviously a local.'

'Born and bred.' She sent a quick look at Ally. 'Aren't you off duty?'

Ally made a small face. 'Looks like I've just come back on.' There was no way she intended broadcasting her new work arrangements. That would happen of its own accord on the hospital grapevine when she gave in her notice tomorrow. She hefted one of the emergency packs. 'See you in a bit, Di.'

'If I'm still on duty!' Diane sent the salutary reminder after them.

'Hell's bells, she's talking as though we'll be out until midnight. How far *is* this Mount Alford road?' Marc frowned the query, lifting the lid of the boot and stowing the medical paraphernalia inside.

'About thirty minutes,' Ally informed him calmly. 'But, of course, we don't know what we'll find when we get there. I'll direct you.'

'I'm counting on it.'

Soon they were in his car, belted up and on their way.

'The casualty's name doesn't ring a bell?' Marc asked as they drove.

'No.' Ally shook her head. 'She's certainly not on our list of midwifery patients. Which leads me to think she may have come in from one of the new acreage blocks up in the high country. Apparently, the city folk have been snapping them up. There's been a lot of building going on in recent months. I was tempted to take a look myself.'

'So you're considering putting down roots here?'

She jerked a shoulder dismissively. 'Maybe. Maybe not.'

Marc frowned, his gaze riveted on the narrow country road ahead. What kind of an answer was that? For a second he felt curiously displaced. Just when he thought he was getting marginally closer to her, Ally skipped away into the shadows again.

'Something's still puzzling me.' He changed gear to accommodate the steep incline.

'What's that?' Ally tilted her head towards him.

'I know I left my mobile number at the hospital but I'm just wondering how they knew I was back in town.'

'Someone on the shift probably saw your car at the bottle shop.'

He huffed a dry laugh. 'I guess that's something I'll have to get used to, then. Realising my movements are being monitored.'

'Only in the nicest way,' Ally explained. 'You're the doctor. The title means something in a rural community.'

'So you're saying I'd better keep my nose clean?'

'And your socks,' Ally added with a husky laugh.

They travelled in silence for a while, until Ally broke it with an explosive command, 'Slow down, Marc!' She thrust her head forward to peer through the windscreen. 'If Di's instincts are correct, we should be able to see a sign of the car any minute.'

'Hell, I'd forgotten how dark the bush can be.' Marc changed down to a lower gear. 'Let's just hope our Tiffany Fields has managed to activate the hazard lights on her car, or it could take us ages to locate her.'

'Over there—stop!' Ally pointed through the windscreen to where several pinpoints of light and the bulk of a white sedan were just visible through the scattering of thin saplings.

'Well spotted, Ally.' Cautiously, Marc turned his car off

the road and eased it forward as far as the belt of spindly bushes would allow.

'We're going to need as much light as we can get,' Ally said practically. 'Perhaps, if you could angle your head-lamps over the crash scene?'

Marc grunted. 'I'd already thought of that.'

Ally clamped her lips together. Of course he had.

In seconds they were out of the car and gathering their gear from the boot.

'Can you manage that?' Marc handed over one of the emergency packs and a groundsheet he'd found in the boot. 'I'll bring my case as well.' He flicked on the powerful torch they'd been given. 'OK, let's see what we're up against.'

The moon had flooded the place with a pale silvery light, the surroundings taking on a ghostly appearance, and it was difficult to see just what damage had been done to the small car. But they could ascertain that the bonnet was hard up against the trunk of a large gumtree.

With Ally following, Marc went forward, pushing back a fringe of trailing vine, holding it aside to let her pass. A few more paces led them to the wrecked vehicle.

'Tiffany?' Marc tapped on the slightly open driver's window. 'We're from the hospital. Are you hurt?'

A soft keening was his only answer.

Ally's heart lurched. Please, she implored silently, just guide us towards a successful outcome...

'I'll have to try to get her out.' In an abrupt movement Marc dropped his pack and handed Ally the torch.

'Let's hope the door's not going to be a problem.' She looked swiftly around to gauge whether there was a clearing large enough to lay the groundsheet. 'It might be buckled with the force of the impact.'

Marc curled his fingers around the doorhandle. 'Only one

way to find out.' Despite his best efforts, the door showed a cantankerous resistance. 'Come on!' He thumped the metal with the heel of his hand, then shoved his knee against it to gain some extra leverage. Finally the lock gave and he was able to jerk the door open.

'My baby…' Tiffany's voice faded to a sobbing little whisper. 'It's not due for two more weeks. I got these pains, and then everything— Oh!'

'Shh, you'll be fine now. We're here to help you. I'm Marc and this is Ally.' Marc felt gently to ascertain that nothing was broken, a sense of relief sweeping over him that the young woman's legs were not caught on any protruding metal.

'I'm going to lift you now, Tiffany. Can you put your arms around my neck? Good work…' Marc's voice and actions were gentle as he eased back out of the car and laid the pregnant woman on the groundsheet Ally had hastily thrown down.

'No sign of the ambulance?' Marc rapped the question as Tiffany's soft moans began again.

'No.' Ally knelt beside the young woman. 'We'll hear them long before we see them. How much time have we got?' she murmured as an aside to Marc.

'Not long.' Marc's hands palpated the pregnant woman's stomach gently. 'I'd say the baby's well on its way. We'll need to make Tiffany more comfortable.'

'Right.' Ally was immediately in her nurse role. She squeezed Tiffany's hand briefly, hitched up the woman's long skirt and pulled down her panties. 'You're doing great, Tiffany.'

The young woman's eyes were wide with uncertainty. 'The baby's early.'

'Two weeks either way is usually not a problem,' Ally

said comfortingly, brushing the damp hair back from her patient's forehead.

'I feel c-cold…'

'Blankets.' On cue, Marc's bulk dropped beside them. 'My mother read somewhere Hillcrest has severe winters.' In the muted light, soft humour gleamed in his eyes. 'I remembered they were still on the back seat of the Jag.'

'Thank heavens for mothers,' Ally murmured. Grabbing one end of the blanket, she helped Marc fold it in two and then again. Seconds later, they were gently rolling Tiffany first on one side and then the other and sliding the makeshift mattress under her.

'Can you see enough to cannulate her, Ally? I'd like to get an IV in as a precaution. Normal saline.'

'Will do.' Sensing there was no time to waste, Ally tossed him a pack of sterile gloves and snapped open her own.

As though they'd worked together for years, they began talking Tiffany through each contraction, co-ordinating their skills, their actions dovetailing silently and efficiently.

'Not far now, Tiffany,' Marc encouraged quietly. 'Let your breath come out freely, don't jam it in your throat.'

While Ally helped Tiffany into a more comfortable position, Marc prepared to deliver the infant.

Tiffany's head thrust back as she strained. 'I—can't do this…'

'Yes, you can, honey.' Ally tightened her grip on the young woman's shoulders. 'Just think, you'll have your baby to hold soon.'

'Head's crowning. We're almost there.' Marc looked down at his hands. The infant's head lay there, streaked and glassy in the torchlight, the dark perfect curls pressed wetly against the tiny skull. 'Gentle push now, Tiffany— terrific. And one more. Don't strain, ease back… Well done… Oh, boy!' The diffused torchlight caught the whiteness of his grin as he looked up. 'It's a girl!'

The offended little squawk was the best sound Ally had heard in a long time—second only to the muted wailing of the ambulance in the distance.

There was no need for Ally to wait but she did. They'd followed the ambulance back to the hospital and Marc had disappeared with Di Castaldi into the midwifery suite.

Ally knew he'd want to check Tiffany and her baby over thoroughly and tidy them up. She would have accompanied them if she'd dared, but she was off duty and it would have caused rumour and speculation. Neither of which she or Marc needed.

She glanced at her watch. The evening was still young enough for them to go somewhere for a meal—that was if he wanted to, of course…

'Ally?'

'Oh—hi.' Ally swung to her feet as Marc walked into the softly lit patients' lounge and stopped short.

His dark brows shot up. 'You waited.'

She flashed him a wry smile. 'Sentimental me. I just wanted to know they were both all right.'

'Mother and babe are doing fine.' Marc lifted his arms to half-mast in a relaxing stretch. 'I couldn't have managed without you tonight, Ally.'

'Rats, you couldn't.' She gave a smothered pleased laugh. 'Is there a husband and new father we have to contact?'

'Mmm. Matt Fields. He's in the army but away on peace-keeping duty in Timor for the next month or so. Di's emailing him at the base as we speak.'

As if by mutual accord they began to walk towards the

rear exit. 'Does Tiffany have a name for the baby yet?' Ally asked, as Marc held the door open for her.

'I didn't ask.'

She gave an exasperated tut. 'Typical man.'

He laughed. 'Well, this *man* is starving. Let's pick up a pizza and take it to your place. OK?'

A thousand uncertainties jumped into Ally's mind. Was he already seeing them as a couple rather than work colleagues? If he was, it was too much too soon. 'We could eat at the pizza place.'

'I suppose we could.' He lifted a hand to place it casually across her shoulders as they walked towards their vehicles. 'But it might be nicer to eat at home. And I suggested your place because mine doesn't feel like home yet. Would you mind?'

She did mind, of course, but she could hardly say so.

'The idea doesn't please you.' His fingers moved, tightened, making a warm ring of flesh at her nape. 'You'd rather eat at the pizza place.'

Ally bit her lip. Was she so transparent? And she was acting like a ninny. Making a fuss about nothing. And he was probably tired. He'd driven miles today, and then the baby... 'No, it's fine,' she said quickly. 'We'll go to my place.'

They stopped by her car. Ally juggled her keys to get the right one. 'The best pizzas are at Maroni's,' she deflected quickly. 'I'll lead the way, if you like.'

'I'm not about to jump on you, Ally,' he said with gentle reproach.

She dragged in a shaky breath. 'I know that.'

'Good.' He grinned suddenly. 'So, what kind of pizza does Ally Inglis like?'

An imp of mischief danced in her eyes. 'Ally Inglis likes enormous ones. With every topping under the sun.'

'I'd never have guessed.' Marc chuckled, pretending to cast a discerning look at her figure. 'But whatever the lady wants, the lady shall have.' He gave an expressive shrug. 'Got to keep my practice nurse happy.'

CHAPTER SIX

ALLY woke on Friday morning far from refreshed. Her night had been full of restless images, mostly of a dark-haired male about six feet tall.

'Oh, get a life, Allegra,' she ordered herself grumpily, rolling out of bed and under the shower.

It wasn't as though Marc had stepped out of line last night either. In fact, it had turned out a very light-hearted evening. Without ceremony, they'd eaten their pizza in front of the television, because Marc had wanted to catch a late news bulletin.

She'd watched amusedly and he'd set about his pizza as though he hadn't eaten in a week, pulling out a long curl of melted cheese and eating it with exaggerated relish.

'What?' He'd caught her look, his grin a bit lopsided. 'Am I being a pig?'

'Quite revolting,' she'd teased, although in reality she'd been turned on by the very unfussy, masculine way he did everything.

'I haven't eaten pizza in months,' he'd confessed with a lack of inhibition. 'Come on, eat up.' He'd shoved the box across. 'Before it gets cold.'

And when he'd left... Ally closed her eyes, turning her face up to the warm spray of water. He hadn't even tried to kiss her.

Not that she'd wanted him to.

Oh, make up your mind. She blew out a controlling breath, pulling on her uniform of navy trousers and corporate-style shirt. She had less than fifteen minutes to get to work and Fridays, for some reason, were always busy.

At the nurses' station, she took the report from the night sister and then, as her first priority, went across to Midwifery to check on Tiffany.

'Hi.' Ally popped her head around the door. 'How's the new mum?'

'Oh, hi.' Tiffany's eyes lit up. 'It's Ally, isn't it?'

She made a small face. 'Last night is all a bit hazy. But I remember your voice. You were great.'

'No, *you* were great,' Ally told her, picking up the chart at the end of the bed. 'Did you have a reasonable night?'

Tiffany put aside the brush she'd been using to tidy her hair. 'I was a bit too excited to sleep much, I think. And Matt managed to call me.' She beamed mistily.

'Well, no wonder you couldn't sleep.' Ally gave a low laugh, lifting her patient's wrist and looking down at her watch to check Tiffany's pulse. 'Everything's fine.' She smiled and laid the young mother's wrist back on top of the counterpane. 'You'll probably be able to have the bub with you as from today.'

Tiffany's eyes widened in query. 'There wasn't a problem, was there?'

'No.' Ally shook her head. 'But in view of her rather rapid arrival, Dr Ballantyne thought it advisable to keep her in the nursery overnight. Do you have a name for her yet?' she asked with a smile.

'Still tossing a few around. I'll get to know her a bit first, I think.'

'Good idea,' Ally said approvingly. 'Just let us know before you leave hospital. We've all the paperwork here to register her. Now, I see on your chart Dr Ballantyne would like to keep you for a few days. Will you have someone for support when you get home?'

'My mum's coming from Brisbane tomorrow,' Tiffany said. 'She can stay until Matt gets home.'

'Well, that all sounds very positive.' Ally smiled. 'And *that* sounds like breakfast, so I'll leave you to it.'

Marc stared down at the warm timber of the benchtop, relishing the luxury of having time to finish his morning coffee.

He'd unpacked after a fashion—the stuff he needed anyway. The rest could wait. He checked his watch. There was just time to throw himself under the shower before he got together with Jenny McGill at the surgery. They'd need to do an inventory and he had a supply of drugs arriving some time today that would have to be checked and stored properly.

Slipping off the kitchen stool, he rinsed his mug at the sink and thought it would have been ideal if he could have had Ally's help. He wondered if she'd given in her notice yet.

He went through to the bathroom, mentally replaying last night's events. Ally had switched on a table lamp, its subdued light drawing the room into a soft intimacy. And they'd sat side by side on her sofa, their pizza spread out on the coffee table in front of them.

He took a deep breath, almost smelling the subtle clean scent of her skin, seeing the distracting curl of her pink tongue as she'd daintily set about her unwieldy slice of pizza.

His heart tripped. Stop right there, his head warned. If he and Ally were going to work successfully together, he had to keep a professional distance. No matter what other messages his heart gave him.

On a groan of impatience with his prolonged self-analysis, he turned on the shower.

* * *

Jenny McGill was already at the surgery when Marc arrived. 'I like to get an early start.' She smiled. 'Now, do you prefer tea or coffee? And do you prefer it as soon as you get in, or later in the morning?'

Marc's eyes twinkled. 'Glad you have the priorities right, Jen. Probably tea during the morning, I think. But could we play it by ear?'

'Lord, yes.' Jenny gave a slight laugh. 'In this job, you learn to be flexible if nothing else. Now, there's quite a bit to be done and I've a list a mile long, so could we put our heads together shortly and start pulling this place into a medical practice?'

'You bet.' Marc felt a lift in his spirits. Erika had spoken highly of Jenny McGill, describing her as 'a gem'. He guessed he was already experiencing the truth of those words. 'I'll just dump this stuff,' he said, indicating his medical case and a long slim package he had tucked underneath his arm.

'The whole place has been cleaned and instruments sterilised,' Jenny said some ten minutes later in Marc's consulting room. 'And all the linen and scrubs should be delivered from the laundry some time today.'

Marc blinked. 'Right.'

'And Cameron is sending someone over from Maintenance to take down the "for sale" sign. Not that you've actually bought the practice,' Jenny went on, 'but the sign lends a kind of temporary, down-market appearance to the place, don't you agree?'

'Oh, quite.' Marc nodded in compliance, already in awe of his receptionist's organisational ability. 'I've had my own sign made, actually.' Leaning across, he flipped out the brass plate from its wrapping.

'Oh, that's splendid.' Jenny nodded in approval. 'That

looks very professional. We'll have Maintenance position that for you as well. Now, I suggest you place a discreet notice in the local paper, announcing you've taken over the practice. The sooner the patients know, the sooner they'll start coming back.'

'And the sooner we can all start making a living,' Marc concurred with a grin.

They worked steadily through the morning. Around twelve-thirty, Jenny disappeared into the staffroom to make sandwiches and brew a huge pot of tea.

'Chicken, avocado and cos lettuce on wholemeal.' Jenny offered him the plate of freshly made sandwiches. 'OK?'

'Very OK.' Marc realised he was starving. And he suddenly realised something else—he hadn't felt so upbeat, so hopeful in a long time.

Not since Karla.

His jaw tightened and out of nowhere a blurred picture of them together in his bed infiltrated his mind. And he remembered how, when they'd be running late for work, she'd sit up suddenly, sweeping her dark loose hair up from her neck and letting it tumble back around her bare shoulders...

'Marc?'

'Sorry?' He blinked his way back to the present, realising Jenny had addressed him.

'You were away with the fairies,' she teased. 'Missing your city life?'

'Hell, no!' he said derisively. 'The tea tastes so much better here.'

Jenny gave him an odd look and decided she must have missed something in the translation. 'Must be the local water,' she deadpanned.

*   *   *

Ally finished her shift at three o'clock. Handover was brief and she took off into the staffroom to freshen up.

'You in a hurry?'

Ally's eyes widened as Rosie's reflection joined hers in the mirror. 'A few things I need to do. What's up?'

'Nothing,' Rosie said with a grin. 'I just wanted to say congratulations on your new job. I'm pleased for you, Ally, if that's what you want.'

Ally coloured faintly. 'Thanks, Rosie. I…just felt it was time to move on a bit.'

Rosie spun round to lean against the benchtop. Arms folded, she looked at her friend. 'Let's just hope Marc decides to stay, then.'

Ally lifted a shoulder dismissively. 'That's a chance I'll have to take. For different reasons, we both want to make a new start, so at least that's positive.'

Rosie's eyes narrowed. 'Well, I know what your reasons are but what about his? You have to wonder what's got him running so fast from everything he's obviously worked for—and been good at, from what we've seen so far.'

Ally closed her cosmetic bag with a snap, her sensitivities suddenly ruffled. 'Stop looking for a drama, Rosie. These days people chop and change jobs all over the place. As far as I know, Marc was fed up with the pressure that goes with working in a big city hospital. Nothing more sinister than that.'

'Mmm.' Rosie looked unconvinced. 'You're as trusting as a newborn babe about men, Ally. Just don't get hurt again, that's all I'm saying.'

Ally made a swift exit to the car park. Rosie didn't know what she was talking about. Marc wouldn't hurt her. Rosie hadn't seen the soft look on his face when he'd talked about his nephews and nieces. And when he'd delivered the baby last night…

With an angry little turn of the ignition key, she started the engine and shot her car towards the exit.

A few minutes later she popped her head round the door of Marc's consulting room. He seemed engrossed, his dark head bent over the computer keyboard. She swallowed. 'Hi—it's me.'

His head came up, his expression moodily distant.

'Uh, Jenny said it was OK to come in.' Ally hovered uncertainly.

He snapped the distracted look off like a light and beckoned her in, casting a quick look at his watch. 'Is it that time already?'

'My feet are telling me it is.' She sent him a wry look, taking the chair opposite him. 'Am I interrupting? You seem a bit preoccupied.'

He gave a lopsided grin, passing a hand across his face to massage his temples. 'Jenny accused me of being off with the fairies earlier.'

'And were you?'

He gave an impatient twitch of his shoulder. 'Old history raising its head.'

Old *bad* history, Ally interpreted silently. Her breath spun out on a tight little sigh. She should never have come running over here like an eager puppy at the end of her shift. She should have been more circumspect and waited for Marc to come to her.

'So…' A dark brow flicked up. 'Are you just touching bases with me?'

'Kind of, I suppose. I wanted to let you know I gave in my notice at the hospital this morning and they've accepted it.' Looking across at him, Ally gave him a guarded smile.

'So you're on board?'

'A week from next Monday. Marc!' She gave a muted shriek as he bounded to his feet and pulled her upright. She threw her head back, her hands pressed against his chest. 'What are you doing?'

'Just this.' Laughing softly, he whirled her in a circle, then gathered her in, his eyes on her face with the intensity of a camera lens. 'I have a very good feeling about this partnership,' he said with conviction.

'Me, too.' Ally's heart gave a giddy lurch. Just the look in his blue eyes had the power to reduce her to mush.

His hands stayed locked around her waist and hers had crept up to rest on his shoulders.

This felt too good to be real. Marc's warning to himself clanged inside his head. But his heart wasn't listening. His hands tightened.

Ally gave a strangled laugh and felt herself colour softly. 'We must look like we're about to dance.'

'No music.' A strained little smile pulled at Marc's mouth. 'But we could try.'

Ally licked her lips. What they were saying made no sense at all. They both knew that. Yet neither of them seemed inclined to break away. To end the silly game.

Instead, awareness leapt between them, tightened, shimmered like a high wire under a circus top.

'What are we going to do about this, Ally?' Marc looked at her through half-closed eyes, his voice a little rough around the edges.

She shook her head, her breath catching, and she found herself shaking, powerless beneath that moody blue appraisal. 'Perhaps I shouldn't have come here?'

'Of course you should.'

His kiss came seconds later, a long exquisite shiver of a kiss that first twined through her body languidly like smoke haze, then built like fire through dry wood to a raging crescendo.

A broken little breath left Ally's mouth and she knew

she should pull away. But they were in too deep now and she wanted it. Wanted him.

Marc deepened and steadied the pressure of his mouth, tasting her over and over, branding her with sensations she knew she'd never felt before. He eased her closer, so that her breasts were pillowed against his chest and she could feel the bump of his heart through the soft stuff of his shirt.

Her fingers found their way to the back of his neck, rode the corded muscle, feathered through his short hair. A convulsive shiver ran through her as his fingers found the bare skin at her midriff where her top had pulled away. His touch was like an electric current. Slowly, exquisitely, he began to stroke slowly down the ridges of her backbone...

Marc was the first to break the erotic contact. He drew back from her slowly, his breath rapid and shallow, his eyes asking a thousand questions.

Ally felt like a rag doll. Her hands fell to her sides. She could hardly breathe. Wrapping her arms around her body as if for protection, she looked distractedly at him and stepped away. 'This can't keep happening, Marc.'

'Just what *is* happening, Ally?' His mouth kicked up in a mocking little twist. 'Let's put a name to it.'

Her breath caught and fire flooded her cheeks.

'I can't.'

He let out a controlled sigh, then shrugged. 'I recall on the morning we first met, you said something about moving on with your life. Well, the ingredients for that to happen are all here. More to the point, I'm here and you're here and neither of us finds the other repulsive, do we?'

She pressed her fingers to her mouth and then let them fall, alarmed at the way he confused her, probed to the heart of her, set her senses on fire...

She got no further. A sharp rap on the door had them both turning, and Marc stepping swiftly in front of Ally to shield her. Jenny popped her dark head in. 'Sorry to break up your conference,' she said, 'but you have your first patient.'

'Ah…' Marc acknowledged the receptionist with a token smile. 'Who is it, Jen?'

'Brian Treloar. It's a dog bite. Nasty brute sank its teeth into his leg. I've put him in the treatment room—the patient, not the dog,' Jenny qualified. 'Oops—there's the phone. It's all go today.' With a flap of her hand, she was gone.

Marc looked a question at Ally. 'Like to give me a hand? Our patient might need a calming influence.'

Was he joking? Ally's gaze clouded. She'd never felt less calm in her life. She nodded, the lump in her throat not allowing much else. Dragging her thoughts together, she followed him along the corridor to the treatment room.

'Brian?' Marc introduced himself and Ally.

'Saw the sign.' Dressed in a bush shirt and shorts, Brian Treloar looked agitatedly from Marc to Ally. 'I hope it was all right to come in?'

'That's what we're here for.' Marc could see at once the man was in considerable shock. 'What happened exactly?'

'I run a lawnmowing service,' Brian explained. 'New client—dog on the loose. When I bent over to pull the starter on the mower, it was on me.'

Marc's mouth compressed as he examined the man's injuries. There was an ugly tear wound on his calf and a series of deep punctures typical of a large dog's bite. The surrounding skin was already swelling and dark blue with bruising. 'It didn't miss you, did it?'

'No.' Brian attempted a cracked laugh. 'Lucky I had the rake handy. I whacked him with that and he backed off.' He took a shaky breath. 'I couldn't get out of there fast enough, I can tell you.'

'So, where are the owners?' Marc went to the basin to wash his hands.

'Dunno. Work, I guess.'

Marc considered their options. 'We're obliged to let the police know. And it'll be up to them to contact the owners and sort things out. But you could find you'll lose them as clients.'

'Yeah, well, can't be helped. I'm not a troublemaker but the dog's dangerous. Imagine if it had been a kiddie.'

Ally suppressed a shudder and looked at Marc. 'Would you like me to follow it up? The sooner the dog is impounded the safer we'll all be.'

'No, I'll take care of it.' He put a hand briefly on her arm. 'If you'd make Brian more comfortable? Then we'll get him treated.'

Ally was already gowned and masked when he returned. She'd drawn up lignocaine and opened the suture packs.

'Thanks.' Marc tugged on the sterile gown she had waiting for him, thanking his good luck she'd been here for the emergency. Already she had their patient looking much more relaxed. He picked up the lignocaine. 'This'll sting a bit, Brian,' he apologised, infiltrating the man's wound with the anaesthetic. 'How's your tetanus status these days?'

Brian grimaced slightly. 'I've been a bit slack, Doc. Haven't had one for yonks.'

'In that case, we'll need to give you a jab.'

Marc sought Brian's reaction after several minutes and judged the anaesthetic had taken effect. 'Right, let's flush with normal saline, please, Ally.'

'Do you have Betadine on hand?' she asked, knowing they'd need an antiseptic to follow once the wound had been flushed clean.

'I've done a restock.' Marc indicated the wall cupboard above her head. 'Fortunately everything arrived today.'

'Am I gonna need stitches, Doc?' Brian asked, as Ally swabbed the last of the wounds with the antiseptic.

'As a general rule, we don't stitch puncture wounds, mate. But the flap of skin will need a suture or three.'

In fact, the jagged tear took fifteen stitches. Almost an hour later, Marc accepted another length of fine nylon thread from Ally and inserted the final stitch. Tying it off, he straightened to survey his work.

'You're very neat.' Ally was generous in her praise as she placed a non-stick dressing over the wound.

Marc stripped off his gloves. 'I'd like you back in on Monday, Brian. We'll take a look and replace the dressing. Any problems over the weekend, go to Casualty and I'll see you there, OK?'

'Sure, Doc.' Brian got gingerly to his feet. 'Thanks,' he added a bit awkwardly. 'Can't remember when anything like this has happened to me…'

Marc looked keenly at him. He still looked groggy. 'Jenny was ringing your wife. I imagine she's outside, waiting to take you home.'

Brian sent out a crooked smile. 'I live only a couple of streets away and the van is an automatic, I reckon I could've got myself home.'

'Probably.' Marc counted out a supply of pain-killers into a plastic bottle and scrawled some instructions on the label. 'But why put yourself under more stress when you don't have to? Now, take these only if you need them.' He handed over the tablets. 'But don't be a martyr.'

'No worries, Doc.' Rather sheepishly, Brian pocketed the small bottle. 'I'm not one for fuss but I hear you.'

'I'll see you out, Brian,' Ally offered quietly.

'Everything OK?' Marc asked a short while later, when Ally returned to the treatment room.

'Mmm. Brian's safely in his wife's care and apparently the police and the RSPCA have things under control regarding the dog.'

'It might be an idea to keep an eye on Brian for PTS,' Marc said.

'Post-traumatic stress?'

He shrugged. 'It can happen with snake bite and shark attacks.'

'I imagine it's quite possible, then. He did seem quite shocked. We'll certainly keep a look out as well, if Brian shows at the hospital next week. Oh.' She looked around in surprise. 'You've tidied up.' She could see he'd already discarded the sharps they'd used and stripped the treatment couch. 'Thanks, but I could've—'

'Forget it,' he came in sharply, reaching to rub at the nape of his neck. 'You did me a huge favour, staying to assist, when you'd already done an eight-hour shift at the hospital. I appreciate it.'

'You're welcome.'

'Uh, do you have plans for the weekend?'

Ally's mind went blank. His question might have been the innocuous kind you threw around to your colleagues late on a Friday afternoon but somehow she didn't think so.

And in view of what she could only see as his rather confrontational remarks earlier, she needed time to think. Time to regather. Time to decide what she wanted from this involvement with Marc. In a nutshell, did she want what he obviously wanted?

Something closer and deeper.

Just the thought made her all fingers and thumbs as she pulled a fresh sheet from the pile, sliding it onto the treatment couch. Smoothing it into position, she turned to Marc, her hand on the neat, tucked-in end, and said the first thing that came into her head. 'I'll be out of town. I'm driving to the Darling Downs to visit my sister.'

'Right.' His blue gaze narrowed slightly. 'Take care, then. I'll probably catch up with you next week at the hospital—or elsewhere.' His voice had a husky little catch in it and she felt the strength drain from her legs purely because of his nearness.

And immediately afterwards felt guilty for deserting him. But then she rallied. He was the new doctor, single, a presentable male in a country town. He wouldn't be short of female company.

If he wanted it.

She was running scared, Marc decided. Hell, it had been all she could do to meet his eyes back there. He sighed and dragged his hands through his hair, turning away to look through the window of his consulting room.

Part of him felt guilty for confronting her like that about her feelings, but somehow the words had just tumbled out. And as for her weekend plans—if she hadn't invented them off the top of her head, he'd walk backwards to Bourke. She was wary. That much appeared plain. Occasionally, he'd caught her almost haunted look.

Was something in her past still weighing her down? Well, he'd been there. His eyes were flint-like for a second. Perhaps they could help each other.

If she'd let him.

CHAPTER SEVEN

'I'LL drive up in the morning, then—if that's convenient?'

'Of course it's convenient, you ninny!' Anne Belzar laughed off her sister's somewhat tentative enquiry. 'Couldn't be better timing, actually. Dirk's off on an overnight camp with his year tens and Holly has a birthday party sleepover, so it'll give us time and space for a good old catch-up.'

'Yes. Um, Annie, I know it's short notice...' Agitatedly, Ally rubbed at the edge of the kitchen bench with her thumb. 'But do you think your hairdresser could fit me in tomorrow some time?'

Anne cackled. 'What's going on here, Ally, a makeover? You haven't touched your hair for yonks.'

'I have!' Ally defended. 'I have it trimmed all the time.'

'Hmm.' Anne's wry chuckle sounded as though she was less than convinced. 'I'll call Greta first thing,' she promised. 'If she's not doing heads for a wedding, it should be OK.'

'Thanks, Annie. Tell Greta I'll just get some foils or something.'

'Will do. Drive carefully, kiddo.'

'Oh, I think we can do more than just foils,' Greta said next day, lifting Ally's fall of honey-blonde hair and letting it slide away. 'It's in great condition but, heck, Ally, no one wears their hair in a mop like this any more.'

'I hadn't noticed.' Slightly ruffled at having her hairstyle described so unflatteringly, Ally gripped her hands together under the protective cape. She blinked uncertainly. 'So, what do you suggest?'

'Decisions, decisions…' Greta made a small reflective moue, making partings and flipping strands this way and that, considering her options. Then she grinned disarmingly. 'Why don't I surprise you?'

Ally closed her eyes for a second and then opened them and looked at herself in the mirror. She swallowed nervously. 'Well, OK, I guess.'

Two cups of coffee and several glossy magazines later, Ally was ready for the great unveiling. With a surge of panic she'd watched as Greta had snipped and shaped, had seen lock after lock tumbling to the floor. Then had come the foils to add 'a few subtle highlights', as the hairdresser had put it.

Now Greta was all business as she towelled off Ally's hair and settled her back in the chair. *What if I hate it?* Ally agonised, watching the hairdresser reach purposefully for her blowdryer and brush.

'Stop looking like that, Ally,' Greta chastised laughingly. 'I know what I'm doing.'

And it seemed Greta did. Ally loved her new look. Almost shyly, she turned her head experimentally and smiled.

In the mirror, Greta smiled back. 'I've relaxed the curl and shaped it into your head so it's sleeker and sassier.' She grinned. 'A new you, in fact.'

'It's fabulous, Greta.' Ally touched her fingers to the newly defined edges, not believing how the pretty gamine style accentuated the clarity of her green eyes and high cheekbones. 'Thank you.'

'My pleasure.' With a flourish, Greta whipped off the cape and ushered her client through to the front counter.

'Hot date tonight?' she asked cheekily, taking Ally's credit card and swiping it.

'Not tonight.' Ally shook her head and blushed. But maybe some time. Some time soon...

'Oh, hi, honey. You're back. Thought I heard your car.' Anne spun round from her meal preparations at the bench as Ally walked into the kitchen some thirty minutes later. 'Well, well.' Anne's dark head tipped sideways, her eyes popping with speculation. 'I thought you said it wasn't a make-over.'

Ally showed the tip of her tongue. 'Like it?' Suddenly full of confidence, she spun round like a fashion model.

'You look gorgeous,' Anne said generously. 'A huge improvement on that poor little waif who arrived this morning hiding under all that hair.'

Was that what she'd been doing? Her sister's comments brought Ally up short. 'You know, I actually *feel* better somehow. Isn't that weird?'

'Not so weird.' Anne gave her younger sister an old-fashioned look. 'So, are you going to tell me about him?'

Ally blushed softly. 'Nothing to tell.'

'Allegra...' Anne warned, picking up a kitchen sponge threateningly.

'Later, all right?' Ally waved her hands about. 'So are we going out to eat or staying in?' she sidetracked quickly. She'd been Greta's last client and already the afternoon had given way to dusk.

'Oh, in,' Anne said promptly. 'I've just picked a load of fresh veg. I thought we'd do a stir-fry with the works—if that suits you?'

'Mmm, sounds yummy. Should be cool enough for a fire, too. I'll just go and get changed. Oh, I got these for after.' Ally slid a box of chocolates onto the table.

'Imported, no less.' Anne raised an eyebrow. 'What are we celebrating?'

Ally twitched a shoulder and then said airily, 'The new me, perhaps?'

'Well, mate, I don't know who you are,' Anne murmured a bit later, throwing an assortment of vegetables onto a chopping board and taking up her chef's knife, 'but my heartfelt thanks for giving my little sister a reason to look forward instead of back.'

Ally prepared to leave midafternoon the next day.

'Ring when you get home,' Anne directed, watching her sister stow her weekend bag into the boot of the car.

'I will.'

'And I hope your new job goes well.'

Ally gave a short laugh. 'It'll be odd after working shifts for so many years.'

'Well, make the most of it,' Anne said lightly. 'Indulge yourself occasionally, like you have this weekend.'

'You mean the hair?' Ally grinned, touching the soft layered ends for the umpteenth time. Her new reflection in the bathroom mirror this morning had surprised her all over again. And pleased her. But for some reason it made her feel vulnerable, too.

'I'm referring to living life, Ally.' Anne was suddenly earnest. 'Responding to what feels good and going with it. OK, enough lecture.' She made a wry grimace and stepped back. 'Just make sure you visit us again soon. And bring Marc. We'll show him some real Downs hospitality.'

Ally's heart gave a rather uncomfortable jolt in her chest. 'Yes, well, we'll see. You know, I think I may take up riding again.'

'What a good idea.' Anne beamed. 'You know Mum still

has all your little cups and ribbons from your pony club days? Are the Faulkners still running their stables in Hillcrest?'

'As far as I know.' A little awkwardly, Ally took the car keys from her pocket and inserted them in the lock. 'Anne...don't go imagining Marc and me as a couple or anything,' she said carefully, then let her voice rise. 'I mean, we hardly know each other!'

'I know, I know.' Anne flapped a hand. 'But, honey, you talked about him nonstop last night.'

'Did I?' Ally looked appalled. 'You should have stopped me.'

'Why? It was wonderful to hear you so interested and involved. And *funny*—the way you used to be. And seeing we're talking about the new you, why don't you go the whole way and ditch that damned wedding ring?'

A heavy beat of silence.

'Anne, I know you never liked Simon,' Ally said quietly, with an expression her sister couldn't read.

'No, Ally, I never liked what he *did* to you,' Anne countered. 'Can't you see, by hanging onto his ring, you're still linking yourself to the past and all its unhappy memories? For heaven's sake, Ally, he dumped all over you! Left you nothing but a mountain of mental agony and enough self-induced guilt to stop a speeding train! Oh, lord.' Anne bit down on the corner of her bottom lip. 'Maybe I shouldn't have said all that.'

'Maybe you shouldn't,' Ally agreed, her voice tight. 'But, then, maybe I needed to hear it.'

Anne wound her arms around her middle and tightened them. 'I just want you to be happy again, honey.'

'I know.' Ally blinked a bit. 'Now, give me a hug and let me go,' she said in an over-bright tone. 'I want to get home before dark.'

Anne hugged her sister fiercely and then stepped back, a tiny frown between her brows. 'Are you sure you're OK to drive?'

Ally pretended to study her legs and arms. 'Nothing broken.' She pulled open the door of the car and swung into the driver's seat. 'Annie, stop worrying about me,' she pleaded. 'I'll be fine.'

'Ring when you get home,' Anne said again, stepping away as Ally reversed and took off down the driveway.

As she drove, Ally tried to untangle the strands of emotion inside her. Her sister's frankness had certainly given her food for thought.

It was true Simon had left her with no happy memories of their time together. He'd abused her trust. And he'd lied to her—oh, how he'd lied...

Her hands tightened on the steering wheel and she waited for the familiar pain and hurt to begin seeping through her mind, hurting her head. She waited and waited but somehow it didn't happen.

She took the deepest breath, a sudden light flooding her mind. Was it possible? Perhaps subtly, without her even having been aware of it, the healing had at last begun. Thoughtfully, she teased at her bottom lip. Now, she just had to think of some further ways to help speed it up...

A few kilometres from home, Ally slowed her speed, took a side road and gently eased her car to a halt. Getting out, she made her way purposefully towards a narrow wooden bridge that spanned a section of the river that fed the farmlands around Hillcrest.

Her loafers made a hollow thump on the rounded timber logs that formed the bridge's base. Halfway across she stopped and walked over to lean on the gnarled railings.

She looked out beyond the water to where the leaves of the trees shivered and danced under the sharp breeze. Then she lifted her gaze towards the mountains and beyond them again to the magic of a vividly pink and gold sunset.

Now!

In a second she felt her heart racing against her ribs. It was essential she do this quickly without another mental inquisition to add to the several hundred she'd already indulged in over the past months.

The narrow gold band slid easily from her finger. Lifting her arm, she threw it as far as she could, watching it arc against the setting sun and disappear into the river.

Ally blew out a calming breath and switched off the ignition. After she'd left the river, she'd got back onto the highway and driven straight to Marc's place, telling herself if he was out, it was no big deal.

But one look across at the large timber house that had been converted into two flats told her Marc was home. His Jaguar was parked in the driveway.

Beating back the slow crawl of nerves in her stomach, she swung out of the car and made her way along the path, up the shallow steps and onto the verandah. The front door was open and she could hear music coming from the lounge room.

He'd never hear her knocking, she thought vexedly. Oh, lord, what on earth was she doing here? She must be crazy. She turned to leave and then hesitated on the top step. She had to stop all this self-doubt. She'd merely called here to see a *friend*, she rationalised. So, why was she making difficulties when there weren't any?

Moving purposefully back across the verandah, she called a greeting through the doorway. And proceeded to wait, her heart banging like a drumbeat inside her chest.

There was no reply. Warily, she took a couple of steps along the hallway to the door of the lounge room and looked in, her lips parting softly on a tiny gasp of air.

Marc was stretched out on the sofa, his eyes closed. Ally hesitated, a primitive kind of tingle prickling along her skin. His short hair was rumpled, sticking up in little spikes. Her hand went to her heart, clenching. He looked absurdly youthful, so vulnerable in sleep. And as sexy as—

'Ah!' She made an involuntary little sound and took a step backwards as his eyes suddenly opened, their direct blueness flooding her with warmth.

'Ally.' He blinked a bit and then jackknifed to a sitting position. 'How long have you been there?' he asked huskily, working his face muscles as if trying to wake up properly and tunnelling his hands back through his hair.

'Not long.' She gave a tinny laugh to cover a sudden attack of nerves. 'Sorry if I'm intruding. Your front door was open and I—'

'You're not intruding.' He jerked to his feet, walking across to the sound system to turn down the music. 'Come in.'

'It's Sarah Brightman, isn't it?' Ally tilted her head enquiringly towards the player.

'Mmm. With the London Philharmonic. Great sound for relaxation.' He turned then and looked properly at her. And frowned. 'Your hair's different.'

'Like it?' Ally gave an experimental twirl, laughing a little as her legs tangled and she almost lost her balance.

'It's great,' Marc said economically. 'New job, new hairstyle, was it?'

'I thought it was time for a change, that's all.'

'It looks good on you.'

'Thanks.' Ally smoothed back a tiny tendril, catching sight of her left hand with its bare ring finger. See what else I've done? she wanted to tell him. *I'm really getting the gist of this moving-on business...* Instead, she asked, 'Uh, how was your weekend?'

Lonely without you, he was tempted to reply. But how could he admit that? Especially when she seemed to be so upbeat about her own weekend. Perhaps she'd found a new lover. She had that air about her—a kind of inner excitement. His mouth grew taut. He hated the thought of that scenario. Waving her towards one of the easy chairs, he dropped back onto the sofa, leaning forward to link his hands between his knees.

'So...your weekend?' Ally prompted, perching a little awkwardly on the edge of the chair.

'Couple of call-outs,' he said dismissively.

'Serious?'

'A young biker came to grief about a kilometre out of town. Busted femoral artery. Pete Delgado took him across to Warwick.'

Ally nodded. Pete was one of the town's long-serving ambulance officers. 'And the other?'

'Query appendicitis. Seven-year-old boy. Brought in at five-thirty this morning.'

'Did you operate?'

'I *am* allowed to, you know.' Dark humour spilled into his eyes and pulled at the corners of his mouth.

'That's not what I meant.' Soft colour licked along Ally's cheekbones and she added throatily, 'I meant, was it necessary to operate?'

Marc gave an impatient twitch of his shoulder. 'He was on the point of rupture when I opened him up so, yes, it was necessary to operate.'

'Thank heavens you were here, then.' Ally touched the small medallion at her throat. 'Who scrubbed for you?'

'Your replacement, Brooke Jeffreys. She's had considerable theatre experience apparently.'

Ally swallowed unevenly. 'So things are slotting nicely into place, then, aren't they?'

'Depends.' His mouth tightened fractionally. 'What *things* are we talking about exactly?'

Suddenly Ally felt vulnerable, her new-found confidence teetering. 'Things in general, I suppose,' she waffled, her mouth drying.

A beat of silence.

'Sorry—where are my manners? I must be still half-asleep. What about something to drink? Glass of wine?' He leapt to his feet and gestured towards the kitchen.

'Just a fruit juice, thanks, if you have it.' Taking a steadying breath, Ally rose and followed him. And found herself automatically wandering out to the rear deck.

Marc opened the door of the fridge and located the jug of fruit juice, giving the cans of lager a rueful look before he closed the door. It had begun to hit home rather forcefully that in his new role he was going to be on call twenty-four seven. Not that he'd ever been into binge drinking but he'd have to be aware of his alcohol intake and make sure he was never unfit to operate in an emergency.

Pouring the juice into two tall glasses, he shook his head as if to clear it, admitting how off guard he'd felt when he'd woken and seen her there. Hell, for a split second he'd thought he'd dreamed her up! How crazy was that? He gave a huff of self-derision. Perhaps not so crazy, he reasoned, when she'd been on his mind for most of the weekend.

Picking up the glasses, he went outside to the deck and joined Ally at the railing.

'Mmm, I can really use this.' Turning, Ally took the glass he handed her.

'Long drive?' Marc removed his hand quickly before their fingers could touch.

'Couple of hours,' she said, careful not to add the extra time she'd taken for her detour. 'But it was worth it.'

'So, good weekend, then.' Marc motioned her into one of the canvas chairs and dropped into the other, placing his drink on the wooden table.

'Yes.' Almost subconsciously Ally touched a hand to her hair. 'Anne's husband and daughter were away overnight so we managed to have a girls' night in. Had a few drinks, a few laughs…'

'As you do.' He smiled and dipped his head, feeling the knot in his gut begin to unravel. It didn't sound like she'd gone out partying and fallen into bed with anyone. 'And Anne is older than you?' he asked politely.

'By about five years.' Ally drew her mouth into a wry little moue. 'When I was growing up, I sometimes felt I had two mothers. But Annie has always looked out for me and most times her advice is spot on.'

'Sounds like my sister, Roz,' he said, a reciprocal amusement stirring in the depths of his blue eyes. 'I missed you,' he added, barely audibly, and raised a hand to cup her cheek. 'Do you mind?'

Ally could hardly breathe. Unable to stop herself, she turned her mouth into his palm to taste him, once and again. 'I missed you, too,' she murmured and gave a soft embarrassed chuckle. 'Anne said I talked about you nonstop.'

A smile nipped his mouth and he reclaimed his hand. 'Was she bored rigid?'

'Don't think so.' Ally took a hurried mouthful of her drink. 'She said I was to invite you for a weekend some time.'

He looked suddenly rueful. 'I might be long gone before that can happen.'

Ally's stomach tightened. So he was still unsure whether he'd made the right decision to practise in Hillcrest. Her mouth drooped slightly. Well, he'd never hidden the fact from her that his stay could be temporary. Perhaps she should take what was on offer—whatever that turned out to be.

And let tomorrow take care of itself.

At the thought she shivered involuntarily.

'Cold?' Marc was all concern.

'Mmm.' Crossing her hands, Ally rubbed her upper arms. 'I have a jumper in the car—'

'Stay there.' His hand fell on her shoulder. 'I'll lend you one of mine.' He was back in a flash with a bulky knit in a soft earthy colour. 'It'll be a bit big,' he said, his gaze running assessingly over her. 'But at least it'll keep you warm.'

'Thanks.' Feeling her skin prickle alarmingly, Ally stood and pulled the jumper over her head, snuggling into its softness. 'Winter's really coming on quickly, isn't it?' A little jerkily, she moved to the railings again, noticing the early evening light had already begun transforming the stark shapes of the mountains into towering castles of purplish black.

'So I've been told by the locals.' Marc dug his hands into the back pockets of his jeans and leaned back against the railings, looking at her. 'And accompanied by wild storms, too, I believe.'

'Real beauts.' A teasing smile nipped Ally's mouth. 'They come in off the mountains. A part of the roof was blown off the hospital last winter. Pandemonium for a while until—'

'Enough!' Laughing, Marc whipped out a hand and placed two fingers over her mouth. 'Don't tell me any more!'

Her hand came up and circled his wrist, gently easing his fingers away from her mouth. 'Might make you cut and run, Doctor?' she asked softly.

'No…' His stared at her, his eyes darkening with need. 'Never for those kinds of reasons, Ally.'

In a second the atmosphere between them was shivering with tension. Wide and slightly startled, her eyes met his and her lips parted on a tiny sigh.

It was too much for him. With a hard indrawn breath, he folded her into his arms and lowered his mouth to hers.

She tasted like nectar or forbidden wine. He didn't know which, groaning softly as her lips, so warm, so giving, parted to give him access. Her arms were around him now, the feel of her ripe, firm body enough to drive him over the edge.

But that was not the way.

Instead, he ended the kiss, turning his head a little, smudging his lips across her temple, her eyelids and into the soft curve of her throat. And then cradled her as though she were infinitely precious.

Finally, his chest rose in a long sigh and he slowly untwined the hands she'd looped around his neck and drew back from her. Lifting his gaze, he stared down into her wide and slightly troubled eyes.

Ally licked her lips. She had to get out of here. Love and desire rolled into one wild surge was swooping through her body and out to the tips of her fingers and toes. Love? The idea brought her up short. Was it really love she felt for Marc or something else entirely?

Perhaps it was merely gratitude. How did you tell? She had no great experience with men. Simon hadn't done her any favours in that direction. She caught back a bitter laugh. So much for thinking that just by ditching his ring she could rid herself of his shadow. 'I should go, Marc.' She gave him a crooked, brittle smile. 'Thanks.'

He frowned heavily. 'For what?'

For making me feel like a woman again, she could have told him, but that would have been too revealing. 'For being here, I guess.'

Marc saw the heartbreaking emotion that froze her face for an instant and something inside him shifted. 'I'm here for you any time, Ally. Believe that.'

'I should go,' she repeated. 'Let you listen to the rest of your music in peace. Oh, your jumper.' She crossed her arms and went to pull it over her head.

'Ally, stop,' he said gruffly, pulling her gently in against him.

For a long time they just stood there, Marc rocking her like a child.

Finally Ally felt her body relax and she breathed deeply. After the longest time she drew back, looking at him, her eyes welling. 'Thank you.' The words trembled on her lips. 'But I'm OK now.'

Of course she wasn't. Moving fractionally, Marc put his hands to her wrists, pushing up the sleeves of the outsize jumper to enclose her forearms. 'Stay and have an early dinner with me,' he said. 'We can have some of the food you brought or I can knock us up an omelette. Probably not as good as yours, though.'

Hardly aware of what she was doing, Ally let her head rest against him. 'I'm game if you are.'

'Good.' He breathed in, absorbing her scent, utterly aware of her and the reaction of his own body. 'I'll get a fire going and open the bottle of red wine. One glass apiece won't put us over the limit, will it?'

'Shouldn't think so.' Her teeth bit softly into her lower lip. 'I'm glad I came.'

'Me, too.' A solemn light came into his eyes and he brushed the pad of his thumb against her cheek. 'I'm here if ever you want to talk, Ally.'

Dazed, she watched the small lifting of his throat as he swallowed, feeling a surge of oneness with him, a flood of happiness she couldn't hide. She managed a tentative smile. 'That's good to know.'

With their hands linked, they went through to the kitchen.

'I had another visitor this afternoon.' Marc went to the sink to wash his hands. 'A friendly lady called Mavis. She presented me with those.' He pointed to the trough of greenery on the windowsill. 'And some of her free-range eggs.'

'Isn't she a gem?' Ally felt a guarded light-heartedness, eyeing the brown speckled eggs he flourished in front of her. 'Mavis is one of our very best home carers.'

'Well, I must confess I felt very cared-for. This would never happen in the city, would it?'

Ally's mouth folded in on a wry smile. 'Not usually.' She looked up from searching in the cupboards. 'You don't have a proper omelette pan.'

He raised an eyebrow. 'Do we care?'

'Probably not.' She chuckled, digging out a run-of-the-mill frying pan and placing it on the cook-top. 'What can I do?'

'Can you open the wine?'

'If you've a proper opener.'

He gestured vaguely. 'In the drawer. Glasses on the shelf beside you. I take it these are herbs?' He swiped the tops off several of the leafy plants along the window ledge. 'I thought I'd chuck them in our omelette.'

'Hmm…' Ally chewed the inside of her bottom lip, stopping a chuckle. Some of the curly leaves looked suspiciously like marigolds. But on the other hand, perhaps they belonged to one of the new varieties of parsley. 'I'm sure Mavis wouldn't have given you anything that wasn't edible,' she contributed lightly, and then sobered.

The world and its problems seemed light years away and she couldn't remember a time when she'd felt so happy.

CHAPTER EIGHT

IT WAS the second week of Ally's employment at the surgery.

'I can't believe the variety of cases I've seen in such a short time,' Marc said.

'Is that good or bad?' It was Jenny who spoke, her watchful gaze linking the doctor-and-nurse team as she placed the lunch tray on the table between them.

'It's good.' Marc gave a rueful smile. 'Just means I have to do a lot more homework in certain areas. Lunch looks wonderful as usual, Jenny. Sit down. I'll pour the tea.'

Jenny needed no second invitation. 'Well, the patients are very pleased with you.'

'They've told you?' Marc looked disconcerted.

'And me,' Ally chimed in. 'Only had one complaint— Cedric McMahon called you "a young whippersnapper" when I took his BP this morning.'

Marc snorted. 'Wouldn't have anything to do with me telling him he had to stop hauling bags of spuds around on his back, would it?'

'Most likely.' Ally gave an arch look, resting her chin on her upturned hand. 'I recall he showed up at the hospital a few times, mostly at his wife's instigation. We managed to convince him a course of physio would help his back pain but he only attended once.'

'Oops, there's the phone.' Jenny sprang to her feet. She popped a couple of sandwiches onto a plate and picked up her tea. 'Oh, leave room for some chocolate cake. One of

105

the patients brought it in. I thought we'd have it for afternoon tea.'

Marc stifled a groan. 'I'll be as fat as a pig if this keeps up.'

'You can't be mean to Jenny.' Ally sent him a prim little look. 'Anyway, I heard you're one of the regulars at the gym these days.'

He twitched a hand. 'Exercise is a good antidote for all manner of things. Didn't you know...?' Their eyes locked for an endless moment, the tension ending only when his mouth kicked up in a crooked smile. 'So, tell me, what do you do for exercise?'

'I work out to my step-aerobics video, very privately in my lounge room.'

'What time?' An air of mischief gleamed in his eyes. 'I might look in.'

'What part of *very privately* didn't you understand, Doctor?'

'Spoilsport.'

'Surely you're not that desperate?' she countered with a chuckle.

'No.' His mouth tilted into a slightly rueful smile. 'Just mildly hopeful.'

'What are you going to do about Cedric?' Ally changed conversational lanes adroitly. 'He did seem in quite a bit of pain.'

'I sent him over to the hospital for X-rays. But from my examination, I'd say he's been lifting incorrectly for most of his farming life.'

'It's hard for these men to break the habits of a lifetime,' Ally pointed out. 'Basically, Cedric needs rest.'

'Which he's not going to get. I'll have more idea of his situation after I've seen the X-rays. But at the moment I'm inclined towards starting him on a nonsteroidal anti-inflammatory medication and between us we might be able to coax him back for some physio. What do you think?'

Ally looked at him over the rim of her mug. 'We can but try.'

'So, how is everything going?' Marc leaned back in his chair and folded his arms. 'Job-wise, I mean.'

'Very well. Far busier than I thought it would be—but that's good.' She tinkled a laugh. 'I can't believe I've been here two weeks and it's already Friday again.'

'Probably time for some relaxation.' He sent her a narrow look. 'Got plans for this evening?'

'Rosie and I are getting a take-away and renting a video.' Her mouth crimped at the corners. 'You're welcome to join us but I should warn you, you'll need to bring a supply of tissues.'

Marc rolled his eyes. 'Think I'll pass. What about tomorrow night, then? Care to join me for dinner at Lavender Farm?'

Ally's heart thumped. Since their emotion-charged meeting, when she'd stumbled into his flat unannounced on that fateful Sunday, they'd met only in the surgery in the course of their working days. And she'd thought perhaps it was the new order of things. That Marc was waiting for her to take the initiative if she wanted a deeper, more personal relationship with him.

And she still hadn't made up her mind about that.

Had he become restless with her inaction? Just the thought made her nerves tighten alarmingly. It certainly sounded like he'd picked up the ball and was running with it.

She brought herself together with a snap. He was waiting for an answer and she couldn't think of a plausible reason to say no. And, realistically, what harm could it do? Heaven knew, there was little enough social life in the town and he still didn't know many people… Abruptly, she got to her feet and pushed her chair in. 'Dinner sounds lovely. I'll look forward to it.'

He raised an eyebrow. 'Seven o'clock? I'll pick you up.'

'Fine.' Ally began to clear up their lunch things.

'Need a hand?' Marc offered.

Ally waved him away. 'Go and do your doctoring.' She smiled.

As he walked back to his consulting room, Marc realised she'd been constantly in his thoughts. Just being around her and willing himself not to touch her was frustrating him like hell.

Out of nowhere, desire, blade-sharp, twisted his gut, bringing with it a replay of the way they'd been together on that Sunday, when she'd gatecrashed his sleep. He blew out a long controlling breath. Perhaps Saturday night would bring some answers. He certainly hoped so. Before he turned into some kind of nutcase.

Marc's last patient for the day was Marnie Civetta. 'I don't know where to start,' the young woman said a bit awkwardly.

'The beginning is usually a good place.' Pushing his chair back, Marc stretched out his legs and smiled disarmingly. 'How old are you, Marnie?'

'Twenty. And I think I might have Huntington's disease.'

A genetic defect of the central nervous system, which causes the premature death of brain cells. Marc recited the medical definition in his head and then said cautiously, 'That's a big call. I take it you haven't been tested?'

Marnie shook her head. 'It's…a long story…'

'Take your time. I don't have to be anywhere else.'

The young woman's throat jerked as she swallowed. 'I'm adopted. And I've begun tracing my birth parents…'

Marc frowned, his lips pursed in conjecture. 'What have you found out?'

Marnie lifted a hand and held it to her throat. 'That my paternal grandfather had Huntington's. But my father didn't.' Her mouth trembled infinitesimally. 'So maybe it's skipped a generation and come to me.'

'Research is still very slow on this disease,' Marc said carefully. 'And the disease itself is relatively rare. I've only seen one case in all my years of medical practice. Are you aware the symptoms usually don't start showing until somewhere between the mid-thirties to fifties?'

Marnie chewed her bottom lip. 'Are you saying it's better to wait and not find out, Doctor?'

Marc swiped a hand across his cheekbones. He had to tread carefully here. It was very likely his young patient would be unprepared in the event of a positive diagnosis. And afterwards there would be no question it would have to be a struggle for her to maintain a healthy and positive attitude. But whatever she decided, she was going to need all the support available to her.

'Tell me a bit about your background,' he said, deciding to take an overview of things before he discussed Marnie's options in any detail. 'For instance, how have your adoptive parents reacted to your search for your birth parents?'

Marnie's whole expression lightened. 'Mum and Dad have been great, encouraged me all along the way. My birth mother agreed to meet me rather reluctantly. She has her own family now and didn't want to upset their lives. And I can understand that...' Marnie hesitated and blinked a bit. 'But she did give me my father's name and I've since caught up with him.' A tiny dimple flickered in Marnie's cheek as she smiled. 'He was delighted to meet me, even though he had to pass on the possibility of the Huntington's. He hadn't known anything about me, you see, and he doesn't have any other children, mainly because of the disease.

'I've written to my birth mother and told her everything. I've asked her to get back to me with any medical history on her side. She hasn't replied yet but Mum says to give her time to get her head around it all.'

'That's quite a story.' Marc's mouth softened in a gentle smile of understanding. 'And quite a lot for you to be handling. Before we go any further, I'd like to get your parents in and have a family conference.'

'That's going to be kind of difficult.' Marnie lifted a hand, curling a strand of auburn hair around her finger. 'I'm at uni in Brisbane. I've to be back on Monday. But Mum's outside.' She looked up hopefully. 'Could we talk now, do you think?'

Marc's jaw tightened fractionally. If he had still been at McAuley, he could have had Marnie referred immediately by pushing a few buttons on his phone pad. But he wasn't, so he'd better get his act together and do the best he possibly could for his patient. But again caution prevailed.

'I could refer you to someone in Brisbane with more expertise in the field than I have, Marnie. How would you feel about that?'

'That would take ages, wouldn't it?' She interlocked her fingers and held them against her chest. 'Since I heard about all this, I haven't been sleeping well. Mum told me there was a new doctor in town so I gathered up my courage and made an appointment. I'm sure you can give me all the information I need.'

Marc smiled a bit grimly at the not-too-subtle pressure his patient was exerting. He sent her a level look. 'What are you studying at uni?'

She looked back innocently. 'Psychology.'

He gave a cracked laugh. 'It figures.' Picking up the

phone he said, 'Jen, would you ask Mrs Civetta to come through, please? And shoot off when you're ready. I'll be a while.'

Almost an hour later Ally heard movement outside in the corridor and Marc's voice, low, deep, a reassuring rumble, and guessed he was seeing Marnie and her mother out.

Automatically, she turned aside from her paperwork and got to her feet. He'd need to debrief or at least have someone to share a coffee with him before he went home.

She looked around at the little corner she'd made for herself in the smaller of the consulting rooms, tidied a few things away quickly and then made her way along to the kitchen.

'Ally, you're still here?' Marc poked his head in, his gaze widening in surprise. 'You didn't need to hang about.'

'I know.' She smiled a bit uncertainly. 'But I had some paperwork to finish anyway. And I thought you might like to wind down a bit. Huntington's can leave such a sad legacy…'

He shot her a curious look. 'You knew why Marnie was here?'

'I hope you don't mind.' Ally made a small face. 'Mrs Civetta asked me if she could have a quiet word. I think she needed to unload some of this stuff they're going through with Marnie. And I do know Bella Civetta quite well. She's actually the inspiration behind most of the fundraising efforts for the hospital. And oddly enough, I happen to have some personal knowledge of Huntington's. The father of one of my colleagues was diagnosed when we'd just started our training. It was pretty soul-destroying for the whole family.'

'I can imagine.' Marc's mouth straightened into a grim

line and he took the mug of coffee she handed him. 'Was your friend tested?'

Ally shook her head. 'She took the attitude to live day by day. Her dad died a couple of years ago and I believe Louise and her mum upped stakes and moved to New Zealand. So I don't know how it turned out. How old is Marnie now?' she asked, watching him pace to the window, peer out and then almost rearrange all the muscles in his face before he took a slow mouthful of his coffee.

'Twenty. It's a hell of a thing to have to tell someone just starting their adult life that there's no known cure and few medical treatments for the disease. And if she's found to be a carrier, she has to face up to progressive worsening mobility, to say nothing of the cognitive impairment.' He peered out into the gathering darkness again and shrugged. 'She seems a gutsy kid, though. And her mother will be a huge support from what I observed.'

'And it may never happen.'

'No.' He turned his head and smiled wryly at her. 'You're a lovely acquisition to this practice, Ally Inglis, do you know that?'

She laughed and twitched a shoulder modestly. 'How did you leave things with the Civettas?'

'I've given Marnie details of the Huntington's Association in Brisbane. She'll be back in the city for uni next week so I figured they'd be the best people initially for her to get the kind of support she'll need. And, of course, I'll refer her on, if that's what she ultimately decides she wants to do.'

'Right. That's enough for today. What do you say we get shot of this place, Doctor?' Briskly, Ally plucked the empty mug from his hands and rinsed it quickly with her own.

'See you tomorrow night,' Marc said from beside her as they made to part ways in the car park a few minutes later.

'Tomorrow night,' Ally echoed, and wondered why somehow the words had a magic sound.

In the soft early evening light, his eyes burned into hers and then he turned and with a brief wave strode across to his Jag.

'I got grilled barramundi and chips,' Rosie announced on her arrival at Ally's place that evening. 'You just home?'

Dressed in a comfortable tracksuit, Ally had a towel wrapped turban-like around her head. 'Mmm. Marc had a late consult.' Ally beckoned her friend inside. 'Fish and chips sounds wonderful. And I got the video and some wine.'

'Bliss,' Rosie sighed dramatically. 'My feet are killing me.'

'You weren't even at work,' Ally reminded her dryly.

Rosie grinned. 'Went over to Warwick, shopping for clothes, didn't I?'

'Damn you, Rosie,' Ally grumbled. 'You could have waited until tomorrow so I could've gone with you.' And could've bought something new and stunning for her date with Marc tomorrow night, she tacked on silently.

'I'm on a late tomorrow,' Rosie said blandly. 'Half a day is no use when you have to travel there and back, as we've found out before to our cost.'

'I could've done with something new,' Ally moaned, as they went through to the kitchen.

'Something special lined up?' Rosie prompted with interest, transferring their food into the warming oven. 'Or should I say *someone* special?'

Ally flushed. 'Marc asked me to dinner at Lavender Farm tomorrow night.'

'Oh, OK…' Rosie bit down on her bottom lip and looked thoughtful for a second. 'Well, I got some nice things so feel free to borrow something if you like.'

'No, it's fine. But thanks.' Ally made a small face. 'I'm just being precious. Now, give me a minute to comb my hair and I'll be right back.'

'Which wine?' Rosie called after her departing back.

'The Chardonnay. It's already opened.'

Rosie took far more time over pouring the wine than she needed to. But she needed to think. Should she say something or not? How serious was Ally about Marc?

And if she was serious, could she bear to hear that kind of stuff about him? Despite her perky front lately, Rosie guessed her friend was still rather fragile.

'You haven't said how the reunion went,' Ally said later that evening. Rosie had gone to Sydney the previous weekend for a nurses' reunion.

'Same old, same old.' Rosie threw tea bags into two mugs. 'There were only a few there from our graduating class.'

Ally twitched an eyebrow. 'No gossip?'

'Jane Saxelby's had twins.'

'And that's it?' Ally gave a disbelieving laugh.

Rosie's heartbeat escalated. 'I suppose there was one other thing…' Carefully, she poured boiling water into the mugs. 'Giselle Landros has moved to Newcastle. She's actually working at the McAuley.'

Ally's eyes widened in query. 'Marc's old hospital? Did she say if she knew him?'

'Well, they worked in different departments,' Rosie prevaricated. 'Marc worked in A and E and Giselle has always stuck to midwifery. But she'd run across him, of course, as you do…' Rosie fluttered a hand and gave a nervous laugh.

'Thanks.' Ally took the mug of tea, wrapping her hands around its warmth. 'What are you not telling me, Rosie?'

Rosie looked uncomfortable. 'Giselle was a bit gob-smacked to hear Marc was working here in Hillcrest.'

'And?' Ally's brow creased slightly.

'Apparently, before he left McAuley, there was a fair bit of gossip about him and one of the surgeons, Karla Costain. According to Giselle, they had a pretty hot affair.'

'That's nothing new among hospital staff,' Ally said dismissively. 'It's like any other workplace. Some people pair off and have relationships.'

'Of course they do. But it was the way this one ended that had the tongues going into meltdown. Apparently, Marc and his surgeon went from being inseparable to having a very public break-up in the hospital coffee shop.'

Ally felt slightly sick. She could imagine the almost ghoulish tangle of excitement the scene would have presented to the onlookers.

And she was no exception, she admitted with stark honesty, feeling, as she did, both fascinated and appalled. And wishing like mad she could put her hands over her ears and tell Rosie she didn't want to hear any more. Instead, she asked carefully, 'So what happened?'

'Apparently, Marc was pretty upset about something. There were raised voices and then Karla slapped him.' Rosie gave a tinny laugh. 'Um, I guess it would explain why he didn't want to hang around at McAuley any longer than he had to. I mean, it must have been pretty embarrassing.'

Ally pressed a hand to her forehead. 'So what's the message I'm supposed to be hearing from all this? That Marc engenders violence in women or something?'

'Nothing like that! Oh, sweetie.' Rosie's face softened.

'Just keep your head screwed on, that's all I'm saying. Marc could be on the rebound.'

Marc could be on the rebound.

The words stayed with Ally long after Rosie had gone. And when she woke next morning they were there again, like a niggling headache.

When it was time to get ready for her evening out, she ran a scented bath. But even soaking in the soothing, fragrant warmth didn't quieten her unease. Did she wish Rosie hadn't told her? She asked herself the question for the umpteenth time and stifled a sigh.

Why was it that when life was going relatively smoothly, problems jumped out of the shadows to obscure your way?

What to wear? She frowned a bit, her hands moving over the clothes in her wardrobe, stopping at her black evening trousers and a silk shirt in softest cream. As she got dressed, she realised some of her light-hearted anticipation for the evening had gone. Now the nerve ends in her stomach felt like so many fine wires all going in different directions.

She shouldn't be torturing herself like this.

Surely Marc's past relationships were his own business and she was crazy to let what she now knew colour her own attitude towards him?

She made a face in the mirror. Too much thinking was tying her brain in knots. And she felt as nervous as a cat on a high wire.

How was she going to hide it from Marc that she knew of his reasons for leaving McAuley? Would her manner give her away? How on earth could she act naturally around him until it was all out in the open?

But on the other hand she didn't want him thinking she'd been gossiping behind his back. Though in truth she had been, hadn't she? She could have stopped Rosie. *Should* have stopped Rosie.

She closed her eyes to try to make it all go away. Moments later, when the phone rang, she nearly jumped out of her skin. The residue of her muddled thinking made her voice crack, as she answered, 'H-hello?'

'Ally, it's Marc. You OK?'

'Ah…yes.' She felt her throat tighten. 'I'm quite ready. Did you want to come over early?'

'Can't, I'm afraid, Ally. That's why I'm calling. There's been a two-car pile-up on the main highway. I'm needed.'

'Oh, I see. Can I help?'

'No, it's fine,' he said quickly. 'Providentially, both ambulances are available. But perhaps you could call the restaurant, tell them we'll be a bit late.'

Automatically Ally touched the silver medallion at her throat, her gaze dropping to her new pointed-toe shoes. 'Yes, fine.' She firmed up her voice. 'I'll do that. I hope it's not too bad when you get there.'

He made a sound between a grunt and a cynical laugh. 'I'll keep you posted.'

Almost two hours later, Ally had had no phone call from Marc and feared the MVA had been a bad one. The facilities at their small hospital would not be able to cope with a multi-trauma so Marc would have had to send the injured across to the regional hospital at Warwick. Perhaps he'd had to go with the ambulance himself.

Deciding their plans for the evening had been well and truly aborted, Ally went back to her bedroom, emerging a few minutes later in comfortable jeans and a thick, baggy sweatshirt.

She'd wait for Marc. She was certain he'd come to her eventually. No matter how late.

The intensity of her feelings, combined with a feeling of restlessness, drove her out onto the verandah. She stood at the railings, gazing out towards the mountains with a sense of misgiving. A streak of lightning was snaking across the night sky, the wind bending the trees, swirling their foliage into a mad dance in the wake of its rushing passage.

Ally drew in a sharp breath, a wave of unease causing her to clench her fingers. That was all they needed—one of Hillcrest's wild winter storms. And the first thing to go would be the electricity.

She crossed her arms, rubbing at her upper arms. She'd better prepare for the worst and start locating candles and torches. There was something decidedly eerie about fumbling your way around in pitch-darkness.

Barely thirty minutes later the storm hit with ferocious intensity. More disturbed than she cared to admit, Ally wandered aimlessly from room to room, stopping at random to check the windows were firmly closed against the driving rain. And then doing another round and checking them all over again.

Although she'd been expecting it, she jumped when the lights flickered and went out. Tamping down her unease, she groped her way back to the kitchen, grasping the lantern torch from where she'd positioned it earlier on the end of the counter top. Convulsively her fingers wrapped around the handle. She switched it on, spraying the walls with comforting light.

Taking a shallow breath, she reached for her portable radio, hoping for an update on the storm's progress, but the static made it impossible to get any reception. Ally felt her stomach heave.

She'd never felt so lonely in her life. And scared. With the power gone, her landline telephone would be dead. She exhaled tightly through her teeth, touching the back pocket of her jeans, reassured to feel the outline of her mobile through the tough denim.

When it rang only seconds later it took her a moment to comprehend. With hands that shook she fumbled it out of her pocket, activating it and putting it to her ear. 'Hello?'

'Thank God, you're all right!'

'Marc?' Ally's mouth trembled. 'Where are you?'

'I'm at the retirement home. Can you get over here? The roof's gone. We need all hands to get the residents out.'

CHAPTER NINE

ALLY wasted no time in speculation.

Fuelled with a new energy, she methodically changed her footwear, discarding her loafers for a pair of sturdy boots with thick rubber soles, figuring she wouldn't be much use in a rescue situation if her feet were slipping all over the place.

On her way to the front door, she plucked a rain slicker off the peg rail and tugged it on, pulling the hood up over her head. She let out a huge breath. So far so good. She tapped the pockets of her jeans, withdrawing her car keys, relieved that earlier, before the lights had gone out, she'd had the foresight to tuck them into her pocket.

In a few seconds she was out of the house armed with her lantern torch and running through the blinding rain to the garage.

The retirement complex was on the outskirts of the town. Ally knew its history. Long ago, someone with money had donated the rambling old home and several acres to the council with the proviso that it be used to house the senior citizens of Hillcrest when they felt the need to relocate to a more sheltered lifestyle.

Over time a group of self-contained units had been built on the grounds and the old home itself had become a kind of community centre.

Suddenly Ally felt sickening dread in her stomach as she realised that at ten o'clock on a Saturday night, that was where most, if not all, of the elderly folk would be gathered. If not for company during the storm, then for one of the many social activities that happened there on a regular basis. Oh, lord. She bit her lips together. They could be looking at broken limbs and heaven knew what else...

But as in all rural communities, there was a plan for situations like this. The state emergency service would, no doubt, have been called. And their volunteers had the kind of practical skills that would quickly bring a semblance of order to the possible chaos.

The thought brought a sliver of reassurance to Ally as she parked her car behind others whose owners had obviously already arrived to help.

Swinging out of her car, she locked it and pocketed her keys. Then, bracing herself and conscious there could be downed electrical wires, she made her way carefully across the lawn and into the house.

To Ally's relief, the SES people were already on the scene, their bright orange overalls lending a sense of security. Emergency lighting was being put in place and several of the men were organising tarpaulins to keep out the rain.

For a second Ally hovered uncertainly. 'Ally! Over here!'

It was Marc.

In a few strides Ally was at his side. 'What've we got?'

'A bloody nightmare.' Marc's brows jumped together in sudden irritation. 'Apparently the back-up generator didn't kick in.'

Ally's hand went to her heart. 'What about the one at the hospital?'

'It's fine, thank heavens. They've sent over trauma kits and what staff they could spare.'

'What are we doing about triage?' Ally hunkered down beside the elderly lady Marc was tending.

'It's a bit difficult. The night manager is still trying to

account for everyone who was here. Hopefully, most of them are uninjured, except for Beryl here who was hit by a flying piece of debris.'

'Where are the others now?' Ally asked practically.

'Di and Brooke have escorted them over to the hospital. We can accommodate them there for tonight. And at least they can get dry and have a hot drink.'

'Why on earth didn't you call me earlier?' Ally asked, *sotto voce*, placing steri-strips over the cut on the elderly woman's temple.

Marc's jaw tightened. 'I only just arrived back from Warwick myself.'

Immediately Ally noticed his eyes were shadowed and faintly strained. Oh, lord, the MVA. Ally gave a silent grimace at her thoughtless remark. It must have been terrible if he'd had to go with the ambulance. 'Just stay still for me, please, Beryl.' She addressed the elderly woman gently. Then turned to Marc. 'This'll need stitching.'

'I'll fix it later at the hospital. Put a pressure bandage on it, please. And check her vitals.' He hitched up his medical case. 'I'd better see where else I'm needed.'

Marc didn't have to go far. Kyle Matthews, one of the SES volunteers, hurried towards him. 'We've just located an old guy trapped underneath a beam, Doc. It's a hell of a mess. Think you need to take a look at him.'

'Where is he?' Marc went with Kyle, nimbly sidestepping a ladder and dodging another tarpaulin that was being swung into place.

'There's a bit of a library in one of the back rooms,' Kyle said. 'Apparently, he'd taken himself off in there instead of playing cards like the other folk. Bit of a loner from all accounts.'

Marc shook his head. It seemed no one was free from scrutiny in a country town. He guessed he hadn't missed out either, and wondered thinly what the residents of Hillcrest had managed to put together about *him*. 'Do we have a name, Kyle?'

'Tom Cobley.'

'You're kidding me!'

Kyle shone his powerful torch into the room. 'Old sailor, apparently.'

'Hell's bells,' Marc said softly, his eyes reacting like a laser beam as they assessed the degree of possible injury to the elderly man. He turned sharply to Kyle. 'What's the score about getting this great lump of timber lifted?'

'A couple of the guys have gone for a trolley jack. They're trying the garage first.'

Marc frowned. 'How long will that take?'

'Hard to say, Doc. They'll have to knock the owner up first.'

Marc swore under his breath. 'Don't you have anything among your own gear?'

Kyle lifted a shoulder. 'Nothing big enough.'

Marc swiped a hand through his hair in a gesture of frustration. 'OK...but see what you can do to speed things up, will you?'

'Sure thing, Doc. Uh...' Kyle's eyes brightened. 'We thought you'd like to know we've found a room with the roof still intact.'

'Well, that's an unexpected bonus, I guess. Organise a few stretchers, mate. We'll use it as a casualty bay.'

Marc took a deep breath and began picking his way amongst the debris, finally squatting close to where the injured man lay. 'I'm Marc Ballantyne, Tom. I'm a doctor. We'll have you out of here pretty soon. Can you tell me where it hurts?'

'Every-bloomin-where...' Tom's voice was thin with strain. 'I think me leg's a goner, Doc.'

Marc shot upright. 'We can't wait on this, Kyle. He needs pain relief and I'll have to get it to him somehow. Could you locate Ally Inglis? I want her here.'

'Oh, Mavis!' Ally had never been so pleased to see anyone in her life.

'Just came to see what I could do to help.' Mavis bustled over.

'Do you have your car?' Ally asked.

'Outside. What do you need me to do, love?'

Ally looked down at her patient. 'I'd like to get Beryl here over to the hospital.'

'Walking wounded, eh?' Mavis observed practically. 'No worries. I managed to nip into a parking space practically outside the front door. And I've brought my beach brolly. That'll keep the rain off.'

'You're a gem.' Ally's look was grateful as she wrapped the blanket more securely around Beryl's thin shoulders.

'Jason's on deck in the hospital kitchen,' Mavis said chattily. 'And the Meals on Wheels folk are mobilised as well. There should be food and hot drinks over here directly.'

Ally smiled weakly. The generosity of these country folk never failed to move her. And amaze her... She felt a tap on her shoulder and turned sharply. 'Kyle—what's up?'

'Doc wants you, Ally.' Kyle took in the situation at a glance. 'I'll give Mavis a hand if you like.'

'That would be a great help.' Ally relinquished her guiding hand on Beryl's shoulder. 'Where is Marc exactly?'

'Library—long room at the back.' Kyle gestured with his thumb. 'Do you know where to go?'

'Yes.' Ally leapt away. She'd been in and out of the place countless times in her role of co-ordinator of the seniors' keep-fit programme. Collecting one of the trauma kits, she made her way carefully to the rear of the building.

A tarpaulin had been used to erect an odd kind of teepee over the injured man. Ally popped her head into the cave-like space. 'It's me,' she said quietly.

'Ally.' Marc's head was bent over his patient. 'I need your expertise here.' In an aside, he began to explain the situation. 'Obviously, I can't examine Tom properly until the beam is lifted and no one seems to know when that will be. But more than likely we're looking at a compound fracture of the leg.'

'So pain relief is a priority?'

Marc nodded. 'I'd like to get the jab in his thigh but the way the beam has fallen, I can't get to him. My hands are too big for the limited space.'

'So you want me to try.' Ally caught on quickly.

Marc began drawing up the dose of morphine. 'His competency seems OK so we're in no danger of destabilising him with the drug. But there'll be no room for error, Ally,' he warned. 'And the last thing you need is a needle-stick injury.'

Ally steeled herself. 'I'll be careful.' She edged closer and squeezed the old man's hand. 'Hang in there, Mr Cobley. Help is coming to get you out but meanwhile we'll give you something for the pain, all right?'

'Ta, darlin'...' Two lone tears creased down his weather-beaten cheeks.

Poor old man. Ally held back her own distress. 'I'm going to make a slit in your trousers, Tom. That will help to relieve the pressure on your leg. I'll be as gentle as I can.'

With Marc shining powerful torchlight on the area where she needed to work, Ally went ahead, her face set in concentration as she slid her hands under the beam, doing everything in slow motion. Every movement painstakingly and carefully orchestrated.

Grasping the small scissors, she made one long slicing cut in the fine woollen fabric of Tom's trousers to expose the pale skin of his thigh. Swabbing the site took barely seconds and finally she was able to shoot home the injection.

'Good work.' Marc's breath came out in a relieved gush, and he rested a hand on Ally's shoulder and squeezed. 'Now, let's get a drip in and alert the CareFlight chopper.'

'You'll send Tom to Brisbane?' Ally disposed of the spent needle in the sharps container.

In a weary gesture Marc rubbed a hand around the back of his neck. 'There's no doubt he's in for a pin-and-plate job. And Warwick's overloaded. I had to send four casualties from the MVA over there. The Royal Brisbane is our best bet for Tom.'

Ally sighed. 'He's going to be a long way from home, then. And he doesn't have any family to speak of.'

'We'll get him back as soon as it's feasible, Ally.' Marc's voice held an edge of irritation. 'If the funding allows it, we can keep him here in one of our high-dependency beds until he's well and truly on his feet again.'

Ally gave a dispirited little huff. 'Seems to me patient care should be about *more* than the availability or otherwise of *beds*.'

Marc's mouth compressed briefly. 'I'm not a member of the government neither do I run the health department.'

So, in other words, she should take her concerns elsewhere. Ally curled her mouth into a cynical little moue. And thought, What a very inappropriate time and place to be having this discussion.

She looked at Marc uncertainly. He seemed jaded and fed up. And who could blame him? she thought fairly. In his role of the town's only doctor, the past few hours would have seemed like the stuff of nightmares. 'Do you want me to stay with Tom?'

In the half-light, Marc stared at her broodingly. He felt frustrated beyond belief, grumpy and out of sync. And there was little comfort in telling himself that earlier today he'd more than likely saved a young person's life.

He certainly hadn't expected his evening to have been turned on its head like this. Not after he'd spent most of the day pleasuring his senses, imagining a long, intimate evening with Ally…

He gave a silent click of disgust at his self-indulgence. He was the town's medical officer and he had a job to do.

'Marc?' Ally frowned at the curiously arrested expression on his face.

'Ah…no.' His mouth drew into a quick straight line. 'Let's see if one of the ambulance crew can take over here. I need you with me. Somehow I don't think we've seen the last of the injuries yet.'

Marc was right. One of the residents had missed her footing in the semi-darkness and tumbled down the steps. She was severely shocked and had to be treated for a suspected broken ankle. And Francine Carmody, the night manager, had herself sustained an injury by trying to catch the same, rather heavily built resident in an effort to curb her fall.

'It's a dislocated shoulder,' she said resignedly, her teeth clamped with pain.

'I believe you.' Marc looked up swiftly from his examination. 'But let's get you across to the hospital. I need to make sure you haven't done any more damage.'

Fran rolled her eyes. 'Trust me, Doctor. That's all it is. I play netball. I've probably had more dislocated shoulders than you've had hot dinners. Tell him, Ally.'

'She's right.' Ally's mouth tucked in on a grim smile. 'Ask any of the nurses. We're all highly skilled at popping Fran's shoulder back in.'

'Well, all right.' Marc frowned heavily. 'I can see I'm being railroaded here. But I'm not letting you get away without a pain-killer first.'

'Oh, please! Just do it! I'll cope.'

'Famous last words,' Marc muttered, motioning Ally to the head of the stretcher.

They worked instinctively, Ally steadying the injured woman while Marc repositioned her shoulder. On a signal from Marc, Ally nodded and braced herself for Fran's yell as the limb clicked back into place.

'That's it,' Marc said briskly. 'Now, I'll leave you something for the pain.'

'Don't trouble.' Fran waved away his concern. 'I've analgesics on hand.' She struggled to sit up and then sank back.

Ally noticed her sudden pallor. 'Are you all right, Fran?'

'Seems not.' Fran's tone held a muted resignation. 'Just give me something for the pain, would you, please? It looks like it will be a long night.'

'You can't possibly be intending to stay on duty?' Ally remonstrated.

'Try and stop me.' Fran swallowed the pain-killers with several gulps of water. 'They're my people, my responsibility.'

Marc growled, 'Alternatively, we could arrange for an ambulance to take you home.'

Fran's chin came up in a jutting little gesture. 'Don't fuss, Doc. I'm a tough cookie. Even if I can't do much physically, at least I can give the orders and see they're carried out.'

'Then I'll save my breath.' Marc clamped his bag shut with a gesture of resignation.

'Uh, could I have a word?' Kyle poked his head into the circle of light. 'The guys are ready to lift the beam off Tom.'

Marc let out a relieved breath. 'Good, we'll be right there.'

Kyle looked across at the night manager. 'We still can't account for one of the residents, Ms Carmody—old Hans Van Duin.'

Fran clicked her tongue. 'My residents are not *old* anything, Kyle Matthews,' she rebuked. 'They're senior citizens to you.'

'Sorry.' Kyle's face was on fire. 'Then I'd like to report that Mr Van Duin is missing,' he said formally.

'He's away for the weekend.' It was Fran's turn to look embarrassed. 'My apologies—I should've told someone.'

'No worries.' Kyle spread his hands in a forgiving shrug. 'I'll let the guys know. So, that's everyone accounted for, I reckon.'

'Terrific.' Marc clapped a hand across Kyle's shoulders. 'What's the news on the chopper, mate?'

'Lucky for us, the base was able to divert one from Toowoomba. It's on its way.'

The rain had stopped, Ally thought thankfully and the tarpaulin had been moved away, allowing easier access to the injured Tom. 'How will they go about this?' She turned a questioning look at Kyle. Suddenly the place was buzzing with purpose.

'We'll stack these concrete blocks and use them as temporary walls,' Kyle enlightened her. 'Once the beam is lifted, we can rest it on the blocks and get the trolley jack out of the way so you and the doc will be able to get to Tom.'

'Ingenious. What on earth would we do without you guys?'

'We train all the time for emergencies like this.' Kyle shrugged away Ally's praise. 'There she goes now!' He leant forward eagerly as the men began to pump the jack and the heavy beam began its slow journey upwards.

At last they were free to work on Tom.

'Poor old chap didn't need this.' Pete Delgado, the ambulance officer, moved aside to allow Marc access.

'No.' Marc's face was set in grim lines. 'Are you still with us, Tom?'

The elderly patient's voice was barely a thread of sound but at least he'd comprehended.

Marc glanced at Ally. 'Drip holding?'

'So far so good. He'll need another bag of fluid before we put him on the chopper.'

'I'll top up his pain-killer as well. Go easy while we splint, please. He's had enough.'

The scudding rain clouds had cleared the sky, leaving the night as clear as a bell. Ally made the observation as they stood tracking the blinking lights of the departing chopper across the pale sky.

Tom was at last on his way.

'I'll nip back to the hospital now, see what else needs to be done.' Marc's voice had an edge of weariness. He turned his head sharply in Ally's direction. 'Coming?'

'Part of my job, I would have thought.' They walked back to where they'd left their cars. 'Have you had anything to eat?'

'Cup of tea and a quick sandwich before I left Warwick. I was hurrying home to take you out, wasn't I?'

Ally swallowed the sudden dryness in her throat. 'Well, I guess there'll be other times in future.'

'As long as you haven't gone off me by then,' he muttered, flicking the remote to open his car. 'See you over there.'

Ally unzipped her rain slicker and threw it into the boot of her car. She gave a fractured little sigh and heard her tummy rumble. What a barrel of laughs the evening had turned out to be! she thought.

Marc was obviously frustrated and out of sorts and there was probably a list a mile long waiting for him at the hospital.

But sometimes life sends us a pleasant surprise, she was to think later. When they got to the nurses' station, a beaming Rosie met them.

'Shaun O'Connor's come across from Wattle Flats,' she said. 'He's worked his way through most of the casualty list and delivered Tara Petani's baby. I think you can take the rest of the evening off, Dr Ballantyne. Things are under control.'

Marc looked startled. '*Dr* O'Connor?'

Rosie smirked. 'That's what I said.' She threw a speaking look at them. 'I must say, you look like a couple of refugees. For heaven's sake, run along to the kitchen, both of you,' she clucked. 'Jason has left lashings of hot food for the workers.'

'Looks like the gods have kicked in on our side at last.' Marc raised a dark brow in Ally's direction. 'I know it's not Lavender Farm, but we could still have our dinner together...'

Ally's heart gave a sideways skip and she gave an off-key little laugh. 'Yes, I suppose we could.'

'But first I'd better go and make our Good Samaritan's acquaintance.' Marc worked his shoulders as if to slough off fatigue. 'Then I'm going to hit the shower. See you in a bit.'

'I'd kill for a shower myself.' Ally looked ruefully at her mud-stained jeans. 'But I don't have any spare clothes here any more.'

'I do, though,' Rosie said. 'Just track pants and my brother's old football jersey. But at least they're clean.' Her eyes lit with humour. 'Probably not what you were intending to wear out to dinner.'

Ally wrinkled her nose, pulling her damp sweatshirt away from her chest. 'Sounds like high fashion to me. Thanks, Rosie. You're a star.'

'He's a real babe, Al.' Rosie leaned forward confidentially.

'Mmm, I know.' Ally turned from watching Marc disappear down the corridor to the wards.

'Not *him*, dopey! I meant Shaun O'Connor!' Rosie's gaze had a far-away look. 'He's tall and tanned. Nice crinkly smile. And he's not married and he's not gay.'

'You asked him *that*?' Ally squeaked, the words strangled in her throat.

'Hey, I was subtle.'

Ally couldn't help it. Her soft laugh rippled. 'You wouldn't recognise *subtle* if it sat up and bit you. But I'm grateful for everyone's sake Dr O'Connor came to help out. It must be over a hundred k's from Wattle Flats.'

Rosie lifted a shoulder dismissively. 'Piece of cake, Shaun said. He'd heard a newsflash on the radio about our troubles and shot across. He's got one of those state-of-the-art Land Cruisers,' she added chattily.

'Nice.' Ally blocked a yawn. 'Now, if you'll excuse me, I'm off to the shower.' She sent back a fluttered wave. 'Have fun with the visiting heartthrob.'

Hospital food had never smelt so good, Ally decided, looking around the big old-fashioned kitchen. Moving across to the Aga, she lifted the lid on a huge pot of soup Jason had provided. And then discovered there were a stack of mini-pizzas in the warming oven and a tray of thick beef and pickle sandwiches that would stave off anyone's hunger.

'Fabulous food.' She looked up with a grin as Marc joined her in the kitchen seconds later. Her eyes widened in query. He was dressed in jeans and a white bulky jumper.

'Old A and E trick.' His face softened and he smiled. 'Always keep a spare set of clothes at the office.'

'I'm wearing Rosie's hand-me-downs.' Ally was smiling broadly.

Several expressions chased through his eyes and then he looked away. 'Is that soup I can smell?'

'Mmm.' Ally got down bowls from the shelf. 'Looks like a chunky vegetable.'

They ate their food mostly in silence. Probably because they were starving, Ally supposed. Or was it that suddenly out of nowhere they felt uneasy with one another?

'So, did you meet Shaun?' she asked, pouring them each a mug of coffee from one of the thermos flasks Jason had prepared.

Marc nodded. 'Seems a nice guy, pretty clued in. Still finding his feet in Wattle Flats, of course.'

'Same as you, then.'

'Not quite. He's bought the practice over there.'

'Oh.' Ally felt her nerves tighten. 'But you'd have a lot in common surely?'

'As in trying to understand life in a rural community?' Marc met her question with one of his own.

'I meant more that you're both sole practitioners,' Ally clarified.

He sent her a dry smile. 'I know what you meant, Ally. Just don't try so hard, hmm?'

Ally felt put in her place. What did he mean? Don't try

to make him *like* being in rural medicine? Or perhaps don't try to convince him to stay in Hillcrest? 'I wasn't aware I was doing that,' she replied stiffly.

There was a beat of silence and then Marc drew in a ragged sigh and said slowly, 'Sorry. Rough day. I didn't mean to take my frustration out on you.'

'Forget it.' Ally gave an over-bright smile. 'Let's just enjoy our coffee, shall we?'

'Then I'll see you safely home.'

Ally's heart swooped like a drunken butterfly. 'You don't have to do that.'

'The power is still out,' he came back practically. 'I want to check everything's in order.'

'Oh, OK. Thank you.'

CHAPTER TEN

'OH, HELP!' Ally exclaimed, as they fumbled their way in through her front door. 'This stupid torch has almost given up.'

Marc kicked the door shut. 'Do you have some new batteries for it?'

'Don't think so. But I've candles. I left them just here on the mantelpiece. And matches beside them.'

'Good. Let's get some light in here.'

She watched as he struck a match and lit several of the tall church candles.

'I'll just do a quick check and make sure no water has come in.' Marc lifted one of the candles, cupping his hand around the flame. He was back in a few minutes. 'Seems very snug.' He put the candle back on the mantelpiece and glanced at his watch. 'It's late. I suppose I'd better make tracks…'

Ally steadied her breathing with difficulty. Her senses were whirling. Without stopping to think of the consequences, she said, 'You don't have to go, Marc.'

He blinked uncertainly. 'Do you know what you're saying, Ally?'

Probably for the first time in a long time.

'It's been an awful few hours,' she said softly. 'Longer for you. And it's no fun going home to a cold, dark flat.'

'So you're just being kind to me?' His eyes narrowed slightly as he stared at her, having noticed her tiny nervous swallow as he'd voiced his question.

'There's plenty of dry wood,' she waffled. 'We could make a fire. Relax over a glass of wine, perhaps...?'

He hesitated then nodded. 'OK. I'll get a fire going and you find the wine. Deal?'

She lowered her gaze, at the same time feeling her skin heat up and tingle. 'Deal.'

What the hell was he doing? The knot tightened in Marc's stomach as he hunkered down beside the hearth and set about getting a fire started.

What on earth was she doing? Ally shivered, not from cold so much as the implication of what she'd set in motion. It was as though the curtain had risen, the scene was set and the actors were about to take up their positions on stage.

In her haste she spilled wine on the counter top and hurriedly began mopping it up, jumping when Marc poked his head around the door.

'Everything OK?'

'Fine.' She gave a cracked laugh. 'Just wish I had more light to work with.'

'Here, I'll help you with that.' He pulled off a length of paper towel and finished mopping up the spill. 'Now I'll go ahead with the candle. Can you manage the wine?'

'Without spilling it, you mean?' she asked, striving desperately to lighten the atmosphere.

'Something like that.' Marc caught up the bottle of wine and took it with him. 'In case we need a top-up,' he explained. 'I think we've earned it after the kind of day we've had.'

They sat side by side on the sofa.

'Shame we can't have any music.' Ally had kicked off her shoes and now held her feet out towards the fire.

'We could always hum.'

'Oh, please.'

He chuckled. 'Talk to me instead, then.' It seemed the most natural thing in the world when Marc reached out and drew her in against him. 'Comfy?' he murmured solicitously.

'Very,' she replied. And she was—deliciously so, with his arm around her, her head tucked in against his chest. And they sat on in a silence that was companionable yet filled with an odd kind of tension.

After a while Marc remarked quietly, 'I notice you're not wearing your wedding ring these days.'

'I threw it in the river.'

'Pardon?' He swivelled his gaze to stare at her. He watched her withdraw, pulling herself in tighter, and then she dragged in a shaky breath and looked down into her glass.

'My marriage was a farce,' she said quietly. 'Every time I looked at his ring on my finger, I thought of Simon and of all the bad stuff. It was Anne's idea, really—to get rid of the ring, I mean. She knew I was still crippled with guilt after Simon died.' She stopped.

'Do you want to talk about it, Ally?'

'If you want to listen.'

He hugged her warmly. 'Of course I'll listen.'

She began hesitantly, 'Simon was an anaesthetist at St Vincent's. He was ten years older than me, very good-looking, and I was dazzled, I suppose. We had a whirlwind kind of courtship and then we got married.' She gave a tragic little laugh. 'I don't know why he bothered, really. He certainly had no intention of staying faithful.'

Marc could hear the breath escaping from his lips. He had prepared himself for something like this but nevertheless her words rattled in his ears. He said carefully, 'He obviously took advantage of your relative youth and vulnerability.'

'And naïvety!' Ally gave a huff of self-derision. 'I had no idea. I should have known—shouldn't I?'

'Why should you?' Marc asked sharply. 'In my book, if you marry someone, you should be able to trust them, otherwise what kind of relationship do you have?'

'Not much of one.' She broke off and took a mouthful of her wine.

Marc looked at her, his eyes full of compassion. 'You really don't have to tell me any of this, Ally. If it's too painful...'

She shook her head. 'It's better if I do.'

'All right.' He smudged a kiss across her temple.

She took a steadying breath and continued, 'We'd been married barely a year when I found out he'd been unfaithful. I had proof and he couldn't refute it. He was contrite and said it had been an aberration on his part.'

'And you believed him.'

'For the sake of our marriage.' Ally gave a bitter laugh. 'Of course I believed him.'

Listening to her, Marc felt a leaden weight in his stomach at what she'd had to deal with. Then he asked gently, 'How did he die?'

'Car crash on the way to the airport,' Ally said unemotionally. 'He was on his way to a conference in Perth. I'd thought it might be a chance for us to have some quality time together and suggested I go with him but he said I'd be bored rigid.'

I'll just bet he did, Marc fumed silently, holding her more closely as if to absorb some of her pain, and guessing what was to come.

'The ambulance reported there were two casualties from the same car. As luck would have it, I was on duty in A and E, when they were brought in—Simon, and the woman he'd invited to go to Perth with him.'

'Oh, lord! You must have been gutted.'

Her shoulders lifted in a huge sigh. 'It was awful. Simon and his *friend* were rushed into Resus. Needless to say, I wasn't allowed anywhere near them. In the middle of it all Simon's parents arrived and his mother took me to task, insisting if I'd been a better wife, her precious son wouldn't have felt the need to stray…'

'Oh, Ally, Ally. I don't know what to say.'

'Don't say anything,' she whispered. 'Just hold me.'

Ally wasn't sure when the wordless comfort changed or even if it did. Perhaps it just grew and took on a life of its own, encompassing all their emotions.

She shivered when Marc's hands began to smooth her back and shoulders until in the end his fingers were bracketing her head and his hands were holding her with infinite gentleness while he kissed her tenderly, all passion reined in.

She made a little sound in her throat and moved against him and let it happen. His kiss deepened and she loved it, opening her mouth under his, wanting more and more.

Suddenly, out of nowhere, she felt an enormous sense of freedom. Wild, too, in a way she'd never let herself feel before. And when he ground out, 'You're beautiful, Ally,' she felt so *physical*, so alive.

Marc felt the shudder that ran through her. She arched up with a little cry and he told himself to take it slowly, but he couldn't hold back. The soft waistband of her track pants came away to allow him the access he craved. With the utmost gentleness he traced the bowl of her pelvis and lower… Oh, yes…so feminine, so much a woman…

'Touch me, Ally,' he breathed throatily. 'Touch me,' he repeated, and with a trembling hand she reached out, sliding her fingers under his jumper to his bare skin to stroke along his belly and dip into the shallow nook of his navel.

Her heart gave a wild skip as the press stud on his jeans came away and her fingertips were free to roam, to mesh in the soft swirl of hair, so much a part of his maleness.

Suddenly Marc made a gravelly sound of protest, jamming his hand over hers to stop its movement. 'We can't do this here,' he muttered hoarsely. 'Come to bed with me, Ally—if that's what you want, too?'

It was.

At her affirmation, Marc scooped her up and then lowered her to her feet and for a long time they stood entwined, lost in the essence of each other, in the shape and feel of each other's bodies.

There was a charge like an electric current between them and Ally wanted to pull off her clothes. And his. And wrap herself around him, claim him all over, feel his heat. *Love* him and never let him go.

Suddenly it was urgent. This need to be together.

Marc picked up the candle and they made their way to the bedroom.

Their clothes fell away.

'Ah…forgot this.' Marc hooked up his jeans with his foot and slipped something from the back pocket.

Ally felt herself trembling, crossing her arms tightly across her rib cage. A tiny jagged laugh left her mouth. 'Another old A and E trick?'

For answer, he traced the tip of his finger over her lips, along her jaw, down her throat and between her breasts, cupping her so lightly that his touch felt like the brush of a butterfly's wing.

'I'd never want to leave you hurt, Ally—in any way.'

They barely made it to the bed and were both far too needy to take it slowly.

Their lovemaking was wild. An explosion of the senses,

a fever of hands and mouths that caught them up in a storm of sensation urging them on, until there was no going back.

Ally arched under her lover, trying to draw him even deeper, wrapping her legs around him. When his final thrust touched her soul, she convulsed around him, whirlpools of sensation dragging her under and then tossing her higher than the highest star.

Ally woke to find the room suffused with early morning light. At once memories of their lovemaking flooded her mind and she reached out to touch him. But he wasn't there.

'Marc?'

'I'm here.' He ambled into the bedroom and parked himself on the side of the bed next to her.

'Hi.' She saw at once he was dressed and reached up to touch his hair, finding it slightly damp. 'Have you had a shower?'

'Mmm. I was looking for something to leave you a note.' He took her hand and raised it to his mouth, trailing several kisses over her knuckles. 'The power's back on.'

'Oh, good.' Struggling upright, she dragged the sheet up to her chin. 'Do you have time for a coffee?'

'Probably not. I'd better make an appearance at the hospital, check over the walking wounded from last night. I'll call the Royal and check on Tom as well.'

'Last night seems like a dream now, doesn't it?'

He huffed a dry laugh. 'Or a nightmare.' He saw her uncertain look and added quickly, 'Oh, not what we shared, Ally.'

She flushed. 'I feel as though I've been turned inside out.'

'That makes two of us,' he said softly, and knuckled her cheek.

She placed her hand over his, trapping it there. Where

did they go from here? she wondered. But obviously now was not the time to pursue it. 'Did you find the spare toothbrush?' she asked instead, cringing inwardly at the mundane quality of her conversation.

'Yes, I did. Thanks. Ally, I should get moving.' He gently reclaimed his hand.

A frown touched her eyes. 'Perhaps I should go in, too.'

'Let me see how things are first. If the units at the retirement village are undamaged, the residents will be able to go home.'

'I could help co-ordinate that, couldn't I?'

'Possibly. Why don't I call you from the hospital?' He reached out to touch her hair, curving his hand so that his thumb brushed along the side of her face. 'Meanwhile, what about easing yourself into the day? Have a leisurely breakfast.'

A breakfast they should have been sharing together. Her mouth drooped for a moment and then she nodded. 'OK.'

Sensing her disappointment, Marc said softly, 'There'll be other times for us, Ally.' He hesitated for a moment, as if wanting to add something, but then said nothing, instead bending his head to kiss her with lingering tenderness. 'You're so special,' he murmured, before he pulled himself upright and left quietly.

Ally heard the sound of his engine as it started and then the Jag's soft purr as he pulled off. Sighing, she leaned back against the pillows. He had made love to her as if he really cared, not as if he'd just been slaking his own needs. He had put her pleasure first—something she'd never experienced before.

Tears filled her eyes and for the first time she realised just what she had opened herself up to.

Was she in love with him? She bit her lips together. The thought was too scary to give voice to. And would he say it back? Possibly not. Probably not. There was so much still unanswered.

And she hadn't yet asked him about Karla.

Ally gave her head a little shake as if to clear her mind. There was no sense in pre-empting the future. A bit stiffly, her body exhausted by emotion, she climbed out of bed and threw herself under the shower.

In the hospital kitchen, Marc wolfed down several pieces of toast and hurriedly drank his mug of tea. Damn the storm and all the extra workload it had left in its wake.

He hadn't wanted to run out on Ally like that. If only he'd woken earlier…

Now she was probably full of indecision. He frowned down at the residue of tea in his mug. Of course she would be. Hell, he hadn't had time to marshal his *own* thoughts. But being with Ally had been wonderful. And they'd been so in tune…

'Ah, here you are, Doctor!' Brooke popped her head in and queried cheerfully, 'Ready to do a ward round?'

There'd been no phone call from Marc but Ally decided to go across to the hospital anyway. She found an organised kind of chaos. 'What's there for me to do?' she asked Rosie, who'd come back on duty at seven.

'Well, we've a full complement of nurses and Marc came in earlier, so we're covered here. But we do need a responsible body to get the old folk back to their homes.' Rosie gave her a hopeful grin.

'Actually, that's where I thought I might be useful,' Ally agreed. 'I take it their units are safe?'

'Basically untouched apparently. The SES guys are busy securing tarps over the roof of the centre—or should I say where the roof used to be. And the insurance assessor will be here first thing tomorrow.'

'So we'll be back in business before we know it. Have the seniors had breakfast?'

'Lord, yes.' Rosie rolled her eyes. 'Apparently, they were rattling round the kitchen at five o'clock this morning.'

Ally chuckled. 'Old habits die hard. Getting up early is something to do with rural folklore, I believe. What about you?' She raised a brow. 'Did you manage any sleep?'

'Enough. What about you?'

Ally willed herself not to blush and flapped a hand. 'As you say—enough.'

'Marc was in pretty early.'

'So you said.'

'I noticed he was dressed in the same clothes he had on after the storm.'

'Is that significant?'

'Dunno.' Rosie screwed up her face in speculation. 'Just wondered if he made it home at all last night.'

'Why don't you ask him?' Ally deadpanned, her stomach beginning to churn.

'Yeah, right.' Rosie clicked her tongue to show what she thought of that suggestion.

'So, how are the seniors getting home?' Ally deflected, looking warily over her shoulder as she heard footsteps approaching and breathing a sigh of relief when she saw it wasn't Marc.

'Dave Berry has offered the use of the school bus,' Rosie said. 'And he'll drive, of course.'

'Great, I'll start getting folk organised.' Ally turned away with something like relief. Rosie was like a terrier with a bone when she wanted to find out something. 'But first I'll just see if Marc's had any word about Tom Cobley.'

'I saw him heading into Sister's office a couple of

minutes ago,' Rosie offered. 'You'll probably find him there.'

Ally's heart was revving like mad when she tapped on the office door and popped her head in. She blinked uncertainly. Marc was parked on the corner of the desk and, by the sound of it, just finishing his call.

He looked over his shoulder and their eyes locked.

'Hi,' he mouthed. He waved her in and she went and stood by the window, looking out at the startling blue sky and the tiny drifts of clouds that sat like fairy floss along the tops of the mountains. It all looked so serene, she thought, so normal that last night's storm might never have happened.

'Ally.' Marc put the phone down. 'You didn't need to come in.'

She spun round to face him. 'I thought I might be useful…' She nibbled the edge of her lip. 'And I wanted to see you.'

'Oh.' He frowned a bit. Was she having second thoughts already? Hell, he hoped not. 'Are you OK?'

Her mouth curved. 'Don't look so worried. Of course I'm OK. In fact, I'm brilliant.'

'Ah.' He reached up, clamping his head between his hands, his eyes never leaving her face. 'That's good. I, uh, thought you might have gone off me already.' He laughed, relief showing in the tender look he sent her.

'No chance.' Ally walked across to him and right into his outstretched arms. 'How's Tom?'

'They did his leg early this morning. He's presently in Recovery. And for his age, doing well, the surgeon said.'

'That's wonderful.' She hugged him and he hugged her back. 'Guess what?' She tilted her head to smile at him. 'I'm about to escort the seniors home. And we're travelling on the school bus.'

He chuckled. 'Is there an anachronism hidden in there somewhere?'

'Possibly.' Her mouth turned down wryly. 'Are they all OK to go?'

'With the exception of Therese Darby.'

'The lady who fell down the steps and hurt her ankle?'

'That's the one. I'm keeping her until we get her reasonably mobile. And Mr McGregor's insulin shot is due at eleven, if you wouldn't mind doing that?'

'No problem, Doctor.'

His hands slid down her arms, then shackled her wrists. 'What are you doing for the rest of the day?' he asked softly.

'Depends.' Her throat suddenly dried. 'What did you have in mind?'

'Come to my place. Let's grab the rest of the day.' His eyes locked with hers, his meaning clear.

She licked her lips. 'All right.'

'And, Ally…' He drew back, smiling a little and brushing a tiny curl off her forehead. 'Bring some clothes for work tomorrow as well.'

Marc was already home when Ally got to his flat. He came out to greet her and took the backpack she'd brought while she carried her work clothes on their hangers.

'Seniors get home all right?' he asked, looping his arm around her shoulders as they made their way inside.

'Yes. Sorry it took me so long.' She sent him an apologetic smile. 'I had to make sure none of their food had gone off while we were without power. The last thing the place needs is an outbreak of salmonella.'

'Amen to that. So, much damage?'

Ally shook her head. 'Not really. None of them keeps a huge supply of perishables. I just advised them to throw out any leftovers to be on the safe side. And they all seemed to have something on hand in the pantry until the shops open tomorrow.'

'You're lovely.' His look was tender. 'So sweet and caring. We're in here.' Without embarrassment, he pushed open the door of his bedroom. He placed her backpack on the bench seat under the window and together they found a space where she could hang her clothes. 'Are you hungry? We could rustle up some lunch…'

Instead of answering, she turned into his arms. In seconds they were kissing hungrily. Moments later they were naked in each other's arms. Then, with a growl, Marc swept her up and carried her to his bed.

'Tell me I'm not dreaming, Ally.' His voice was rough-edged, husky against the skin of her throat.

'If you're dreaming, I must be dreaming, too,' she murmured as he rolled her beneath him.

Their loving was wild and sweet and touched with bright sunlight. They hadn't bothered to close the curtains and Ally marvelled at how hard and powerful his body looked in the clear, pure light of day.

That day marked the beginning of a blissful couple of weeks. Ally was to think later that it was as though they had reached a place where nothing could touch them. A place very warm and safe, an oasis of pure happiness.

And it continued…until the day she decided to ask Marc about Karla.

It was late afternoon on a Sunday and they were sitting under her pergola, enjoying a cool drink. Marc had mown her strip of lawn and they'd done some winter pruning.

'The peach tree is already starting to flower,' Ally remarked.

Lounging back in his chair, Marc looked indulgently at her. 'Perhaps we'll get an early spring. The seasons are so clearly defined here, aren't they? Much more so than at the coast.'

Ally chuckled and gave him an old-fashioned look.

'What?' He arched a dark brow.

'I can't believe we're talking about the weather of all things.'

'We were talking about the *seasons*,' he said.

'OK. Seasons, then.' She leant across to stroke his jaw, loving the slight rasp of his beard. 'Are you open to a complete change of subject?'

'Fire away—as long as it's not shop.'

'Tell me about Karla.'

As soon as the words were out, she wished she'd thought things through more thoroughly. Suddenly he seemed to go still and his mouth tightened into a straight line.

'Who's been talking?' He delivered the question very quietly and lethally.

Immediately Ally felt wrong-footed. 'I didn't go searching for information about you,' she said defensively. 'Someone went out of their way to tell me.'

He gave a bitter laugh. 'Warn you, you mean.'

'I form my own opinions, Marc.'

His jaw tightened. 'What do you want to know?'

'Your side of the story,' she said resolutely.

Silence came down like a wall between them for a few moments.

'OK, these are the facts,' he said starkly, as if he were about to recite them in a court of law. 'Karla came to McAuley on an exchange from the States. She's a surgeon.'

Ally nodded. 'I knew that.'

The ghost of a dry smile nipped his mouth. 'I met her on her first day at work—in the hospital car park of all places. She was still trying to get the hang of driving on the left-hand side of the road and in a bit of a panic about where she was entitled to park.'

'And you were her knight in shining armour, I suppose?' Ally felt sickening black jealousy raise its ugly head.

'Perhaps,' he admitted reluctantly. 'And she did have a cute accent.'

Oh, please! Ally's lip curled.

'We clicked, I suppose.' He lowered his gaze, his fingers toying with the coaster under his glass. 'I showed her where to get her ID organised and made sure she knew the short route to Theatres.'

'Surely there were people assigned for that?' Ally said sharply.

He looked at her steadily. 'I'm trying to tell you how it was, Ally. Do you want to know or not?'

She drew a deep breath. It was painful to listen to. More than she could have realised. But at least he was confiding in her. Surely that meant something? 'Sorry,' she said quietly. 'Go on.'

'Within a week she'd moved in with me,' he said heavily. 'I think we were both surprised at the speed at which things happened. I know I was. She told me she was legally separated from her husband and that as far she was concerned the marriage was over.

'We'd been together a couple of months when she got word her father was seriously ill in the States. She took compassionate leave and flew home. It was another month before she returned to McAuley. I tried to pick things up again but she said she needed time to think.'

'How long did this go on?'

He finished his drink and put the glass down. 'A few days—but to me it seemed like an eternity. I felt I was getting the run-around and I was puzzled. And hurt,' he admitted. 'We'd been so close.'

'So how did the situation resolve itself?' Ally asked tentatively.

He gave a bark of cynical laughter. 'It was bizarre really. I happened to be at Reception when this guy came in and asked where he could find Dr Karla Costain. When he was asked for some ID, he said he was her husband and that he wanted to tell her he'd found them a "swell" apartment.'

Ally flinched. She could see it all now. How vulnerable Marc had felt. How hurt. And on a much deeper, instinctive level, she now understood the reasons why he'd let his anger show when he'd confronted the woman. Looking at him now, at his closed expression, Ally felt a great wave of empathy wash over her. 'So you had a showdown with Karla?'

'You could say that. I demanded to see her as soon as she had a break. She said she'd meet me in the hospital coffee shop.' A fleeting frown crossed his face. 'I suspect she thought there would be less chance of things getting out of control if we met in a public place.'

'But things did get out of control, didn't they?'

'I see the story has lost nothing in the retelling,' he drawled.

Ally made a throw-away movement with her hand. 'These things hardly ever do—they're more likely to become embellished.'

'You're probably right.' He laughed harshly. 'Anyway, to cut a long story short, I put it right on the line to Karla. She said as soon as she'd got home to the States, she'd realised she'd been a bit hasty about leaving her marriage. She and her husband had been reconciled. She hadn't known how to tell me.'

What a cow! And what a pathetic excuse! Ally bit hard on her bottom lip. 'I imagine you were angry.'

'Damn right I was angry. I accused her of leaving my

bed to go to his—and a few other things she took exception to.' He shook his head as if he still didn't quite believe it. 'She slapped my face. It was all very public and very messy.' He looked directly into Ally's eyes. 'So, there you have it.'

Ally swallowed. 'Where is she now?'

'Still fulfilling her contract at McAuley, I imagine.'

'Is that why you left, Marc—because of what happened?'

His chin came up defensively. 'I felt betrayed. And on reflection I suppose my pride was battered. And the gossip about us was rife. But I was pretty fed up with the intense nature of emergency medicine any way. The break-up with Karla merely hurried my decision along.'

Ally wondered if she could entirely believe the reasons he'd given. Perhaps that was what he'd been telling himself. Perhaps just the thought of Karla and her husband together had been enough to stampede him into leaving his very senior position and heading for the bush.

And if that were the case… Ally finished her drink and replaced the glass carefully on the table. Was he really over Karla Costain? And in view of her own relationship with him, where did that leave *her*?

'I'll get dinner started, I think.' She rose quickly to her feet, scooping up their empty glasses. 'I'll put something together in the slow cooker and we can have it later when we feel like it.'

'If you don't mind, I'll take a raincheck, Ally.' As if he had to be somewhere in an awful hurry, Marc shot to his feet. 'I have to go to the surgery for a while.'

'I can hold dinner.'

'Thanks, but no.' The muscle in his jaw worked for a second. 'I've a bit of homework to catch up on. I could be a while.'

Ally knew he was making excuses. For his own reasons

he obviously didn't want to be around her tonight. Swallowing the hurt, she brought her head up and forced out a semblance of a smile. 'I'll, um, see you at work tomorrow, then.'

He stared at her in silence for a moment, his jaw clenched, the muscle jumping again. 'Fine. I'll take off.' Raising his hand in a brief salute, he turned and began making his way quickly along the path at the side of the house.

Ally went slowly back inside. 'Well, he seemed pathetically eager to be shot of me,' she fumed, placing the glasses carefully in the dishwasher. 'And I'll just bet he's not going anywhere near the surgery. I'll bet he's going home to drown his sorrows and think of his lost love!'

On a little howl of frustration she opened the freezer and pulled out a tub of ice cream. Why on earth had she brought up the woman's name?

CHAPTER ELEVEN

NEXT morning Ally dragged herself to work, wishing it was Friday instead of Monday.

Uncertainty was sending the nerves of her stomach into overdrive. Where did she and Marc stand now?

Jenny was her usual chatty self and Ally was leaning over the counter in Reception, listening, when Marc strode in. He barely looked at either of them, wishing them a curt good morning before shutting himself in his office.

Ally felt the sharp pain of rejection. 'What's eating him?' she muttered—as if she didn't know.

'He's probably just a bit stressed.' Jenny was kind. 'I believe he was called into the hospital in the early hours.'

Ally shook her head in rueful conjecture and wondered whether she'd ever get used to the way news, good or bad, was telegraphed almost before it happened in this small community. 'How do you know all this, Jenny?'

'I live next door to the police sergeant,' Jenny explained. 'He was just coming off his shift when I left my house to come to work. We usually have a bit of a chat.'

'Oh—I see,' Ally rejoined faintly. 'Was it very bad, do you know?' she added, and knew she should have been asking Marc instead of their receptionist.

'Brad didn't say—well, they're not supposed to, are they? He just said it had been a very busy night and the doc had to be called in to attend to someone after a bit of a domestic upset.'

Perhaps a battered wife, Ally thought sadly. 'I'd best get

on.' She gave Jenny a token smile. 'I've a procession of walking wounded due in today for various treatments.'

'And I'll take Marc a cuppa and a piece of my cherry slice,' Jenny decided. 'That'll perk him up.'

If only life were as simple as that. Ally's mouth tightened as she left Reception and made her way along the corridor to the treatment room. Somehow she'd have to get through the day. Maybe Marc would lighten up and talk to her. And maybe he wouldn't...

By late afternoon Ally had had enough of Marc's stand-offishness. She clicked her tongue in disgust. He may as well have been wearing a 'do not touch' sign for all the communication they'd had. Checking with Jenny that he was through for the day, she knocked on his surgery door and popped her head in.

'I'd like a word, please.'

'Ally...' He turned from looking out of the window and swiftly rearranged his expression. 'What's up?'

She stepped inside and closed the door and then moved to stand as close to him as she dared. 'I want to apologise for yesterday,' she said quietly, before she could lose her nerve. 'I shouldn't have asked you about...your past. It was none of my business.'

'No need to apologise.' He folded his arms and leaned back against the window ledge.

'I made you rehash everything, though. It...must have been painful.'

He stared at the floor for a while then looked up at her, and his eyes were bleak. 'It hurt like hell. Much more than I ever imagined it would. But you were the first person I'd actually spoken to about it, so perhaps that's the reason.'

'I'm sorry,' she said numbly, feeling tears clog her throat. Her inquisition had probably wrecked everything.

'Ally, you've nothing to be sorry about.' Suddenly his

arms were around her. 'It was time I faced things and got them out into the open, instead of leaving them to fester.'

Ally blinked against the tight lens of tears across her eyes. 'If you're sure… I'd never want to hurt you, Marc.'

'I know that.' He swallowed. 'I should apologise for running out on you the way I did. I acted like a clod.'

'Enough of that.' Ally snuggled closer. 'We've both apologised so we're squared away, right?'

'Right. Let me take you out to dinner.'

'No, you look tired.' Reaching up, she curled her fingers in the soft warmth of his hair. 'We'll get take-away.'

'Sounds good.' His mouth lowered to her throat to kiss the tiny pulse that beat frantically beneath her skin. 'I've missed you.'

She tilted her head back, her mouth opening with sensuality at his touch. 'It was only one night.'

'One night too many.' He buried his face in her throat again, his hands sliding beneath her shirt to roam restlessly across her back. 'Let's go home.'

They'd made up but something still wasn't quite right between them. The knot of uncertainty tightened in Marc's gut. It was three weeks on from when they'd had that stupid misunderstanding.

He knew now he should have kept his own counsel about Karla. It was over, finished. Relating the sorry business had only served to make Ally wary around him. She hadn't needed all that stuff dumped on her, especially when she'd barely recovered her own emotional strength after the demise of that rat of a husband and the travesty of her marriage.

He sighed and dragged his hands through his hair. One would have imagined they'd have unlimited time to spend together after hours but somehow lately it hadn't happened.

A tight little smile drifted round his mouth at the frustration of it all. It seemed being the sole practitioner in a small rural community made him the target for being invited onto all kinds of committees.

And he hated the talk-fests that seemed to precede every decision, when his own reaction was to cut through the red tape like a knife through butter. His eyes glinted with dry humour. Rural medicine certainly had its moments.

But he'd got right off the track. Suddenly he spun off his chair, his manner filled with purpose. It was time he and Ally had a decent night out.

He found her in the treatment room, taking an audit of their supplies. She looked up as he propped himself against the doorframe and asked, 'Hometime, is it?'

'Way past, actually. And it's Friday.'

'So it is.' Ally made her last notation and closed and locked the door of the drugs cupboard. 'We need a few replacement items. I'll fax an order through.'

He lifted a shoulder impatiently. 'Can't it wait?'

'If I do it now, they'll be able to dispatch it first thing on Monday,' she explained shortly, making her way through to Reception. Jenny had long gone, so Ally fed her order form into the fax machine and punched out the number.

'What about dinner at Lavender Farm?' Marc had followed her through.

'What about it?'

His face became expressionless. He knew they'd lost touch a bit but that was hardly his fault. 'I'd like you to have dinner with me,' he rephrased carefully. 'That's if you'd like to, of course.'

'And then fall into bed afterwards, I suppose. Why bother going out to dinner at all?'

He felt taken aback. 'Where is all this coming from, Ally? You know how crazy things have been lately.'

'You've managed to make time for certain things.' Ally turned away, her hands shaking as she began unnecessarily tidying some papers in Jenny's filing tray. 'It would be nice to feel I was more than just a convenient lover to you, Marc.'

A beat of silence.

'I'm sorry you feel like that, Ally.'

Ally's stomach shook. 'Yes, well, so am I.'

'I thought you trusted me.' His jaw worked briefly. 'I thought we trusted each other…'

She turned, determined not to melt. 'But that's just it, Marc. I can't trust you to be honest about your feelings for me when you're still hung up on Karla.'

'You think I'm on the rebound?' His eyes were stormy. 'That I'm using you?'

'I didn't say that. I'd *never* say that.'

He stared at her in silence for a moment, his jaw clenched. 'Then what are you saying, Ally?'

Her eyes clouded. 'Things haven't felt right since you talked about Karla…'

'You wanted to know,' he reminded her harshly.

'So you're saying it's *my* problem?'

'The way you're interpreting things is the problem, Ally,' he said flatly.

All the strength drained from Ally's legs like water from spaghetti, and her knees were shaking so much she could hardly stand. But she managed to, knowing she couldn't leave things like this. With so much strain between them, her job as his practice nurse would become untenable.

'I don't want to fight with you.' She forced the words past the dryness in her throat.

'Then don't.' He gave a ragged sigh. 'God knows it's

the last thing I want. Look, why don't we both go home, shower and change and meet at the pub for a counter meal? Spend the evening as friends, colleagues or whatever you want? No pressure.'

Ally dropped onto the edge of Jenny's desk as if all her muscles had suddenly let go. She nodded. 'All right. I'd like that.' She gave the ghost of a wry smile. 'Whoever gets there first buys the drinks, deal?'

'Deal.' The backs of his fingers briefly brushed her cheek then he turned and left quietly.

'Apparently, it's karaoke night,' Marc said, as they settled at their table in the beer garden. He'd got there first and ordered a glass of red wine for Ally and a light beer for himself. 'Got to keep my wits about me,' he said, when she'd queried his choice of drinks.

'Mmm...' Ally's mouth turned down. 'You're really never off duty, are you?'

'Comes with the territory, I suppose.' He leaned back in his chair, his loose-limbed frame oddly tense. 'You look nice.'

'Thanks.' In a nervous gesture she lifted a hand, fingering the collar of her new red top. 'This is fun, isn't it?' she tacked on, looking around at the happy Friday night crowd.

'We'll do it more often in future.' Marc put out his hand towards her. 'You're very special to me, Ally.'

She held her breath, looking straight into his eyes, feeling the sensual charge of his thumb running over the top of her hand. Every nerve in her body was singing with sensation. Her heart thumped against her ribs and she wondered whether this evening would mark the beginning of a whole new understanding for them.

They were halfway through the karaoke part of the evening and Ally was laughing and clapping along, when Marc touched her arm and indicated that his mobile had rung and he was stepping outside to take the call.

He was back within seconds, his face grim. 'Sorry to break up your evening, Ally, but we're needed over at the high school.'

Ally didn't waste time in conjecture. She knew from Jenny there was a dance being held that night for the students. There must have been a mishap and serious enough for Marc to have been called.

'We'll take my car,' he rapped as they hurried outside. 'That was the school principal, Aaron Hart. One of the male students has collapsed. Sounds like drugs.'

Ally's hand went to her throat. 'I never thought that kind of thing would happen here.'

'It's a global problem, Ally,' Marc growled. 'Why should Hillcrest be the exception?'

The school principal seemed relieved to see them. 'This is a catastrophe for our school community,' he said, visibly upset. 'Is there any way we can keep it under wraps?'

'We can try.' Marc's reply was clipped. Privately, he imagined the dogs would be barking it by the morning. 'Do we have a name for the casualty, Aaron?'

'Jarrod Knightly. He's relatively new to the school.'

Marc's mouth pulled tight. He should have realised. 'Where is he?'

'In the male toilet block. We didn't like to move him. Our PE teacher, John Ferguson, is with him. John has his advanced first-aid certificate but obviously this needs skills way beyond that level.'

Marc nodded. 'I'm sure you've done everything you could.'

Ally heard the music start up and she and Marc exchanged startled glances.

Aaron Hart grimaced. 'We're doing our best to keep the

incident quiet. Thought it best to try to keep things as normal as possible for the sake of the other students. Here we are.' He opened the door of the toilet block. 'The doctor's here, John.'

The teacher barely looked up. His face was tense as he carried out CPR on the boy. 'No pulse, no breath sounds,' he gasped.

'Bloody young idiot…' Marc swore softly, but there was no time to sit in judgment. 'Ally, take over the CPR, please. John, you've done well.'

Ally's gut clenched and clenched again. This was trouble of the worst kind. She hunkered down beside the boy.

'I'm giving adrenalin.' With swift precision, Marc shot the drug already prepared in its mini-jet into the lad's inner arm. 'Keep the CPR going, Ally. I'll start bagging him and see if we get a result.' In seconds Marc had the resus bag attached to the small oxygen cylinder and was manually ventilating their patient.

'Anything?' Ally felt her heart like a jackhammer against her ribs.

Marc shook his head, his face like granite. The kid was barely fifteen years old. He'd been told Jarrod was getting counselling. Obviously they still had a long way to go. 'OK, we have a pulse.' Marc's expression was taut. 'Still no breath. And where on God's green earth is the ambulance?'

'Wait—there's something happening!' Ally bent to place her cheek near the boy's mouth. 'We've got him! Marc—atropine! Quick!'

Marc's hands moved like lightning, drawing up the drug that would stimulate the boy's heart. 'Don't close down on us, sunshine,' he muttered, sending the jab home swiftly.

'Oh, thank God.' Ally rested back on her heels, almost seeing the injection work before their eyes. 'Pulse back to sixty,' she relayed evenly. 'He's waking up now. Take it easy, Jarrod. You're OK.' Ally's voice was softly reassuring.

The boy's eyes flicked wide open. 'W-what happened?'

'You tell me, Jarrod.' Anger like a loaded spring coiled in Marc's chest. Snatching the empty syringe up off the floor, he held it in front of the boy's face. 'What did you use this time?'

'Stuff you!' The boy turned his face towards the tiled wall. 'Just get off my case.'

Ally looked sharply at Marc to judge his reaction, seeing his jaw tighten, before he said brusquely, 'OK, let's get him to hospital. Is the ambulance here?'

'Just arrived.' Aaron was grim-faced.

'Has Jarrod's mother been notified?' Marc asked, helping Ally tuck a space blanket around the youngster.

Aaron nodded. 'She'll meet us at the hospital.' His eyes flicked to the student. 'It's a bad business all round.'

More sad than bad, Marc thought bleakly, but kept his own counsel.

'You've treated Jarrod before, haven't you?' Ally had made the connection with the domestic incident Marc had been called to several weeks earlier. Now, as they left the hospital, the picture of the boy's mother was still vividly in her mind. Mrs Knightly had looked numb and rather lost. Ally's heart had ached for her.

'I was called to the home a few weeks ago in the early hours of the morning. Jarrod had shot himself full of equine growth hormones.'

Ally's hand went to her throat. 'Whatever for? Is he trying to increase his sporting ability?'

'If only it were that simple.' In a weary gesture, Marc

tugged a hand through his hair. 'Jarrod's parents have split up. I'd say it's his way of protesting about the situation.'

Poor kid. Ally's heart went out to the youngster. 'Is there any way we can help him?'

'I'm not sure.' Marc unlocked the door of his car and they scrambled in. 'After the first episode I referred both Jarrod and his mother for counselling. It would appear the kid hasn't sorted out his feelings to any great degree.'

'What about his father?' Ally asked. 'He doesn't live here, I take it.'

'He lives in Sydney—with his new partner. Mrs Knightly was reared here. She returned after the marriage break-up, thinking having extended family around and the rural environment would help Jarrod.'

'Instead, he's resentful,' Ally surmised. 'Blaming his mother for upsetting his world.'

'And his present behaviour is his way of rebelling,' Marc added grimly. 'Mind you, his father isn't helping matters. Apparently, he's overcompensating by providing Jarrod with more money than a kid of his age has any need for.'

So that was how the boy was able to buy the drugs. Ally shook her head. 'Looks like you'll have to involve the father in some family counselling, then.'

Marc grunted. 'That's if he'll co-operate.'

'Surely he will?' Ally gnawed at her bottom lip. 'If his son's health and welfare are at stake?'

Marc sighed heavily. 'I'll give it my best shot. Somehow I'll have to get through to him that if he doesn't start pulling his weight as a parent, his son's on the way to nowhere.'

'So that's it, guys,' Marc said during their lunchbreak almost two weeks later. 'As from next week I'm declaring the surgery closed at midday on a Wednesday.' He looked from Jenny to Ally and grinned. 'You can both start planning what to do with your half-day off.'

Ally looked surprised. 'Can the practice afford it?'

'The accountant says we can.' Marc placed his hands palms down on the table in front of him. 'We might have to streamline how we're allocating our appointments to some degree. But that shouldn't be too difficult, should it, Jen?'

'Piece of cake.' Jenny flapped a dismissive hand. 'Some days we run right over, as you both know. And it's not because we've overloaded with patients, it's because some folk think they can wander in twenty minutes late and it's OK. Well, they'll have to start to realise it's not OK.'

'Way to go, Jen!' Marc grinned. 'I can safely leave the administration changes in your hands, then?'

'I'll get things moving right away.' Jenny looked full of purpose as she rose to her feet. 'A mail-out advising the new surgery hours for starters and a notice in the paper wouldn't go amiss. And I don't even have to think how I'll be spending my half-day off,' she said happily. 'I can be a regular at my midweek tennis club. They're always short of players.'

'What about you?' After Jenny's departure, Ally's gaze swung to Marc. 'What are you going to do with your half-day?'

His head tipped back and he looked at her, the expression in his eyes fathoms deep. 'Depends on you.'

'Me?'

'Mmm. I thought perhaps we could spread our wings a bit.'

Her mouth tipped. 'Go flying?'

'If you like.' Marc took her comment literally. 'I believe there's a flying school not too far away.'

Ally pretended to shudder. 'No, thanks.'

'But there must be lots of other things we could do to-gether,' he said softly. 'Like exploring the district. There are some beautiful little B&B places over Warwick way. We wouldn't have to be back until Thursday morning.'

'Oh.' Ally's heart thumped and raced. Ever since the night they'd been called to attend to Jarrod Knightly, Marc had distanced himself from her. Well, why wouldn't he? She'd practically accused him of taking her for granted. Her lashes fluttered down and then up. 'Sounds like fun.' She swallowed unevenly. 'We, uh, haven't seen much of each other outside the surgery lately.'

There was a short, significant silence, a silence that to Ally was so palpable it had the effect of making the hairs on the back of her neck stand up.

'No, we haven't…'

Ally twisted her hands in her lap. 'I don't know where we stand any more, Marc. You've made no effort to see me after working hours.'

'I was waiting for some sign from you.' His jaw worked for a second. 'I thought…'

'What?'

Marc let his breath go in a harsh sigh. 'I had the impression you wanted to slow things down.'

Her stomach lurched and she rattled out impulsively, 'But not to grind to a halt!'

Surprisingly, he laughed. 'Ah—no.'

'Oh, lord.' Ally put her hands to her burning cheeks. 'That sounded awful. But you know what I mean. I want things between us to be—I don't know—*real*, I suppose, like they were before.'

Before she'd asked him about Karla. The words lay unspoken between them.

But only for a second.

Until Marc leaned into her, painting a brushstroke of a

kiss across her mouth with his lips. 'You're right, Ally Inglis,' he said throatily, coming back for just one more taste. 'Let's get real. I have to attend a regional seminar at Warwick on the weekend so let's make plans for next Wednesday afternoon.'

'And night,' Ally murmured, and blushed.

'Sounds clandestine, doesn't it?' His voice dropped a little and his blue eyes held a secret gleam. 'We're going to have to pack quite a lot into a few hours, aren't we?'

Ally felt excitement begin to mount inside her. 'What would you like to do? I mean, really.'

He gave a rakish grin. 'I've a few ideas.'

'But apart from those?' she countered. 'I know—we could pack a picnic lunch for starters. And there are lots of tiny villages we could explore. Do you like antiques?'

'Love them.'

'And we could possibly fit in a short wine tour. Oh— and afternoon tea, somewhere with a log fire. What do you think?'

His eyes crinkled in soft amusement. 'I think you should start promoting tourism for the district.'

'So my itinerary works for you, then?' She slanted him a smile, content to devour him with her eyes.

'Beautifully.'

'Let's pray for an emergency-free day, then,' Ally said jerkily, suddenly feeling vulnerable and uncertain under his gaze. She swung to her feet, taking their mugs to the sink. 'Oh, by the way,' she threw back over her shoulder, 'your first patient this afternoon is Marnie Civetta.'

Marc's look was suddenly closed, as he stood and pushed his chair in. Marnie's visit could mean only one thing. She'd decided to go ahead and be tested for Huntington's.

The kid had more guts than he'd have had in the same

circumstances, he thought grimly, making his way slowly back to his consulting room.

For a moment he stood at the window looking out, feeling his gut tighten. He hated this part of being a doctor. Marnie was young, full of vitality and by rights she should have had the prospect of living her life to a ripe old age. Instead, there was a fair chance she was looking at having that life drastically reduced and altered in ways she couldn't begin to imagine.

Nevertheless, he had to stay professional…

'Surely it's not vacation time again, is it?' Marc forced a cheerful note into his voice as Marnie took the chair in his office.

'Wish it was.' She rolled her eyes. 'Then I'd have my next lot of exams over. No…' She hesitated and then said in a rush, 'I'm just home for a couple of days. Something's happened and I needed to talk to Mum and Dad about it and then Mum said I should speak to you before I left again.'

Marc leaned back in his chair and folded his arms. 'Fire away. I'll do whatever I can to help.'

'You remember all that stuff I told you when I was here before?'

Marc nodded. 'Of course. It wasn't something I was likely to forget.'

'No. Well, the thing is, I've heard from my birth mother again. And it seems my natural father is someone else entirely.'

Sweet God…

Marc frowned. 'So are you saying this knowledge will put an end to your fears you might have Huntington's?'

'Looks like it.' With trembling fingers Marnie extracted a photograph from her purse. 'My birth mother sent me this and I can see now where I got my auburn hair…'

Marc took the photograph and studied it. It showed a couple of teenagers, no more than seventeen if he was any judge. They were straddling a powerful-looking motorbike, smiling into the early morning sun as though the world belonged to them and them alone.

Marc glanced up at Marnie's rapt expression and asked gently, 'So what's the story?'

'Christine, my birth mother, grew up in a country town…' Marnie's voice seemed to come from far away. 'Her parents were very conservative, especially her dad. She'd been going with John—that's the guy that I *thought* was my natural father—from when they were fifteen and because he was from a family they approved of, it was OK.

'Then Rhys—that's the guy on the motorbike—came to the school. Christine said he was very good-looking but a bit wild. They fell for each other big time. She dropped John but didn't tell her parents.'

Marc's eyes narrowed. 'So, obviously, Christine fell pregnant and let her parents think the father was John?'

Marnie met his sharp question with a nod. 'Because she'd only known Rhys for a little while and her parents would have been totally shocked. And, anyway, his family had already left town and she didn't—still doesn't, in fact—know where he went. Anyhow, to Christine's relief, her parents didn't want John or his family involved at all. She said they just wanted the whole thing hushed up and sent her away to have me and then I was adopted.' Marnie stopped and sobered. 'She didn't go home again and she's kept the whole thing to herself ever since. It was only when I told her about the possibility of the Huntington's that she decided she had no choice than to tell me the truth.'

Marc rubbed a hand around his jaw in silent disbelief. One lie had caused so much mischief, so much unnecessary heartache. He looked at Marnie searchingly. 'So, what happens now?'

'I can understand how scared Christine must have been when it all happened. She was hardly more than a kid herself. She grasped at straws.' Marnie looked down, pleating the denim across her thigh. 'She wants everything out in the open now. She's going to tell her husband and children about me…'

'Is that what you want, Marnie?'

She flexed a shoulder. 'I guess. I think I'd like to meet them—well, the children are only nine and ten so they'll be satisfied with a simple explanation.' She dimpled a smile. 'I'll be their big sister.'

'Yes.' Marc responded with a guarded smile of his own. 'And your birth father, Marnie? Any plans to find him?'

'Not yet.' Her reply was unequivocal. 'I've enough to be going on with, I think. One day, perhaps.'

'And John?'

'I'm sad about that.' She made a small face. 'But Christine said that's her responsibility to sort out.'

'You and your parents must be very relieved about all this.'

'Yes…' Marnie blinked a bit. 'They've been fantastic. It's brought us even closer together.' She got quickly to her feet. 'Thanks for your time today and for listening and everything, Dr Ballantyne. I'm glad I won't be needing a referral for that other business.'

Marc swung off his chair and walked to the door with his patient. 'I'm glad, too, Marnie. Very, very glad.'

CHAPTER TWELVE

ALLY couldn't believe how quickly the longed-for Wednesday had come round. For the past couple of days she'd been conscious of a kind of sick excitement in her tummy. Now all she and Marc had planned was about to happen.

'I've kept the list as short as I dared.' Jenny looked at Ally with an air of conspiracy. 'You and Marc are planning a getaway this afternoon, aren't you?'

'Is it that obvious?' Ally gave a shaky laugh but didn't bother to deny it.

'With emails from bed and breakfast places arriving daily for Marc? *Please!*' Clutching several files to her chest, Jenny sighed theatrically. 'I think it's wonderful! You and Marc. Takes me right back to when Noah and Erika got engaged.'

'Steady on, Jen!' Ally protested, bemused by the ease with which Jenny had their future all mapped out. 'We're miles away from anything like that.'

'The signs don't lie,' Jenny countered sagely. 'I've seen the way you look at each other.'

'I think it takes a bit more than that,' Ally deadpanned.

'Oh, go on with you!' Jenny flapped a hand dismissively. 'I'm never wrong about these things.'

Ally put the treatment room to rights for the second time that morning. At this rate they were going to get through easily by noon.

And then she and Marc would be away.

Oh, lord.

Air whistled out of her lungs, ending in an explosive little gush of air. When she'd greeted Marc that morning, she'd pretended to be serene and unruffled while inwardly she'd been trembling. Were they expecting far too much from these few hours away together?

The feelings of apprehension rushed at her again and it was almost a relief when the extension phone rang beside her, breaking the relentless cycle of her thoughts.

'Ally, you'll never guess who's just been here!' Rosie's voice heightened with dramatic emphasis.

'Who?' For some unaccountable reason Ally felt a cold river of dread run down her spine.

'Karla Costain. She came to the hospital looking for Marc. I've redirected her to the surgery.' Rosie paused for emphasis. 'I thought you should know in case you want to warn him.'

Ally's throat closed tightly. Warn him? 'Uh, I suppose I— What should I say?'

'Heck, I don't know, honey.' Rosie's voice softened in empathy. 'Just tell him, I guess, and then make yourself scarce.'

'I can't—morning surgery is still going on.'

'Oh, help, I should have stalled her,' Rosie wailed. 'Said Marc was out of the place or something.'

'I don't think that would have put her off!' Ally gave a tragic little laugh. 'I think the lady is here on a mission.'

Ally put down the phone, almost numb with disbelief. What a fool she'd been, believing him when he'd said it was over with Karla. Like hell it was…

Feeling her skin crawl with dread, she snatched up the phone again, pressing the number that would connect her with Marc's consulting room.

When he answered, she said crisply, 'I need a word urgently. I'm in the treatment room.'

In the seconds until she heard the sound of his tread in the corridor outside, Ally felt as though her heart was jostling for space inside her chest.

Marc knocked once sharply and came in, shooting a swift glance over the spic-and-span area and then returning to Ally. 'I thought you must have had someone bleeding to death in here. What's up?'

Ally opened her mouth but nothing came out. Indecision was suddenly eating her alive. I can't do this, she agonised. I can't tell him his former lover is about to arrive on his doorstep.

'Ally?' Marc's tone held faint impatience. 'What is it?'

Ally's heart jerked again but this time when she opened her mouth the words came out flat and unemotional. 'Rosie just called from the hospital. Karla's been there looking for you. She's on her way here.'

Marc went very still, all his energies reined in. Then he paced to the window, looked out and then spun back. 'Right…' He drew the word out on a long breath. 'My next appointment has cancelled so I've a few minutes to talk to her.'

Although she'd vowed she wouldn't do it, Ally just had to ask. 'Why do you think she's come?'

'I don't know, Ally. I guess I'll soon find out, though, won't I?'

'Perhaps she wants you back.'

His cool, dark look told her what he thought of that. 'Trust me, Ally, all right?' Then he was gone.

Ally was locked in indecision. She glanced at her watch. Karla must be only seconds away and the female part of her was urging her to go out to Reception, to be there when Karla walked in. She shook her head. That wouldn't be sensible. Marc was probably there himself—waiting for her.

It's all so sordid, Ally thought in disgust, making her way to her little corner in the second consulting room. How dared she come here? Anger carried her through the next half-hour, then jagged into a tight little knot of apprehension when Marc opened the door and came in.

Her throat lumped. 'Well?'

'She's gone.' Marc was tight-lipped. 'She needs to rest. I've sent her along to Lavender Farm.'

But that's *our* place! Ally wanted to yell at him. Instead she said, 'Why does she need to rest? Is she ill?'

'She's pregnant.'

Pregnant. The word spun round and round in Ally's head, thumping intolerably like a physical pain. Her fingers whitened with the pressure of gripping her upper arms. 'Is it yours?'

'No.' His mouth twisted. 'Of course it's not mine.'

'H-how can you be sure?'

'I always used protection for one thing, and the timing is all wrong for it to be mine.' He looked down briefly. 'Anyway, that's not up for discussion. It's her husband's child without a doubt.'

Ally could hear the clock on the wall ticking, ticking. Very slowly and very loudly—almost as loud as the blood pounding in her ears. 'So, why is she here? Has he left her?'

'No, nothing like that.' Marc shook his head. 'She's felt unhappy about the ways things ended with me…'

Ally's disbelieving huff filled the room.

In a gesture of a man almost at the end of his tether, Marc raised his hands, ploughing his fingers through his hair and locking them at the back of his neck. 'Karla is not a bad person, Ally. Her contract has finished at the McAuley and she's flying back to the States next week.'

Ally's mouth thinned. 'So, she's come here to beg your

forgiveness and put her own little world in order before she leaves the country, is that it?'

'Something like that.' He lifted a shoulder dismissively. 'I would have thought it took some guts, actually.'

'Yes, well, you would!' Ally swung to her feet and thrust some paperwork into a waiting tray. 'Because you're still in love with her!'

The silence between them lengthened and became thicker.

Marc stared at her, just watched her, and then said flatly, 'You believe what you want to believe, Ally.' He glanced at his watch. 'I've only one more appointment and then we'll shut up shop. We should be able to get away in an hour or so. What do you think?'

Ally's eyes flashed. Surely he was joking! 'I think you've got a damned hide, that's what I think, Marc Ballantyne. I wouldn't go anywhere with you. Ever again!'

A heavy beat of silence.

'Suit yourself.' His mouth snapped shut, his tightly clamped lips a harsh line across his face. 'I'll have lunch with Karla, then.'

'Do that!' Ally dragged in a shallow breath, feeling her control shattering by the second. 'It'll be like old times. You'll probably end up in bed together!'

Marc's face went pale under his tan. 'I'm not like your faithless late husband, Ally. You might like to consider that when you've calmed down.' He went to the door and left quietly.

Once the last patient was safely in with Marc, Ally grabbed her things and went through to Reception. Jenny gave the semblance of a smile and for a second the two women looked awkwardly at each other.

Ally held up a hand. 'Don't ask, Jenny.'

'Can I do anything to help?' Jenny looked torn.

'No.' Ally gave a faltering glance around the soft lilac walls, the neatly set-out office equipment and Jenny's little vase of sweet peas on the counter. She loved working here. Now she'd have no choice other than to leave.

There was no way she and Marc could be around one another now.

'I'm taking off, Jen.' Ally swallowed the lump in her throat. 'I may see you tomorrow. I may not.'

Jenny went to say something, then closed her mouth. She shook her head, turning blindly to answer the phone as it rang.

Ally stepped outside, shivering in the sudden gust of chilly wind. Well, that matched the chill in her heart, she thought sadly, scooping in a lungful of air. It was the only way she could stop from weeping.

She drove home, hardly knowing what she was doing, and shut herself in the bedroom.

'Damn you, Marc Ballantyne.' She hugged her arms around her shoulders and rocked herself gently in the middle of the bed. How could he have done this to her? To them?

Finally, exhausted by emotion, she threw herself off the bed and under the shower. She'd make her own plans for the afternoon and to hell with men!

Out of the shower and dressed, Ally was startled by banging on her front door. She brought her head up with a snap. If that was Marc... Her heart revved, as she went to the window and peered out. Rosie's battered little four-wheel-drive was outside. Ally's heart did a U-turn back to its rightful place.

'What on earth's going on, Ally?' Rosie almost fell inside in her agitation. 'I called the surgery and Jenny said you'd left and looked terrible, and then not ten minutes later

Marc came to do a ward round and I swear you could have used his jaw for a granite benchtop!'

To her horror, Ally felt her eyes fill. 'It's finished, Rosie.'

'Oh, Al—' Rosie stretched out a hand and tugged Ally down beside her onto the sofa. 'Perhaps you're just misreading things,' she offered, sensing her friend's abject misery.

'He's having lunch with Karla.'

'That's hardly a hanging offence,' Rosie pointed out coaxingly.

'You don't understand…' Ally sniffed and shook her head. '*We* had plans for this afternoon—and tonight.'

'You and Marc?'

'Yes.'

Rosie raised a finely etched brow. 'Are you saying he cancelled in favour of Karla?'

'No!' Ally shook her head. '*I* cancelled! I wouldn't walk down the road with him now.'

'Oh, my stars.' Rosie snorted inelegantly. 'No wonder the poor guy looked like he'd swallowed hemlock. Oh, Ally, you're a goose. Marc is nuts about you!'

'You couldn't be more wrong.' Ally gave a quiet little sniff and got to her feet. 'Are you on lunch?'

'Mmm.' Rosie sprang upright. 'And I'd better get back. Are you off somewhere?' For the first time she noticed Ally's smart tweed trousers and fine wool jumper.

'I'm going down to the stables. Hopefully, I can hire a decent horse for the afternoon.'

'Well, be careful. The weather's a bit iffy today.' They walked to the door together. 'I'm off at three so ring if you want to meet later. Ring anyway,' she qualified, 'so I know you're home safely.'

*   *   *

'You know I'm not altogether happy about you taking Misty out today, Ally.' Cherie Faulkner looked dubiously at the sky as they made their way to the stables.

Ally managed a passable smile. 'But Misty's a dream to ride, Cherie. She's so high-spirited and eager. And I *am* a competent rider, you know.'

The stable-owner gave a wry laugh. 'So are most of the jockeys who take tumbles on the racetrack. I'm not doubting your ability. It's just that Misty hasn't been ridden for a while and that wind is worrying. There could be a storm brewing.'

'Stop fretting. I'll keep a look out for any change in the weather. And to put your mind totally at rest, I won't stay out too long, OK?'

'I guess…' Cherie went forward and began to saddle the flighty black Misty. 'Just keep to the trails as a special favour to me.'

Ally was true to her word for a while and kept to the riding trail but suddenly her spirit needed to break free and the call of the high country was too much to ignore.

Misty was happy to oblige. In perfect rhythm, horse and rider took off across the winter-brown paddocks, climbing higher and higher until Ally decided they'd gone far enough.

Wheeling the young mare to a halt, Ally closed her eyes, breathing in the woodsy tang of eucalypts and pungent lantana blossoms. 'Isn't it fabulous, Misty?' In an absent little gesture she tapped the filly's neck and urged her forward. There was a watercourse higher up and the little mare deserved a drink after her long gallop.

At the stream, Ally dismounted. She'd let Misty graze for a while, she decided. The sun was warm on her back and she stretched, letting go some of the tension that had been tying her in knots for most of the day.

It was lovely here. Feeling her spirits begin to lift, Ally dropped to the grass at the edge of the stream, wedging her back comfortably up against the trunk of a gnarled old paper bark and pulling her knees up to her chin…

Almost an hour later, Ally woke with a start. Dazedly, she straightened, rubbing at the crick in her neck. How bizarre to have fallen asleep like that. For a second she panicked and then blew out a sigh of relief. Misty was still grazing nearby.

Ally scrambled upright, a new kind of unease running along her nerve ends. Unless she was mistaken, those were stormclouds swirling up from the valley and speeding across the mountaintops.

All her reflexes sprang into overdrive. Horses were notoriously spooked by storms and she knew it was going to take all of her skills to handle a youngster like Misty.

Whatever it took, she had to get them both safely home.

But Misty's senses were on high alert. She didn't want to co-operate, shaking her head and stamping restively. Ally's fears began to rise as she cautiously approached, calling, 'Come here, girl… Come, Misty…'

It took precious minutes to reclaim the young mare and the first heavy drops of rain were already beginning to fall as Ally swung into the saddle.

Ally knew she had to keep her head. Reining Misty in, she accomplished the run down to the plateau without mishap. The young mare was skittish, over-eager, knowing she was going home. But then what Ally most feared happened.

The sky was split by a jagged chain of lightning and a huge clap of thunder ricocheted through the valley.

Like two springs uncoiling, Misty's ears flattened back against her head. Nostrils flaring, she reared, lurching sideways. Ally cried out as she spun helplessly out of the saddle, landing with a sickening thump amongst the coarse bush ferns.

The rapid build-up of the storm was already sending sheets of hard, driving rain to earth. Ally was wet through in seconds. And the worst of it was that Misty had bolted. The ride that she'd begun with such anticipation was now the stuff of nightmares.

Ally bit down on her bottom lip. What a mess. She was miles from home. Now there was nothing for it but to start walking and hope she'd get home before dark. With both hands she pushed herself upright, only to sink quickly back onto the ground. A sickening, numbing pain shot through her ankle.

She waited, steeling herself against the wave of crippling black nausea. When it had passed she began pulling herself on her bottom to the shelter of an overhanging rock. Her choices were all gone. The bleak thought struck her forcibly, exacerbating her solitude.

'Oh, Marc, please, find me…' she whispered, as tears of pain and futility squeezed out and ran down her cheeks to mingle with the steady drip of rain through a gap in the crevice above her head.

Marc thought he was going crazy. The horse had returned to the stables, riderless. Ally was somewhere out there in the storm, hurt—or worse. His stomach heaved at the thought of the latter possibility.

In a few anguished seconds he recalled the events that had led to him being here at the Faulkner stables and the terrible uncertainty that now confronted him.

Sick at heart at the way they'd parted, he'd gone to Ally's house. She wasn't there. About to retrace his steps, he'd seen Rosie's Jeep pull up outside and she'd come flying in to join him on the front verandah.

'She's gone riding,' Rosie had said. 'I asked her to call me when she got back but she hasn't. I've been trying her mobile but she's not answering. Something's wrong, Marc. I can feel it.'

Marc had felt his blood run cold. 'Are you saying she's out there in the storm somewhere? On a *horse*?'

'Maybe she got back and she's taken shelter at the stables.' Rosie tried to put a positive spin on the bleak scenario they were facing.

'Then let's get out there.' Marc had pushed back his terror. 'Can you direct me?'

When they'd got to the stables, Cherie Faulkner, dressed in an oilskin jacket and wellies, had come running to meet them. She was obviously upset. 'The mare arrived back not five minutes ago. I think Ally's been thrown. I was about to call the ambulance and the SES.'

Marc felt the tentacles of fear grip his insides and squeeze. He made quick introductions. 'I'm a doctor and Rosie's a nurse. Could we start to search?'

'Not unless you know the country.' Cherie led them inside to the big farmhouse kitchen. 'I advised Ally to keep to the trails but, judging by the time she's been gone, I'd say she's obviously gone further.'

'So she could be anywhere?' Marc's lean rugged features were stretched tautly.

'I'm afraid so.' Cherie picked up the phone and began punching out the emergency number. In a few short moments she seemed to have things organised. 'The ambulance is on its way and Kyle Matthews is heading a team from the SES. He's on his way to mobilise them as we speak.'

'We'll get ready to follow.' Marc had gripped Rosie's arm and begun to propel her back outside.

'Wait!' Cherie held up a detaining hand. 'No offence,

Doctor, but we'll make better progress in my Land Rover. It's equipped with a two-way radio. But we don't go anywhere before the others arrive. Kyle will have a search plan, so we'll be guided by what he has to say.'

Marc felt frustration rip through him. While they messed around, Ally could be lying injured…

'At least the rain's stopped,' Rosie said a little later, breaking the crippling tension as they waited on the Faulkners' back verandah.

'I should have never let her out of my sight!' Marc's hands were interlocked, his knuckles straining white.

'For heaven's sake, don't start beating yourself up,' Rosie sighed. 'There's been enough of that, from what I hear.'

'How was she when you saw her?' he asked, trying to keep the panic from his voice.

'Upset.' Rosie shrugged expressively. 'I must say, you could have handled things better.'

'Don't remind me.' He looked at his watch again. 'What the hell's keeping them?'

Rosie touched his arm. 'Here are the guys now. Kyle must have moved fast.'

'Do we have any idea what Ally was wearing?' Kyle asked. The group had gathered in a tight little knot on the verandah.

'Unless she changed after I saw her, she had on dark trousers and a red jumper,' Rosie offered.

'And a loose scarf.' Cherie pressed her hands to her cheeks, thinking hard. 'White, I think.'

'Was she wearing a safety hat?' As he spoke, Kyle was unfurling a map of the district across the outdoor table.

Cherie looked affronted. 'I don't let any riders out without one.'

Marc let himself breathe again. Perhaps at least they

could rule out any head injury. 'Could we get a move on?' He looked desperately at Kyle.

'Yeah, mate. We'll be on our way directly.' Kyle pored over the map. 'The trail winds back in a circle from here.' He indicated a shaded portion on the map. 'So I figure she's gone to the high country. Except for the wind factor, the weather was sunny and clear. Nice day to be out riding.'

'What's your point?' Marc could hardly contain his impatience.

Unfazed, Kyle carefully folded the map and shoved it into the pocket of his windcheater. 'My point is that it shouldn't be too hard to find her. There's only one direction she would have gone. We'll fan out, go very slowly, keep calling. Right, guys, let's go. We've got only about another hour of daylight.'

'Kyle, I don't want to labour the point.' Marc pushed the words past the lump in his throat. 'But what if we don't find Ally before dark?'

'No worries, Doc.' Kyle promised. 'We've equipment that seeks out body heat. We'll find her.'

'All-ee!' The sound carried from somewhere. But it was far away. Too far.

'I'm here…' Ally whispered a response uselessly into the near-darkness surrounding her. Oh, God, it had to be a search party. It had to be!

But they'd never find her stuck here against the rock face. Somehow she had to make her presence known. But how? For the umpteenth time she chastised herself for leaving her mobile phone behind. But she hadn't been thinking properly…

Enough! The strong Ally, the nurse Ally, came to the surface and began to think rationally. A signal of some kind—that was what was needed here. But what? Think!

The answer came to her in a flash. Her white scarf. If somehow she could crawl into the clearing, hoist her scarf on something… She looked around, telling her brain to focus. A tree branch—that would do it. Thank heavens for the spindly she-oaks that grew everywhere in this part of the country.

Half crawling, half sliding, she managed to make it across to the small stand of saplings. Pulling herself to her knees, she chose one of the long whip-like branches and endeavoured to tug it free from the main trunk. The branch was tough and sappy, unwilling to let go. Finally, it gave way, peeling off in a long sliver of green bark.

The relief Ally felt was almost overwhelming. She sank back onto her bottom, steadying herself until she felt able to get on with the next stage of her plan, which was to remove her scarf and tie it to the end of the branch.

At last it was done. Again the sound of her name being called rang out. This time it seemed closer. Or maybe she was hallucinating. Steeling herself against the pain from her ankle, she turned on her good side and began inching herself across into the clearing.

Now she could see headlights coming slowly towards her. 'Please, find me…' It was Ally's desperate whisper. They had to see her. They just had to. From her sitting position she grasped the tree branch tightly and held it aloft. Tears ran down her face, unchecked, as her white scarf began billowing gently in the breeze.

'It's all right, Ally. You're safe, sweetheart. I'm here… I've got you…'

The words echoed and spun through Ally's head as she was gathered into protective arms. And held. 'Marc?'

'Yes. You're safe now.'

She buried her face against his shoulder. 'It's almost dark. I thought I'd be out here all night...'

'I wouldn't have let that happen.' His voice shook. 'I'd have found you—whatever it took. I love you.'

'We should get a move on, Doc. Get her to hospital.' It was Kyle's voice this time, his tone brooking no argument.

'Yes, yes.' Marc tightened his hold on Ally. 'What am I thinking of? I haven't even checked to see—'

'It's just my ankle...' Ally managed a wobbly smile. 'Otherwise I'm fine.'

'I'll be the judge of that when we get you back to the hospital,' Marc growled, and kissed her swiftly on the lips. 'Rosie's here, too.'

Ally closed her eyes and let the trained hands take over. 'Of course she is...'

'They're my best trousers,' Ally protested weakly.

'Sorry, honey.' Expertly, Rosie sliced along the outside leg seam. 'Has to be done, otherwise we'd never get them over that brute of an ankle.'

They were at the hospital and Rosie had appointed herself Ally's private nurse. 'You're soaked through anyway,' she tutted. 'Hold up your arms so I can get your jumper off.'

Ally gritted her teeth. 'I am *not* wearing one of those awful hospital gowns, Rosie.'

'Relax, would you? I'll pop you into a scrub suit.'

'Where's Marc?' Ally grizzled.

'He'll be here directly.' Rosie prepared a cold pack for Ally's injured ankle. 'I have to say he was in a right old state when we found you were missing.' She gave a lopsided grin. 'Wasn't a ruse on your part to bring him to heel, was it?'

Ally snorted. 'Yeah, right! As if I'd deliberately go out and put myself through this by choice— Ouch!'

'Sorry.' Rosie was all contrition. 'We'll have you more comfy soon. Ah…' She looked up and grinned. 'Here's your doctor now.'

'How are you?' he asked softly, pulling up a chair and taking Ally's hand.

'She'll live,' Rosie supplied cheekily, elevating Ally's ankle gently.

'Have you done her obs, Rosie?'

'Both pupils equal and reacting. A few bruises, none serious. Probably suffering from wounded pride, though.'

Ally made a face. 'I'm a good rider,' she insisted. 'Under normal conditions.'

Listening to the interplay between the two, Marc's shoulders lifted in a relieved sigh. His girl was already bouncing back. Thank God. 'You've been fantastic, Rosie. Thanks for everything.'

'You're welcome,' Rosie answered cheerfully. 'Now, if you don't need me for anything else, I'm out of here.' Tilting her head, she looked from Ally to Marc and grinned. 'Let me know in plenty of time, won't you?' Executing a quick tidy-up, she began singing under her breath, 'Here comes the—'

'Rosie!' Ally and Marc threatened as one.

'Just going.' Rosie turned, her expression all innocence. 'Nighty-night.' She fluttered them a two-fingered wave. 'Be good.'

'Not much chance to be anything else.' Ally chuckled, looking ruefully at her injured ankle.

'How are you feeling—really?' Marc asked, his entire heart in his gaze.

'Much better now the pain-killers have started to kick in.' She paused and touched his face, stroking the marks of strain around his eyes with gentle fingertips. 'You're not going to keep me in, are you?'

'No. As soon as you've rested a bit, I'm taking you home to your own bed.'

'That's nice.' She looked into his eyes, her gaze alight with love. 'Will you stay with me?'

'If you'll have me.'

She dropped her gaze shyly. 'I'll need someone to help me into the shower and stuff. At least for a couple of days.'

Marc felt the knot in his chest begin to unravel. It was going to be all right. 'Oh, I think I can manage a bit longer than that.'

Ally bit her lip. 'Did it wreck your afternoon terribly—coming to search for me, I mean?'

'Where else would I have been?' His voice shook. 'I nearly went crazy with worry when Rosie told me you'd gone out riding and hadn't come back.' He took a deep breath. 'Promise me you'll never do anything like that again.'

'I…just had to get away,' she proffered by way of explanation and blinked a bit. 'Can you understand how it was for me?'

'I can now,' he admitted ruefully.

She sniffed. 'Sorry I was so nasty about Karla. Did you have lunch with her?'

His mouth tightened. 'I never intended to. I'm ashamed to say I just hit back because you'd scuttled our plans…'

Ally wailed her disbelief. 'We acted like a couple of adolescents.'

'Insecure ones at that. Oh, sweetheart…' Marc leaned into her, kissing her softly, tenderly. 'Karla may have been in my life once but she was never in my heart. Not the way you are…'

'And you're in mine,' she said, tears welling helplessly. 'I love you, Marc.'

'Then we should start making plans.' He looked suddenly youthfully eager. 'Are you off marriage altogether or would you like to try it again? With me?'

Her lips twitched. It wasn't the most romantic proposal but it meant the whole world. She looked at him, her eyes shining with love and some unshed tears. 'I'll give it my best shot.'

'So that's a yes, and we can start making plans?'

She nodded, reaching up to touch his face, and Marc bent towards her. Their lips met and their kiss sealed the moment, sweetly, tenderly.

'So, my love,' Marc asked a bit later, kissing her nose and then her eyes and her cheeks and her chin, 'are we going to make a life here together?'

'You really want to stay as a country doctor?'

He gave a wry chuckle. 'For a while at least. Whatever else, Hillcrest is never dull.'

'No.' Smiling, she stroked her fingertip across his lower lip. 'But what about the workload?'

'It's not crippling like it was at McAuley. And I've had a word with Shaun O'Connor. He's interested in working out some kind of reciprocal arrangement where we'd provide cover for one another.'

'So we could escape on our own from time to time?'

'Plus, we'd have our Wednesday half-days,' he added, and a slow smile curved his lips.

'Altogether, not a bad life, then?' She looked at him, her eyes shining with love and pure happiness.

'Not bad at all,' he agreed. 'Ready to go home now?'

'Mmm.' She nodded. 'Can you commandeer a wheelchair?'

'Rats to that,' he growled. 'I'll carry you out to the car.

Come on, Ally Inglis, put your arms around my neck and let's get out of here.'

She smiled serenely. 'Masterful, aren't you?'

'Only when the occasion demands it,' he countered, his voice gravelly with laughter and his eyes filled with love.

4 FREE

BOOKS AND A SURPRISE GIFT!

We would like to take this opportunity to thank you for reading this Mills & Boon® book by offering you the chance to take FOUR more specially selected titles from the Medical Romance™ series absolutely FREE! We're also making this offer to introduce you to the benefits of the Reader Service™—

- ★ FREE home delivery
- ★ FREE gifts and competitions
- ★ FREE monthly Newsletter
- ★ Exclusive Reader Service offers
- ★ Books available before they're in the shops

Accepting these FREE books and gift places you under no obligation to buy, you may cancel at any time, even after receiving your free shipment. Simply complete your details below and return the entire page to the address below. You don't even need a stamp!

YES! Please send me 4 free Medical Romance books and a surprise gift. I understand that unless you hear from me, I will receive 6 superb new titles every month for just £2.75 each, postage and packing free. I am under no obligation to purchase any books and may cancel my subscription at any time. The free books and gift will be mine to keep in any case.

M5ZED

Ms/Mrs/Miss/Mr ....Initials ....

BLOCK CAPITALS PLEASE

Surname ....

Address ....

....

....Postcode..................................

Send this whole page to:
UK: FREEPOST CN8I, Croydon, CR9 3WZ